Noëmi's Shadow

K McCity

ISBN: 9798766624455
Imprint: Independently published

Dedicated to my 'Guy' with every bit of my love.

ACKNOWLEDGMENTS

Ever grateful thanks to Emma City for the awesome cover artwork; it's the best. Thank you to Babe, who is indeed my 'Guy', for the never-ending love, belief, support and for reading this first.

Cover by Emma City ©emmacityart.

CONTENTS

Noëmi's Shadow

PART ONE – REASONS

Aimer, voilà la seule chose qui puisse occuper et remplir l'éternité - Victor Hugo

PROLOGUE

MRS EVAN McKENZIE

3 September 2018.

"Do you think I'm falling for you?"

Marcus

Dr Marcus McKenzie was in fine form; life had blessed him. His ambitions and dreams were unlimited. Just the week before, in the review of his first year of junior doctor training, he had been graded outstanding. His gym session that morning had invigorated him; weights increased for his reps and a personal best run over 5k.

'To be honest, I feel invincible, now I just need to find the perfect flat to buy', he mused, as he strolled up to Newcastle Royal Victoria Infirmary (RVI). Marcus popped his sunglasses on top of his head and bounced into work. His shift would begin at 5pm but he was in early for a special meeting. Today his department would be introduced to Alex James, the new Accident and

Emergency Trauma Consultant and to Evan St-John-Jones, the new Patient Care Manager.

'Two hyphens in a name seems a bit much!' Marcus thought to himself. A notification pinged through on his phone about a flat available in the Jesmond area.

Arriving at the meeting room, he saw the rows of blue hospital chairs with their itchy woollen seats. The familiar 'refreshments' table had been replenished with water, tea, coffee and a few basic biscuits. Marcus grabbed a hot drink and waited with his colleagues for the introductions. Amongst complaints about the long-life milk, he found out a registrar was leaving to work in Singapore. Life was trundling on.

Suddenly the door opened. Everyone turned around. The room fell quiet. The hospital director walked in. Intently he was studying his notes. Accompanying him were a tall, fair-haired man and a fine figured, blonde woman. Marcus noticed that his colleagues seemed inquiring and he suspected it may be that some were trying to work out who was who.

'That's Alex! I can't wait to work with him! He's just the kind of mentor I need!'

Prepared as ever, Marcus had researched Alex James' career thoroughly.
The hospital director made the introductions and Alex addressed the group first.
"I'm overjoyed to be taking this role at RVI. I've been leading the emergency department at King's, a large teaching hospital in London. I'll be starting a number of research projects and lecturing advanced trauma skills to our medical students. We'll be looking to continue the project, set up this summer, with

4

doctors treating neglected tropical diseases. I intend to chat to you all individually; get to know you better. Our work is never easy, so we need to be open, supportive and help one another. We are a team and we are all to be valued with equity."

Pushing his fingers through his hair, Alex looked a lot younger than his forty-nine years. Leaning on the presentation lectern, smiling broadly at the room, Alex was all friendliness. Marcus felt air beneath his feet.

The young woman was tall, long legged and immaculately dressed in designer clothes. She was blue eyed, with a honey complexion and red dewy lips. Her long, silky blonde hair was pulled back in a ponytail that swung as she walked. Unlike her colleagues she did not smile but surveyed the room with an air of superiority.

Evan then spoke with a cut glass English accent.

"I would like to echo what my colleague Alex James has said."

'Here we go, that voice reminds me of just one person...Sophie!' Marcus thought.

She continued, "I'm here to improve our operation, ensure the best care for our patients and keep our highly valued team motivated."

Marcus nodded. *'All sounds perfectly reasonable.'*

Intently, he listened to their presentations detailing their backgrounds and visions for the hospital over the next five years. The meeting ended. Evan circulated the room shaking hands and then eventually got to Marcus.

"Hello, Evan St-John-Jones, how's your day going?" she proffered a delicate, red tipped, manicured hand.

"Hi, I'm Marcus McKenzie, second year junior doctor, specialising in emergency medicine, pleased to meet you!" He returned her pleasantness.

"Likewise, I hope to find out more about your work and will be visiting from time to time."

"Absolutely fine, I hope I can be of assistance if you need further information, Evan." He beamed.

"Yes, very good, thank you." Evan went to walk away but as she did Marcus also turned and she bumped right up into him. He put out his hand, catching her just above the waist to stop her falling. She put her hand on his arm to steady herself and looked back up at him.

"I'm so sorry are you okay?" he asked sincerely, concerned in case she was put out or thought he had been careless.

"Looks like I'm falling for you!" Evan joked as she went a bit pink. Marcus laughed genuinely.

"I must apologise, it's my fault." His brows knotted.

"No, I'm fine," she righted herself and walked off.

Marcus thought to himself, '*I need to be less clumsy. I wonder if that flat will be any good? It's really time to get onto the property ladder.*' He checked his phone.

Evan

Her hair cascaded round and slipped onto his shoulder. Body warm against hers. Her breast pressed into his arm. Kind face. Firm muscles. She was safe. Jolted; she felt a frisson of desire throughout her whole body. She drank in this handsome doctor. Evan savoured the feel of his hand on her side.

'*Do you think I'm falling for you?*' she said to herself as she relived their encounter again and again. Her hand slipped down to her waist where he had held her. '*Dr Marcus McKenzie, I need to get to know you better…Mrs Evan McKenzie…*'
She had definitely seen something in his eyes.

"That was no accident."

CHAPTER 1 - GOOD THINGS

3 September 2018.

Evan

Heart beating, mind racing, Evan arrived at A&E and found Alex and Marcus examining some X-rays.

"Two months old, broken femur." Marcus shook his head.

"Non accidental by the looks of it. Good God." Alex gave a sigh.

"I'll get on with the report and bleep the safeguarding team." Marcus settled at a computer at the urgent care centre staff base. As he logged on, Evan moved to his side. Marcus looked up. "How's it going?" he returned his eyes to the screen.

"Excellent, I had to see you. I read your review on safeguarding systems in emergency care." She perched on the side of the desk; Marcus moved a folder of patient notes considerately.

"And I'm just using that new process!" Marcus, eyes fixed on screen, typed and talked.

"Truly excellent work, particularly the section on vulnerable patients and also the part on whistleblowing, well done." She swung her hair round and crossed her leg over one knee.

Marcus looked up, "Thank you so much!" His brown eyes were wide.

"Has no one commented on it?"

Quickly he gave a shrug, "I just think everyone's frantic, you know, clue in the name, emergency department!"

"It's an outstanding piece of work. I'm taking it to the hospital board, I'll make sure that you get the recognition you deserve." Standing up she put her hands on her hips. Pushing her chest out, she gazed at him.

"Amazing Evan, I'm chuffed, no one's ever said that...thank you! You know that makes just three of us who have ever read that report! Things are beginning to change for the better!"

"I couldn't agree more, Marcus."

* * *

Noëmi

Since summer 2016, Noëmi McAllister had been working at St Wolbodo's school in Durham. She was a teacher of maths and now, rather surprisingly, French. Quite how she had been persuaded to do this, she was unsure.

On the first day of term, she studied her new teaching timetable. Sitting in the staffroom, good friend Frank Sprague was at her side.

"I'm tired already, my summer relaxation was proofreading Marcus' safeguarding report for his department. It came with us to Nigeria and Italy! He put his heart and soul into it!"

"I love how into every bit of each other you are!"

"We used to help one another like that at school, it's in the DNA! By the way Frank, what's this FR code on my timetable in 8XFR5?"

"Seriously, which university did you go to again?" he asked as he sipped his coffee then brushed a speck of dust from his patent leather shoe.

She bristled. "Anyhow...must be French, obviously...I knew that. Year 8."

Frank raised an eyebrow.

A message pinged through from Marcus. Timetable to one side, busily she replied.

"Got a flat to see." She told Frank.

"Nice, where is it?"

"Jesmond, not far from Avanti, that Italian restaurant, the one that did the catering for our engagement party."

"Ah now that was a good night!" Frank gave her a smile.

Thursday 15 February 2018, seven months earlier…

Marcus

One more day to work before a full three days off and Marcus could not wait. It was his and Noëmi's engagement celebration that weekend. A party was to take place at Noëmi's father's house with all their friends and family. A number of their university friends were coming up and staying with him; he was excited.

Arriving at work, his mind was soon back on his job. The icy February weather meant that A&E was fuller than usual with people having slipped over on pavements or skidded in their cars.

Felicity Gomez

One casualty was Marcus and Noëmi's former history teacher, Mrs Gomez. She had retired from the chaotic Newcastle Green Academy the summer before. This year was her first one when all she had to worry about was her garden and the holiday she would take to Greece, to see the ancient ruins. Whilst dividing her herbaceous perennials, she had managed to trip over a planter and fall, embedding her hand deep into an upturned garden fork. Her panicking husband took Felicity Gomez and the entire fork to the emergency department to get her treated.

Marcus

The bizarre sight made Marcus grin as he saw the couple waiting to be triaged.

'*Oh look who it is! Our Newky Green history teacher!*

"I'll take this one Pen," He told his colleague Penelope Rivera

who smiled. "She used to be my teacher! I've often wondered how it happens if you know someone who comes in!" He went over and began his job.

. "Hello Mrs Gomez, how are you?" Unable to shake her hand he shook her husband's.

"Oh my God Marcus McKenzie!" was all she could manage as she stared incredulously.

He laughed and replied; "Don't worry I'm qualified, a junior doctor."
He guided her and the garden fork into a treatment bay.
"Sorry doctor...sir...oh Doctor McKenzie."

He laughed some more and she continued. "It's so lovely to see you. I taught your sister Tianna last year, she did very well getting the top grade in her history GCSE. She told me you were a doctor now but I didn't know it was here." Mrs Gomez sat on the bed, still staring at him.

"Tianna's results were awesome, thank you for all your hard work." He knew this as he was part of the McKenzie family entourage who had attended Tianna's GCSE awards' ceremony.

"Let's get this looked at. Then you can let me know all the

trouble Tianna has caused you and I'm sure my mum will get you a letter of apology."
Marcus gently removed the fork from her hand.
"Oh yes I remember, quite funny all that business."

"You'll need a tetanus jab and some stitches, hold on there a minute, I need to clean it all up first." Fetching the trolley, Marcus chatted with Mrs Gomez as he patched her up.

His former teacher did not feel a thing because she found it impossible to take her eyes off the handsome, capable young man taking such fine care of her.

"There you go Mrs Gomez, remember to take the antibiotics and see your GP as soon as possible. Contact the out of hours service if there are any signs of infection over the weekend. Of course, if you have any cause for concern, come straight back here," he said, giving her a leaflet with the instructions for her care.

"Oh, call me Felicity," she said all aflutter as her husband rolled his eyes.

"Of course, Felicity and take care in the garden; they can be dangerous places!" Marcus had a natural charm.

"Thank you so much. Can I ask, what became of everyone in your class?" Mrs Gomez looked nostalgically at him, not wanting to end the appointment just yet.

"Yes a lot of people are still around and some in London. Rob Barr's a financial consultant!"

Mrs Gomez pursed her lips together. Slowly she got off the treatment bed.

"And your classmate, the one that went to Cambridge when you went to Oxford, Noëmi?"

"She's well and working in Durham, she's a teacher now, maths, at St Wolbodo's."

"Oh no, someone needs to talk to her about that! Does she not want a life?" Mrs Gomez shook her head.

"I'll tell her that," he laughed, as he tidied the trolley away.

"If she needs any advice, from an old timer, please ask her to get in touch, she can contact me via the school. Even though I've now finally left, they'll pass it on seeing as I spent almost forty years there. I did become quite a fixture at that place!"

"Oh, I'm sure she'd like that very much, I'll let her know, and less of the old please!" He stood and looked warmly at her.

"I remember you two were so funny together sitting next to each other in my history classes, competing so fiercely with one another, then helping each other. You both used to lean all over the other... such lovely temperaments. Always laughing with each other."

Marcus

Marcus smiled at the memories; they only ever wanted to work in history by sharing a text book together. If Noëmi was getting on with an exercise he would just casually rest his elbow on her back or play with her hair. For her part she would lean into his shoulder quite naturally when they were listening in class.

"Well hopefully that'll continue for many more years to come as we've just got engaged to each other."

Mrs Gomez was amazed.

"You're engaged to Noëmi McAllister! That's so perfect." Tears welled up in her eyes.

"Yes, we're having a celebration on Saturday, and actually when we get married you must come along. Let me show you a picture of us now!" He got his phone from the main desk and showed her the one they had taken on New Year's Eve, the night they got engaged.

"I feel very blessed," he added.

Felicity

More tears filled Mrs Gomez's eyes as she looked at how well they had turned out and how sweet they looked together. Marcus was clearly so very proud.

"No, no I can't cope with any more tears! Really, I mean it!" he joked and they all burst out laughing as Mrs Gomez wiped her eyes.

Felicity and her husband left along with their garden fork, and she took her husband's hand with her uninjured one. She felt a warm glow throughout her soul. Good things really did happen.

CHAPTER 2 - GUY

Thursday 15 February 2018.

Yumi

Six miles or so away from Newcastle RVI Hospital was the headquarters of the Northumbria police force, the workplace of Marcus' best friend Guy Castle. Similarly looking forward to the party that weekend, his day was also brightened by a visitor.

An effortlessly elegant woman walked into the reception area. Her glossy hair swung gently over her shoulders as she walked.

"Excuse me, is Guy Castle available please?" She asked the receptionist.

"Name?" He asked without looking up.

"Yumi Watanabe."

"I'll just see." He made a call.

"A visitor for Sergeant Castle in reception, Ms Watanabe."

Finally looking her way, he addressed Yumi, "He won't be a moment, please take a seat."

Yumi sat on a dark brown, corduroy covered chair in the echoing hall of the police headquarters' building. Guy was now based here as he was completing his detective training.

Footsteps got faster, a door swung open, and Guy almost fell into the reception area, knocking a large Yucca plant with his stumbling body. Catching the leaves, he heard Yumi before he saw her as she burst out laughing.

"Yumi! You're here already!" he gasped. He ran and hugged her, she smiled.

"Yes, sorry I didn't want to disturb your work," she nodded to indicate that the receptionist was staring coldly at the pair. Guy regained his composure and stood back more formally. They went outside the building.

"Are you okay? Shouldn't you be at school?" his brow furrowed.

"I need to talk to you. I've been offered a new job." She could not look at him.

Guy

Guy felt his throat tighten, although they had only known each other for six weeks, he was hoping that this would be a serious relationship. Yumi had become Noëmi's best friend when they met during their teacher training at Oxford. Guy and Yumi's romance was quite magical for the four of them. However, the pair had very sensibly tested their feelings to be sure they were not falling together because of these friendships.

"Oh right, interesting, where's the job then?" They sat on a bench outside the somewhat municipal looking building. He tried to sound casual.

"Well, that's the thing, that's why I had to come here, I wanted your advice."

"Where's the job?" He asked too quickly.

"You see it does involve me moving from London."

He felt the skin on the back of his neck. Images of her at the airport leaving for Tokyo filled his head. '*Why's there a problem when I've finally found someone who excites me the way she does? The chemistry between us is unbelievable; nothing I've ever experienced before.*'

"Where?"

"Durham!"

"Oh my God, I thought you were going to say Japan! Oh Yumi, that's just brilliant! Will that be from September?" Running his hands through his hair, his guard dropped completely. She could not help her smile either.

"They want me to start at Easter, I'll need to learn how to flip a burger."

"No way! That's just brilliant!" Guy was a grin on legs.

"Wiping the counters will be an important part of my job, I'll need training."

"Durham! This is the best news ever!" The grin was growing.

"Guy, are you even bothered about what my new job is?"

"Sorry but it's in Durham UK, not Durham USA, right?"

"Guy you're spending too much time with Marcus! Yes Durham, in the grey skyed northeast of England, Great Britain, UK. It's actually an excellent job too at a private school, called Mountford. I'll teach maths and Japanese. Although you don't seem to care a jot about that!"

He regained his composure, "That sounds like a dynamic career move for you at this stage…"

"…whatever and because I've no exam classes, my current school has agreed to let me go at Easter. *They're not best pleased* as you would say." She liked the odd English turn of phrase. "So do you think I should say yes? You know how much I like London..." She looked teasingly at him.

"Oh, obviously it's your decision, the fact that I would love you to be up here is hugely important though!"

"I'm keen to be closer to Noëmi, she *is* my best friend after all…" Yumi mused.

"Absolutely Yumi, that's the perfect reason to move up here!"

"Aghhh I've already told them I'll take it! We should celebrate!" He enveloped her in a huge hug.

"Well done, tell me all about it tonight, I've got to go back, got a big case on. Here take my key I'll see you back at the flat. Yumi this is the best news ever!" Guy started to go, stopped, turned around, went back to kiss her again and sped off.

Yumi

Evidently buoyed up by the news of Yumi's imminent move, Guy arrived home with a bottle of champagne to celebrate her job offer. Now twenty-six, Guy was settling into his work as a detective sergeant and was on his way to becoming a plain clothes investigator, which was his dream. Having had a couple of hours to spare, Yumi had made enchiladas and herself at home. Throwing her arms around him as he arrived back at his flat, Yumi told him. "Watashi wa anata no tame ni ochite iru to omoimasu."

Guy stroked her cheek and said," We English are lazy! We make it so much simpler; I think I'm falling for you."

Yumi was melting inside, her feelings for him were returned in full measure.

"So how do you say, 'I love you' in Japanese?" Guy was inquiring.

"Watashi wa, anata o aishiteimasu."

17

"See what I mean!"

They could not do without each other.

Having finished his shift at 9pm, Marcus called in on Guy to return the weights he had borrowed when he was unable to get to the gym. He rang the bell, waited and rang again.

Eventually Guy popped his head round. "Sorry mate, bit busy, you okay?"

"Yeah, all good, can I just drop these in a sec?" Marcus pointed at the box of dumbbells he needed to deliver.

"Ah thanks man," Guy looked unsure what to do so opened the door just enough for Marcus to pop the weights inside. In an instant Marcus took in the scene; two champagne glasses, the remnants of dinner and clothes everywhere. Clearly, he was interrupting.

"You've got a bit to clear up before Yumi gets here tomorrow." He told his friend.

"No, no, you don't understand." Guy appeared flustered.

Marcus gave a loud sigh. "Look Guy, I really don't want to sound moralistic but Yumi's not only Noëmi's best friend but she's my mate too. She really means a lot to me. Just last weekend you told me you're official and now this! I don't want her to get hurt, know what I mean?" Marcus' voice was firm.

Guy ran his free hand through his hair and opened his mouth to talk when Yumi poked her head out of the bedroom and shouted.

"Marcus it's so good to see you! How I've missed you!" she beamed, taking the awkwardness out of the conversation in the way only she could.

18

Relieved but cursing himself, Marcus replied, "Yumi! Of course, I should've realised. God I'm sorry mate, I should've thought..."

Guy smiled, "No worries, buddy, touching little speech there!"

Yumi arrived at the door and jumped in, "I came up a day early! Marcus you mean a lot to me too, what do you say we ditch the other two and go for it?"

Shoving the box of weights through the door with his foot, Marcus gave Yumi a nod. "Right, it looks like things are back to normal so I'm off, see you both tomorrow, I'm sure."

Hardly had the door shut, before he heard Guy and Yumi laughing, no doubt back in each other's arms.

CHAPTER 3 - YUMI

Guy was on a high. Yumi was planning a future with him and he loved that she was being proactive. The last six weeks had changed his life. After having met Yumi on New Year's Eve 2017, he was smitten. On New Year's Day, he had raced back over to Noëmi's flat, where Yumi was staying, armed with all the ingredients to cook everyone brunch. Surprisingly refreshed after the evening before, he wanted to see Yumi for as long as possible before she went back to London. Lying on the sofa bed in the sitting room, Yumi was delighted to see him arrive and rushed off to the bathroom to get ready. Guy made himself useful in the kitchen. Busy and buzzing he set up juices, croissants, different servings of eggs and bacon and had even brought Yumi flowers.

Yumi

She sat down, opposite him. Looking at him, his fine physique, kind eyes and irresistible sense of humour, she felt a bit jittery.

'*Why am I nervous? I'm never bothered by anyone or anything. Never have I felt butterflies like this, not even as a teenager. My sharp wit will pull me through, always.*'

They both reached for the orange juice at the same time, their fingertips touching. Electricity went from one to the other. Feeling self-conscious she pulled her hand back.

"Sorry, you go."

"No, no after you, please."

Of course Guy was a gentleman.

Everything in Yumi's life was planned, measured and exact. Here she was in an unfamiliar world of excitement, uncertainty and surprise. She sipped her juice.

"I know where everything is because the three of us hang out so much together. Although you should know I was Noëmi's friend first," No doubt Guy thought that this would make him more appealing to Yumi.

"My best friend has great taste. She's always picking up fit men," Yumi replied as she would to Marcus who could handle almost nothing she threw at him, even after so much practice.

However, Guy blushed, which shocked her as he seemed so confident. Now Yumi was embarrassed.

"Have some tea. I've brought green tea if you prefer? Not that I'm giving into stereotypes or thinking that because... I just remember when I was in Japan..."

"That's lovely, thank you."

They looked at each other and smiled.

"Any sign of the old married couple?" Guy asked, nodding towards the bedroom.

Yumi sighed, "Not yet, I'd go and see but I'm banned from going in there. And if we all stay in Newcastle, I'm banned from his bedroom too."

Guy almost choked on his tea from laughing. "What?"

"Oh, it's just Marcus, he gave me some big talk about boundaries. Now I have to knock and all that kind of thing, so boring, I only want to talk to Noëmi."

"Might be a good idea Yumi, believe me, it's hard to unsee things."

"Yes, but when Noëmi and I lived together in Oxford it was just like we were sisters, so much fun. I suppose he makes her happy, even if he does get in the way," she said with a sly expression.

Guy's grin got broader.

"Anyway, it's great news about their engagement. I'm hoping to be a bridesmaid. I guess his sister will be as well, but otherwise I can't think of any other competition!" She carried on.

"Damn I was hoping to be one too!"
Yumi could not stop smiling.
A door closing broke their gaze from each other.

"Oh, good morning, is this to impress me then Guy?" Marcus said as he appeared in the kitchen, wearing a black towelling robe.

"Of course, you're the one, it's always been you." Guy turned to look at his friend.

Marcus laughed. "Don't let me interrupt."

"I hear you keep chucking Yumi out of your bedroom!" Guy said.
Marcus looked over at them and gave Yumi an old-fashioned look as he waited for the kettle.

"You do overreact Marcus!" she muttered, glancing over her shoulder.
Marcus made two cups of tea. As he walked out to go back to bed, he said with a smile,

"Hopefully Yumi will have a different bedroom to invade pretty soon."

Yumi went bright red.

Guy suddenly jumped up, "Better get these roses in a vase."

So that Easter Yumi made the move to Durham, a mere fifteen miles from Guy who lived in Newcastle. Everything fell into place. Noëmi had moved in with Marcus so Yumi took over her friend's old flat in Durham. Within a week she was starting her new job at the renowned Mountford School. Guy was delighted for her.

One evening he strode into his flat to find Yumi had let herself in. Legs curled under her, a cream-coloured throw wrapped around her, she was sitting quietly on the brown leather couch.

"Yumi! What's happened?"

Forlornly she wiped her eyes with tissues from a box she was holding. Dropping his backpack, he rushed over to her and hugged her tightly.

Sighing, she began to tell him about her first two days at Mountford School, Durham, a prestigious private school with a strong academic tradition. If Yumi were honest the school's fine reputation meant extraordinarily little to her, as she would have taken a job anywhere to be in the same twenty-mile radius as Guy. She had been like a woman possessed, searching for a teaching job near Newcastle. The stars aligned and this impressive school was advertising for both a maths teacher and, in a separate advertisement, for someone who could teach Japanese. Yumi was the answer to their prayers. Having a British grandfather meant that Yumi was better adapted to life in the UK. However, whatever her heritage, nothing could have prepared her for some of the students that English schools had to offer.

Her first day went swimmingly. Yumi was the epitome of elegance and natural charm. With her long, silky hair, lovely bone structure and perfect figure, she could have turned up in a hessian sack and still commanded the room better than anyone else. The next day Yumi met her tutor group who were in the final year of sixth form. Every bit a professional, Yumi had her room ready and everything in place a good thirty minutes before the arrival of these students. She had planned her pastoral session meticulously, especially as she was replacing their well-loved tutor who had left on maternity leave.

"Good morning please come in," she had welcomed them.
Fourteen of the fifteen expected students had arrived and Yumi began her session: discussing exam preparation and final revision strategies.
About ten minutes in, the door was flung open by a confident looking student who strolled in and relaxed into his seat.
"Excuse me?" said Yumi, eyebrows raised.

"I know I'm late to the party but I've just passed my driving test! Yes! Finally!"
Students smiled and called out congratulations.

"Whilst I'm pleased for you, I can't ignore the fact you're late…"

"Miss, come on! It's taken three attempts!"

Yumi felt herself getting hot. *'Rules, a school is built on them. Relationships, they underpin everything.'*
"Mr Deehan, I take it?" She checked on her screen.
"Yes, Christopher. And you are?"
"Miss Watanabe, replacing Mrs Winter for the summer term."
Yumi was firm. "I appreciate your honesty but when you have a job you'll need to make up for time lost due to tardiness."

"Tardiness! What century is this?" Christopher leant back and looked around the room for support. The other students sat unblinking.

Yumi felt breathless. "The sanction for lateness is a detention at lunchtime. I'll see you here at 12:30pm." She looked away and noted this in her register.

"God you're stressy, Mrs Winter would've been chill, but then she's a good teacher." He gave the chair in front a kick.

"Christopher, I'm not sure that's fair. I have my job to do. Rules are rules! We all have to learn how to be. If I didn't care about you I'd let you do what you liked! You could at least apologise!"

"Well, I'm *so* sorry for being late *Miss Wat-a-knob*." The rest of the class tutted, groaned or sniggered.

"And that's now a second detention for rudeness."

Yumi thought to herself. '*In my previous so-called 'rough' east London school no one ever made fun of me or my name. There the students were as polite as those in Japan. And how those students' families often struggled financially. Yet they treated me with complete respect.*'

"Class, please read the information on the board." Yumi continued her lesson.

Guy

Guy listened as she described the rest of her day. "At lunchtime, he comes to the detention and just stares at me. His face was white, his cheeks were shaking with hatred and rage. I cut the detention short as I felt so vulnerable. Then walking out of the gate at the end of the day a small silver car buzzed right close to me. I had to jump out of the way!" Her face relived the moment.

"Did you get the car details?" Guy was in detective mode.

"No, it was so fast, probably my imagination but what did I ever do wrong?"

"Not easy upholding rules, even though everyone needs them!" Guy stroked her hair gently.

"And everyone wants them, the minute something's not fair you never hear the end of it!"

"You're the best. Remember at your old school that kid whose father was ill and all you did for them. And the sponsorship you got for the football team? You're paying it forward, one day they'll remember your help!" He put his forehead on hers and gazed lovingly into her eyes.

"I just don't know if teaching's for me. Maybe the burger bar would be the answer."

"You'd love serving burgers!" His voice was teasing.

"The kids say all I serve up is rules!"

"Yeah, leave teaching to robots with no feelings." Guy nodded.

"They call me A.I. The kids say I'm automated." He could see she was not joking.

"No! You're in the slump, remember that goodbye card? Those messages? That's the tip of the Yumi kindness iceberg."
She sat up.

"They call me sub-zero, saying I've got no feelings."

Guy ate a laugh. "How long have you been there?"

"Two days." She was deadpan.

"Let's give it a bit more time, eh?"

CHAPTER 4 - BACK TO WORK

Frank and Noëmi - 3 September 2018.

Noëmi

Noëmi was beginning her third year of teaching and was busier than ever having taken on more responsibility. *'At least this year the school will be more settled.'*

Since the John Dyer scandal was revealed in July 2017, the whole leadership team had either been sacked or morally forced to resign. Temporary solutions were hastily arranged. Frank Sprague, Noëmi's dear friend, had been given the leadership role that John Dyer had snatched from him the year before. Frank's husband Valentino Trombetta was resolutely unimpressed by this promotion.

"His workload and our fun are inversely proportional," he would complain to everyone. Nevertheless, Frank did a fine job. The school was gradually returning to normal, although this was never a word that could really describe St Wolbodo's.

Noëmi had arrived early for the first teacher training day of the term. Her friend and fellow maths teacher, Brianna, joined her in the staff room and gave her a hug.

"Well hello *Deputy Head of Sixth Form!*"

"Bri! Indeed and this year I'm going to be professional and organised!"

Noëmi sat on one of the coffee-stained chairs and started hunting for a pen in her handbag. It was the bag Marcus had bought her during their very first trip to Italy. It was a bright mustard colour and onto it she had fixed a beaded charm she had bought in the market in Sokoto. Frank walked in, gave them a wave and went straight to fix himself a coffee. Cup of caffeine in hand, he sat down.

"I love that bag. Val has a cashmere sweater in the same colour. Very classy."

Noëmi was still frantically searching. "This bag is a time capsule of my life, I've just found all these bits of paper right at the bottom, look!"

"And what are those?" Frank asked, sipping his drink.

"My change of address slips, complete with mobile number!"

She cringed at the strapline: **Newcastle watch out! She's back!**

Noëmi's moving in with Marcus!

"That was Easter! Don't you ever clear that thing out?" Bri shook her head.

Noëmi ignored the comment.

"Oh well, we can use the blank side for motivational speech bingo during those interminable meetings," Frank sighed as he stirred his coffee and gazed out at the September sunshine.

"*Ofsted, consistency, results, best teacher you can be!* Can we use phrases?" Bri asked.

"Absolutely extra points!" Frank was amused.

"You're leading one of these meetings. I hope you're going to include some of these buzzwords." Noëmi reminded him as she finally located a biro, then grabbed a glass of water.

"Of course, did you think I'd forgotten? My session's called, '*Let them know you know they know*' slash let's all fall asleep. I can hardly wait! Actually, I'm quite looking forward to yours."

Noëmi was going to present on making the End Noma Campaign the school charity of the year. "Anyway N, drink this evening? I'm going to need one."

"Absolutely, the Swan and Three Cygnets must have missed us all summer."

"Its takings will have plummeted." Frank rolled his eyes in mock horror.

Noëmi laughed.

Pat Davies, school secretary, walked slowly into the staffroom.

"Oi, **No-enemy** you've got a visitor." She called out.

"Pat, who is it?"

"That Stoney mother, she walks in unannounced, looking for you. The barefaced cheek. In my day you waited and spoke when spoken to." Pat was red with anger. "She got banned from that primary school, my friend, the one who works at Asda, knows all about it. Nasty business."

Noëmi put her glass down and turned to Frank, "Should I see her?"

"Yes, come on, I'll go with you. Back up."

Noëmi smiled at Frank gratefully. She gathered her things, deciding to meet Mrs Stoney and then go onto the main hall for the meetings.

Mrs Stoney was standing in the school foyer shifting from foot to foot, handbag under her arm. Upon seeing Noëmi she fixed her stare.

"Mrs Stoney, how can I help you?" They stood in the reception area.

"Freddie's having nightmares about your persecution of him." Mrs Stoney gave in one breath.

Noëmi noticed Frank turn away and cover his mouth. "Excuse me," he said as he moved back around.

"Oh, I'm sorry to hear that, but I don't think that's the correct choice of word Mrs Stoney. I follow the St Wolbodo's behaviour policy, that's all!" Noëmi was professional.

"We've had a private child psychologist's report done and it appears that Freddie is traumatised and at risk of becoming a school refuser." Mrs Stoney's eyes were wide and wild. Noëmi heard Frank cough and maybe mutter something.

"I'd be happy to look at it, but please rest assured that everything is a clean slate and I really want Freddie to do well, he's a bright boy, gifted in maths." Noëmi was sincere. "I have no problem with Freddie, only his behaviour choices."

Mrs Stoney was dumbfounded. She shifted her soft burgundy leather bag to her other shoulder. "Well as long as you don't ruin his chances Mzzz McAllister."

"Absolutely not, why don't we keep in contact and have regular meetings to help Freddie. Here let me write down my school phone number, I have a direct line now that I'm Deputy Head of Sixth Form."

Noëmi had her own handbag over her arm. Fishing in her handbag Noëmi, found an old piece of paper and wrote her school email and direct line on it. Mrs Stoney took the small note and popped it into her bag.

Mrs Stoney left.

Noëmi turned to Frank, "I know exactly what you want to say!"

"That saves me the bother!" Frank quipped. "Freddie's sister Elizabeth caused me endless problems and his brother Jude is keeping all the wrong company."

"That must be my fault too! But does she realise that us teachers never give up on kids?"

"Indeed!" He sighed.

He put his hand on her back and they went towards the hall for the staff meeting.

"Anyway, onto the important things in life. Don't forget the bingo!" He mused.

She gave Frank a knowing look and went to settle down to hear about how *'exam results could be improved by personalised feedback.'*

Within minutes the teachers were back into the routine of crowded classrooms, busy corridors and endless marking. Most were already counting the weeks until the next holiday.

Alex and Marcus - 3 September 2018.

Marcus

Over at Newcastle RVI, Mr Alex James, new Trauma Consultant and Dr Marcus McKenzie had an opportunity to catch up straight after their first shift together. The pair moved into Alex's office, just behind the busy A&E staff desk. Calls, bleeps and Tannoy announcements faded into the background as Alex shut his door, sat back in his burgundy leather chair and enquired.

"What brought you to Newcastle RVI then Marcus?"

"I thought it was a good-sized teaching hospital in a large city where I could take on more responsibility by being in a smaller department." Marcus delivered the perfect answer.

"And then you can tell me the other reason, when I let you know I worked closely with your friend Mohammad down at King's."

Alex's eyes sparkled impishly.

Marcus laughed, looking down for a moment, "Okay I had a relationship I needed to sort out. I had to do that otherwise it was going to distract me massively and I figured I'd worked so hard at Oxford that I've got lots of time to focus on my career. Junior Doctor training is pretty much the same everywhere as long as it's a good-sized hospital. It doesn't mean I'm not ambitious, quite the opposite." He sipped his coffee.

Alex leant forward and the afternoon light made his blonde hair appear halo like.

"I understand, as you know I was at Oxford too, a couple of decades before you! It's so much work. I'm glad you know the importance of personal happiness; we have the most stressful job and you can't do that without support. Mohammad has told me how brilliant it is to work with you, that your temperament is well balanced, that you're a team player. To hear first-hand how much you do for your patients is the best testimony. I'm delighted."

"Thank you, I must say the team here is awesome. I'm learning all the time; everyone plays such an important part." Marcus put his coffee cup on the side table.

"And you get on with everyone. Plus, I looked over your academic record, it's most impressive."

"I've also researched what you've done, which is really outstanding and I'm very pleased to have you as my mentor."

Alex leaned back again and popped his foot onto the opposite knee.

"Talking to my predecessor I hear that the amount of praise everyone gave you became quite overwhelming!"

Marcus was embarrassed, "I wouldn't say that…"

"But you know there's been a complaint about you." Alex interrupted.

"What?" The blood drained from Marcus' face; he was visibly shaken.

"Oh my goodness, you look mortified, I'm sorry I'm being a bit naughty! A patient complained about their doctor being involved in a very public display of affection at the hospital entrance last year! Anecdotally the team were all highly amused, actually *relieved* is the word your previous mentor used."
Marcus twigged.

"Oh! They never told me about that! Honestly…"

"Said relationship I take?"

"Yes, yes, only her. Noëmi. They could've told me… all this time…oh now those big smiles that Monday morning make sense!"

"Ah a mischievous bunch hey? So what, you're engaged?" Alex finished his coffee and grimaced as he risked drinking the dregs.

"Yes, getting married next year to Noëmi, she's a maths teacher in Durham."

"I'm married to Cathy; she's a midwife and she's also working here now. We have three daughters who spend all our money.

You know I've led trauma and A&E departments at Kings plus

I've been an expert witness in a number of cases. I love to cycle, play squash, all that sort of thing."

"Busy! Expert witness, that sounds fascinating."

"It is when they listen to the evidence. Had a case a while back where the victim clearly did not get justice. It still keeps me awake to be honest."

"That's tough. We never give up on our patients, eh? I like to play squash too; we should have a game sometime."

"You'll destroy me!" Alex relaxed back into his squeaky chair.

Alex explained that he had made a difficult decision to leave London. Having fallen in love with the area when his daughter attended Durham University, he felt their lifestyle would be better up north, plus he was finding the commuting tiring. They chatted some more and spoke about the work Marcus had recently done at the End Noma Campaign Hospital, in Nigeria, and how they could build on that in the next few years.

CHAPTER 5 - NIGERIA 2018

Noëmi

Back in their old hometown of Newcastle, life was turning out so much better than expected for Noëmi and Marcus. Having joined forces to fundraise when they were together at Oxford, they had finally fulfilled their ambition to help first hand with the fight against the neglected disease noma. Spending four weeks, during the summer of 2018, at the End Noma Campaign (ENC) hospital in Nigeria, Noëmi and Marcus had taken on active roles for the charity. Marcus had carried out medical assessments, initial interventions and small surgeries as a doctor. Noëmi worked with the health promotion team. Marcus was given two of the four weeks off as special leave because he was involved in a medical project.

27 July 2018.

After the arduous journey, during which they had to change planes three times, Noëmi and Marcus finally arrived in Sokoto, Nigeria. Hit by the heat and the hardship of the people, nothing could prepare them for the poverty that perpetuated the suffering of the population.

They were just sorting out their bags when they saw a familiar figure.

"Jesse!" Marcus' face dropped.

Jesse strolled over, hands in pockets, huge grin on face. Tanned, hair bleached by the sun, teeth dazzling; he was looking great.

"Noëmi hello! Welcome to the ENC Ritz! This is about as good as it gets!" He put his hands out to gesture around at the hospital buildings. "If you're lucky I'll be keeping you company at night, not the snakes!" He gave her a wink.

Neither had expected to see Jesse as he had said he would be in the UK when Noëmi informed him of the trip.

Since his spectacular disappearance from her life two years earlier, their contact had been quite formal so she had not disclosed the change in her personal circumstances. Therefore she had described her travel partner quite simply as an 'emergency specialist, one year into junior doctor training.'

'Why do I now wish I'd explained that I was bringing my fiancé?'

"Hi Jesse, which is more dangerous then? You or those creatures?" she tried to joke his comment off but felt suddenly uncomfortable.

'No obligation to talk to Jesse about my private life, especially as he's not part of it.'

Ignoring Marcus, he raised his sunglasses, smiled at her and gave her a big, long hug. Finally releasing her, he turned to a tight-lipped Marcus.

"And you must be the doc, I'm a nurse so we'll be working together for the month," he shook Marcus' hand eagerly.

"Brilliant!" replied Marcus, only Noëmi could hear the sarcasm in his voice.

"Yes Marcus, you know Jesse, from the charity ball."

"How could I forget?"

Noëmi gave him a look although she could understand that the four weeks with Jesse would probably not be something he would be looking forward to.

"We really can't wait to help and do what we can," Noëmi stated, to remind Marcus of the reason for their trip.

"Absolutely, now I've worked in A&E, doing minor surgeries. I'm qualified in many ways," Marcus clearly heard her message.

"This is awesome, let's leave your bags and I'll show you around, it really helps that you're friends too."

There was still something for Jesse to understand.

The buildings were clean, simple and well aired. The wards were functional and somewhat sparse. Hospital beds with their blue mattresses, all fitted with the very necessary mosquito nets, were set out in rows. The End Noma Campaign was providing well for the patients and was fully supported by the Ministry of Health in Nigeria. Starting the tour straight away, Jesse put his arm around Noëmi and led them through the buildings, which were all coming off a central courtyard. This is where patients could relax during the long rehabilitation time after their facial reconstructive surgeries. Jesse smiled and waved at all the Nigerian staff who made up ninety-five per cent of the workforce. Many well qualified doctors and nurses cared for patients. Volunteer helpers visited throughout the year offering new training and expertise whenever they could. Noëmi had managed to free herself from Jesse as they walked back into the courtyard. Jesse turned to the pair, but basically ignored Marcus.

"How are you, Noëmi? I'm really sorry about what happened.

I've turned my life around, you know, stopped drinking, exercise is my new obsession." He lifted his top to show off his abdominal muscles.

"That's amazing Jesse! The lifestyle changes and the abs!"

He laughed and put his arm around her again. Marcus looked on unimpressed. Noëmi was very conscious she was not wearing her engagement ring as they had decided to leave it at home because of 'the hands-on nature of the work'. Turning to her, Jesse went straight to the point, as if Marcus was not there.

"I really regret what I did and how I treated you, Noëmi. If I could turn back the clock I would. When I got sober I thought of you at that station, just wondering what the fuck had happened. Then I was so rude to your friend when she came to check on me, sorry is not enough, I behaved badly." He scuffed his trainer on the earth as he spoke.

Marcus

Marcus decided to stroll over to look at the trees, newly planted in the fight against desertification.

"Jesse, remember I ended it before that weekend. But I was terrified when I couldn't reach you. Anyway, it was, what? Two years ago now."

"Yeah I messed up big time."

"Jesse don't worry, I know it was a terrible time for you, I understand."

"I've been so looking forward to seeing you again, counting the days..."

"Jesse I have..."

"Do you think it would be impossible for us to try again?" He looked at her sincerely.

"Jesse, I don't think you realise, my life has moved on. I'm engaged..."

"Oh my God, I didn't know." His face froze.

"Yes I'm sorry, we're good though, you and me, good friends."

"Friends is not really what turns me on, who's the lucky man...or woman?" Jesse sighed and looked to the skies.

"The doctor, Marcus…"

"The guy from Oxford? That one over there? Your old mate? No way, why did you choose him? Did you see the shelf looming or something?"

This was all loud enough for Marcus to overhear from his tactful vantage point under a Nigerian Acacia tree.

The most awkward of silences came over them. Jesse glanced between them both.

"Sorry! Hey just ignore me, the sun gets me a bit crazy, let's get you guys to your digs. Sorry you know there's no mixing. The local religion doesn't allow that. It's like boarding school, single sex dorms, lights out and all that!"

Jesse had attended one and probably assumed they had too as they had been to Oxford. Neither Noëmi nor Marcus would know anything about such schools given that their alma mater was state comprehensive, Newcastle Green Academy. Their old school did not enjoy the most prestigious of reputations, slumbering at the bottom of most league tables.

Determined to make a worthwhile contribution they both got to work straight away. Marcus was skilled in the intricate minor surgeries that could help in the process of repairing the faces of the youngest victims. As part of the decision to allow him special leave, his mentor had thought it would be good to link the project up with the training aspect of the hospital. In doing so, it would encourage surgeons and trainee doctors to spend time supporting the fight against neglected tropical diseases.

The vagaries of the Wi-Fi meant that Noëmi and Marcus found it hard to keep in touch in spite of only being metres apart. However, Jesse seemed to have no problem getting his messages through to Noëmi.

By the end of the first week Marcus and Noëmi fully immersed in the incessant work and only catching glimpses of each other here and there. One evening Jesse called the whole team to a meeting to make arrangements for the following week.

Marcus was reminded of when he would look out for Noëmi at school. During sixth form, they used to have group sessions about personal development and relationships. Students saw these as 'pointless', as did the teachers. The usual format was a quick video and then 'pair work' where students would 'discuss the topic'. Everyone was happy with this; teachers would catch up on work and students could chat.

One such session was arranged for the final year students. Noëmi had appeared in an outfit perfectly recreated from one of her mother's favourite Eighties videos. The pedal pushers, striped t-shirt and black pumps that she had meticulously put together, were not typical sixth form attire. Her old tormentors laughed, as usual, so she quickly sat down. Marcus then stood up and walked all the way across the room to get the seat by hers.

"Did you not see I had a chair for you?" he said as he dumped his rucksack down.

Going pink, Noëmi got her folder out and turned to him.

"Everyone saw you do that!" She whispered.

"So? I want to talk to you and this is the only lesson you can get away with that, at the insalubrious Newcastle Green Academy!"

"Insalubrious!" she laughed.

"I'm preparing for my Oxford interview by eating words! I got the letter today!" Marcus leant back in his chair and stretched out his legs.

"They'll see right through that! I've not heard yet if I've got an interview for Cambridge, stressful!"

"Mrs Gomez says I'm one of the first to get an interview probably because it's medicine and they have so many applicants. Don't worry." He sat forward and put his hand on her arm to reassure her.

"Bedside manner already Dr McKenzie!" Noëmi looked appreciatively at him and sighed.

"Oxford, Cambridge, they're next to each other right?" He looked quizzically at the worksheet as he asked.

"No idea, it's all happening so quickly. All those colleges! That nearly finished me off trying to choose one."

They then tried to focus on the video that was playing about statistics for teenage pregnancies in the northeast.

"They were laughing at my outfit. If they don't shut up, next time I'll wear the *Italians do it better* t-shirt from the video, if I can find one." Noëmi grimaced.

Marcus laughed, enjoying her spirit. "Do it! I'll get you one! Ignore them, you're the only one with any style around here." He passed her a hand-out that was coming round about emergency contraception.

She informed him, "This is from the *Papa Don't Preach* video. Does it look that bad?"

"Perfectly themed for this lesson then! You always look good to me whatever you wear!" He leant across and whispered something in her ear. Confident he relaxed back again into his chair.

"What are you like!" She rolled her eyes and tried desperately not to join his smile.

Jolted back to reality in Nigeria, he listened as the session began. A large ceiling fan wobbled slowly above their heads and the orange glow of the lights faded momentarily from time to time. Electricity from a solar powered generator was temperamental. A few insects buzzed around as the group sat in the hospital office on the low benches. Jesse leant against a heavy looking chipped wooden desk.

"Noma is a disease that shouldn't exist. Our aim is to achieve that zero noma goal. Now today, we need to think about our work in the community and the stigma on survivors. Their disfigurement often means they're shunned by their own communities. We need to reach out, work with traditional healers and encourage victims to get to hospital sooner. Next week a group of us will be away so that we can spread awareness in the remote rural areas. The team will be myself as trip leader, Esperance on security, Maduka as driver and Noëmi organising the outreach. In my absence, Tayo will be in charge here. So guys all get packed. We leave at 5am tomorrow. See you in the courtyard."

The meeting dispersed and Marcus looked round for Noëmi, worried that she would be out away from the hospital. Jesse was explaining the itinerary and gave her some maps and a walkie talkie to charge.

"Wow that'll be an adventure," Marcus said to her when he finally got close.

"Mmm I'm a bit scared, it all looks so easy from a distance but I'm not as brave as I thought I was. Snakes scare me now that I've read up on them!"

He was jolted by colleagues moving some boxes through the office for the trip.

"Don't worry they'll look after you, Esperance and Maduka are right on their game and I think Jesse has a bit of a vested interest! Watch out for the sleeping arrangements!"

"Don't worry I can hold my own. Let's keep focused on what we're here to achieve hey?"

Given the lack of privacy they did not give each other a goodbye kiss which left him a bit unquiet.

Noëmi

The week on community outreach was extremely important. The group checked the water points, distributed information leaflets and gave out free hygiene products such as toothbrushes. A screening programme was set up to look out for malnutrition which was one of the contributing causes of noma. Building trust and awareness enabled the team to get the message to some of the most isolated communities.

After a long week on the road, the group reached their last stop in the Sokoto region of Nigeria. Arriving at their accommodation, Jesse took one last shot at persuading Noëmi to return his affection. Sitting, sipping homemade lemonade, in the small lobby of the guest house, he turned to her.

"So, Miss McAllister, as those school kids call you, where do you want your life to be in five years' time, when you're thirty?"

"Jesse I have no idea, I take each day as it comes at the moment! What about you?"

"Settled down, with someone like you, or even actually with you!" He looked at her across the table of the small village guest house where they had stopped for the night.

"Mmm that might be a bit crowded Jesse! I'm already settling down with Marcus. That's decided." She tightened her ponytail.

"Why him?"

43

"Love Jesse you know that old fashioned thing! Anyway, I'm sure you'll find the right person too. Where are Esperance and Maduka?"

"They know people in the village so they're staying with them, just us here. Some people from another organisation too." Looking over her shoulder, she checked the clock.

'*How convenient*,' Noëmi thought to herself.

The ceiling fan whirring above them reminded her of Marcus' flat which she had just moved into a few months before. Her mind drifted to how well they were enjoying living together. Suddenly she remembered Jesse was there.

"Shall we get food?" The small kitchen did not give a choice but offered a meal of the day and a cold can of drink. They chatted and when they had paid up Noëmi wanted to go to bed. Locking her door behind her, she looked around the small room with its bowl and bottle of water for washing. The bed looked clean with a mustard yellow candlewick bedspread and of course the essential mosquito net. A Qur'an lay on the bedside table and the shutters were firmly closed. Gingerly she checked with her torch for any creatures she did not wish to spend the night with. She popped herself into bed, mosquito net tightly in place, walkie talkie at her side.

The next morning, she was up bright and early having slept well. The street outside was alive with the sounds of the Muezzin, markets and motorbikes. Feeling positive about the work they had done, she was now keen to get back to the hospital. Hers and Jesse's rooms had been on the upper floor and the only other room was occupied by a worker from another charity, not involved in their work. As she settled their bill, she was surprised to see the other aid worker walk downstairs with a young local woman whom Noëmi had not seen before. Noëmi watched as this man had a final conversation with his new friend, smiled at her and waved her off.

Jesse appeared yawning, "Sleep okay?"

"Yes, thanks, you?" She was looking past him at the pair.

Nodding over his shoulder at the aid worker, Jesse sighed, "You get some real wankers in this business. Don't worry, Esperance and I have reported it; whistle blowing. He'll be getting a visit soon from the law enforcement here. They won't be all touchy feely about his rights and all that shit, like they are in the UK. He's probably abusing others. I won't accept any of that crap from any of my guys. We run a clean operation. If anyone crossed the line, they'd be out, straight away, everyone knows that. We have top class safeguarding and don't tolerate little shits like that arsehole there. Of course it would've been fine for me to share my bed with you, if you'd been willing. That's quite different."

"Yeah, I get what you're saying Jesse."

After a final stop, to talk about mental health support, at the last village on their itinerary, the group made their way back to the hospital. Having taken her bags back to her dorm, Noëmi then settled in the administration office to write up the report from the trip. Marcus walked past in his blue scrubs on his way to theatre and looked visibly relieved to see her back safe and sound. She wondered whether he had been worried about snakes as they seemed to be everywhere.

CHAPTER 6 - OPPORTUNIST

4 September 2018.

Marcus

RVI, A&E, Marcus was assessing a child with a fractured arm.

'What I wouldn't give for tea, water, anything...every minute another ambulance! That waiting room will be packed by now.'

"So young man a bit of extra yummy Calpol to stop this arm hurting and then we're going to use a special camera to look right inside your body like Superman!"

The child gave a toothy grin and Marcus signed the paperwork for the radiographer.

'Shift over. Debrief home.'

Walking to the meeting room he saw new manager, Evan, pulling two large boxes along the corridor. Her soft, golden hair swayed like a shimmering sunset as she tugged.

"Whoa! Let me help you with those!" He ran to her side. Sweet lilies filled his nostrils.

"Thank you! We need these for paediatrics. They're comfort kits donated by a conglomerate of companies." She stood up, tucked her shirt into her skirt and took a breath.

"Nice one, what's inside?"

"Not sure but the last ones were awesome, we can take a look. Just need to get these to the store cupboard over there!" Her voice strained as she heaved.

Pushing as she pulled, together they got to the doorway. Evan jolted the cupboard open with her butt and reached her hand in to turn on the light.

"Here we go!"

Marcus wedged the door open with a broom.

'*Need to make sure she feels safe!*'

They got the boxes in place and stood back to admire their work. She put her hand up for a high five. Marcus slapped in celebration of a job well done. The door slammed shut as the broom gave way.

"Let's take a look!" Evan's eyes sparkled as she dived a hand into the first large box. Pulling out a drawstring bag there were puzzle toys, crayons, a model ambulance and a neon pink squidgy ball.

"Did they donate all that?" Marcus could only imagine the children's faces.

"Absolutely, I used to get these for St George's and they're working with me here too! All free, another ten boxes are arriving tomorrow. Where will we put them?"

"We'll find space, that's so brilliant, well done Evan!" Marcus was overwhelmed as he thought of some of the young patients. Evan giggled and drew herself up. In the dim light her eyes were shining. Playfully she threw the soft ball at Marcus, who instinctively put out his hand and caught it. "Good catch! But I bet everyone says that about you!" Evan gave him a coy look.

"Hey!" Marcus laughed.

She grinned back and put her hand on his arm to steady herself. Together they closed the box. Turning out the light they headed back to the corridor.

"What are you doing now?" Soft red lips asked him.

"Debrief then home, it's past eight already! But what about you, don't you finish at six in those cushy office jobs?"

Evan raised her eyebrows, "Cushy? Dr McKenzie? I don't think so! No, I need to get a lot sorted in patient care. I have so many ideas, you know!"

He looked at his watch and put a kick in his heel, "Dedication! I love that! See you tomorrow!"

"Looking forward to it!" Evan called as Marcus moved ahead and disappeared into his meeting.

5 September 2018.

Tianna

Tianna McKenzie, Marcus' younger sister, walked along, drinking in the bright September sunshine. She was returning from her first day of the autumn term at Newcastle Green Academy. She was now entering her final year. The pressure of expectation was pushing down on her entire being. Fifteen years of McKenzies at '*Newky Green*' would be coming to an end.

Every teacher made the same, '*Ah the final McKenzie*' comment. In addition to the attention at school, she was now alone in the family home as her brothers were all away. The silence and space were unnatural to her; two bedrooms stood empty where the three boys had alternated the sharing combinations. Tianna had found herself through squabbling and holding her own with her brothers. She knew they loved her dearly and she missed them viscerally.

48

A surprising relief to her was that Marcus was only twenty minutes' walk away. She would pass his flat on her way to school, often popping in for breakfast or tea depending on his shifts. She had his whole rota on her phone and knew it off by heart. When it was school holidays Noëmi would be there and she could spend time quietly with her too. Never had she ever imagined that she would appreciate her annoying and over serious eldest sibling as much. He had grown into a fine man and was blessed with a partner whom she adored.

On her way home she stopped off. Sitting at their kitchen table she sipped mint tea and ate a ginger biscuit as she looked at the late evening sun streaming through the French windows. She hugged a cushion, curled her feet under herself and felt happy to be chatting to Noëmi.

"Thank you for taking me to Italy, you know it was my first time abroad. I had such a lovely time apart from that baby nearly drowning. Your grandparents were so kind to me."

"Think about what your family has done for me and my dad! We're all one big family now!" Noëmi looked up from her teacher's planner.

"It was so exciting to fly!" Tianna took another biscuit.

"I remember! I'd only been to Italy when I was your age. So for me it was awesome to go somewhere like Nigeria."

"Nigeria! For the same money you could have gone to New York or LA, you know somewhere decent. I hear the shopping in the US is unbelievable."

"Ha! Nigeria was an amazing place. We had a purpose. Plus there was shopping. Look at my handbag charm, so different!"

Tianna looked curiously at the beaded souvenir. "It must be nice to be with someone you love, you know in the sunshine, by the sea. Even if it is my brother," she gave a sly smile.

49

Noëmi laughed. "What's going on with you then?"

Tianna opened her heart about all the unwanted comments from teachers. The assumption from her parents that she would emulate her brothers' success. Friends who were bothering her. Social media that was driving her crazy.

"They want me to go for Oxbridge." She played with the packet of ginger biscuits.

"What do you think?"

"I'm scared of not getting in." She finished her tea.

"Yeah, I felt like that too. Marcus is free on Saturday, why doesn't he chat with you, take you shopping or something? He's got money now, give me a break from him!"

"Perfect! I'm in!"

Noëmi packed her work away and picked up a bridal brochure.

"I don't know what I'd do if you weren't so close," Tianna said.

"Make sure you choose a decent colour for those bridesmaid's dresses, I want to wear it to prom too, I like rose gold, that would look good on me."

"I love rose gold, so that's decided then."

"And another trip to Italy?" They smiled at each other.

CHAPTER 7 - ITALY 2018

Noëmi

Tianna had reminded Noëmi of their trip to the Amalfi coast that summer to visit her mother's parents.

24 August 2018.
With their work in Nigeria complete, Noëmi and Marcus were travelling from Sokoto to Italy to meet up with friends and family. Arriving at Naples airport, the heat was thick; the August sun burned down from the cloudless sky. It seemed even hotter than Nigeria and the mercury confirmed this. Climbing into a cool taxi they had time to admire the heat hazed hills on their way to her mother's parents' villa.

As they arrived, Noëmi's grandparents, Giuseppe and Francesca, were a picture of pure delight, the minute they saw her. Running to greet her, she was whisked into their arms as Marcus paid the driver and collected their bags. Donnie McAllister looked relieved and was especially happy that his daughter and her fiancé had survived this far off land. Marcus's seventeen year old sister, Tianna, had travelled with him, along with their friend Sarai Bianchi and her baby. Friends, Frank and Valentino, were staying in a neighbouring villa. Guy and Yumi had been busy that summer, moving in together, and had also just arrived, straight from Guy's sister's wedding. Donnie helped Marcus with the bags and took them to their rooms. The chatter of the happy group echoed into the olive groves on the hillside.

Tianna had never been abroad before and was excited to be in Italy. Noëmi's grandparents treated her as their own. Neither could not understand much of what the other said but the smiles told everything. Yumi and Noëmi, especially, took her under their wing. Sitting outside on the terrace, Yumi was checking a map of the local area.

"We've hired a car so I'll take you shopping," Yumi told Tianna, "Looks like I need to take your future sister-in-law shopping too, what are those shorts?" Lowering her sunglasses, she looked over at Noëmi.

"My main bag's still in Nigeria, can I borrow some of your stuff?" She looked down at her Bermuda's, which now seemed very boy scout-like compared with Yumi and Tianna's short shorts.

"Absolutely, for all our sakes! You look like an aid worker!" Tianna burst out laughing, "Can I have wine tonight?" Tianna asked, sipping a bottle of water.

"Yes, but go steady, drink water too, I'll keep an eye on you. Make sure Marcus doesn't see. We've got this." Yumi gave her a nod and repositioned her sunglasses.

"I heard all that, you two!" Noëmi let them know.

"She's morphing into a female version of Marcus isn't she!" Yumi joked to Tianna, who pulled down her fashionable sun shades to match her elegant new best friend.

Noëmi

A morning spent in the artisan shops of Amalfi delighted Tianna and revamped Noëmi. Having enjoyed fresh pizza and local gelato, Marcus, Noëmi, Tianna, Guy and Yumi had stopped off for a late afternoon swim on their way back to the villa. The sea was a deep blue green, and the only sound was the gentle swish of the waves lapping the beach at the local lido. Under one of the brightly striped umbrellas, shielding from the blazing temperatures, Tianna, Yumi and Noëmi were barely able to move. Guy and Marcus went to buy drinks.

"What are you doing?" Tianna asked as she noticed Noëmi searching on her phone.

"Looking up the What3words for this place."

"You're such a word geek!" Tianna rearranged herself on the raffia chair.

"Just a geek!" corrected Yumi, poking her friend playfully.

"Compromises, delimit, cityscape! That's quite a good one!" Tianna balanced her ill-fitting fashion sunglasses on her face.

"Looking good in those!" Yumi encouraged.

"They're just cheapo rubbish, this is what I need!" Tianna pulled them off and replaced them with her brother's polaroids.

"Don't put any finger marks on those!" Noëmi warned her with a smile.

Yumi laughed out loud, "He's so meticulous! But this time, he'll never know!"

Noëmi took a photo of Tianna. "Evidence!"

Marcus' sister wrestled to delete the photo.

Grabbing the sunglasses, Noëmi put them on herself. "Whoa these are good!"

Their playfulness was interrupted by a concerned voice calling out, "Matteo! Matteo!" A crying woman was running along the beach, seemingly searching. Noëmi gazed out into the distance to see what the problem was but saw nothing. Then the polaroids did their job. Suddenly Noëmi's heart stopped. In the sea she saw a dark shape bobbing up and down." She shouted at Tianna, "Call an ambulance right now, use my phone, the number's 112, location tell them, compromises, delimit, cityscape, got that? 112, do it right now tell them to come to this Lido, there's a child drowning! Yumi come on!"

Marcus

Seeing them tear towards the shoreline, Marcus dropped the drinks and started to go to Noëmi. He heard her shout, "A child, in the sea!"

Yumi accelerated up and began to make furiously for the infant, who was about four metres out. Her speed through the water was breath-taking. Grabbing the small child, Yumi turned back. Noëmi and Tianna were now right behind. Between them it was a struggle to hold him out of the water. They righted him and pulled him from the waves. Marcus shouted from the beach as he ran to the shoreline.

"Check his airway? Start giving mouth to mouth now!"

They got the child onto the sand and by now, having heard their shouts, a small crowd was forming. Exhausted from their mammoth effort, Yumi and Tianna caught their breath. They looked on as Marcus and Guy got to work. Having laid the infant on his back, Marcus checked his airway.

"He's not breathing. I'll give the rescue breaths. Five to start then you give 30 compressions, centre of his chest, one arm, go down 4 centimetres. Then it's two and 30. Got that?" Marcus shouted to Guy, who gave him a nod. Marcus gave the breaths and Guy gave the compressions everything. Noëmi was holding the mother who was screaming hysterically, hardly able to breathe, "Matteo, Matteo, Dio per favore! Dio per favore!"

"É un dottore," Noëmi reassured her that Marcus was a doctor.

"Come on, come on," Marcus begged as the pair repeated the routine.

"His name's Matteo!" Noëmi offered.

"Matteo! Matteo!" Marcus kept calling.
Noëmi held the trembling mother in her arms.
After what felt like an eternity the tiny Matteo coughed, sicked up a lot of sea water and began to cry loudly. Putting him into the recovery position Marcus checked his pulse and his breathing. Matteo's mother collapsed with joy.

"Thank God," said Marcus, sitting back on his heels. Guy fell back onto the sand.
By now the ambulance had arrived. Racing to the scene in full uniform, the three medics took over and were able to give oxygen. Noëmi translated. "They say thank you and well done. There are lifeguards but apparently there's a nasty rip current so they're impressed you got to the child Yumi, Tianna."

Through her tears Matteo's mother, still bent double, thanked the group. She was gently helped into the ambulance to go to the hospital with her child.

Noëmi

The crowd clapped, one of the bystanders, a rather jolly looking, middle-aged man, came over and shook all their hands furiously. Eventually the onlookers dispersed, and the cafe owner brought them some bottles of ice-cold water. A feeling of calm came over the beach after the drama of the ambulance arriving and the paramedics rushing to help. Noëmi and her group sat in silence on the sand in the burning heat, recovering.

"I wouldn't do your job for all the money in the world. Nearly gave me a heart attack!" Commented Guy.

"Yeah well, you just did! It's a bit different being away from the comfort of the hospital where you have all the machines and medicines to help. Anyone not breathing, it's a three-minute window. Terrifying."

"Will he be okay?" Tianna asked, drawing a face in the sand.

"He looked good but it's dangerous, that secondary drowning thing."

"They're going to update us later." Noëmi said. "Yumi, you can swim!"

"I swam a lot as a teenager, but that was tough, treading water like that. He was so far out, I nearly lost him, he was going under, thank God you and Tianna were there!" she wiped her face as Guy put his arm around her. "As a teenager, I became a little obsessed with swimming. 2011 affected me badly, I've told you about my friend. Ridiculous really there's no way to beat a force like that."

Everyone was still; taking in what had happened.

Arriving back at the villa the group were emotionally exhausted. The non-family members were staying in the little guest house in the grounds of the villa. They returned to rest before the evening. Being Marcus and Noëmi's turn to cook, they arrived in the family kitchen almost immediately and explained the events to her grandparents.

The house where Noëmi's mother, Manon, had grown up was a typical Italian country farmhouse. The kitchen was enormous with an ornate fireplace. On the chimney breast was a fresco style painting of two Roman nymphs carrying wine jars. The walls were pale buttermilk, the ceiling was slatted with solid mahogany and a majestic iron candelabra hung down from it. French windows gave out onto a terrace from which you could see over the whole valley of vineyards, olive groves and lemon trees. It was perfect for long evenings of outdoor dining in the late summer sun. Between the group, they arranged for each pair to cook and clear up one time during the week. By taking turns, the week was very pleasantly catered. Tianna, enjoying the lack of chores on this holiday, quickly engineered to do as little as possible, keeping baby Lucia occupied and disappearing from any episodes of domesticity. By the end of the week everyone wanted to stay forever.

Giuseppe and Francesca listened to Noëmi's account of the beach rescue and were astounded and impressed by the actions of their young guests. Little by little the rest of the group arrived and they all sat down to eat. Wine was passed around and Giuseppe handed out cold beers. Subdued chatter started and freshly baked olive bread, hot from the oven, was shared.

Noëmi's phone rang. "It's Matteo's mother! Pronto!" she replied.
Everyone stopped as they heard the background sounds of Matteo's mother talking.
Noëmi relayed the conversation as they spoke;
"...è fantastico...he's going to make a full recovery...domani? He can be discharged tomorrow! Gelato...he says he wants the ice cream he was promised at the beach! ...resta in contatto, se mai visiti Newcastle in Inghilterra, vieni a trovarci!"

They heard Matteo's mother breakdown, "non piangere va tutto bene..." Noëmi reassured her. "She can't thank everyone enough. She feels terrible, poor woman. She let little Matteo run ahead for what felt like a second, when she stopped to put some rubbish in a bin. She says she can't forgive herself. The terror is overwhelming."

Everyone could hear the mother crying as the phone call ended.

Sarai leant over and stroked Lucia's head.

"Lucia is never to be let out of my sight," she announced dramatically to Donnie who was sitting next to her.

"Sarai, I understand. I used to feel like that with Noëmi. Even now I'd put a tracking device on her if I could."

Hearing this Noëmi got up and went over to her father. Standing behind his chair, she put her arms around her father's neck and kissed him on the cheek. He put his hand up to hers. Together they looked at the little one year old sleeping peacefully in her pushchair.

"Noëmi, where have the last twenty-five years gone since you were born?"

"Come sei bella, come una stella!" She whispered to her father.

"How beautiful you are, like a star!" He translated.

"That's what you and mum would say to me every night before I went to sleep, remember?"

She felt a warm tear fall on her hand.

CHAPTER 8 - DRIVEN

Marcus

"And the weather will continue to be stormy with sudden showers, a six degree high then thundery towards the evening. Have a great day everyone!"

Capital North East radio kept Marcus company as he drove along. Remembering the days when he had to trudge through the rain, he felt snug and warm in his vehicle and sorry for those outside. Suddenly he recognised Evan battling along with an umbrella and a laptop bag. He pulled over, leant across and opened the car door.

"Hey Evan! Do you want a lift?"

"Oh, thank you so much Marcus, you're a lifesaver," her sweet, lily perfume filled the car.

"Now that's always the aim!" He joked back. They both laughed.

'*I just love being able to help people!* Marcus felt triumphant.

"And now here's one for those of you in love today, forget about the weather outside, snuggle up together in the warm and listen…"

The strains of Ed Sheeran's **Perfect** started. Marcus started humming along, "I like this one," thinking the lyrics reminded him of his journey with Noëmi.

"Me too!" smiled Evan, glancing across at him.

Their eyes met.

"How are you finding Newcastle? Takes some getting used to!"

Evan laughed, "I've found a suitable place in an area called Jesmond."

"Oh wow! That's where I live! There's a great deli cafe. I often go there after a run on my days off." He turned to her as they stopped at the traffic lights.

"Oh, where's that?" Her eyes found his.

"Cake Stories, the coffee is *so* good!"

"I'll make sure I try it. What about pubs for a night out?"

"Bar Blanc is good for a romantic drink, but Quattro to watch the football! Something for everyone! You'll love it!" The lights changed and they were on their way.

"Thanks for the tips, we should all go out some time, I don't really know many people yet!"

Ed Sheeran was still singing.

He glanced over at her, just as she looked at him.

"Right...of course," Marcus smiled.

Arriving at the hospital staff car park, Marcus popped his permit onto the dashboard and asked Evan. "What's the problem with your car then?"

"Oh, just in for a service."

"Hope that's not too expensive!"

"Oh, it's definitely worth it, thank you for the lift, which way are you going? I'll walk your way."

Marcus strolled with Evan.

"You seem to be settling into RVI. I saw your work on choice of language with regard to patient well-being. That was excellent. It really does help!"

"Thank you, we're all potential patients after all. We need to think about how we would wish to be treated when vulnerable."

They reached the doctors' changing rooms.

"Absolutely! So true! On that note I'm off to scrub up and make that difference!"

Evan lowered her head and gave him a little wave, turned on her heel and sashayed off.

Marcus went through to prepare and sent Noëmi a quick text:

'*You're perfect xxx*'

'*You've been listening to that song again! xxx*'

He smiled and got changed for work.

'*Great partner, great colleagues, great job! Life's just perfect!*'

* * *

Frank and Valentino were adjusting to Frank working as a Senior Manager at St Wolbodo's school. Not one to hide his displeasure at his husband's sudden promotion, Valentino increased his hours at his dental practice to avoid being alone at their house. Val did not like to be apart from his husband and would sulk if Frank was late. Marcus' hospital was but a stone's throw from Valentino's dental practice. Indeed, working close to each other, Val and Marcus would meet up every now and then for a drink. Marcus found that going out with Val was always an experience.

Valentino received endless tips about where to get the best drinks from his faithful lady patients. This time it was a small Tapas bar, La Ilusión, just along from where they both worked. Previously it had been a pole dancing club.

61

"So glad all that tackiness has gone, but still not sure I want to touch anything!" remarked Val as they walked into the swish place.

"Absolutely, that stuff was for a different generation I think," remarked Marcus.

"Still too much red velvet for my liking, I hope they've industrially cleaned this place. Anyway, what do you fancy? I'll get these, you know, just in case I ever need any emergency treatment someday!"

Val could watch series like **ER, Casualty, Grey's Anatomy** endlessly and he absolutely loved the fact that Marcus was an A&E doctor. He would tell all his clients about his clever friend.

"You know our services are free Val! You just want to make sure you don't have any accidents! Someone came in today because they'd tripped over their clothes drying rack in their kitchen!" Marcus passed him the plate of free olives, but he shook his head.

"God! One would hope to go in more glamorous circumstances don't you think!" Val joked.

They laughed and shared the problems of dealing with public health issues. Next, they made plans for another trip to Italy as they had all enjoyed the last one so much.

"Let's take a selfie and send it to Frank and Noëmi, they have a parents' evening. It'll annoy them!"

Val transmitted the happy picture of them in a dimly lit cocktail bar to their partners who were in a brightly lit school hall for *Year 7 Meet the Teacher Evening*. As they discussed St Wolbodo's school, Marcus and Val were interrupted.

"Marcus!"

They looked up. There was Evan, shimmering in an electric blue, figure hugging dress.

"Oh Evan! Hello! How are you?"

"I didn't know you came here!"

"Val, this is Evan our new Patient Care Manager, Evan this is my friend Val, he's a dentist."

"Hi Val, you must treat Marcus; he's got great teeth!"
Marcus had no reply.

"Yes! He has, and excellent hygiene!" Val proffered a hand, "Lovely to meet you Evan."

"I think it says something about someone, good teeth!" Evan's long silky hair cascaded over her shoulder as she leant in towards them.
Val gave Marcus a sideways glance.

"Doesn't it just!" Val replied, "teeth are so important!"

"Evan's just moved to the area; she's settling in!" Marcus finally joined their conversation.

"Yes, I must say everyone's been extremely friendly at work, socially things are a bit lonely but I'm sure it'll pick up in time." She flicked her hair back.

"Are you here on your own?" Val was curious.

"Yeah, I'm waiting for a friend who's passing through some time this evening, they're being kind. I think they've sensed how alone I am up here."
The dull sounds of piano bars began.

"Oh...I see...er do you want to wait with us?" Marcus suggested.

"That's so kind, thank you." Evan sat down on the stool next to Marcus. Somehow her dress had risen up and her long, slender legs were on full display. As she put her bag to one side Val gave

63

Marcus a look and his friend shrugged his shoulders. Val's phone rang.

"Frank! Oh, is she angry? Put her on!" Val gave Marcus a sly smile, "Pronto! Ti è piaciuta la foto? Sei solo gelosa!" Val laughed as he rang off.

"Are you Spanish?" asked Evan?

"Sono Italiano!"

"Right! I've never been to Italy!"

"Was that N?" Marcus asked.

"Yes, furious that we're in a cosy bar and they're in a draughty school hall!"

"You got the Italian rage version! Actually Val, I'm thinking of taking some Italian lessons so that I can chat with Noëmi's grandparents. It's just finding a class that fits with shifts." Marcus finished his drink. "Alright my round, Val same again?" He paused, then awkwardly added, "Evan what would you like to drink?"

"Vodka and slimline please no garnish."

Marcus went to the bar past the low tables filled with a few midweek customers. Soft piano music caught his ear in the silence.

"So where were you living before Evan?" Val asked.

"London."

"As an undergraduate I take it!"

"Charming, but no, actually working. I did my degree there too, although I *had* the grades for Oxford, like Marcus."

"Of course," Val smiled.

Returning with the drinks, Marcus looked at his watch.

A strained silence fell. Marcus made an effort, "Evan, how are you finding the hospital?"

64

"Busy, I *am* managing a number of the departments. How's your second year going Marcus?"

"Very well, thanks. I'm putting together a proposal for overseas' outreach, based on the work of a charity I've got involved with."

"Amazing. I would love to hear more about that. You know I'm all about charity! I'll book some time for us to discuss it." Evan reached for her phone.

"To be honest it's probably best if you talk to my girlfriend, she's really the one in charge of that." Marcus picked up his drink.

"Well fine, maybe she can come in during the school holidays or something."

"Good idea, I'll mention it to her."

Evan sipped her drink and checked her phone. Reading the message she knotted her eyebrows, knocked back her vodka and stood up.

"Thank you for waiting with me, I need to go. It's been delightful to meet you Val. Next time, Marcus, I'll buy you a drink, okay?" She leant down, pecked him on the cheek then turned and shook Valentino's hand. Phone in bag. Gold snake clasp clicked shut. Off she wafted, leaving a trail of sweet, lily perfume.

"No kiss for me then!" Val said fancifully.

"You can have mine!" Marcus said, sighing.

"Not like you to go telling everyone you went to Oxford!"

"I don't, you know I never do. Only if I get asked directly and no one has ever asked at RVI. My new mentor, Alex, knows but he's seen my hospital records. He mentioned it because that's where he went too."

"I think you've caught her eye!"

"Don't be silly! It's a fluke she's here too. A chance meeting. She's an important contact at the hospital. Very professional so it's all harmless!" Marcus loosened his collar and sat back.

Val examined his hand, "Actually you're right, but if I'm out with Frank, he gets very, very upset by friendly people!"
Marcus smiled, "Shows he cares!"
"I was thinking of telling her you were with me. But then, as it was your work, I thought you may not appreciate it. Could start all sorts of rumours, but it usually sends them packing!" Val gave him a wink.

"Val to be honest I wouldn't have minded! Feel free to claim me for yourself anytime!" Marcus touched his arm playfully.
"Stop it!"

"Val you're blushing!" Marcus laughed out loud,

"Stop it, you're not caring about my sensibilities! I shall use a drill very badly on you next time you're in my chair!" Val replied with a wry smile.
They caught up on their week and plans for the following one. They marvelled about what a gem the tapas bar was, how it was so very well hidden and tucked away down a side street.

Marcus

Early the next morning, rushing out of the door, Marcus went through the week's schedule in his mind. Aware he had missed the gym; he made a mental note to organise his exercise sessions during his morning break. He got to the car and did a double take. The whole side had been keyed. Looking to the skies he mentally calculated the cost of the repair and the mentality of someone who would do this.

'Just what a teacher and an NHS worker cannot afford.'

He now had to spend his morning break looking for the best deal on paint touch ups.

Later that week, with the car at the garage, Marcus was walking to work. Reliving his familiar journey made him nostalgic. Suddenly a silver sports car screeched to a halt next to him.

"Jump in!" smiled Evan who reminded Marcus of a fly in her huge sunglasses.

"Hey Evan! Look I'm happy to walk, you know, get some exercise. Plus, it's lovely and sunny for once!"

"You're running late I can tell!" Evan was persuasive.

Finding it awkward to say 'no' he obliged. He was sad to leave his time with his memories as he was enjoying walking along with them.

"Good weekend?"

"I'm still getting used to the area. Not really finding any friendly people if I'm honest, but work keeps me going." They pulled up at a red light.

"Mmm work can do that!"

"You?" The gleaming, silver car screeched off.

"Oh yeah, just a quiet one." He did not want to share the great time he and Noëmi had enjoyed. They had been with a large group of friends, including Guy and Yumi, on a night out in the Newcastle clubs. He smiled as he remembered how Yumi loved to tease him,

'Let's do some shots and learn Marcus' secrets! We say in Japan, sake ga shizumu to kotoba ga ukabu, when drink goes down, words come up'

'Why do you think I've got secrets, when you sussed me out the first time we met Yumi? You could just ask N anyway!

'She doesn't tell me anything interesting. Maybe there's a big joint secret, my sixth sense tells me this. Dairokkan, we say!'

'Maybe it's time to learn your secrets Yumi!'

'Marcus, there's no way you could handle those!'

"I really need to spend some time in A&E mapping the patient journey." Evan interrupted his daydreaming.

"Ah! More of a haphazard stumble than a journey! It's frantic most of the time!"
He glanced at his watch wondering how much of the drive was left. His phone pinged.

'Mate, the only camera in the area shows a kid in a grey hoodie by your car. Looks like they did it but how many thousands of people in the Toon fit that description! No face shots, sorry, insurance claims 4 U!'

'Cheers Guy, see you later'
He popped his phone away.

"What's your week looking like?" She asked.

"Ah who knows what delights A&E will serve up for us all today eh?" He tried to be jolly, "Last week we had a woman come in because she couldn't get her false nails off; you know those plastic extension things!" As his mouth shut, he saw Evan's manicured hands glinting red in the sunlight. "But it's nice of course when women look after themselves!" He winced at the coincidence.

"Definitely, I keep myself in shape."

"Yes! I can see that." They stopped at a pedestrian crossing near the hospital.

'God what did I just say?'

"Admiring the view are we?" She put her sunglasses onto her head and revved the engine.

"No, not like that! I mean I can see you take care of yourself…"

She jumped in. "That's funny but it can go too far! At St George's we had a woman come in as she put a bulb of garlic up her vagina and couldn't get it out! What would you do in that situation Marcus?"

She glanced over at him.

Marcus gave a nervous laugh. "Not sure. That's some herbal remedy! Er...what do you think of the new printer system?"

"Fine but it's not going to stop the crackpots putting allium up their snatches, is it?"

Burning up, he replied, "I think the change is effective. The printer system that is."

Evan threw her head back and shook her hair.

"Change is always good, Dr McKenzie, got to be ready to try new things. There's a whole world out there!" Her red lips were glistening in the early morning sun and her blonde hair shimmering. Eyes fluttering like the wings of hummingbirds, Evan gently put her hand on his arm.

CHAPTER 9 - EXPECTATIONS

Marcus

Fast fashion shops, Eldon Square, Newcastle. This was the last place Dr Marcus McKenzie would choose to be at 10am on a Saturday. Usually if he had a weekend off, he would stay in bed until then, go for coffee with Frank, go jogging with Val, play squash with Guy, cycle with Noëmi, watch football, even go fishing with his dad, a million things before shopping.

Today was about his sister, Tianna. By 10:15am things were looking up as he had met a few people from the hospital, busy doing their morning errands. Nurse Penelope Rivera was one such colleague; she was out shopping with her son Joel. Having been unceremoniously moved on from St Wolbodo's the previous summer, Joel Rivera had joined the local Durham technical college. There he thrived and he had achieved outstanding exam results. This all meant he would be off to university the following summer and he was now taking a gap year.

"My God! Marcus! Shopping? Sorry, sorry I mean hello! How are you?"

"Pen! Great to see you! I'm fine and you? As you can see, I'm hoping to get myself a new outfit!" He pointed at the mannequins dressed in crop tops and tiny shorts, in a nearby shop window.

Penelope burst out laughing, then regained herself. "This is my son, Joel, we're getting a smart shirt. He's got an interview for a Health Care Assistant position at RVI next week."

"Great to meet you Joel, your mum's told me how well you did in your A Levels."

"Oh, he did!" She turned to her son, "Marcus, here, went to Oxford! Joel's looking at Oxford but only Oxford Brookes."

"Hey Pen stop! Oxford is Oxford! I have friends from both places, the fun lot are the Brookes guys! Joel, you'll love it. Good luck for the HCA interview, I did that a few times in the holidays. This is Tianna, my sister, she's applying to Oxford too."

The teenagers smiled at each other warmly. Joel's face lit up.

"Joel, Marcus' girlfriend, is a teacher at your old school, Miss McAllister!" Penelope added.

"Oh yeah I know, she was kind, a bit scatter-brained, I mean in a good way! She used to help me in the after school catch up sessions. She always smelled nice... not like some teachers!" Marcus felt proud of Noëmi.

Tianna agreed, "Oh she's lovely, far too good for this one here!" Everyone laughed.

Joel asked Tianna what she wanted to study, and they began their own conversation. Marcus took advantage of the fact the teenagers were no longer listening.

"Pen, can I ask you something?"

"Of course! Anything!" She pulled her jacket to stop the draught from the shopping centre doors that kept opening.

71

"Did you hear something, the summer I joined, about a complaint against me?"

She burst out laughing. "Oh my God yes! That was hilarious, the funniest thing ever, I won the sweepstake…er…steak that's what we're having for dinner, yes…just going to get some…from the butcher. If there *is* one round here?" She looked away, then back at him and saw his face, "Okay, I made fifty quid."

"What! How many people were in this little betting circle?"

Penelope looked to the ceiling as she counted in Portuguese, "Nine of us, the consultant entered twice, a fiver each, I won, but it's because I got to the Doodle poll first…"

"Doodle poll!"

"Marcus, come on, you know the department! Anyway, I got *'bounce in like an excited puppy on Monday morning!'* Madhav got *'recreate the Titanic scene at RVT',* not a chance and no one was going to win with *'ridiculously romantic smoke skywriting message.'* I mean we don't really have the weather for that do we?"

"Clearly the only reason that option didn't win! Doodle poll! Go on, tell me the title of it!"

"No, I can't! We'll get sacked! There'll be no A&E department." She looked genuinely worried.

"Pen!"

"Er…er…okay…it was…*What next for Dr McKenzie?"*

"Oh really! You lot came up with something that unimaginative?" Marcus folded his arms and gave her an old fashioned look.

"Can't quite remember anyway…it was along those lines, got to dash, shirt shops may shut soon!"

"Pen it's twenty past ten in the morning!" He laughed as she scurried away.

Joel shrugged his shoulders endearingly at Tianna. "Gotta go buy my shirt!"

Marcus' perspective changed; he stopped checking his watch and began to enjoy himself. They went for coffee in the food court.

"Thanks bro you're the best!"

"You need to treat those trainers before you wear them, they're leather. The protective spray's in the bag too, I got them to add that." He studied the instructions' leaflet.

She blew on her drink to cool it down.

"Honestly, Oxford, will I get in?" Tianna had to move her chair in as a lady with a buggy negotiated the gaps between tables.

"Noëmi and I can help you. We made it our entire focus. I couldn't have done it without her and vice versa. What I'm saying is you have to really want it."

"But then will I fit in? Remember when I visited? They all go to Dubai on holiday, not Seaham by the sea!"

Marcus rubbed his face, "Yeah, I think I know who you mean."

Tianna bowed her head, "She made comments about my hair and make-up."

"What! No! Tianna, why didn't you tell me?" He banged the table with his fist.

"I'm telling you now!"

"I swear I'll sort it out, how dare she!" Marcus felt his body seize up and shut his eyes. *'If I'm haunted by Sophie, I deserve it, but not Tianna.'*

She shook her shoulders and changed the subject, "Maybe I should take up rowing, then I'd have something in common with the posh lot."

"You shouldn't have to change yourself, Tianna! There's a way more diverse intake now! If you have the grades to study biology at Oxford, you should go for the best." Marcus put their cups together, ready for the recycling bin. They chatted some more, then Marcus wandered, bemused, around fast fashion shops buying things for his sister. Making an effort, he picked out a dress.

"You can only wear that if you've got blonde hair."

"What?"

He found a pair of jeans that he'd seen were popular.

"They're not for a figure like mine, you have to be skinny."

"Tianna, seriously?" Marcus was stunned.

"You don't understand, boys only like a certain type of girl!"

"Well, if that's the case the population would be falling, not rising!"

"Some of us need to just fit in!"

"Tianna be who you are! *Head up, be proud, be seen!* What Mum says, she's right!"

Tianna smiled faintly at her brother, "Sure, will do."

After a few hours they went back to Marcus' flat and found Noëmi chatting with Guy. He had popped by to get food and watch the football before playing squash with Marcus. Tianna showed off her shopping haul and Noëmi looked on, giving her approval. Guy shared a few of his shoplifting stories; "The minute they see me or hear the alarm, they go! Used to keep me so cardio fit!"

"I know a bunch at Newky Green, in Year 10, annoying as they get us all banned from city centre shops. I can get you a list of names if you want?" she offered.

"Tianna, I have to catch them red handed! It's all about evidence.

You'll not believe how much scheming people will lie." Guy

handed her the TV remote and got up to leave for the sports' club with Marcus.

Guy smashed the ball down and there was little chance Marcus could get to it. Running on, he stretched out only to miss and hurtle into the wall. Bouncing off it he spun round to see Guy grinning. "And that's how it's done! Yes!"

Once again his friend had beaten him.

"I got a few more points off you this time at least." Marcus gasped as he caught his breath.

"Yeah, well done, you just need more practice."

"No, I just suck at this game, even Alex, my new boss beat me the other day."

"Ha, same time next week? Does that work with your shifts?" Guy laughed, grabbing his towel, delighted with his win.

"Yep, I'll be here for you to thrash me once again! Fancy a beer?"

"Absolutely let's go."

They came out of the court and walked towards the changing rooms. At the end of the corridor, they noticed a group waiting for a spin class.

"Hi Marcus!" cried a voice dressed in leggings and a tight sports' top.

"Oh Evan … hello!"

She moved to talk to them. "I didn't know you were a member here too!"

"Yeah, I joined a while back." He put his towel around his neck.

"Someone's fit!" She put a hand affectionately on his bicep.

Marcus heard Guy suddenly cough behind him. He shot him a glance over his shoulder.

"Guy this is Evan, our new Patient Care Manager." Marcus recoiled to remove her hand.

"Pleased to meet you, Guy. *This* is how I take care of that body of mine!" Evan pointed at the spin bikes, "It's brutal!"

"Right! Don't let us hold you up, enjoy your class!" Marcus said and started to walk off. Guy caught him up and unburdened his mirth.

"Someone's popular!" He had tears in his eyes as he put his hand on his friend's shoulder to steady himself. Marcus ignored Guy.

"That's Evan, she's new at work, she doesn't know many people here."
Regaining his composure, Guy wiped his face with his towel.
"Seriously, she's a stunner!"
"Sorry, your point is?" Marcus replied purposely.
Marcus strode ahead into the changing rooms, kicked off his squash shoes, pulled off his sweaty kit and showered. Close behind Guy followed and did the same, saying no more.

They walked out to a bar across the road from the gym, chatting about their plans for the coming week. The road was busy with early evening traffic as the city prepared for Saturday night. Settling down for a well-earned pint, they were sharing an anecdote about Noëmi's map reading, when Marcus noticed Evan come in.

"We should definitely all go back to Italy, I know you're off to Japan soon but a summer trip would work, don't you think?" Marcus spoke quickly.
"Sounds great! Yumi suggested that too!" Drinks in hand they went to find a seat.
"You and Yumi are perfect together; the chemistry between you two is something else, true love eh?"
"I've never experienced feelings like this before, it's nuclear."
Guy was far away for a moment. "My only complaint is that it took our useless best friends four months to introduce us!" Guy playfully flicked a bar mat at Marcus.

Catching the bar mat in one hand and flicking it back, Marcus laughed. "Yeah, we were a bit wrapped up in ourselves! Actually, are you and Yumi ok for Saturday the 20th?" Marcus started to get up to go to the bar.

"Sure, can't wait. I've got that weekend off."

As Marcus stood up, he suddenly found Evan blocking his path. "I owe you a drink Marcus," her sweet, lily perfume filled the air.

"Ah Evan! Really no, don't worry, we're good thank you!" Marcus was all politeness.

"No, I insist! Sorry Guy, we've been sharing lifts to work. Plus, we were out together last week for a drink and Marcus paid for everything!"

Without looking Marcus could see Guy's face.

"Really, it's fine Evan, a kind thought but there's no need!"

"Come on, you like the draught beer don't you?"

Marcus' jaw dropped but he remained silent.

"Next time then!" She leant over and pecked him on the cheek and sashayed out of the bar.

"Right…" Guy said as they watched Evan leave.

Marcus crossed his arms. "It's not what it looks like." He sighed heavily.

Guy laughed.

"You're not helping Guy."

"Sorry mate, I feel for you, I do. What a problem to have!"
Marcus went to get them another drink and returned with two pints of Doom Bar some minutes later. They settled back down. Marcus explained.

"I was out for a drink with Val after work last week and she happened to be in the same bar on her own, that's all."

"And have you done anything to encourage her?"

"Sorry?" Marcus looked directly at his friend.

"You know what they say, you have to crush a crush."

Lost in thought, Marcus took a long sip of his drink.

"What does Noëmi think?" Guy was inquiring.

"What? There's nothing to *think* about anything!" Marcus snapped.

"You've not shared your *work problems* with her then?"

"I don't have any work problems!"

"You do. Evan seems keen to make something happen." Guy's voice was firm.

Marcus looked away, ignoring his friend's comment and started thinking about the party he was planning.

"Who's playing Newcastle next? They're really struggling…"

Guy's words faded into the low hum of the bar.

'*She's a stunner…what a problem to have…*'

.

78

CHAPTER 10 - CHRISTOPHER

Christopher

A clock ticked loudly in the heavy silence.

The Dean's letter had been quite clear. 10am, his office, formal attire. Christopher walked along the corridor of the college to the appointment. Over the top of her glasses the Dean's secretary indicated for him to take a seat. He felt the weight of the stillness. The dark claret carpet was absorbing him and the heavy, walnut clad walls were bearing down on him. Sitting on what looked like a one hundred year old chair, the just nineteen year old felt restless.

"The Dean will see you now." The secretary announced and she opened the office door.

Christopher walked in.

"Mr Deehan, please take a seat."

The Dean, in the presence of Christopher's college tutor, went through the decision of the board given the evidence and witness statements.

"Christopher, possession of a class C substance contravenes the acceptable behaviour policy as detailed in the student handbook.

Even though you state it is for personal use, the drug is still not permitted in college. You agreed to this when you signed the student university contract before beginning as an undergraduate. I do need to note that there were two cases this week, at your college, of involuntary ingestion of the same drug. Both victims were hospitalised. Neither can recall where they were or how they got the substance. It may well be a very unfortunate coincidence. I know the police investigation is frustrated by a lack of evidence. However, it is with regret that I have to tell you that your contract with Oxford University is terminated. These events will not prejudice your reapplying to university for next year and indeed the university hopes you can take advantage of the support offered in order to address your habit."

Christopher had a thumping head and a raging thirst. He listened to the Dean's voice in the vacuum of his thoughts. The Dean had stopped and Christopher had nothing to say. He was handed a letter and he left. His undergraduate days were over after just ten days. Remaining silent he walked out of the office, undid his tie and cursed his bad luck. In one moment, Christopher left his parents' dreams in ruins and Oxford University.

Rufus

Later that same Saturday, Christopher's father, Rufus, waited as the electric gates opened. He drove into the driveway of their expansive home just outside Durham. The journey with his youngest son had taken place in silence.

Walking into his kitchen, he saw his wife nurturing a glass of wine. Rufus kissed her head, poured himself a glass and sat on a stool next to her. He broke the silence.

"We're lucky he wasn't prosecuted. It's just us with the sentence of failure and despair."

"Shhh don't cry Rufus." Rufus took a deep breath. "I'm just tired."

The granite work surface reflected the stems of the wine glasses to look like two elegant swans.

"Wendy, I just don't understand it, the other two have not put a foot wrong, not even a parking fine, and now this!"

"He was top of every class, polite and exceptional, where did it all go so wrong?" Wendy's voice was faltering.

"Arrogance, he's always been that way, he tells us how stupid we are." Rufus loosened his collar.

"When we told him to get a summer job and so on?" Wendy sipped her drink and held onto the glass.

"Yes and I actually think that Oxford offer was a curse, we gave in to all his whims to protect his grades, you know everything he wanted, anything…"

"He used it over us, there were warnings…"

"You never wanted to rock the boat; the entire year has been dominated by that bloody Oxford offer. Maybe we should've thought about the whole picture, not just one accolade."

"Everything he wanted, tutoring… we should've just left him to get on with it."

"I know Wendy, we're both guilty, it became *our* obsession, finally a child who would make that grade." Rufus ran his finger around the rim of his now empty glass.

"He did get the grades, remember, some good came out of it. He will now have to reapply… somewhere."

"The letter did say they would not prejudice him in a future university application, he needs to understand how serious this is. He's not fully spoken about whatever this other 'incident' was."

"And no one will tell us because of his age...it's up to him and he won't say a word."

"He owes us an explanation at least surely?" Rufus stood up and looked out at his garden.

"Rufus, I think he doesn't feel he owes us a thing."

"It's the army for him if you ask me, he needs discipline, if they'll have him that is."

Wendy began to cry and went to phone her daughter.

Christopher had gone straight to his room which Wendy had got ready in spite of Rufus insisting that she *'merely leave the sheets on the bed for Christopher to sort out.'* If Christopher felt any remorse, he had no intention of showing it.

Rufus looked skyward for an answer and found none, the silence in their smart kitchen deafened him. For once in his life he had no sense of optimism. He walked out, turned on the football and sat full of his own thoughts.

The following week, Rufus pressed the key to close his gates and walked into his marble walled hall after a long day of meetings in London.

"Where's your car Wendy?"

"Christopher's taken it to go out to see his friends."

"Did he do his application?" Rufus sighed and looked at his wife.

She was silent. Faced with the bleak reality of Christopher's disappointing behaviour they had decided to make an action plan to which they would all agree and adhere. It was written down:

- **Christopher to re-apply for university.**
- **Each day Christopher to make one application to find work.**

- **Grounded for a month in order to face up to the enormity of the recent fall from grace.**

Three days into this contract Christopher was unleashed.

"How did he get the keys?"

Wendy burst into tears, "He came right into my face calling me a 'useless mother', I just wanted him to stop, I couldn't bear it.

What's happened to my son?" Rufus held her as her sobs soaked his shoulder.

"We need to get some psychiatric help I think, I'll talk to our GP. I'll see him on Sunday at golf."

"For him or for us?" Wendy asked.

"Indeed, I'm not sure, all of us probably." He put his arm around her and passed her a box of tissues.

"He's nineteen, no one will talk to us about him, he's an adult, apparently." Wendy wiped her eyes.

In their beautiful home they sat in silence as the evening drew in. Rufus could not focus on the television and went to water the flower beds. His mind jumped from problems with a tricky client at work to Christopher.

Wendy

Christopher did not return that evening and in the morning, Wendy was shaking with fear. With no message and no reply from her son's phone, nervously she rang the local police to find out if there were any reports of accidents. After some toing and froing, she discovered the truth. A pleasant sounding DS Guy Castle had told her

'Christopher's been arrested on suspicion of driving under the influence of drugs. He's refusing to talk. He's now in a cell awaiting further questioning. As an adult there's been no need to contact any next of kin but you're

welcome to come down to collect the car and see if you can help break his vow of silence.'

Guy went into the interview room to find Christopher refusing to cooperate with the duty lawyer. He steeled himself, they had met before.

"Shouldn't you be more gainfully employed these days Mr Deehan? And how can you afford such a nice car?"
No reply.

"Your passenger was taken home. Aren't you a bit old to hang around with seventeen year olds?"

"Jude's a good mate."

"What happened to your plan to go to uni?"
"I got kicked out."
Guy raised an eyebrow and then groaned as this meant Christopher would never get out of trouble or his judicial area.

"Do you want to tell me about it?" He sat down opposite him and handed him a bottle of cold water.

"Thanks, I got into Oxford, then I got blamed for a class C substance that was doing the rounds." He unscrewed the bottle top and took a swig.

Surprised at his candour, Guy wondered what hope there was with Christopher.

"These substances could've killed you and your friends. You do realise that?"

"Yeah, but the plan was for some fun...so I was told."

"There are other ways to have fun."

"Don't start the old natural high school assembly with me."

"This is serious, you need to tidy up. Plus, you're actually lucky not to be in jail, Christopher. So what's your plan now?"

"Reapply for uni and hope no one asks any awkward questions. Get a job."

"Indeed, I appreciate your honesty. We have your test results and you're a very lucky young man; they've come back negative this time. Is that a lab error? Were you under the influence of any substances whilst driving last night?"

"Obviously not PC Plod! That really would be the end of any uni chances!" He finished his water.

"Actually not necessarily, believe it or not we value you and I'm not giving up on you. A drug conviction just means there are some courses you can't get onto, those involving safeguarding; Medicine, Teaching, Social Work, Law of course."

"Like I want to be some underpaid doctor, teacher or police officer! I want to be rich."

A picture of all the people dearest to him flashed into Guy's head.

"Anyway, have you thought about rehabilitation? I want to expedite the therapy for you, help you get your life back on track. Focus on keeping busy, find work and take up a sport maybe? They're looking for more younger rowers at this club, here's a leaflet, why not give it a go?"

"Okay but it all sounds a bit middle aged." He took the flyer and stuffed it into a pocket.

"You need to face reality; the whole of society is trying to help you and you just keep throwing it back. Are you still taking drugs?"

"Excuse me, I have the right to privacy!"

"Of course, I'll call you tomorrow to discuss your rehab, now I need to get the paperwork processed. Your Mum's come down to collect the car. She says you can walk home." Guy scooped up his papers and walked out.

Christopher looked aghast. Having heard the details of his latest debacle Wendy was, it would seem, at the end of her awfully long tether.

CHAPTER 11 - BOUNDARIES

Marcus

The following Saturday night, Noëmi was out with friends and would not be back before midnight. They were celebrating Deanna's birthday. Marcus had been made well aware what these get-togethers with her former Newcastle Green schoolmates were like. Noëmi had described the pattern.

"Towards the end of the evening, when they're all bevved up, one of them starts. The intro is always astonishment that we're together, you know, me being such an awkward geek, you being the school *simbolo del sesso*…"

"Sesso?"

"Exactly, then it's followed by all these fantasies they had about you when we were in sixth form."

Marcus rolled his eyes. Noëmi continued,

"You wouldn't think I was there! Details! Oh my God!"

"Yeah but you and me, we know the truth." Marcus put his arm around her and grabbed the TV remote.

"Sure but they've still got these flipping fetishy fixations about you!"

Marcus put his hands behind his head and smiled at her. "Sounds interesting!"

Noëmi scowled and threw a cushion at him, "God, you love it really don't you!"

Noëmi

Saturday did not disappoint.

In the Slug and Lettuce, Quayside, Deanna threw her arm around Noëmi and thrust a glass of wine into her hand. "I've not seen you for ages! You've been abroad most of the summer!"

"Happy Birthday Deanna," Noëmi gave her friend a kiss.

"How's living together then?" Deanna had a glint in her eye.

"It's great! One week I put the bins out, then the next week he does...are those the kind of things you want to know about? Or is it our cleaning rota?"

"Oh, shut up!" Deanna's arms enveloped her in a hug. They sat down looking out through the window at the Tyne Bridge. "Don't you get so exhausted..." She whispered to Noëmi.

"Deanna! Stop!"

Her friend creased up. "Bet he's bloody tireless, you lucky thing!"

Noëmi threw her arms up, "We've been here five seconds and you're off already! Maybe I'm the tireless one! How's work going Deanna?"

"Yeah that would make sense! Work, big sigh, it's alright, car showrooms are so slow at the moment. Plus I've got issues with my manager, we had a bit of a thing going on..."

The girls caught up as they waited for Ruby and Charlotte to arrive.

Evan

On the other side of town, Bar Blanc was buzzing. Pushing the door open, Evan jumped in from the rain. Quickly she brushed the drops from her coat and shook out her hair. Surveying the bar, she quickly saw Bri. Rushing over she threw off her coat and hugged her friend.

"Good to see you darling!"

"Get this down you and tell me everything!" Bri pushed a tequila shot Evan's way with the necessary salt and lime. The girls knocked them back. Bri lined up the next.

"Bri, I love my new job!" Evan gushed.

"You actually love your work this time? Alrighty who is he?" Bri gave her a sly look.

"Stop! Yes, I've met someone. Bri this time it's someone decent. Someone my equal!"

"Amazing, tell me about it!"

"My first day, we have a big department meeting and I notice him straightaway. Sitting there, tall, fit, kind eyes. Then he bumps into me with his great body. Now that's no accident, is it?"

"Definitely not! A classic invitation to hook up!" Bri pointed at Evan emphatically.

"I see it in his eyes, that mutual attraction. Next thing I know he's stopping to help me at work and giving me lifts! Then I pick him up!" Evan puffed out her chest.

"Always picking people up!" Bri joked.

"But this is the real thing, he's the one! A doctor too. Clever, considerate and he works out!"

"Ah Evs I'm so pleased for you. Finally a chance for happiness!"

"There's a problem though Bri…"

"Oh no what?"

"He's got a partner." Evan's voice was low.

"You can take them on! When have you ever failed to get what you want?"

Evan's brow darkened. "I checked him out on the HR system; she's his next of kin and her mobile is his emergency contact. Same address. Looking up personal information is a bit naughty! I'd be sacked if they find out! To be honest it's the only thing I've read since I got there. I just skim titles and tell everyone how brilliant their work is!"

"My friend's boyfriend works there, he's a doctor. I could ask them to find out about this guy and his girlfriend. What's his name?"

"Too early for those details Bri. I'll tell you when we're official, but I'm not put off."

"Did you check them out on social media?" Bri fixed her make-up in her compact mirror.

Evan rolled her eyes. "There's not much but she looks pretty plain and boring." Her look became faraway, "I've made him feel flattered and he loved it! I know I could make him happy. Physically we'd be a match."

"You go for it; you deserve some happiness after all that happened at St George's." Bri's voice was thin.

"Best not to mention that, so glad I'm out of there. Their divorce was not my fault. If they'd been a strong couple, they'd have got over it. Only a bit of fun, nothing serious." Evan knocked back another drink.

"True, but this time it sounds like the real thing! Go for it, you can't stop love after all now can you?"

Evan beamed, "I'll need to be quite scheming with this one!"
Bri gave a screech and passed Evan another shot.

Marcus

Finally arriving home Marcus was quite happy to be alone; he was looking forward to watching Match of the Day on catch up. Tired he flung himself on the sofa with a beer, thinking he would eat something later on. Suddenly his work phone pinged. He had meant to turn it off; his shift was over and he was not on call. Only in the case of a national emergency would he be summoned in. Looking, he saw it was Evan. Surprised, he wondered what was going on so he clicked on the message. *'Has something happened at work?'*

*'**Marcus help me, I can't get into my house, I've locked myself out.**'*

*'**Are your neighbours in?**'* Immediately he regretted answering.

*'**They're all out. Anyway, I'm scared and all alone...please!**'*

He looked up to the ceiling and cursed his good nature. *'**What's your address?**'*

*'**It's so cold, I've got nowhere to go.**'*

*'**Okay I can break in.**'*

'Why am I suddenly the only person who can help?'

He was only one sip into his long awaited beer. He put it down with a groan.

'Maybe Guy would have some tips? Damn it, I can just go, get her in and come back to the match pronto.'

91

Pulling up outside her flat, it was dark. Marcus rushed out, not even bothering to lock the car behind him, '*Let's just get this over and done with.*' Evan was all dressed up, smelling of her sweet, lily perfume. Marcus went over to examine the set up and how he could get her into her flat. '*I need to leave as soon as possible.*'

Evan

Seeing him disappear, Evan quickly opened his car. Surreptitiously she slipped off her knickers and leant into the car. Opening the glove box, she left them as a gift for Noëmi and Marcus. '*You're welcome. Job done, doesn't matter which one of you finds my token of appreciation. Excite one? Enrage the other?*'

Marcus

He went round the back and saw a half-light window open. Hauling himself up, he put his arm in and opened a bigger window through which he could then climb into the kitchen.

'*That was easy,*' he thought to himself. Looking around he found the light and turned it on. The kitchen was tidy with a table covered with psychology books and notes. A large bookcase had an impressive array of imprints, all the classics plus medical reference books and Italian language books. A cookery book was open with a delicious looking recipe that Evan was undoubtedly about to make. Her washing was drying, and Marcus noticed, '*not your usual domestic scene but all neatly arranged thongs and bras*'. He bristled seeing it. Moving through the hallway he noticed a pile of coats and hoodies on the bannisters. He went to the front door to let her in.

"There you go."

"Thank you so much, what would I do without you! Can I fix you a drink?"

"No, I need to get going, glad it's all worked out for you," and he turned to leave.

Suddenly Evan burst into tears.

"Evan, are you alright? Look, sit down."

"I'm sorry, I shouldn't ...please I'm fine, you just go." She put her head in her hands.

Marcus bit his lip and checked his watch.

"Shall I make some tea?"

"That would be wonderful Marcus. Earl Grey please." He looked around the kitchen and got all he needed. She dried her eyes and looked up at him as he brought her a cup of tea.

"It's just that there are so many problems, my mother's ill, work's incessant and I'm so lonely."

"I'm sorry to hear that your mum's unwell. Does she have a good specialist? Please let me know if you need any advice regarding her treatment." He looked at his watch. A message pinged through from Noëmi.

'Back from NG reunion, where r u? xxx'

'Helping someone from work who locked themselves out! xxx'

'More over sharing, fairly sure those offers are still on the table if you're ever tempted! xxx"

'U need to protect me! xxx'

'Love u xxx'

"I need to go, is there someone I can call for you?"

"No, don't worry, I'll be fine, it's only two days until Monday when I'll see people again."

Marcus rolled his eyes as she lowered hers.

"Who have you just been out with? Can they come over?"

Evan cried some more, "That was my ex, he scares me so much, it was an abusive relationship."

Marcus was bemused as to why he was now Evan's confidant and carer. She had looked absolutely fine when he arrived to rescue her. She dabbed her eyes some more and took a sip of tea.

"Listen I have to go but why don't you call a friend?" He began to move to the door.

"You're my friend. We could grab a coffee over the weekend so that I'm not all alone?" Looking up at him, her eyes seemed bright.

"Why don't you see how you get on, hey?" Marcus was walking out.

"I'll message you!" She cried after him.

He left the flat wondering whether he had been clear enough.

'Maybe she won't text.' He said to himself. *'Don't be naïve. I'll turn off my work mobile, no I'm on call tomorrow, damn!'*

Next morning at 8:30am his work phone pinged. Before he could move, Noëmi reached right across him from her side of the bed to his bedside cabinet and picked it up. He felt her soft, smooth skin on his. "Don't worry you don't need to go in, just some dude called Evan says he can meet you for coffee at Cake Stories."

She passed it to him. Leaving her body draped on his, she snuggled up to him and went back to sleep. Marcus lay wide awake and silent.

'Evan it's not possible for me to meet work colleagues during my time off.'

'There, done. That's the end of that.' He said to himself.

Putting down his work mobile he breathed a sigh of relief. He looked at Noëmi; her long hair was all over him, her warm body was next to his. He pulled her closer in.

CHAPTER 12 - PARTY PARTY

20 October 2018.

Tianna

'Do you want to earn some cash Ti?'

'How thick are you?'

'Nice one, I need a couple of you to serve drinks and keep things tidy at our housewarming.'

'I'll bring Shanice, our rates are high, given the quality of our work ;)'

'£10 an hour each sound okay?'

Marcus let his sister and her friend in as Noëmi blow dried her hair. He showed them where all the glasses, plates and drinks were.

"How is this a housewarming when you've lived here for over a year?" Tianna pulled a face.

"It's to celebrate N moving in."

"That was months ago!" Tianna turned to her friend. "See Shanice, how soppy they are!" Her friend put her hand over her mouth.

"Never mind. You need to top up glasses, tidy up plates and stuff. Keep the place looking tight." Marcus checked his list of jobs.

They looked around, taking in the set up and nodded.

"And no drinking!" Marcus added as the doorbell rang.

"Sure, we'll just stick to weed!" Tianna called back. He gave her a look, she rolled her eyes. Shanice smirked.

Friends started arriving and soon the mood was bubbling. Having spent the day cooking, cleaning and sorting out the music, Marcus and Noëmi were ready to relax.

Marcus

Guy and Yumi had arrived. Hearts and arms full, they offloaded hugs and booze. As Yumi chatted to Noëmi, Guy sidled up to his friend.

"How's that work problem? God she's not here, is she?" He looked around in panic.

Opening a bottle of champagne, Marcus gave him a stare. "No!"

"Of course, she'd be by your side telling you how fit you are!" Guy took a swig of his beer and slapped his friend on the shoulder.

"Friends only tonight!" Marcus was unsmiling.

"Yeah, she wouldn't fit in, she's not interested in the friend zone!"

"Your imagination is so overactive." Marcus was dismissive.

"I'm a detective." Guy said simply.

Noëmi joined them, "Marcus, come on, introduce me to your work friends! I'm desperate to find out what goes on there!"

Drinks in hand they circulated, finally getting to Marcus' consultant mentor.

"Noëmi, this is Alex and his wife Cathy!" Marcus felt a frisson of excitement that they were all meeting. Tianna busily filled their glasses.

"Ah Marcus never stops talking about you!"

"And I can say the same!"

Hugs and kisses followed.

Marcus shared details, "Alex is a major trauma specialist."

Noëmi joked, "Alex that's quite a title! It's lovely to see you socially, but I don't think I ever want to meet you in a professional capacity!"

Eyes twinkling, Alex laughed, "The feeling's mutual Noëmi!"

"And Cathy's a midwife!"

"Ah now one day!" Noëmi gave Marcus a sly look.

"Yeah, let's get the wedding done and a house sorted first alright!" He put his arm around her.

"Marcus likes everything very structured and ordered." Noëmi teased as she took a gulp of her wine.

Alex jumped in, "I had noticed! But it's you I wanted to talk to about the noma charity. I hear you were the driving force!"

"No Marcus' enthusiasm motivated me!" Noëmi went a bit pink.

"We're actually looking for a project to support, working on neglected tropical diseases. It's a bit of a two-way thing. Our doctors can go out and help upskill other healthcare workers but gain valuable experience too."

"Yes! The End Noma Campaign hospital would be perfect. Marcus did so much; intricate localised surgeries, skin grafting."

"It helps enormously that he's already been there, gives our proposal a head start! Right, we'll get on with moving that forward. Let's organise a proper meeting."

"We can get the hospital manager on a call too. Marcus became such good friends with the Nigerian medical staff, everyone loves him!"

Alex then leant in to whisper to her, "He's the best colleague I've ever had. I'm the one learning so much from him."

She whispered back. "Don't tell him he'll never shut up!"

"Don't worry his colleagues don't miss an opportunity to lighten the mood!"

"The doodle poll…"

Bursting out laughing, Alex looked delighted as a dutiful Tianna passed by again and filled his wine glass.

Tianna

"Bunch of old soaks, where do they put it all!" Tianna whispered to a giggling Shanice as they grabbed more wine to fill up the glasses. Soon Tianna and her friend busied themselves tidying up and sorting out the empties. Shanice was collected at 11pm, leaving Tianna alone to clear up what she could in the kitchen. She looked out at the crowd in the flat; some had spilled out into the small terrace garden. Everyone was laughing, drinking and dancing. She sighed, '*No one young here.*'

The doorbell rang and she was the only one to hear it.

"Hi, I'm collec…Tianna, how are you?"

"Joel! You remember me! Did you get the job?" She all but shrieked.

"Of course to both."

She could not help her grin and opened the door as wide. He shook the cold from his shoulders and stepped inside.

"I'm here to collect my parents." He looked into the lounge and saw his mother filling her glass. "They're still going for it! Can I wait with you?"

Tianna nodded and they weaved their way through the separate groups to the kitchen. Finding a chair each they sat down.

"I'm supposed to be the waitress tonight but I've done enough! They're all so drunk they can sort themselves out!"

Joel laughed. The lighting was soft, she noticed his olive skin, kind eyes of conker brown and stylishly cropped dark hair. He was easy on the eye.

"Ever since I passed my driving test, I've become their personal chauffeur. They like a drink! Look at them!" He gestured towards his parents who were laughing with Alex James in the hallway. "Such wastrels!"

Tianna passed him a coke. "I've got mum's taxis picking me up! It's like she's got me electronically tagged!"

Joel gave a throaty laugh. "What did you decide about uni then?" He fixed his eyes on her.

"Yeah, I'm applying to Oxford, see what happens? You?"

"I got my offer from Oxford Brookes, so I'm going! Hopefully, I'll see you there then!"

"Fingers crossed, it'll be good to have some normal friends."

"Ah! Do you mean poor?"

Tianna felt herself blush. "Oh no, I mean…"

"You're so easy to mess with! I'm teasing. They'll be all sorts at all unis, don't stress. Next Friday I'm off to visit some of my friends at Manchester uni. We're going to destroy the town! Oh, look they're drinking up, I'd better get them home!" He looked over his shoulder at his mother slightly unsteady on her feet. Jumping up he went to her side. Tianna followed him with her eyes as he went to fetch his folks. Waving, he gave her a wink, then he took his mother's arm.

'He's a year older, he just thinks you're Marcus' little sister. Soon he'll be out in Manchester partying, clubbing…meeting girls.' Her phone pinged and a merry Marcus saw her to their mother's car. Tianna deflated into the passenger seat and thought about the pile of homework she had to do.

* * *

Marcus

'Thanx for a fun time you two xxx'

'So much fun! Lovely evening see you soon X'

'Hungover, had a fab nite, missing you already x'

The messages came in the next day as Marcus and Noëmi lay in bed, recovering from their 5am bedtime.

"Why does Guy never dance?"

"Oh, he's Mr laidback isn't he? Doesn't ever make a fool of himself."

"I love your boss, Alex and his wife Cathy, they're so much fun,"

"They're just the best, he's going to invite us back, and he's got some big party next year."

"We're doing well back in our old hometown. Who'd have thought!"

"I would never have believed it!" He rolled over and hugged her tight.

101

"I need tea, so dehydrated,"

"Nice that Sarai came along, how did your dad get on babysitting?"

"Fine I think. She's giving up work she says it'd cost her more in childcare than she earns."

"You need to help her get what she is entitled to, she keeps thinking someone will take Lucia away if she asks for help."

"You're right I'll keep an eye, do you want tea?" She got up slowly and went towards the kitchen. "My head's throbbing, have we got anything?"

"Advil in the bathroom cabinet." He called back to her.

"I think I'm going to be sick." She sprinted to the toilet.

Noëmi

Monday morning both rushing to get out of the flat. Noëmi's heart raced and her skin was clammy as she wretched over the toilet.

"I'm still throwing up!" '*How* am I going to teach?'

Moving slowly to the sink she brushed her teeth, spat out her toothpaste and called out to Marcus, "I've just been sick again you know! I'm never drinking again. Should I take another day's pill?"

Marcus

Marcus was hurrying and trying to find his phone, '*What did she say? Should I take another Advil?*'

He called back, "What? No! No more pills, you don't want to overdo it. Where are the car keys? If you want a lift to the station we need to go like five minutes ago!"

"Hang on, I'm ready, just one sec." She sped out of the bathroom, grabbed her laptop bag and gave him a nod.

Leaving through the front door he told her. "You still look pale."

"Alcohol poisoning." She added dramatically.

"Enjoy that Year 9 class this morning!"

She looked sheepishly at him. "And of course you're fine."

They ran down the steps.

"The difference between disordered and super ordered!" he quipped.

"Of course, everything has to be at a higher level with you!" She strode ahead, put her nose in the air and swung her mustard coloured handbag over her shoulder dropping its contents behind her.

CHAPTER 13 - ANOTHER ORDINARY DAY

Marcus

Later that day, the RVI emergency department was buzzing and beeping. The shift was busy. Marcus was finishing with a patient who had fractured his skull after falling down a flight of stairs in a restaurant. Unconscious, he was now stable and being moved to intensive care. It had taken him longer than usual as the patient needed a CT scan. Finding a free radiographer had been a struggle. His patient was measuring badly on the Glasgow Coma Scale, '*He really doesn't look good,*' Marcus sighed to himself, biting his lip.

Already two separate RTAs had come in and the place became frantic. Cases finally under control Marcus paused for breath. Within seconds, however, there was an urgent call to say that a comatose male, nineteen years old, was coming in.

Marcus rushed to the emergency ambulance entrance with his team. The paramedic gave the update on the young man who had overdosed on recreational drugs.

"Unconscious, fecally incontinent, very shallow breathing, at risk of cardiac arrest."

The handover took seconds and in an instant the patient was in the bay.

"Secure the airway and central line, let's go." Marcus called to his team, "Then check his vitals. Christopher, we're looking after you, stay with me. Everyone concentrate, adult life support as required."

Frantic checks were made. Marcus looked at the monitor.

"He's gone, everyone prepare for shocking." His nursing assistant handed him the defibrillator.

"Clear the patient, I'm clear, you all clear? Everyone clear!" Marcus was controlled and calm.

Nothing.

"Come on, come on, again, prepare for shocking!"

Still the monitor remained inactive.

"Again, Christopher stay with us? Come on. Christopher, we need you. Everyone clear! Shocking!"

A faint splutter came from his mouth which was foaming. He vomited all over Marcus and Leo, the Emergency Healthcare Assistant. Together the team put Christopher into the recovery position and he was back breathing.

No time for Marcus to wipe the vomit from his apron and scrubs.

"Oxygen, and manual ventilation, let's get on that. Christopher, we're looking after you, don't worry."

Marcus watched his patient's heartbeat stabilise. "Great work, he's back, well done team. Let's keep him steady. We need to get toxicology tests quickly, did anyone say what he took?"

An emergency nurse looked in the notes, "Anecdotally GHB...Gamma Hydroxybutyrate, class C, what a prick."

105

"Thanks, then we can give activated charcoal, keep him on the drip, he's likely to vomit again. Remember we don't know the circumstances of this overdose so let's avoid jumping to conclusions. He may have been given it by a third party." Marcus smiled knowingly at the nurse whose cheeks turned pink. Memories of his drink being spiked, by the Newcastle Green posse, briefly entered his mind.

Looking up in relief Marcus genuinely thanked God. Taking off his apron, he cleaned up and changed his scrubs. Going to another patient, who had cut their hand with a knife when destoning an avocado, he thought about the young lad. Why had he ended up in such a state? Within the hour he had the news that his overdosed patient had indeed been taking a recreational drug; GHB commonly known as liquid Ecstasy.

His young patient had come round; gaunt looking parents were now at his side. Marcus went to see him before getting him admitted onto the ward. "Christopher Deehan, is that right? Date of birth 1 October 1999."
The parents nodded.

"You're a very lucky man, if your friend had not called the ambulance you would've died."

Christopher's mother gave a gasp and a small cry.

"GHB or liquid ecstasy is extremely dangerous, you can enter a coma very quickly. You were unconscious when you came in. Your heart stopped, we got it going again."
Christopher looked at him weakly.

"Now if you were a victim of drink spiking we need a statement for the police. If not, you should know that, apart from nearly dying, you lost control of your bladder and bowels. Not a good party look I'd say. Two of our nurses had to clean you up."

Wendy looked even more shaken. Rufus looked away, seemingly taking his son's shame.

"This is an illegal recreational drug with a bad reputation. I need to inform the police. You'll be interviewed and if necessary, enrolled on a rehabilitation programme."

Marcus did not hold back, '*The truth hurts but death would hurt Christopher and his family more.*'

"Thank you so much for all you've done." Wendy said to Marcus.

"Honestly it's my job, I just hope Christopher follows the rehab programme. I'm not judging him but he needs to know how close he came to death. The rehab is good and it will make all the difference."

"I just wish…" Wendy began to cry.

"Hey, there's hope for the future if he gets the right help. We've all messed up when teenagers. Why not encourage him to get busy, maybe take up a sport?"

"Such a wise head on young shoulders!" Rufus commented.

"I've been well trained. Plus I was a teenager once!" Marcus smiled warmly at them.

"Where did you study Medicine?"

"At university, it was hard work but worth it now!" Marcus was completing Christopher's notes.

"Which one?"

"Oxford actually. Six years!"

"Oh...Oxford…"

"Are you okay Mrs Deehan?"

107

She looked away. "Wendy...yes sorry it's all just been too much..."

"Let me organise some tea for you. I'll get some information that we give to family members, plus some leaflets about local sports clubs. There's a rowing club looking for new members."

"Thank you, you're so kind...such a fine young man."
Marcus nodded and went to get the things promised.

Noëmi

Finally recovered from the weekend, Noëmi longed for the next one so she could sleep. Trudging home from the station the evenings were getting colder, darker and longer.

Going up the three steps to their flat, she grabbed their post and went through to the kitchen. Marcus was on lates. She had time to have a cup of tea, a warm shower and to make some supper before his return. Chucking the advertising leaflets into the recycling, without even looking at them, she opened her mail. A letter from her mobile phone company, a thank you note from Alex and Cathy and a large brown envelope addressed only to her by name, marked 'private'.

Curious, she opened it and put her hand inside to get out the contents. A hot searing pain drilled into her wrist and she yelped. Drawing out her arm she was horrified to see a wasp. She brushed it off quickly. The insect limped across the floor and she looked at the red welt left by the sting. Involuntary tears pricked her eyes from the pain and she put her wrist under the cold tap to relieve the burning. What was this envelope? She put rubber gloves on and took out the brochure. The compliments slip read:

'Dear Miss McAllister, Thank you for enquiring about our services, we hope the enclosed is useful. Roland Barrow and Sons Solicitors.'

108

Looking across at the brochure entitled, '**Personalised divorce solutions for you!**' she began to cry. What was this? Why had she been sent this? She had not asked for this literature. Suddenly shaking, she put it to one side, determined to find out why they had sent her such an ominous folder of '**bespoke services to get the best divorce for you!**'

Undecided if the sting or the nature of the paperwork was making her most angry, she looked at the clock for when Marcus would be home to ask him what he thought was going on.

Marcus

Walking into their flat, Marcus saw Noëmi preparing dinner in the kitchen.

"Yes! So glad it's your turn. Prawn linguine! I love that! Good day?"

The look on her face told him all he needed to know.

"Look what arrived, I've never requested anything like this!" She pushed the mysterious divorce brochure towards him.

Putting his rucksack on the table he examined the booklet.

"It's probably just a marketing ploy, you know, making it personal. Just bin it, that's definitely something you and I'll never need." He leant over and gave her a long kiss.

"Inside was a wasp that stung me."

"Let me see, that's unusual, wasps die off as it gets colder, are you sure it was in the envelope?"

"Yes, definitely."

"N, it was probably just resting on it. There was a big nest in the building last year when I moved in, maybe there's another."

109

"Sure, you're right, I'm just beginning to imagine things! But you know what they say. *If a wasp stings you, it's a sign your foes will get the best of you.*"

He stroked her cheek softly.

"Still hungover! Eh?"

"Stop it, I'm never drinking again. We've had a lovely card from Alex and Cathy, I like them very much."

Smiling at each other Marcus treated the sting with antiseptic and soothed the hurt. Kissing it better, the barbs, both actual and implied, were dismissed as unfortunate coincidences.

PART TWO - REACTIONS

On peut citer de mauvais vers, quand ils sont d'un grand poète - Les liaisons dangereuses, Pierre Choderlos de Laclos

CHAPTER 14 - SPEAK UP

Tianna

Tianna progressed her plan to take up rowing. Marcus had told her there was a club looking for members. It was situated between Newcastle and Durham using the River Wear, so she made enquiries and signed up for a taster session. The Wear Rowing Club was a traditional little club with an excellent reputation. The teams trained, unsurprisingly, on the River Wear.

Nervously she arrived and sat in the car.

"Do you want me to come in with you?" her father asked, as he adjusted the car mirror.

"No Dad, I just need a minute." Presently she got out, knowing her father would wait a few moments anyway. Suddenly she saw Joel striding across the car park.

"Joel!"

"We must stop meeting like this!" he laughed. "Are you getting ready for Oxford then?"

"Kind of, bit predictable, rowing! What about you?"

He opened the door for her, she waved to her father.

"They sent a flyer out to the hospital, looking for new members! Sounded interesting so here I am! I'd like to go further with my fitness."

"Same, Marcus showed me that leaflet."

They walked in together and looked around.

"Over there, new registrations." Joel indicated to Tianna who followed him to where a group was waiting. Everyone began to chat and introduce themselves. One newcomer was Louisa whose previous experience meant she had gone straight into the team squad. She was fresh faced with hazel eyes and a honey blonde ponytail that swung as she walked. Louisa was most interested in getting to know Tianna as they were both in the A Level year. Another was Christopher Deehan. Tianna noticed his rugged good looks, piercing blue eyes and chestnut coloured hair which was flecked blonde in places by the sun. Holding everyone's attention, Christopher introduced himself, "I'm Kit, great to meet you all!"

Happy murmurs of shared expectations and excitement filled the room. Joel stayed close to Tianna and asked her. "How was the clearing up at the end of the party?"

"Not too bad! I got paid!" Tianna's voice was shaking.

"That's the wonderful thing about work, the money! Even if I'm working with my Mum!" Joel handed her the pen for her registration form.

"And my older brother! Rather you than me!" Tianna pulled a face.

"Your bro's really alright though! He's inspired me, I'm going to train to be a paramedic." Joel smiled and signed his form.

The group leader, Alan Kelly, called them to attention and went through the schedule for the evening. First would be a warm up and some instruction on basic rowing technique.

'*God everyone will see how unfit I am*', Tianna was panicking. No time to think immediately they were sent out to jog around the neighbouring field. As the introductory session ended, Squadron Leader Kelly beamed at them and told them how pleased he was with his new recruits. A number left immediately and a few moved to join the older rowers at the bar.

The bar was a typical set up. A brown wooden table top surrounded by a mirrored wall with the usual optics that regular drinkers preferred. No fancy gins, just the trusted ones. Good draft beers like Doom Bar and displays of bar snacks like Scampi Fries and Twiglets. Oars were suspended across the ceiling for decoration and indeed any opportunity to incorporate an oar into a logo, poster or sign had been taken. A large trophy cabinet housed an impressive array of silver shields and medals; the club was successful. A few bar stools, covered with faded green velvet, were scattered around next to some faux leather sofas. Small oak tables were stained with white ring marks. On the wall a few certificates were displayed explaining the licensing laws and club regulations. An out of date first aid notice was next to a defunct looking fire extinguisher.

"Fancy a drink?" Kit asked, directing his question only to Tianna.

Tianna felt a rush of independence and maturity.

"Oh yes please, a coke would be lovely," Kit turned to order a coke and a pint for himself. Tianna turned to Joel, "What do you want Joel?"

"Don't worry I'll get a coke, but thanks for asking. I'm driving, got my Mum's car. I never mix things, but if I'm drinking I'm drinking!" he replied confidently.

Tianna wondered how it worked in pubs ordering drinks and why Joel had not been offered anything. The new members sat down together. Joel shared a few anecdotes about his work that day at the hospital, including a story about a porter with a prosthetic eye who could pop it out at will. Kit mentioned his afternoon scores on PS4 Call of Duty and his intention to, one day, do a Masters in Business Management. Tianna felt a little out of her depth with these two older boys. Feeling she had nothing to say, she was brave.

"Well, I had a day of lame lessons and annoying teachers!"

An awkward silence fell, Tianna felt a lump in her throat, '*I'm so boring.*'

Suddenly Joel chipped in.

"Yeah! That was so me last year! Living the dream eh Tianna?" She could breathe.

Louisa strolled over and pulled up a chair. "You all did well."

Joel smiled at her, "Novice squad dominating!"

Tianna asked her, "Where are you at school?"

"Mountford, just moved there, Dad's job. I used to row for my old school." Her teeth were gleaming.

Kit finished his pint, "Whoa I went there, good school. Who's your tutor?"

"Miss Watanabe, she's *so* strict, she can quote every sanction at will, it's like she ate the rule book." Louisa moaned.

Tianna gave a sharp intake of breath. '*Yumi!*'

"Oh God not her, she was mine too. We used to call her …. Miss What a Knob!"

"God you're horrible but that's funny!" Louisa gave a scoff and laughed, "*What* a name!"

"Someone called her that once and she totally freaked out in Japanese, scariest thing ever!"

"Oh, I'll mention that, it'll spook her!"

They both laughed. Joel was silent. Tianna had a lump in her throat. She thought about Yumi swimming furiously to the tiny

Matteo. Their conversation about the petty rules that sixth formers found tiresome, faded into the background.

'*Why did I not stick up for her?*'

Marcus had offered to pick Tianna up at the end of the evening. He messaged her and tactfully stayed in the car.

'*He remembers these little things are so important when you're seventeen.*' She thought.

Tianna announced that she was leaving and Joel got up to see her to her lift.

"Hey Joel, how are you?" Marcus asked as he saw Penelope's son accompany Tianna to the car.

"Good thanks! See you tomorrow!" He gave the car a tap and went to drive home.

Marcus asked Tianna about the evening as they set off.

"Yes I liked it, I met some great people, they all seem very sophisticated and confident. A couple of them are from that private school where Yumi works. Is it really expensive to go there?"

"About fifteen thousand a year from your net income; you need to earn twenty thousand just to pay for one year. So yes, it is!"

"That guy you work with, Joel, he was there."

"Nice! He's doing well at work," Marcus merged onto the road out of the village.

"Sounds a bit boring." Tianna was feeling quite limitless, she had been invited for a drink.

"Oh, I see like that is it? You're too good for us normal people now! Do your arms ache?"

"No, I'm strong."

"They will tomorrow!"

"Marcus you're so sensible, have you ever done anything like *out there*?" She relaxed back.

"Nothing that I'm going to tell you about." He replied as he turned onto the main A1 road.

"Oh, did you put your revision notes in the wrong folder once then? Use the wrong colour highlighter in your studying?"
He laughed.

"Even when you stayed out all night it was a fail because you couldn't hold your drink."

"Indeed Tianna, I was well and truly roasted as you would say...or is it rinsed?"

"God, that's so tragic you trying to sound like a teenager!" She kissed him on the cheek and jumped out of the car.

In spite of having to drive to Newcastle, Kit began to pick Tianna up in his mother's silver sports car for rowing practice, stating that it was 'on his way.'

Anthony

Kit duly arrived one evening as Marcus and Noëmi were helping Anthony clear out his garage. Tianna was not quite ready. Anthony saw Kit march towards him.

'*Oh, he's confident I see. He needs to get past me if he thinks he's taking my precious daughter anywhere.*'

"Hi Anthony! I'm Kit, here to pick up Tianna." Kit beamed.
Anthony felt his neck prickle. Slowly he moved in front of Kit and pulled himself up to his full six feet. "I see. Have you been smoking anything? Taking pills or the like?" Anthony, unsmiling, was straight at him. "Liquor or drugs?"

"No and the car's just been serviced, I have the logbook here."
Kit pointed to the silver car.

117

"You'll stay in the speed limit, you keep the music off. Stop at every junction." Anthony put an arm out to invite him into the hallway to wait. Marianna came out of the lounge.

"So wonderful to meet you all. Your house is so beautifully decorated Mrs McKenzie. In fact, I don't think I've been anywhere so tasteful."

Marianna looked at her modest semi-detached home with its worn carpets and was rendered speechless. She regained herself.

"Thank you, Kit, the pictures of my children are the things that look best in my mind." She pointed to her hall wall which was covered in photographs, detailing every smiling event in McKenzie history.

Marcus and Noëmi had followed.

"This is my eldest son Marcus and his fiancée Noëmi, they'll be married next year."

"Hey good to meet you Kit. Watch it if you go shopping with Tianna, she goes for distance!" Marcus joked as he shook Kit's hand warmly and gave him a friendly pat on the shoulder. Kit seemed all at once pale. Noëmi jolted with surprise as she was proffered a peck on the cheek by Kit. Raeni appeared from the lounge and also received an uninvited air kiss.

"Oh, you must be Grandma, it's so wonderful to meet you. Grandma, your dress is absolutely stunning," he remarked, "I don't think I've seen such an elegant outfit; no one could wear that jade green like you do!"

"Thank you, Kit," and she seemed uncomfortable.

Kit looked at the photos, "What a wonderful family!"

Marianna explained. "Our third son Isaiah is studying at Imperial College in London, this is an excellent place for science. Jayden was at Cambridge reading history and Marcus went to Oxford;

he studied medicine. He now works as an emergency doctor at RVI, in A&E."

Kit gave a jolt. "Ah none of us want to end up in there!"

Marcus laughed, "Very true! You should see some of the stuff we have to deal with, it's crazy! Anyway Kit, now you've seen the swamp from which Tianna has extracted herself, what about you?"

"You want to go to university?" Anthony added.

"Absolutely, I hope to do some travelling in Europe before university, plus I was thinking of trying for Oxbridge as I got the grades."

"Tianna hopes to go, but her other choices are Imperial or Durham which are also good, we feel." Raeni replied.

"So did you apply for university the first time?" Anthony asked, looking poker faced at Kit.

"Yes, but as I said, I felt I could have gone for Oxbridge, so I declined my place."

"Where will you apply for now?"

"Oxford hopefully, UCL too I'd be happy living in London. My parents have a flat there in Chelsea, so it'd be easy."

"I don't know London but our second son Jayden lives in Battersea, not far from Chelsea I think?" Anthony offered.
Kit smirked.

Tianna appeared down the stairs, looking extremely embarrassed. She grabbed her jacket and they left. Watching them drive off, Marianna, face deadpan, spoke first. "How charming."

"He's older than Tianna," Anthony said thoughtfully.

Marianna added. "Yes, plus it's *that* year, the difference between still at school and nineteen. Free to do as he wishes, drink, go to clubs. What interest could he have in someone who can't join him in that? Besides, Tianna needs to focus on her studies."

"And that car is not just an ordinary coupé, it's the silver sports S type, fast and expensive."

Marcus

Marcus and Noëmi did not comment, Marcus was unsure what to think but knew that Tianna was a clever girl. "I know that guy..." Marcus said.

Returning to the garage, Noëmi added, "I don't get a good vibe.

He told Grandma her necklace was 'stunning.' It's just her everyday gold cross, not the Koh-I-Noor diamond."

"He wanted to know where Dad got his jumper from, even funnier!" Marcus spontaneously burst out laughing.

"Because he wants the same, as if! Doesn't look like he shops in Asda!" Noëmi added as she put some old badminton rackets to one side.

Anthony joined them in the garage. For a few moments he busied himself with a box of old gardening tools, without saying a word. Suddenly he stopped and said quite simply.

"I don't like that boy one bit."

CHAPTER 15 - ANYTHING FOR YOU

1 December 2018.

Marcus

The nights drew in and got darker as the weeks rolled on. Noëmi had a number of events to arrange for her sixth form students. Sitting on the sofa with Marcus one evening, he noticed she was unusually silent.

"Are you okay?"

"Yeah, it's just..." she hugged a cushion and curled her knees up.

"Just what?"

"This careers' fair that I decided to organise for the Year 11 and sixth formers, it's next week and so far I've got 4 exhibitors, one of them being Frank bless him."

"Frank?"

"In case anyone wants to be a teacher, so that's no one."

"Did the hospital not get someone organised? Did you send the details over to the email I gave you? That's our new Patient Care Manager who organises all the community outreach projects."

"I did, three times, to that guy with all the hyphens, but no reply."

"When is it?" Marcus felt a bit flushed.

"Next Thursday at 3pm until 5pm."

Marcus spent a couple of minutes on his phone.

"Alright I can do it, I've swapped my shift with Madhav, don't worry."

"Really! Oh my God, that'd be amazing, thank you so much."

"You're welcome," he smiled and carried on texting.

"I've messaged Pen, she says she can help too. I'll get some banners and leaflets about all jobs in healthcare. There are so many for all sorts of students. Need to motivate them, it's not just about being a medic, those nurses, radiographers, healthcare assistants, porters all do such an important job, something for everyone."

"You've saved my life."

"That's what I'm supposed to do, hold on, have you asked Guy?

He's the link police officer for the school after all! He was your friend first remember! He likes to remind me of that."

"Ahh I didn't think of him."

Marcus messaged some more.

"Yep, he can do it, part of his community work. He says it'll give him a chance to talk to the new management too."

"This is getting better and better," she smiled, "one of the other four is Dad's office so I guess that'll be Dad."

"Sounds like your birthday party list, do you have anyone who doesn't know you?"

"Actually you know the Neglected Tropical Diseases Trust is sending two representatives up from London, can you believe! A human resources specialist and a communications expert, the school's going to make a donation."

"Oh my God, that's amazing, have you seen the work they do? I'd love to chat to them too! This is going to be awesome. Who's the fourth one, Val?"

"No, he completely refused, saying no one ever *wants* to be a Dentist. I'm still hoping he'll relent. It's one of your Dad's colleagues from Marks and Spencer talking about retail, so probably actually your Dad."

"Nice one Dad, it's shaping up N, don't worry!"

"Honestly I'm just so grateful already, you have no idea."

"You're doing a fine job."

Her brow furrowed, "You can't come in scrubs, you know, that'll be too much for me."

He laughed, "We're not allowed to wear them out of the hospital, I'll have to wear a suit"

"And a white coat with a stethoscope?"

"Sounds good! Look like a doctor!"

"Just no scrubs," she smiled knowingly at him.

6 December 2018.

Careers' Day arrived and Marcus knocked on Evan's office door then waited.

"Come in!" Evan was sitting at her neat desk fixing her lipstick.

"Hi Evan! I've just come to pick up the pop ups and leaflets that I mentioned." Marcus looked around the office for them.

"Yes, they're all in the car, let's go." Evan stood up and grabbed her dark blue cashmere coat.

"You're coming too?" Marcus' eyes were wide.

"Yes of course, outreach to local communities is important for the hospital and the next generation. It's vital to do this work." She slipped the coat on. Then she returned her make-up to her shiny black handbag. Gold snake clasp snapped shut, she popped her bag on her arm.

Marcus bit his tongue. '*So, you don't bother replying to Noëmi's emails but now the minute a doctor's giving up his free time you're prepared to drop everything.*' They walked in silence to the car park.

"Penelope's joining us. I just need to pick her up from the department." Marcus reminded Evan.

"I told her not to bother, no room in the car. Plus, she's needed in the emergency department, we're good." Evan's hair shimmered like shiny gold satin.

"What! I can fit us all in my car!"

Marcus was annoyed, Penelope Rivera was a good friend and a fine nurse. She had agreed to be there. Evan's car was a bright silver convertible. Ignoring his comment, she zapped her key. The sparkling car unlocked, flashing its lights.

"I saved and saved to get this."

Marcus wondered why she was making that point, '*How you finance your life is the last thing to cross my mind.*'

They sped off to the school.

Marcus felt a bit awkward arriving with Evan especially as the fancy silver sports car caused a bit of a stir in the school staff car park. He grabbed all the materials and banners and carried them into reception.

Noëmi was there waiting with Frank, and she beamed as she saw him. Marcus' shoulders relaxed. He strode in, dumped the pop ups and boxes on the reception desk and walked straight up to her. Ignoring everyone else, he put his arms around her and gave her a long, tender kiss on the lips. Noëmi, when finally released from his embrace, went bright pink.

Evan gave a sharp intake of breath.

A couple of young students helping on reception, looked at each other and giggled.

"Alright you two that's enough. Teachers are actually humans, you know, some people even like us." Frank told the amused pupils.

"This is Noëmi McAllister, she's in charge of the event. Noëmi, this is Ms St-John-Jones, our Patient Care Manager."

"Noëmi," One of the sniggering students whispered to the other.

"Call me Evan!" She proffered a perfect hand.

"Oh! **Evan**...Evan...Evan it's lovely to meet you thank you so much for supporting us." Noëmi looked straight at Marcus who avoided her gaze.

Evan moved forward to sign in.

Noëmi whispered to Marcus, "That's Evan?"

"Er yes…"

"I got the impression Evan was a guy. What was that coffee the other weekend?" she hissed.

"Nothing, I didn't go, remember?" He did not look at her.

Evan

'*Really no competition,*' Evan thought to herself.

Noëmi was breathless. "We just need to get you both signed in, then one of the sixth formers will take you to set up."

Evan grabbed the pen, marched forward and wrote, '***Marcus &***

Evan, Newcastle RVI' in the visitors' book. She swallowed a

smile as she heard Noëmi's gasp when she looked at Evan's

signing in. Badges were given and car registration numbers
taken.

"Miss McAllister, the hospital lady wants to use the loo." A
student holding a tray of cups interrupted.

"Oh of course one minute, ah, Bella could you please take Dr
McKenzie to set up in the hall?" She sent him a curious look.

"Of course Miss McAllister," the sixth former replied.

After registering, Evan and Noëmi went to the toilet.

"That's lovely perfume Evan, lilies isn't it?" Noëmi commented.

Evan smiled, face dropping as Noëmi looked away. Bri came in.
Noëmi started the introductions.

"I know Evan," she interrupted. "We met backpacking in Asia

years ago. I suggested she look at RVI for jobs and hey presto!"
Bri smiled.

The pair hugged. "It'll be a great event, so lovely of Marcus to

come along and help out."

"Yes absol…" Noëmi began to say.

"Yes it is! He's so kind, but that's just him! One of life's givers!"

Evan spoke loudly over her and disappeared into a cubicle.
Noëmi gave a small squeak.

Bri peered at herself in the mirror pulling on the skin under her
eyes.

Noëmi continued, voice shaking, "Marcus is so thoughtful, and

what about Frank! Can you believe what a star!"

"Ah ha. Take care, you look even more tired than me!" Bri

touched her arm affectionately.

"I know! I don't have any idea why I'm so shattered. Bring on Christmas!" she said, also examining herself in the mirror, "Look at these dark circles!"

During this time Evan had been sizing Noëmi up, *'no hair extensions, no surgery, bit of the girl next door about her, clothes very teacher-like. I can take her on. Damn she has a great figure and good hair.'* Evan came out of the toilet and joined the two teachers at the sinks.

"Work and men, they wear us out right!" Evan remarked to Bri, ignoring Noëmi.

"Too much of one or not enough of the other!" Bri replied.

"And which one are you getting too much of?" Evan laughed chummily.

"Work unfortunately, no man on the horizon. How are your plans coming on?"

"Getting there and he's definitely the full package, education, career, looks."

"We all want the full package in every department!" Bri joked.

"You're working in the right place if Marcus is anything to go by, all those fit doctors!" .

"Yes, there's definitely so much sexual tension in our workplace! Honestly what some of them get up to!" Evan looked cheekily at Bri as she smoothed her hands over her dress.

Noëmi

Her hands felt clammy and her throat lumpy.

"What about you?" Evan turned the question to Noëmi, as she eyed her via the mirror over the sink.

"I...sorry... oh too much work..." She stuttered, her palms got sweaty.

"God how dull and boring!" Evan said coldly at her and walked out.

Noëmi felt her eyes sting and the lump in her throat grow.

They went into the hall. Noëmi focused on Marcus who had set everything up and was standing, hands in pockets, at the healthcare booth.

"We're all set Noëmi," Marcus smiled, giving her a wink.

Evan joined him on the stand. "Hey thanks for getting this all done Marcus," Evan touched his arm in appreciation and positioned herself right up close to him.

"Oh yes...we're nearly ready," Noëmi was frozen to the spot.

*'What's she doing so close to him! She's touching him! Who **is** this Evan woman? Thank God he's moved away.'* Her heart began to race.

There were ten exhibitors and students appeared motivated to find out all they could. Marcus' booth was overrun as healthcare was popular. Noëmi sat with Frank at his empty stand, so he was not lonely.

Frank

"Who's that with Marcus then?"

"Evan, a new manager from his hospital." She glanced back over her shoulder at their packed area.

"Right, okay."

"What does that mean Frank?"

"She seems terribly keen," he bit his tongue and did not add, *'on your fiancé'.*

"I know I'm so glad they came, I'd messaged her three times with no response and then Marcus got it sorted only last week, just like that!"

The sound of Evan's laughter filled their ears.

128

"Really now?" Frank straightened out his **Teaching! Could Do Better!** brochures. "Honestly this is how rubbish our profession is. They can't even get a brochure titled without irony! Anyway, how's the McKenster alliance working out?"

"Yes, perfect! We're about to set a date for the wedding, May half term. Then have a luxury honeymoon in the summer. We're looking at Bali." She ran her finger round the table edge.

"You're not taking work home with you I hope."

"No! Just a bit of marking here and there! Don't worry I'm not boring!" She touched his arm affectionately.

"That's what I like to hear. By the way no one's been to talk about getting into teaching, only a couple of my sixth formers came over wanting to know about the homework I set."

"Sorry Frank, thank you anyway!" Marcus joined them during a short break. Noëmi had to get refreshments for the exhibitors.

"Anyone fancy a *coffee*?" she asked, looking pointedly at Marcus and walked off.

"So thoughtful of your colleague to come along then." Frank gestured at Evan who was sashaying across the hall.

"Yeah, something like that." Marcus did not look round.

"What does that mean?"

"Well N emails her three times, no reply then the minute she finds out a doctor's going she's suddenly keen to join in."

"And not any old doctor." Frank brushed some dust from his shoulder.

"Sorry?"

"Okay I take it Noëmi doesn't realise?" Frank looked directly at Marcus.

129

"What? There's nothing to realise Frank. Evan's my colleague and is actually great at her job." Marcus picked up one of Frank's brochures with pictures of smiling teachers and flicked through it.

"It's awesome that she's so motivated." Frank gave a sigh.

"Frank work's busy. She's important. I need to have good relationships with my colleagues." He put the brochure back, neatened the stack and walked back to his stand where a coffee was waiting for him.

Noëmi

They finished the event and set about tidying up. Evan observed everything and spent most of the clearing up period touching up her make-up in the corner. Noëmi thanked all the exhibitors individually. As she spoke to Raphael, HR Manager from the Neglected Tropical Diseases Trust, he suddenly handed her a gift.

"It's for all you've done on that noma blog. We get so much response from that I can't tell you! There you go, that's for you to enjoy if you ever get a break!"

She looked down at the bottle and felt a tremble to her lip.

"Thank you for being so thoughtful. We really appreciate you coming tonight and for the talk you're doing tomorrow. The students can't wait."

"We'll see you tomorrow, you know we're off now to host an event at Durham University. This has all worked out so well for us Noëmi!"

Raphael and his colleague picked up their bags and left.

She turned to Guy and Evan who were in the school foyer.

"Well done. Nice wine that one!" Guy commented.

"They said it's to thank me for my noma blog!"

Having loaded the banners and publicity materials into Evan's car, Marcus came back inside bringing a cold draught with him. He looked around.

"N are you coming home now?" Marcus asked her.

"No, I've got a meeting with a student and his parents." Her voice was strained; she was already tired.

"Guy?"

"I'm meeting the interim Head teacher, I can drop Noëmi back later."

"I'll take you home Marcus." Evan smiled at Marcus who stood awkwardly not returning Evan's gaze.

Noëmi knew she had to thank Evan. "Marcus, can you take this bottle of Pinot Grigio, it's from the NTDT guys. We're not allowed to keep alcohol in school." She passed him the wine and turned to Evan. "Thank you so much for everything you've done tonight." She looked at Marcus as she said this.

"Marcus and I are always keen to help. Anything we can do!" Evan affirmed. Noëmi took a deep breath. Guy made a comment under his breath she didn't quite hear.

Marcus came straight to Noëmi and gave her a kiss. "See you later at home."

They watched Marcus get into the silver car with Evan.

"Nice car." Guy sighed.

"It's weird her whisking him off, looking like that, in that car. Plus, she invited him for a fucking coffee a few weeks back, on a day off!" Noëmi picked up the leftover leaflets.

Guy put a comforting arm around her shoulder.

"He always does the right thing, sometimes to his own detriment,"

131

"I feel a bit insecure having seen her, she looks like a supermodel and I'm some *boring* washed-out teacher..." Noëmi hugged her **Teaching! Could do Better!** brochures.

"Oh God don't say that! She's nothing compared with you Noëmi, believe me!" Guy ruffled her hair affectionately.

"Yeah I'm such a *good* person."

"...I meant..."

"Oh, my dependable personality."

"...no, I actually meant...oh never mind...anyway you can trust him."

"I do trust him." Noëmi said in a small voice as she wiped her eyes. Guy gave her shoulder a squeeze.

Guy

Guy and Noëmi returned to the flat in good spirits after the drive home from Durham.

"My third time in a patrol car! Hey where's my wine?"

Marcus called from the kitchen, "I left it in my hospital locker, I walked home."

"You know I'm exhausted, can't face food, gotta go nap." She yawned.

Guy stayed with his friend.

Marcus finished cooking as Guy asked uncomfortable questions.

"So that Evan won't leave you alone, will she?" He pulled his chair up to the table.

"No, it's just work." He gave the wok a big shake.

"You need to stop being so naïve. What was this coffee?"

Marcus looked to the ceiling, "Oh God, I didn't go. I'm engaged, everyone knows that! My every other word is *my fiancée this, my fiancée that*. Everyone at work must think I'm as wet as they come, so under the thumb."

"Well you won't need to worry about any of that if Evan has her way." Guy went to the fridge and grabbed a juice.

"There are big projects at work, I have to get on with everyone, be a team player!"

"Boundaries, your favourite word remember! Think if it was the other way around, you'd be pissed off. When that Jesse bloke made his move this summer Noëmi shut it right down!"

"You're getting this out of proportion Guy!" Marcus opened a cupboard to get the soy sauce.

"No, you're being really unfair to Noëmi, she's not comfortable with Evan's attention towards you. You have to crush a crush!"

"There's no crush, she's just a friendly work colleague who's a bit hyper that's all!"

Marcus kicked the cupboard door shut with his foot and served up their stir fry. He looked at Guy who added. "Just be sure Evan gets the message loud and clear! Shut it down!"

Noëmi

Relieved that the careers' evening had gone well, Noëmi was looking forward to the medical charity coming back to the school for assemblies. She was up early and went to grab the post, '*I hope the End Noma Campaign newsletter arrives today. Then I could show it to the charity guys, they'd love to see that!*'

A large brown A4 envelope marked private and confidential, '**For The Attention of Miss McAllister**' was the first thing she saw. Curious, she ripped it open. A letter stated that '**the information requested**' was enclosed. Looking past the letter she saw a glossy brochure;

133

'**Your plastic surgery future!**' with details of various procedures that she could pay thousands of pounds for in order to '**Get the you, you deserve!**' Flinging it down she gave a scream of frustration. Marcus appeared sleepy, looking confused.

"This is not a coincidence or clever marketing," she said pointing at the now on the floor brochure. She stomped towards the kitchen with the rest of the post. Glaring at Marcus, she let him have the best part of her upset.

"Anyway, why are you up now? Coffee time with Evan is it? And why exactly did you not tell me you were meeting *her* on your day off?" Grabbing her flask, she threw a teabag in and lifted the kettle.

"It was just a quick work thing. It didn't happen. Forget about that,"

"It's a bit hard now that I've seen her." She scowled at him.

"Oh so how does what she looks like make a difference?"

"Really you want to try that line of defence? Is it what she looks like or that you didn't mention that Evan was a *she* that bothers me most? Or could it be both? What do you think?" She looked over her shoulder at him.

"N, it was just an awkward situation, trust me."

"You're lucky that I actually do."

Picking up the envelope, Marcus looked at it and went to the kitchen. Another envelope addressed to **Ms McAllister** was in her hand, she trembled as she opened it.

'**Warrington, Barnes and May, solicitors specialising in divorce solutions.**' Noëmi chucked it to the floor and Marcus looked down at the compliments slip. '**Thank you for your call to our offices, we are happy to enclose the information requested.**'

"What's going on? Who's doing this?"

Marcus was dumbfounded.

Noëmi wiped a tear away and finished making her hot drink. She went to the door to leave. She pulled her coat on and brushed her hair, pulling it up into a long ponytail, peering in the hall mirror as she did. She shook her shoulders and was resolved to be in control.

He intercepted her and took her in his arms, holding her tight, "I love you so very much, N."

"Someone out there doesn't love me…" she looked up at him.

"I remember what today is too." He whispered.
Still, they were silent. Suddenly she sighed.

"Twelve years. Let's take Dad out tonight and forget about all this stuff. I'm sure it's just new marketing strategies like you said.

Ignore me! I'm just feeling tired and emotional all the time."

CHAPTER 16 - LOSS

Evan

'*Hey Evs how's the romance? What's happening?*'

'*Bri, we're getting each other Christmas gifts! #gettingcloser!*'

Marcus

Arriving at Newcastle RVI, Marcus caught sight of himself in the reflection of the door.

'*Time to cheer up man!*' he sighed to himself. Rushing to his locker he got changed and moved to check his pigeon hole. A small red envelope. The scent was familiar. His heart stopped. He looked around. Quickly he opened it. '**RVI Staff Secret Santa, you're gifting to…**' he unfolded the bottom part of the note and said out loud, "Evan."

'*Of course I am.*' He looked to the ceiling that never gave any answers, screwed the paper up and chucked it in the bin.

Soon forgetting about the £5 gift he had to buy, he got busy with a tricky case in A&E. A pregnant woman had come in as she had not felt her baby move for a number of hours. An ultrasonographer, Esme, had been called and was on her way with a portable device for an initial look. In order to keep the patient calm her vital signs were taken. Marcus listened for a heartbeat but was unable to detect one. Feeling anxious he was pleased that Esme arrived so promptly and took over the diagnosis. Remaining close by, in order to assist his colleague, Marcus read the images with her and had to deliver bad news.

His patient collapsed inconsolable as the receptionist desperately tried to contact her next of kin. Holding her hand Esme comforted the woman whose baby was nearly twenty weeks gestation. Marcus took over the report and explained what would happen next.

"I'm afraid the diagnosis is not looking positive and it is likely to be bad news. I'm so sorry. We are unable to detect your baby's heartbeat, but we must verify with a more powerful ultrasound before we can be absolutely certain. We'll keep you fully informed at all times. Please let us get you some water and we're contacting your partner."

He came out of the cubicle and cursed the patient's misfortune. Nothing was easy about delivering such news. He had seen the patient's history and knew this was a long-awaited pregnancy. As he wrote the report he could hear the patient sob quietly, and Esme talking quietly to her. He felt wretched.

Drained, he was suddenly bleeped to go to the Patient Care Manager's office.

'What! We're so busy, I'm ignoring that! I'll go during my break. HR admin is the last thing on my mind when patients need help!'

Twice more his pager buzzed.

137

Alex came past, "What's this all about?" Marcus showed him the messages.

"No idea, you're right to just get on with this ever-growing list!"

Finally he had his break and went over to Evan's office. Walking in he saw a large book about neglected diseases in Africa on the edge of the desk.

"You called me?" he was not smiling.

"So important to help, did you know noma is not on the global list of neglected tropical diseases."

"Yeah, I did actually," Marcus did not say any more, the patient whose baby had died in utero filled his mind. "You wanted to see me?"

"Firstly, I wanted to thank you so much for rescuing me the other weekend. I'm sorry to have disturbed you. Here I've got something for you." She handed him a gift bag.

Marcus looked and saw an expensive shirt from an exclusive boutique in Newcastle city centre. Feeling himself blush, his words stumbled out.

"I...I can't accept it. It really is no problem to do the odd favour for a colleague."

Evan looked down. "Why not?"

Marcus looked at her directly. "Well if I'm honest, Evan, it'll be upsetting for my fiancée; she would love to buy me shirts like that, it's too personal. Do you get what I'm saying?" He could feel his heart begin to race.

"Sure, I'm sorry, there I go again, messing things up!"

"No, really don't worry, there's nothing to mess up. Was that it?" Marcus turned to leave.

"Sorry, yes, but no. We need to look at this rota for bank staff, you know when you, Madhav and Alex have your mandatory weekends off." Evan took out a large A3 piece of paper.

"Okay how can I help with that?" He stood and folded his arms.

"Can you all indicate the weekends you request off with reasons so that I can put in the necessary cover."

"Reasons?" The A3 sheet crumpled as he examined it.

"Birthdays, weekends away. So I can prioritise."

"Bit personal," he said looking at the spreadsheet, "no one's ever asked for that before."

"We want to run a more empathetic service for our staff. Say if Alex's children have a birthday that would take priority over Madhav celebrating Diwali and so on."

"Really? I don't get that, you wouldn't know what's important to us. In any case we usually sort it all out amongst ourselves, it's been working fine so far." Marcus was short with her.

"That's too casual I'm afraid."

"But you read my report about safeguarding! Remember that whole chapter? If this information fell into the wrong hands, it's a clear breach of data protection for the department! It could put people at risk!" He stared at her, *'She told me how impressed she was with my review, how could she have missed that section?"*
Evan turned pink.

Marcus took the printed-out calendar and was about to leave when he noticed a brochure about an MSc in psychology placed on her desk.

"Are you taking that course?"

"Absolutely I'm training to be a clinical psychologist, with an intention to go into practice."

"Impressive," he said, immediately regretting this. As he picked it up, an Italian dictionary was underneath. "You speak Italian?"

"Oh yes, I lived in Rome for a bit after I graduated."

"It's a beautiful country," his mind wandered to Noëmi talking with her grandparents. They were having lunch on the sun-soaked terrace of their family villa, overlooking the valley where they grew lemons. A slight breeze stopped the heat from being oppressive and Noëmi was dressed in a short pale blue dress, her skin was soft and tanned, her hair was silky and loose around her shoulders. The panorama was beautiful and the far-off sound of the waves made it the most idyllic spot. She was chatting with her grandfather who held her hand tightly and stroked her cheek. He was laughing at whatever she was saying in Italian and then gave her a huge hug. At that moment he was touched by how much the grandfather loved and cherished Noëmi. The thought of ever being apart from her suddenly scared him.

"Have you been?" Evan's question awoke him from his reverie.

"Yes, not to Rome but to the Amalfi coast, last summer and we're hoping to go back this year sometime, when... anyway I don't need to take up any more of your time, thanks for the schedule planner, I'll discuss it with the others."

Marcus got up to walk out.

"I wondered if you'd thought any more about us all meeting up?"

"Sorry it's not a good idea..."

"Maybe just you and me? Somewhere quiet?" Her hand reached out and touched his arm. Her eyes locked on him.

Marcus slid his arm away from her red tipped hand, "Evan, there's a staff social intranet. There are lots of meet-up groups you may wish to look at." He started to leave her office.

"I have to be careful who I mix with."

"We all do, don't we?" Marcus said emphatically as he left.

'That's shut it down.'

He hoped she had got the hint. A confident, good looking woman, in a managerial position, in her early thirties, could definitely find her own entertainment.

CHAPTER 17 - CHRISTMAS

15 December 2018.

Tianna

Dark evenings also heralded holidays and hurrahs. Events were aplenty. Tianna McKenzie was excited for The Wear Rowing Club Christmas party. She strategically negotiated an extended curfew until midnight when her father would pick her up.

'Time to show everyone who I am; mature in every way.' She was a new woman.

The whole family had rallied round to support her. Her new dress was the sparkliest and shortest she had ever been allowed to wear. Her hair had been styled by Marianna's hairdresser friend Rochelle. Her legs felt tight from all the working out she had done. Marianna had treated her to rose gold shellac nails. Marcus had bought her evening shoes, Jayden sent her new earrings from London and Isaiah, with his girlfriend Jalissa's help, sent her a make-up pallet. Everyone wanted Tianna to feel loved.

Decorating the club room, the social committee had done a fine job. Christmas decorations sparkled and lights twinkled. **Last Christmas** by Wham blared out. A frisson of excitement down her spine, she strolled in with confidence *'believe in yourself Tianna'*.

Very quickly Kit arrived at Tianna's side.

"You look so amazing,"
Tianna was chuffed, no one had ever told her that before.
"Fancy a drink?"

"Oh yeah coke please!" She threw her head back.
"How about some vodka in that?"

Tianna was hesitant "I'm not eighteen...but why not!"

The evening got going and everyone was in the party spirit. The junior squad were all on one very loud table, and the wine was flowing. Tianna was opposite Kit who filled her glass regularly.

"Steady on Kit, she's not a drunk like you!" quipped Joel.

"You need to learn to enjoy yourself mate!" Kit gave back.
A few small glasses of wine in Italy had been her only previous drinking practice. Tianna was not long in feeling the effects of large glasses of Prosecco imbibed at speed. The room started spinning so she stumbled outside to get some air.

Joel

Joel had noticed Tianna's elbow slip off the table. Giggling, she got up but lost her footing. Steadying herself on the back of the chair she pulled her dress down and staggered away. *'Tianna you're not okay'* Joel got up and followed her to the main door. He wedged the door open, *'She needs to know she's safe.'*

The night was dark and still with the faded thump of party music behind them. They stood on the steps of the entrance to the clubhouse, looking out onto the car park.

"Tianna, hold onto me if you need to." His breath glistened in the frozen night.

"Yeah," She grabbed his arm. "Oh God no, going to be sick."
Tianna promptly vomited all over her new shoes. Joel held onto
her and steadied her,

"Hey, sit down, put your head on your knees, I'll get some water
and tissues, just wait!"
She was shivering.
He put his jacket over her shoulders and dashed to get some
water and kitchen towel to clean her up. Rushing back, he
propped her up and got her to drink the water. She threw up
again and began to cry.

"You're okay, don't worry, just take small sips, here..."
Tianna slumped back. The water fell to the floor.
"Tianna, come on," he slapped her cheek gently but her eyes
rolled and her head swung forwards. "Tianna I'm worried." His
heart was pumping, *'I've seen this at the hospital with the patients on a
trolley sometimes.'* He sat with her. She hung her head, she seemed
half sleeping, taking shallow breaths. *'What if she's not okay? What
if she collapses like Stephanie? I need to get help.'*
Twenty minutes later Tianna came round.

"What...? What's going on?"

"You've been sick, it's the wine. I called my mum, she's a nurse,
she told me what to do, you're okay." He smiled.

Tianna's face contorted into a horrified gurn. "What the fuck did
you call your mum for? She'll tell everyone! You fucking idiot,
I'll be grounded for fucking ever!" She struggled up, jacket still
around her, grabbed the shoes Joel had cleaned and stomped
inside.

"Tianna come back!" he ran after her.

Having staggered into the party, Tianna was caught by Kit.

"Whoa careful gorgeous, who've you been copping off with out there then?"

"What? What's copping...off?"

"You come here," Kit pulled her onto a sofa.

"The room...it's torating…" her eyelids were heavy.

"Kit she needs to go home, she's wasted." Joel had followed.

"What? Sure I'll get her back don't worry,"
Merry Christmas Everybody thudded out.
Tianna curled into the seat. One of the older girls went to her with some water.
Joel went to the bar, turned then spun round again.

'*You know what I've had enough.*' Returning into the party room, he saw Tianna snuggled up with Kit. His jacket was abandoned on the floor. Grabbing it, he did not look back.

The frosty evening air was a welcome change from the sweaty party room. His lift home arrived.

"Is Tianna alright?"

"Who knows? Probably, but everything's all messed up," he sighed as he slumped into his mother's car.

"But Joel, you were so looking forward to this evening!"

"It's not turned out quite how I'd hoped. Mum, it's fine, let's go."
Joel remained silent looking out of the car window, the evening was on repeat in his head, his body felt heavy.

"You've got something caught on your jacket, a bit of tinsel or something."

* * *

145

Tianna woke up the next day with no memory of what had happened or how she had got home. She woke up, still in her dress, some sequins had fallen off onto the floor and one strap was broken. Her make-up was smeared over her pillow and her finger hurt as one of her nail extensions had broken off. Sucking her finger to ease the pain she saw the ominous figure of her mother appear at her bedside.

"Good morning Tianna." A cup of tea was placed next to her. Tianna remained silent; she was unsure if she had got away with whatever she had done the night before.

"What's the legal drinking age?"

"Eighteen."

"Do I need to ring the club or should I get that policeman friend of your brother's to talk to them?"

'No one asked for ID and you're allowed a glass of wine with a meal' she wanted to say but knew that she had just stumbled out of last chance saloon. "I'm very sorry Mum, I've been really stupid."

"Stupid, selfish, smug, the list goes on. Do you know there's a reason for these age restrictions? It's based on what will be good for you. Did you enjoy yourself? Do you want to take a look in the mirror?"
Silence.

"Maybe you can't remember? Is that a fun evening? What could've happened to you?" Marianna looked teary. Tianna remained silent.

"I dread to think. If it hadn't been for that Kit rescuing you...You know I was so wrong about him. He explained how he looked after you! He rescued you!"

146

Hazy memories came back to Tianna of Kit's hands on her body. Having little memory and no feelings for Kit it was so far from what she had expected of her first embrace.

'Kissing isn't what I thought it'd be.'

"He did?" A bright memory of Joel wiping vomit from her shoes flashed through her head.

"Yes! In nine months' time you'll be at university, are you ready for that? Think about it. There won't always be someone like Kit around to look after you!" Marianna began straightening out the duvet cover.

"You let Marcus go to uni after his episode. Is it because it was Oxford?"

"Marcus was just as bad, did I not worry about him? You and he are very similar. You need to keep yourself safe, you owe me that." Marianna walked out.

Throat raging, Tianna drank her tea and caught her reflection in the mirror. She saw one of the earrings that Jayden had sent her was still in but could not find the other anywhere. Frantically she looked and realising it was lost, she began to cry.

* * *

Marcus

Penelope was on Marcus' shift the next day in A&E. She stopped at the front desk to collect some forms for the trolleys. Marcus looked up from his case report.

"Pen, are you coming to that Christmas lunch today?"

"Yes, you've got your Secret Santa?" Penelope said in an offhand way.

'Damn no I've forgotten the gift.'

"What? How did Joel enjoy the party? Was it fun?"

"Okay so you don't know? You wouldn't mess with me, can I talk to you?"

Marcus moved to one side with Penelope who explained what had happened at the rowing club party. Marcus was visibly shaken.

"I'm so sorry, she'll make amends believe me."

Rushing to his locker at the start of his lunch break, Marcus called his sister. He was met with an unremorseful Tianna.

"You're so judgy!"

"You need to apologise for your rudeness to Joel."

"Who calls their Mum?"

"Someone with medical training, whose mum is a nurse and who's looking after an intoxicated, underage girl who's on her own and so drunk she can't stand. Plus he'd spent twenty minutes cleaning you up, but you won't remember that will you?"

"You're no better."

"I never said I was. You can learn from my mistakes then."

"Don't tell Mum about this."

"Tianna what planet are you on? Nothing gets past her. Who looked after you when Joel had left? There was still another hour of the party."

"Friends. You know I've got some, unlike you!"

Tianna hung up on her brother. Moving to the other side of the changing room to avoid anyone else listening. He rang her straight back.

"Don't ever put the phone down on me again, that's so rude."

"My life is none of your business."

"It is when you're upsetting my colleagues. Think about other people, Tianna, not just yourself. Joel is a decent person who doesn't need to be sworn at by you."

"I didn't swear at him."

"You were vile to him! He cleaned you up and kept you from collapsing in a heap alone outside. If he hadn't helped you out, you'd still be lying there."

"What! Like you, who couldn't even get home?"

"The difference is I was old enough to drink. Why don't you just benefit from all my fails?"

"You're so holier than thou."

"No Tianna, you're being tone deaf. I'm telling you how to respect others, not upping myself. By the way, I've got the earring you lost, Joel found it and gave it to his mother. You know the nurse who was called so the minor with alcohol poisoning didn't die. It'll be at the flat so next time you visit you can get it. I now need to go to lunch with my colleagues, you know the decent people who tried to help you." Giving an exasperated cry he turned his mobile off. '*Yes that'll do!*' he spotted the Pinot Grigio and grabbed it, '*Secret Santa sorted*'. Marcus charged to the staff Christmas lunch.

Tianna

Rowing was intense. Putting her all into showing her strength, Tianna was exhilarated. The icy wind was biting and early morning frost glistened on the muddy banks. The winter light sparkled on the water. Ducks flew up and away as Tianna's boat cut through the surface. Each stroke pulled her away from the competitors. Her father stood proudly on the bank, moving his arms to keep warm, watching his powerhouse of a daughter win her sculling race. After half an hour Tianna saw Marcus run up to join their father, bringing him a take away coffee. More events took place and Tianna was excelling; every boat she was in won. Her coach was ecstatic.

For all her amnesia of the night of the Christmas party, her brutal put down of Joel was at the forefront of her mind. After Marcus' reprimand Tianna had felt dreadful and had wanted to see Joel to apologise. She began to feel desperate to talk to him so she could regain his lost approval. Having finished on the water, she saw Joel alone preparing one of the boats, she grabbed her chance.

"Hey Joel how are you? Thank you for finding my earring."

"No worries and I'm good thanks, you?" He looked up at her and smiled.

"I feel bad for how I spoke to you at the Christmas party, I was out of order. I'm sorry."

"Yeah, I did feel a bit mugged off." Suddenly he spoke faster, "Tianna, you were set up a bit with the drinking. I'd even say Kit may have spiked your drink? I hear from the others he was all over you. Whatever happened is between you and him but it's actually a crime for him to get with you when you're out of it. You can't consent to anything when you're off your head. Sorry if I'm interfering. Gotta rush, I need to help Louisa with her sculls."

Tianna felt herself blush. She put one foot forward to follow him but he was now speaking at length with Louisa. Something stabbed her heart.

She put her head back. Looking at the two of them chatting she felt her jaw clench.

'He's at her side the whole time. So smug. That's so mean, I've apologised.

What more can I do?' Tianna was downcast. 'I was perfectly nice and

150

he makes a dig. So what if I chose to experiment, I'm allowed my first kiss even if it felt weird. I'm seventeen, not seventy! Although I really can't remember anything…'

Kit strolled by and stopped to chat with Tianna who laughed loudly at whatever he said. Looking over her shoulder every few seconds, she noticed that Joel never once looked her way.

CHAPTER 18 - MEDSOC

Marcus

Marcus and Noëmi were excited for New Year's Eve; the first anniversary of their engagement. Marcus had requested the time off, putting '**Engagement anniversary weekend**' onto Evan's intrusive spreadsheet. A reply came through: '**Request refused, Madhav is off.**'

Marcus messaged Madhav. '*Mate any chance we can swap? I work Christmas day and you do NY's day?*'

'*Sure that suits me better. Esme wants us to go away for our first Christmas anyway!*'

Marcus smiled to himself.

Marcus booked the trip. The first night would be the Medsoc reunion in Surrey followed by two nights in a hotel in London. Marcus had planned some surprises. Having seen much of family and friends over the festive break, the pair were looking forward to getting away alone together. They had an early night in anticipation of the long journey to the south of England.

Lying in bed, Marcus turned and gave Noëmi a kiss.

"Four days off I can't wait."

"Yeah me too! I'm shattered all the time. God knows why!"

Marcus' phone pinged. He grabbed it from his bedside table and replied to a message, then quickly lay back down.
"Is that Evan?"

"Stop it! Tianna's got period pains. Mum wants advice on the best painkillers. Tianna has a regatta tomorrow. I've told her ibuprofen and a hot water bottle!"
"The agony I had with that at her age."
"Yeah, I remember but we all know Mum would never agree to the solution your GP came up with!" he laughed.
"Oh God, that appointment is at the absolute top of my embarrassing moments list. Sitting there with Dad."
Flopping onto her pillow, she yawned, "We should take that bottle of wine, I was given. It's an expensive one, although what makes it special is the thought. I was so touched."
He turned over, put out the light, eyes wide open he felt his stomach lurch. '*And all I cared about was my reputation. I didn't want to be that person who forgot the Secret Santa. Although I can't prove it, I have no doubt who gave to me in return. Those cufflinks were expensive, not a five-pound gift.*'
He pictured the cufflinks exactly where he had left them, by his place at the staff Christmas lunch. '*Someone else can have them.*' He had decided.
Noëmi

Noëmi lay in bed smiling to herself, her mind musing. '*What a hectic half term as Deputy Head of Sixth Form! I've done brilliantly! What*

153

a *Christmas! Poor Tianna, always so painful.*' Suddenly she sat up rigid, heart racing, staring ahead into the darkness.

Wotton House, a country hotel near Dorking, Surrey, had been chosen for the 2018 Oxford Medsoc reunion. Everyone was going. The event was scheduled for the night before New Year's Eve. A frost lay over the early morning as Marcus and Noëmi jumped in the car.

"You're on sat nav duties...actually don't worry I'll do it." He put his keys and wallet in the cup holder beside him.

"So rude." She checked her make-up in the mirror behind the sun flap.

"Come on N, sense of direction was removed from your DNA somehow!"

"I found my way back to you." She flipped the visor back into place.

He turned, kissed her and they set off.

"It should be a good evening. Post-midnight it'll be a bit scraggy knowing that lot!"

"This is the friendship group that kept you and Sophie together!"

"It's the only reason we were ever together. We hardly did anything apart from the group. Just as well, we were bickering most of the time."

They were in slow traffic queuing for Redheugh Bridge. She kicked off her shoes and put her feet on the glove box of their car.

"I still feel jealous." She looked out of the window.

"Don't! We weren't close, zero emotional intimacy. It was nothing like us, a million miles from that. All through Oxford my feelings for you never changed. I always missed you."

"I know that now, when I came to Oxford, I was unsure if you'd moved on or not. Your 21st was a low point."

"Don't mention that evening. Could you not see how I felt whenever I looked at you?"

Soon they joined the A1 road and sped along towards the south. Listening to Ed Sheeran radio, Marcus was singing along. Noëmi became lost in her thoughts.

"Cheer up, it'll be okay!"

"No honestly I'm fine. This place is in the middle of nowhere?"

"Yes, away from it all!"

"Are there any shops nearby?"

"Er not sure, maybe in somewhere called Dorking, what are you after?"

"Oh just a few toiletries, you know the usual stuff. Maybe at the services?"

Driving to the hotel, through the winding country roads, Noëmi was not feeling great, '*I must be feeling nervous about seeing Sophie again.*'

The hotel was a large country mansion set in impressive grounds with a walled garden, pheasants running free and landscaped lawns. They settled into their room which was nicely decorated with wood panelling, in pale green, and buttermilk coloured walls. Their ground floor room gave out onto the ornamental gardens with a raffia peacock statue just outside their window.

Marcus

"*Alcoholic beverage appreciation* at 6pm in the bar." He read the agenda that had been pushed under their door. Marcus looked at the dress code, black tie. They both got ready. Noëmi looked stunning in a long red silk dress. Still not feeling one hundred percent, she went for a soft drink which got a loud groan as she ordered it. Marcus paced himself wondering what the evening would bring.

Sophie, dressed in sequins, strolled in with Charlie.

"Hey Charlie, how's married life? Is it wedlock or deadlock?" A voice shouted. Sophie flipped her middle finger and shouted back. "Fuck you!"

Marcus took a deep breath. *'Here we go.'*

Drinks flowed and they enjoyed catching up with their medic friends; finding out all they were now achieving. Sophie hunted out Marcus. "No surprise about your news Marcus, congratulations!" she said, turning her back on Noëmi. "You better not have been shagging Miss McAllister behind my back." Noëmi rolled her eyes.

"No, you know I was never unfaithful to you." Marcus moved so that Noëmi was included.

His simple reply made her bristle especially as he gallantly did not refer to all her well documented infidelities.

"I'm a GP in Richmond now, so fucking easy compared with what you guys are doing. No shift work. Hope to be a partner soon, go part time. Plus, I'm trying for a baby, Charlie's a busy man."

Seeing them talking, an already very merry Charlie came over and put his arm around Noëmi. "When's the wedding then Cindy!"

"Cindy?" asked Noëmi. She removed Charlie's unwelcome arm from her shoulder and went to join some of the others.

"How's St George's Charlie?" Marcus asked.

"Manic, I'm so tired. Bet you're the same. A and bloody E. Plus we have the TV cameras there the whole time. Hey, you've got one of our old managers at your place now I hear?"

"Evan St-John-Jones?"

"That's the one! She was back down the other day for some pointless meeting. Found out we were at Oxford together, asked loads of questions about you. She was getting personal." Charlie put his arm around Marcus and spoke in a low voice, "I hope you're not messing around with her."

"Good God no! Of course not. Charlie, you know me!" Marcus removed Charlie's arm from his shoulder.

"Sure sorry, it's just she was like, well, obsessed!"

Marcus exhaled deeply. "She's definitely a bit needy."

Charlie spat his drink out as he laughed. "Bit of a bloody understatement Marcus. Be careful, she'll get whatever she wants, I warn you! Caused carnage at George's!"

Turning away he saw Noëmi talking to some of his closest friends. Watching her listening, smiling she noticed him and looked his way.

'Evan can't touch us.'

Noëmi

Dinner was announced and Marcus indicated to Noëmi that he needed a minute. She saw him take Sophie to one side and talk sternly to her. *'Pulling her up on her comments to Tianna.'* Sophie listened, snapped something back at him and flounced off. The group moved into the dining room and a raucous meal followed with the waitress barely able to keep up with all the drinks orders.

After the meal Marcus took her hand and they slipped out onto the patio to be alone. The December night sky was lit by the dining room glow. The grass already glistened and the dull sounds of the group were muffled by an owl in the distance.

"Star Walk time!" she giggled.

"Ha! Yes the stars have aligned. Soon it's 2019, the year we get married!" Marcus was visibly excited.

Smiling back, she was shivering, he put his jacket around her.

"Oh yes the wedding...how many months is it until that?"

"18 May is about four and a half months away. We need to send the invites out by the middle of January, quite a lot to plan. Plus we need to get a place of our own!"

Noëmi's thoughts wandered. With a clatter and a shriek, Sophie crashed out of the door behind them. It slammed shut because of the force she had used to open it. She was wiping her nose and looked high. Seeing them she came over and got a cigarette out.

"Sophie, when did all the smoking start? You're a doctor! I thought you wanted a baby?" Marcus looked astounded.

"You know what Marcus, stop being so bloody judgy. Try and have fun for once." Sophie snapped back. "It's only when I have a drink."

"You definitely need to stop that."

"Actually you and Cinder... I mean *Naomi*, make a lovely couple, you know, well suited for each other, both so bloody boring." She lit her cigarette.

Noëmi shuddered and thought to herself, '*Can everyone just stop calling me boring,*'

"It's Noëmi," Marcus said.

Sophie gave a cackle.

"But that's not really what she's called is it?" Sophie inhaled deeply.

"What do you mean?" Marcus' eyes were questioning.

Sophie exhaled a long draw of smoke. "Guess who I met? Guess who came to visit Charlie and told me all about her sexless time with you! I told her she didn't miss out on anything!"

"I have no idea what you're talking about." Marcus could feel the hairs on his neck rising.

"Shauna Rhodes! Remember her? We had *such* a laugh! Slow off or more like never getting off! Always so bloody proper!"

Noëmi began to feel panicked and started pacing, "I'm cold, I'm going back inside,"

"Off you go, bye then, now what did she say you were called..." Sophie said patronisingly to Noëmi.

"What?... don't!" Marcus said, looking back round suddenly at Sophie. The owl gave out a long, soft call.

"Don't what?"

"Whatever you might be about to say, just don't!"

"I have no idea what you mean!" Sophie had a malicious smirk on her face as she sucked deeply on her cigarette.

Noëmi tugged hard but could not open the patio door to get back in and swiftly turned to find another escape route.

"If you want us to have even the tiniest happy memory of the time we were together just say nothing Sophie. I'm warning you."

"Happy memory, that's a joke! And actually is that a threat?" Her eyes narrowed.

"No, just good advice." The night was still, the owl's hoot, this time, more distant.

Sophie stood back and looked across at Noëmi who was frantically looking how to get back into the hotel.

"What do you think I'm going to say?" Sophie was laughing.

"Sophie, please..."

"Hey Gross Moron, go in through the leisure club, it's round there," Sophie delivered her blow. Noëmi walked off in any direction that would take her.

The owl gently cried out a final time.

Marcus

Marcus turned away, putting his hands on his head. He gave out an agonised cry. Sophie gave a start. Swinging round Marcus strode off to catch Noëmi. Without stopping he called out to Sophie; "You're unforgivable! You can't even imagine what she's always meant to me! She's done nothing to you! She could've got with me in a heartbeat, at any time. Way before she came to Oxford, one word would've done it! And yet she did nothing but respect you and our so-called relationship. Shame on you!"

"You know what? She would've been welcome to you! You ticked a box that was all! Pointless, boring, weak..."

Suddenly Noëmi was storming back. Voice shaking, she cried out.

"Leave him alone! How dare you insult him after all he did for you! He's the opposite of all that you say. You know nothing until you understand that to be kind is to be strong! And what exactly was that box he was ticking? Do you want to tell him or shall I? I heard you at the charity ball, I know exactly what you were doing."

She turned and regained her path. Beginning to run Marcus caught Noëmi up and put his arms around her and they walked off together.

The sound of the bar spilled out as Charlie opened the patio door to find his wife, face streaked with tears. "I really miss you sometimes." Sophie called out.

Marcus did not look back.

CHAPTER 19 - SURPRISES

Noëmi

The next morning Noëmi and Marcus were leaving early for London.

"Right let's put a bit of gel on those," he smoothed some cream into her puffy eyes. "Focus on us."

"Never tell anyone what they used to call me. Can you imagine if Guy knew..."

"Like me, Guy would be right after those bullies, but N, please stop. The shame is on them. Their cold, calculated cruelty defines them. Rejoice in the knowledge you are everything they're not; kind, loving, beautiful, warm, giving, thoughtful, caring and strong enough to be vulnerable."

She nodded but her lip trembled.

"We're going right into the city centre. I've planned something!"

As they drove Noëmi noticed Dorking was bigger than she thought and she spotted the high street. "Do you mind if we stop for a minute, I just need to pick up a couple of things."

"Okay but be quick, I'll wait in the car." Distracted, he studied the route on his sat nav.

161

Quickly she returned.

"All set?"

"Yep thanks." She went to open the glove box but changed her mind and slipped her shopping into her handbag. Feet back on the glove box, she gazed at the leafy Surrey roads as they drove up the A24 into London. The roads were busy as they reached the centre and finally they got to their hotel. Walking through the swish reception, Noëmi felt giddy. "Oh just wow!" He had booked the Shangri-La at the Shard for two nights which included dinner in the exclusive restaurant at the top. They were shown to their room and they were finally able to unwind.

"Time to relax, this is special! Half an hour and then it's time for drinks," he smiled and went for a shower. Noëmi flicked through the TV, she saw a programme about women having babies and sat transfixed. Marcus came out, towel around his waist, drying his hair.

"Have you delivered any babies?" Her eyes did not move from the programme.

"Not myself, I've been at twenty births, whoa, that's hard work for you women all that, look," He pointed at the screen where a woman was moaning her way through second stage labour. "It'd be an emergency if I got involved. Definitely not something I want. If a full or near term pregnant woman dies, we have four minutes to cut the baby out."

"Serious stuff."

"Yes, anyway, why are you watching this?"

"Oh you know I was with Sarai, remember?" She was offhand.

"Don't get any ideas! We've got plenty of time before we have to worry about any of this. I really want to travel. There's a whole world to see and so many things to do before we have babies.

We're far too young. About thirty would be a good age to start all that."

"Yeah absolutely, too young we're only...twenty-five..."

They went up for drinks.

"Let's have champagne, it's New Year's Eve, N, a special day for us."

"I'll stick to tonic water. I've not drunk alcohol since our party."

"Ah come on, you need to up your levels! You can't let me drink it all!" He sighed at the just arrived bottle. Sitting down for dinner they could see the London skyline from their vantage point. The lights of London were twinkling away. Noëmi matched in her silver dress and Marcus was back in black-tie.

"London... no Tower Bridge… and the Gherkin, so impressive, what a view!"

"Thank you for organising this."

"I remember that dress. The charity ball!"

"Okay, Marcus I do need to tell you something."

"Yes what?" he carried on reading the menu.

"No you have to listen, it's important!"

"Actually, N, there's something I need to talk to you about."

She looked at him open mouthed.

"Sorry. You first."

A notification pinged through on Marcus' phone.

"Oh yeah! Brilliant! Jayden and Shreya have sent a picture through."

He showed Noëmi the screen, "Where do you think they are? They want us to guess."

"Anyway, as I was saying..."

"Where do you think they are? Come on…"

"I wanted to say…"

"Do you think they're here?" He started looking around.

"Marcus…"

"Oh my God they are! And Isaiah and Jalissa! Oh this is amazing!"

Before she knew it their meal for two had become a meal for six and Marcus' two brothers and their girlfriends joined their table. New Year was celebrated in style!

Returning to their room, Noëmi was sober and Marcus extremely merry having drunk the bottle of champagne to himself, then wine and shots as he celebrated with his brothers. He fell down on the bed.

"2019 now, we've been engaged for a year N!"

"Marcus!"

He was suddenly asleep in his clothes.

Noëmi removed his jacket and undid his tie and sighed. She frantically searched the internet and finally fell asleep.

Marcus

Waking the next morning, Marcus was struggling.

"Happy New Year!"

"God, I feel terrible. You would be so smug, of course, not drinking, actually why exactly is that? You seem fine to me. God my head."

"Never mind, let's go to breakfast, we can talk then."

Sitting looking radiant, Noëmi studied the menu.

"There's something a bit self-satisfied about you at the moment N." He drank water constantly.

"Really you think? I'm actually scared?"

"What? Last night you said you had a problem?"

164

"I wouldn't describe it as a problem."

"I really don't get it, I need some tea, I'm so dehydrated." He looked around for the waiter. "It's so posh here but getting a simple cup of…"

"For goodness sake Marcus, I've been trying to tell you, I'm pregnant!"

Marcus dropped the menu and his phone fell loudly onto his plate, interrupting the soft piano music. The waiters shot them a look.

"Oh my God, how on earth? That's just brilliant, oh my God Noëmi!"

"But you said we were too young." She grabbed his hand.

"Of course we are but it's the best news ever! Have you done a test?"

"I've done two and I've got another to do with you. I wanted to be sure and then tell you at dinner, that was the plan but…"

Marcus laughed, "N! We're going to be parents! You and me! I'm over the moon!"

"We'll have to go travelling in twenty years' time."

'But that's the great thing, we'll still be young enough, old backpacking hipsters travelling the world, we might bump into our child on their gap year! We could all go together!"

"I realise it must be three months already! But you also said you needed to tell me something?"

"Oh no, just some stuff going on at work, nothing for you to worry about." All he could see was Evan's face as she picked up Noëmi's bottle of wine. Nothing was going to spoil things; they were pregnant and infallible.

The following day, a five hour drive back up the M1 meant the future parents had time to chat about their growing baby. Noëmi relaxed with her feet on the glove box. Back at their flat, forced to sit down whilst he prepared dinner, she looked through the post from the four days they were away. There was really nothing much; pizza delivery offers, window replacement brochures and a large brown A4 envelope addressed to Ms McAllister. Noëmi sighed. Trembling, she opened it.

'Dear Ms McAllister, Please find enclosed the information requested about our services, we hope to hear from you soon.'

Inside was a fold out leaflet on more plastic surgery options from a nearby private hospital.

Marcus snatched the rest of the mail from her leaving her with just half of an Indian take away leaflet in her hand.

"You're not to open any more post! Leave it all for me!"

"Why do marketing companies do this?"

"I shall ring every single one of them and complain, just you see!"

Marcus put a cushion behind her back and went back to finish the salmon risotto he had started.

CHAPTER 20 - HONOR

Noëmi

Early the next day, feeling tired but elated at their unexpected news, Noëmi floated into work. Deciding not to rush, now that she had another life to consider, she daydreamed about the fusion of hers and Marcus' genes.

'What will the baby look like? I hope the baby has Marcus' eyes.'

Almost levitating by the time she reached the staffroom, Frank gave her a knowing look.

"Now what?"

"And Happy New Year to you too!" She replied looking serene.

"Something's going on, tell me." He took the teabag out of his cup and put his foot on the lever to open the pedal bin.

"Ah wonderful news Frank! I'm pregnant!"

"Fantastic, any idea who the father is?" She gave him a look,

"Seriously that's great news Noëmi. Congratulations!"

"Thank you Frank, it was an accident!"

"Gives me great faith in doctors!"

"We're so happy!"

167

"And I am too for you, it's the best news."

Noëmi pondered on whether it was a boy or a girl. Frank began to open his mouth. Stopped. Waited a minute or two. Then said, "My dear friend, I hate to ruin your moment but you do remember who's coming in to see us in about 5 minutes time?" Frank looked at his watch.

"Excuse me?"

"Mrs Stoney."

Noëmi very quickly tumbled from where life was but a soft, fluffy cloud. "Oh Jesus Christ!"

"And you may well need His help."

Honor Stoney, the difficult mother of Freddie, was back.

Frank and Noëmi moved into the school meeting room with its beige melamine table, uncomfortable dark brown plastic chairs and bare walls. The faint sound of children arriving in school and a clock ticked into the silence. They looked over some notes and awaited their visitor.

"Hello Mr Sprague, lovely to see you," Mrs Stoney strode in and ignored Noëmi. Her long brown corduroy skirt swished around her leather boot clad legs. Her waist was tightly cinched by a large suede belt, her long hair flowed onto her tight cream sweater. She was the epitome of middle-class power parenting.

Since Freddie had joined Noëmi's tutor group, in 2017, Mrs Honor Stoney had made herself known. It was almost as if she were in the class next to her son. Every day an email would arrive in Noëmi's inbox at around 6:30pm when, no doubt, Honor would sit down with a 'well deserved' glass of wine. At first the demands were somewhat simple:

'Please could Freddie sit near a window because of his preference for natural light?'

Soon the daily email became a long list of accusations against other students, staff and particularly his form tutor Miss McAllister. Mrs Stoney also seemed to forget that Miss McAllister had twenty-nine other students in her tutor group.
'Could you colour code Freddie's timetable as soon as possible?'
Being Assistant Head Teacher, Frank was copied into these emails and would amuse himself by texting Noëmi possible responses, such as;
'Let me introduce you to our hard-working office secretary Pat who I am sure will be delighted to help with that one,'

At the beginning of December, Freddie's mother had demanded to see Noëmi again. During this meeting she had more or less accused Noëmi of 'picking on' her child. Her 'lack of experience' was undoubtedly the reason for Freddie's 'playing up', in spite of the other students behaving well. Noëmi had calmly explained the disrespect Freddie had for the rules and that she was concerned about his defiance. Freddie's behaviour continued to worsen and Mrs Stoney requested another meeting.

"Happy New Year Mrs Stoney, thank you for coming in," Noëmi began.
Mrs Stoney ignored her.
Frank stepped in, "Miss McAllister and I believe we need to review how Freddie is getting on."
"Yes, Mr Sprague, I think he is being victimised, most concerning. You just don't expect it, he comes home upset each day, telling me how his tutor is picking on him." Mrs Stoney frowned.

"Right, I'm sorry to hear about Freddie's impression of things. Miss McAllister could you please account for Freddie's sanctions?"

"From my records..."

She proceeded to detail Freddie's behaviour choices.

"...when I asked him to pick up the rubbish, he was extremely rude to me."

"I got your email, all he said was *'Can't'*"

"Unfortunately, he got the vowel in that contraction wrong."

"Absolute rubbish you're making this all up!"

Frank covered up his burst of laughter with a loud cough.

"You can't teach, you shouldn't be near children." Mrs Stoney sneered.

Noëmi jolted back in her chair.

Frank took over. "I am afraid to say, Mrs Stoney, that we have surveyed Freddie's teachers and it is the same report from all of them. From today he'll be on report to his Head of Year and to me." Frank's voice dominated the room.

Mrs Stoney sat ashen faced.

"I think if his tutor, Mzzz McAllister, could be positive with him then he would not be behaving this way."

Frank looked exasperated. Noëmi knew he had come across Freddie during a science lesson when he disobeyed instructions and caused an irritant gas to be released which resulted in a lab evacuation. Mrs Stoney complained about the ensuing exclusion and blamed a fellow student. The school curtailed and Freddie was merely kept in one lunchtime for twenty minutes.

"Let's see how he does on report, thank you for coming in Mrs Stoney." Frank stood up to prompt her to leave. Grabbing her handbag, flinging a long silk scarf around her neck, she marched off, never looking at Noëmi. She strode out and Frank followed her to reception to ensure she left the premises.

"Great start to the year, bring on another twelve weeks of teaching!" Noëmi said under her breath. "It's all a bit creepy Frank, I have a bad feeling about this. Plus, there's the French trip soon." Her stomach lurched at the thought.

Frank gently touched her shoulder as they both turned to go to their tutor rooms.

"Au Pas de Calais!" Noëmi was imagining the horror.

"I'll be au bar de Calais if I get half the chance!" Frank smiled and waved goodbye.

CHAPTER 21 - PAS D'ANGLAIS

Noëmi

Each January, Pas de Calais was the lucky recipient of a coach load of 'vibrant' thirteen year olds from St Wolbodo's School. Noëmi had completely forgotten about the annual French trip. More accurately, she had pushed the terror it inspired into her entire being firmly into her subconscious. The trip objectives were '**to open the students' eyes to a different culture and to practise their language skills.**' This is what was written on the permission form, although most knew that the students only wanted to go so they could miss five days of school. The travel time, just to get to the Channel Tunnel, took the best part of the first day, so an early start was necessary. Frank and Noëmi had been assigned as leaders for the trip with a number of other staff helping out including school secretary, Pat Davies.

At 5am, one dark, wet January morning, a huge double decker coach swung into the car park of the school. With its headlights illuminating the rain, its appearance meant the trip was all systems go. A small cheer went up from the 'keen linguists' excited to be off to a whole new world. Noëmi heard Frank curse under his breath.

"You were actually hoping it wouldn't turn up weren't you?" Noëmi challenged Frank.

"Moi? I bet you were too!" he replied.

She gave him a look and got her clipboard out.

Queuing up to get the best seats, the students had their passports checked, gum confiscated and expectations modified. As they settled, hoodies, itineraries and workbooks were distributed. The coach was modern with seatbelts, air conditioning and a microphone for communicating with the enthusiastic students of French. The first person to speak via the sound system was Ron, the lead driver, who issued a graphic description of what he would do to anyone dropping litter in his coach. The most frightening part of this was his assertion that he would have no problem leaving them in France. He then added with equal vehemence, "And no oranges!"

Noëmi asked everyone to tell a member of staff promptly if they felt ill. She then settled into her seat, thinking it was good she had the sick bucket at her feet in case she was nauseous, after all that was what pregnant women were renowned for. Her mind wandered to how many weeks pregnant she could be. She was now pretty sure that the party weekend at the end of October must have been when she conceived and that the pill confusion was the reason why. Marcus had dropped her off early and felt a bit anxious that she was doing the trip when pregnant, however he knew that medically there was no reason to worry.

Thus the happy group were on their way to Boulogne sur mer in the early morning drizzle. Frank managed to sit next to Noëmi for the first leg of the journey.

"Strange absence of actual language teachers on this trip," Frank noted, glancing at the raindrops vibrating on the coach window.

"Yes and I don't really count as I only have a couple of beginner classes, obviously those teachers know better, you should have seen how overjoyed they were when I said I'd lead the trip."

"I think they've not recovered from the 2014 excursion when a whole bunch of the kids got onto a roof."
"What the..."
"Did no one tell you?" Frank smiled and looked at his watch, "No turning back now, we're ten minutes in, only another one hundred and seven hours and fifty minutes to go,"
Noëmi paled at the thought of what these ninety youngsters were going to be able to think up in terms of mischief. Working as a group they would no doubt exceed all expectations in this area.

"I see Pat's turned up. We all had a fiver on her not making it." Frank proffered.

"She's my room mate."

"Noëmi you're sharing? Good luck with that, I've paid extra to have my own room, I'm way past that bonding experience. I can't do bathrooms with anyone but Val. I probably could with you to be fair, as your hygiene is excellent, but no one else."
"Nigeria was interesting for that. We were in dorms."

"Anyway, this is probably more basic, not sure why Pat's signed up, if you've ever heard her rant about 'foreigners'. Probably to get some duty-free wine and cheap cigarettes."
By 2pm British time and 15hrs French time, they had all reached a foreign land.
Arriving at the French end of the Eurotunnel, Ron swapped duties with the second driver Vic who looked even more likely to abandon any miscreant on French soil. Vic hurtled along the smooth French motorways giving the impression that the faster

174

he drove the faster this whole trip would be over. Exuberant students looked keenly out of the coach windows that were peppered with the same miserable rain that they had left behind in their homeland.

"Why northern France in January?" Frank said as he looked at the grey sky.

"It's just like Newcastle!" a voice shouted from the back of the coach. At that moment they passed a large hypermarket with its name posted on a massive billboard, '**Boozers of Calais.**'

"It's so..."

"Underwhelming..." Frank finished her sentence.

"I hope they can speak some French."
Frank burst out laughing, to the point where he had tears in his eyes. "You're not serious?"

"But..."

"Noëmi, sometimes I can't make out if you're genuinely that idealistic or actually that naïve! The only phrase they'll try is '*Où est le Macdonald's*' once they've decided French food is 'infect'. The actual use of '*Où*' by *one* of them, will be a high point in your career. Ah we'll need to be careful in Cité Europe, the shopping centre, a couple of years ago a few of them got arrested for shoplifting."
Noëmi felt her heart racing.

"Frank, why has no one told me all this? The only reason I'm not hyperventilating with terror is because you're here."

"And there was that time when two of them got left at the motorway, sorry autoroute, services..." Frank smiled.

Another voice called out, "Miss, is that the Eiffel Tower?" as they passed an electricity pylon. Frank rolled his eyes and told

175

her not to bother answering. "It's an eyeful of something so it can be whatever they want it to be."

"Anyway I was going to suggest that lots of red wine would calm the nerves but that's not going to work for you! Let's take a selfie of us living the dream and send it to Marcus and Val."

She managed a frozen smile and their image with the caption, '*vivant le rêve*' was sent back over La Manche. Noëmi looked out of the window and saw a bead of rain trickle down the mucky window as the glass shook given the coach's desperate speed. Sighing, she tried to think about the new life growing inside her, only for images of St Wolbodo's children hanging from rooftops, abandoned at petrol stations and incarcerated in French prisons to intrude into her mind.

Within minutes of arriving at the tiny room in the hostel, Noëmi realised sharing with Pat was not going to work. Having to listen to her livestream her thoughts, was one thing, but the smoking out of the window made Noëmi hypersensitive in her state of first time pregnancyhood. She messaged Frank.

"Frank, I know you've paid extra and all that but do you have a spare bed in your room?"

"Only because it's you. Room 221'

In delight she gathered up her stuff, said goodbye to Pat and hurtled to Frank's room.

"Pat, I can share with Frank so you've got the room to yourself!"

Pat sighed and said under her breath, "Still carrying on together, his poor wife Val, some people have no morals."

Arriving in Frank's room she saw a double bed with a pillow down the middle.

"Only for you, up to you if you want to remove the pillow, I feel no danger. N, like I said, I'm very particular, Val and pregnant best friends are the only people I share my bed with. Val knows you're very clean so he's fine with it, I did check."

"Frank, that's so lovely of you, thank you!" She tossed the pillow out of the way.

Later that evening, having spent two hours checking all the students were in the correct rooms, they finally flung themselves into bed and did a group video chat with Val and Marcus.

"It must be nice to have a new life growing inside," Frank said as they put the light out.

"Yes, but scary too, so much responsibility. I've not even told Dad yet, thought I'd wait until the scan and everything's certain, don't want him to worry."

"I guess it moves you into a whole new realm of responsibility, something Val and myself have never had to worry about. Shame really."

"Yes, you two would be the best parents ever, but we're going to share out the joy, you and Val will be Godparents, so be assured, you can have some of the stress Frank!"

"You're too generous!"

"All that white furniture," she smiled and he gave a nervous laugh.

Frank

Frank had assured Noëmi that he would deal with Freddie so that she was not stressed by his antics. The next morning students were experiencing life in France, as breakfast was served. Fresh French bread, jam, Nutella, butter, hot chocolate and orange juice were on offer.

"Sir, Miss, I'm gluten free, lactose intolerant and I've got a nut allergy." Explained one small student.

177

"Don't worry Miss McAllister will let the kitchen know...maybe they've got an apple!" Frank smiled and sipped his coffee. Noëmi began to see how full on a school trip was.

"Anyone absconded?" Frank asked.

"All present! I've just done a register and two headcounts. Now we need to pick up the coach for the snail farm."

"Snail Farm? You're not serious?" Frank had not read the itinerary. After years of these kinds of trips he merely turned up with a waterproof, flask of coffee and noise cancelling earphones, mentally counting down to the end.

"Whose idea was that?"

"The Head of Department put the trip together..."

"And then doesn't show up..."

Noëmi threw her shoulders back and walked off.

Off the group went to the local 'ferme d'escargots' on the Opal Coast. The weather had improved and although chilly, the sky was lit by sunshine, perfect for activities with snails. Students chatted and the odd shriek of laughter was given out; the mood was relaxed. Ron and Vic, the coach drivers, dropped the group off and Pat said she would stay with them as her 'knee was playing up'.

Noëmi

The students were all excitement as they lined up along the roadside. The snail farm was on the other side of a fairly busy road. Noëmi knew this was a time to keep a keen eye on their group. Cars were intermittent but fast.

"Everyone hold on!" Frank called, as a number of cars accelerated into sight.

Freddie immediately went to cross, looking the wrong way.

In the corner of her eye Noëmi noticed him flinch. Instinctively she flung her arms out and pulled him back as a car whistled past.

White with shock, Freddie gaped at his teacher.

"I thought he said *everyone come on*! You saved my life!" his voice shook as he spoke.

Noëmi's heart was racing and she felt adrenalin flow through her body.

"Just wait until everyone else crosses in future Freddie. Please! You nearly gave me a heart attack!" Noëmi took some breaths and mentally calculated the number of hours and minutes left to keep these children safe.

Frank

Strolling off to the farm Frank led the pack. Soon snails were distributed. They began crawling on the students' hands under the supervision of a severe looking French snail farmer, Olivier. Expressions of disgust and cries of horror rose up as the slimy snail trails covered the students' arms. Freddie had been entrusted with a large, grey snail that looked bigger than any of the others. The very moment Frank noticed Freddie with said snail, he saw a grey blob fly through the air. It landed on a little girls' head. Unfortunately she was from another school group. Immediately she screamed and began crying hysterically as Freddie doubled over with laughter.

"Mais qu'est-ce qui se passe?" asked the farmer angrily as the snail looked like one of his best. He grabbed Freddie by the arm.

"He touched me, the paedo touched me!" Freddie screamed.

Irate to the core the snail farmer launched a tirade of angry French at Freddie which Frank very much enjoyed witnessing. Frank thought to himself;

'*It would be rude to interrupt especially as there were so many examples of reasons and justifications in Olivier's extended sentences.*'

179

Freddie, doubtless, understood nothing apart from the sentiment behind the outburst and replied. "Fuck you!"

The farmer, although speaking no English, obviously understood this.

"Freddie! No! Apologise now!" Frank gasped.

Noëmi spluttered, "Je suis vraiment désolée, Monsieur…"

The farmer was having none of this disrespect. Noëmi translated his rant. "He says we must leave without delay and we're banned from returning ever again." Her voice was shaking. "Frank! I've never been banned from anywhere!" Her eyes were wide.

"Never mind, you'll get used to it!" He began shepherding the students away.

"Where have you been banned from then?" Her incredulity was growing. Smiling mystically, he continued to rally the bemused students. The keen youngsters began complaining loudly that they had not had time to visit the gift shop. "Don't you worry, there's plenty more places for you to waste your parents' hard-earned cash." Frank said as he marched the group out of the snail farm.

Presently they got back to the coach to find Ron, Vic and Pat smoking and putting the world to rights. Reluctantly cutting short their break, the doors of the coach hissed open and Freddie was kept to one side.

"We need a plan B." Noëmi sighed, hunting for the risk assessment in her folder.

"Mmm supermarket shopping?" Frank suggested as they had passed a hypermarket on the way. That decided, Freddie was placed under the supervision of Frank for the rest of the trip. Sitting on the coach, Noëmi looked close to tears.

"This is so embarrassing I feel like a failure, this kind of thing never happens to Marcus. The humiliation!" Noëmi's bottom lip was trembling.

"Marcus is not leading a tween school trip to soggy France. Just relax, as long as no one goes missing it'll be a huge success!" Frank assured her as he messaged Val.

'Just got banned from a snail farm in Pas de Calais'

'You're quite the wit! Hard-core, looks like they want pas d'anglais!'

The coach then sped to the Auchan hypermarket where students purchased smelly cheese, different colour berets and lots of chocolate. Ultimately the good times came to a welcome end.

Noëmi

Relieved to be back at St Wolbodo's, with every child safely collected, Noëmi finally sighed with nervous exhaustion. Marcus was there to pick her up. He waited until all the students were gone before giving her a hug. Frank was chirpy as the trip was over and gathered all the paperwork as Noëmi thanked the drivers.

"Thanks for letting her sleep with you Frank!" Marcus said.

Pat raised an eyebrow and gave them a sideways look.

"No worries! Anytime and congratulations!" Frank told Marcus.

"Cheers Frank, exciting times," he turned to Noëmi, "Did they all get to speak French?" Noëmi had talked incessantly of how she hoped the trip would go. Frank laughed again, more tears in his eyes, "Honestly! You two, do you spend evenings together seeing who can be more ridiculously idealistic than the other? And you went to Newcastle Green Academy! That's the funniest part of all this!"

Noëmi tossed her head up, "They're all safe, that's all that matters," she replied, marching off to return the sick bucket to the school office.

CHAPTER 22 - HURT

Evan

'Hey Evs how's the romance? Let's meet up and you can tell me all about it!'

'Bri, watch this space! Things are moving forward!'

Marcus

Early February was unexpectedly warm and Marcus thought back to his engagement party the previous year when the skies had threatened snow. Today A&E was buzzing with a steady load of patients although slightly less numbers with respiratory problems. Marcus and Madhav were both busy taking full responsibility for their cases with Alex observing and advising where necessary.

Alex

Alex looked across from reception. Madhav was organising extra tests for a baby with suspected pneumonia and Marcus was dealing with an elderly man who had fallen. Going over to check everything, he thought to himself, *'I'm so fortunate with my junior doctors; such fine, competent and hard working young people.'*

"Absolutely correct Madhav, keep a watch for sudden sepsis too."

Madhav nodded and checked his notes.

Going to see Marcus, he found him checking the X Rays with the radiographer.

"Perfect, you've spotted that it's a complex fracture, you did well to ask for the other views to be imaged, great work."

Marcus smiled in reply then Alex's attention was seized by Evan, strutting into the department, clipboard in hand. *'To what do we owe the honour I wonder?'*

Stopping at the front desk he heard her speak to the administration assistant.

'Asking about patient wait times and the number of cases per hour?' Alex felt suddenly hot. He marched over. "Morning Evan, how can I help?"

Evan looked directly at Alex. "We're thinking of putting in digital customer survey terminals. Then patients can give a smiley face or sad face response to show what they thought of their treatment in the department, you know, like at the airports."

"Aren't those used for how clean the toilets are?" Alex sighed sarcastically and leant on the front desk. The receptionist looked over her glasses at him and suppressed a smile.

"Exactly, we need to get quick figures on how happy patients are after visiting A&E."

With a hollow laugh, Alex responded, "I imagine most of our patients won't be best pleased, given that A&E is hardly what anyone plans for a day out."

Evan ignored this. "We'll need terminals at different heights for anyone exiting in a wheelchair. We need to be inclusive."

"I can only imagine how delighted those patients will be feeling, especially if they didn't arrive in one." Alex looked back to his list.

"Actually there's a worse way to exit a hospital, in a box!" Evan barked.

Alex jumped back slightly. "I'm sorry Evan, it's far too random and too easily skewed. Anyone annoyed, bored or off their heads can just keep pressing on that sad face. Do join us at 1am on any day you choose. Then you will get an idea of how unhappy almost all of our patients are before, during and after their treatment!"

Evan capitulated "Anyway I shall continue my tour." She walked away. Alex's eyes followed her as she left. He could not fail to notice that her blouse and skirt were skin tight.

'Power dressing par excellence, I wonder whom she wants to impress,' he said to himself.

Marcus

"How's everything going?" Evan asked as she stopped by the bay where Marcus was working on a new patient.

"Good, thank you, this young man has sprained his wrist playing hockey at school," he replied without looking up as he was bandaging the youngster.

"Don't worry you'll be back at school tomorrow," he told his patient who sighed deeply. The mother and Marcus smiled at each other. "Lucky it's not your writing hand, eh?"

The young boy grimaced. The mother ruffled her son's hair playfully.

"Keep the splint on for the next few days and no sport for two weeks and then see your GP..."

185

Suddenly a scream went up and a clipboard flew in Marcus' direction.

"What on earth..." he looked round and Evan was on the blue linoleum floor doubled over in pain.

"Penelope!" Marcus called as he rushed over to see what had happened.

"In my blouse, in my blouse!" she shouted.

Marcus felt his brow get sweaty. *'I'm not going anywhere near her...but I have to do my job. There's no one else here.'*

Finally his prayers were answered, Penelope appeared and began examining Evan. Marcus looked away and allowed Penelope to explain what the problem was.

"A wasp Dr McKenzie."

"Okay Penelope can you cover the patient, take them to bay six and I'll get the trolley."

Marcus went back to his young patient.

Penelope

"Any history of adverse reactions Ms St-John-Jones?" Penelope asked as she helped Evan into the treatment area.

"No, but shouldn't Dr McKenzie be examining me? I'm in pain so I need a doctor!"

"Don't worry, Ms St-John-Jones, I'll take good care of you." Penelope assured her.

Finally Marcus appeared, remaining at a safe distance. Penelope got on with treating the sting and Evan's shock. Evan flinched as she cleaned the sting and rubbed in some antiseptic.

"Sorry, we need to check you suffer no adverse reactions, Ms St-John-Jones. It's a nasty little wound right on your chest."

"Should Dr McKenzie not be doing that?" she asked again.

"No, it's a minor injury, I'm qualified for this kind of thing."

"Of course you are," said Evan, sounding disappointed.

Alex

Outside the treatment area and separated by a curtain from his patient, Marcus wrote up the notes for Evan. Alex stopped by to see what the commotion had been. Evan looked downcast and moody, which he put down to the unpleasant surprise the hospital manager had been dealt. Alex stopped to chat to Marcus.

"How convenient that Ms St-John-Jones was in A&E when she collapsed. Testing our response time no doubt!"

Marcus looked back at Alex and gave him an understanding look, "Indeed, so very fortuitous, she couldn't have planned it better for herself!" he replied.

"However I still think she'll be rating this as a sad face experience!" Alex chortled.

Marcus looked puzzled.

"I'll explain." His consultant smiled and gave him a pat on the shoulder.

Marcus

Arriving home, Marcus was perturbed. He flicked through the post and put his rucksack down.

"Hey, how was your day?" Noëmi called out. She was already home and painting a small cabinet.

"Good, should you be doing that? The fumes and chemicals…"

She put her brush down and grinned. "I love how much you fuss! I've nearly finished. I thought it'd be nice for the baby's room when we finally move! How was A&E then? Any dramas?"

187

"Yeah, fine, the usual." His answer was clipped. Evan's episode pricked his mind.

'*No need to mention that. It's nothing.*'

Marcus busied himself in the kitchen unpacking a few items he'd bought on the way home.

Noëmi's phone pinged. He heard her sigh. Coming out of the kitchen he saw her face darken as she held the screen out for him to read.

'**Naomi, Charlie says I should apologise for calling you a Gross Moron. It was not nice. Sorry. I'll not call you Gross Moron again. Luv Sophie.**'

"That's not an apology, that's just Sophie having the last word. Loving the caps touch." She whacked some paint on the cabinet leg. A bit splattered on Marcus' leg.

"How did she have your number anyway?"

"Medsoc charity presentation. My number never changed even after I stood on my phone."
There was silence and then Noëmi was off.

"How is it that you were ever attracted to her? What were you even thinking? Did you ever have a conversation or was it just because she's so *super sexy*?"

"N, stop, we've talked about all that." Marcus leant against the wall and avoided her stare.

"Have we? I still don't get it!" More paint splattered from the brush.

"N, I don't want to talk about it again." He felt his body clenching.

"You never do, poor Marcus, all lonely in Oxford, fell into the arms of sexy Sophie."

"N, it wasn't like that…"

"Really you must have thought you were so lucky… the popular girl everyone liked! Is that your type? I mean Evan's not dissimilar!" She was not done.
Marcus drew himself up.

"Right stop! You're my type, no one else, I told you that from day one. The only thing that's ever changed is that I love you even more…" His body tensed, "but remember what you did? I'd given you every bit of myself. You threw it all away! Two years I was alone, mourning. All I got was chirpy little messages about how great Cambridge was. I'd lost all hope and I tried to move on. It was actually so unfair on Sophie, knowing I could never love her. Can you imagine how it felt for me to be in a relationship that's not with you? Knowing that there would always be something missing because I wasn't with you. Then all my prayers were answered, two years ago and we were back on track. Then I mucked everything up!"
He walked off through the kitchen and out onto their terrace.
After a few moments he felt her hand on his. Turning they fell into a hug.

"I'm sorry. I felt that pain too. I made mistakes. I thought I didn't deserve you."

"Shhh it was a mess, but we've got through it N. Please just forget about Sophie. All I care about is you, us, all of us."
Holding her waist, he felt her tummy.

189

"Ah someone's growing in there! Look! I can really feel a big bump now!"
She looked down and smoothed her shirt over her stomach.

"Sixteen weeks, so I'd be very unlucky to miscarry now, correct?"
Marcus nodded, his mind flashed to the patient whose baby had died in utero. "True, although you need to take care. I think we have to tell everyone, especially if we're postponing the wedding."

"We're looking to the future and forgetting about the past!" Noëmi was resolute.

CHAPTER 23 - KING AND PAWN

Tianna

Squadron Leader Alan Kelly, top coach at the Wear Rowing club, had called a meeting of the novice squad in the club bar. Sitting surrounded by various papers, he motioned at them all to settle down. Tianna, perched on a hard bar stool with a ripped green velvet seat, was keen to be part of the committee that he wanted to form. Glancing over at Joel, she saw he remained looking ahead, unflinching.

"Right we've cut the dead wood, it's floating away! You're the ones we can rely on. The ones who turn up week on week, the ones who train. You need to get all signed up to become full members of The Wear Rowing Club, or **WeRoC-ers** as we like to call you!"
Tianna saw Joel shake his head at the name.

Alan Kelly detailed the training programme calendar, the upcoming competitions and gave out letters asking for club subs to be paid. Tianna looked at the letter and felt her throat close. Beneath the bizarrely informal WeRoC logo, was a very formal letter written in some kind of legalese that set out the terms and conditions. Phrases such as *'illegal default'*, *'legal action to recoup monies owing*' and '*immediate dismissal*' leapt out at her. The club fees were nearly £60 per month and she doubted that her family could afford this. Joel was also reading the information.

Suddenly Joel asked. "Sir, do you have a concession if your family's on a low income?"

"Absolutely you just need to contact me in confidence and I will give you all the details, not a problem!"

"Great thanks!"

Tianna felt her heart rate slow down until she heard Kit whisper loudly to Louisa, "The club is a charity for benefits street scum after all!"

Louisa shot him a dark look and continued to listen. Tianna looked down and felt ashamed, '*Why can we never afford private school and rowing club fees?*'

On her way home the next day, she called in on Noëmi with the letter. Tianna sat opposite Noëmi at the kitchen table and stared into her coffee.

"It's expensive and if you can't pay you look like a welfare scrounger. Like you're *scum* who live on *benefits street*."

"Wow, a whole new vocabulary there Tianna! All sorts of valuable people are on low incomes; teachers, carers and NHS workers."

Noëmi was puzzled and asked to see the letter. Brow furrowing, she explained. "Look, you qualify for the lower rate. I can call Squadron Leader Kelly to sort it out."

Marcus came home, gave them both a kiss.

"A&E nearly killed me today!"

He grabbed a coke from the fridge and looked over Noëmi's shoulder at the letter.

"If it's a problem Tianna we can pay, don't stress, it's only for one year."

He made his way to the lounge and called out, "Joel was surprised at how much it is. He's paying himself, the full whack, from his wages. There's no way his parents could afford it."

Marcus flopped down on the sofa with the TV remote and he flicked through the channels. Tianna sat drinking her coffee, watching Noëmi note down the details from the letter.

'*Why did Joel even bother asking about the concession if he's paying the full rate?*'

Once they were all signed up, they needed to establish the novice committee. Kit offered to act as President. Joel volunteered to be one of the first aiders, given that he already had training from the hospital. Louisa was suggested for Social Secretary and Tianna was asked to be Treasurer. The first meeting was to take place at his Kit's parents' home and Joel offered to pick up both Louisa and Tianna. Feeling redemption was finally coming her way Tianna was excited.

In spite of Marcus' assurances that Joel was completely trustworthy, Anthony had no intention of leaving anything to chance. Anthony stood by Penelope's small azure blue car.

"Driving licence..." he put his hand out expectantly and checked this carefully. "Any alcohol today?"

"No Mr McKenzie, I've been at work," Joel replied.

"Smoking anything? Taking pills or the like?" Anthony looked straight at him.

"No never,"

"And you won't be taking anything when you're out? Liquor or drugs?"

"Not at all, driving means absolutely no drinking."

"This car's had its service? Been checked? All up to date?"

"Yes, it's my Mum's she's very conscious of safety, she works with your eldest son."

"You stay in the speed limit, you keep the music off and you take no chances. Stop at every junction."

Anthony shook his hand and allowed Tianna to go in the vehicle.

"So embarrassing, who invented parents! It's like the dark ages," Tianna sighed as she climbed into the back.

"Don't worry my dad would've done the same but because he works at the hospital with Joel's Mum he spoke to her instead," Louisa smiled from the front passenger seat. Tianna felt reassured.

"What does your dad do?"

"A&E Consultant at RVI!"

"Oh my brother works at RVI in A&E too!"

"Right, ask him if he knows Alex James, that's my dad, he's in charge of the whole of A&E. He's awesome, I want to be a doctor too."

Joel drove carefully and they got to Kit's house in a gated estate to the north of Durham. They waited as the electric gates opened. Tianna's heart raced and she gasped. Louisa looked round at her and said sweetly.

"He doesn't own this, his parents do. They're just lucky that's all, don't let it bother you."

Kit arrived at the door as if he did indeed own the house. He showed them into a lounge that was just for him and his absent siblings. Beautiful monochrome figures in frames looked down on them from every wall as they sat on soft white leather sofas

"Drinks?"

"Tea please," Louisa said first.

"Have a proper drink!" Kit smirked.

"No way, tea's fine, it's a Tuesday night and I don't see a party going on!"

The others agreed. Tianna admired Louisa style. She was not easily intimidated. Tianna now understood how to respond to an offer of a drink she did not want.

Fidgeting the whole time Tianna played with her fingers and could barely speak. Kit ran through a few decisions. Louisa wrote down some notes. Joel put dates in for first aid training. Having drunk a few beers Kit ordered pizza for everyone and they chatted until it was time to go. Tianna was tongue tied.

'All I have to talk about is school.'

The meeting drew to an end and Kit moved himself closer to Tianna and whispered to her.

"I can drop you home, save that one over there the bother." His breath smelt of pepperoni and beer.

Tianna pulled away. "You can't drive after all those beers."

"They're not strong, it's like drinking water."

He moved his hand onto her knee. Tianna removed it.

"Don't be like that, we should spend some time really getting to know each other."

"I'm not interested!"

She moved further away, putting space between them. She noticed Kit almost sneering at her. Under his breath he murmured something. A chill went through her body. Looking

195

sideways, she checked whether Joel had noticed anything. Joel turned the other way as soon as she caught his eye.

On the way home Tianna remained silent. Louisa was dropped off first. Tianna's heart sank when she saw her parents' home.

Alex James' house was also very fine, with electric gates. Joel took Tianna home last and they stopped outside the McKenzie home. He turned off the engine.

"My house looks so poor,"

"Hey! Don't ever say that! Never be ashamed of where you come from." Joel turned towards her.

Tianna was shocked at how passionate he sounded. '*How do I get nothing right?*'

"Sorry, it's just I'm not used to all that. All my friends live in houses like mine." She looked at the scarlet paint flaking off her front door.

"All our parents work hard, some are luckier than others, that's all. My parents are both nurses. I'm so proud of them and what they do. They save lives. I don't care what house we live in as long as it's us in it. Your house is brilliant and your family is the best. I can't tell you how welcome your brother has made me at work."

Tianna shut her eyes and breathed.

"Thank you Joel, I found it hard tonight."

"Why what's the situation with Kit then?"

"Oh God knows, I have no idea why I... thanks for not telling my brother about that particularly huge mistake."

"Keep away from him Tianna, he's bad news. He's always wasted. Put him in the bin where he belongs." Joel's hands clenched the steering wheel.

"You're right, I just can't figure life out at the moment. I have no idea how I'll cope at uni. Thanks for the lift and for all your kindness, Joel." She was desperate to hug him.

"You know Miss McAllister, your brother's girlfriend, she used to say something to us all at school. I remember, it was; *When the game ends, the king and pawn end up in the same box.*"

"I like that, it makes sense, we're all going to end up in a wooden box one day."

Joel gave a throaty laugh. "Well, I'm trying not to think of that Tianna! I think the saying is more about equality. Remember it's not what we've got or even our power, it's about making the best moves, doing the right thing, a pawn can win a game of chess after all. But anyway, when it's all over we're basically no different from each other and all end up in the box together."

"Kings and prawns are equal." Tianna said firmly to prove she understood.

Suddenly Joel sniggered.

"What!" Tianna was wide eyed. Joel could not talk. She began to catch his laughter. "What?"

"Pawn, it's pawn. You're too cute." He was almost crying.

"Yes of course, I knew that! It was a slip of the tongue!" She collapsed giggling. They laughed together. Smiling warmly at Tianna he got out, went round and opened the car door for her, then walked her to the suddenly bright scarlet McKenzie front door. Watching him drive off, she thought, '*Even when I muck up he makes me feel good about myself.*'

Tianna thought back to her first kiss and wished it had been Joel. As they sat in their meetings she kept surreptitiously glancing at Joel and noticed how she felt almost electrified in his presence. She liked his kind eyes, warm smile and how his hair was stylishly cut. With his physique being sporty, she could see he was strong and broad shouldered; he looked older than his nineteen years. Attempting to find clues about what he would like in a partner, she listened intently to all he said. If he looked over at her, she quickly averted her gaze. Then she would glance back to check if he was still watching but he would turn away so fast she was not sure.

Part of Tianna's role as novice squad treasurer was to collect contributions to the social fund from each of the members and she enjoyed taking responsibility for this. In order to be on top of things she typed all payment details into an overly detailed spreadsheet. Every piece of information about every note she kept. In addition, she bought a lockable box with two keys, giving the spare to President Kit. With any money stored away in the little cash box, she placed it in the safe. '*Nothing could be more secure,*' she smiled to herself.

CHAPTER 24 - OOH GOD

25 February 2019.

Noëmi

Winter was passing quickly and it was almost March. Monday morning, Marcus grabbed his overnight case, laptop bag and headed for the door. Noëmi kissed him goodbye as he was leaving early for the station to travel to London.

"Send Jesse my love!" she grinned.

"Yeah, I'll say hello to him for you! That alright?" He cupped her face in his hands and kissed her. As she opened the door for him to leave, the postal worker passed by and gave her a bunch of mail.

"Don't open anything N," Marcus reminded her. She smiled and placed it all dramatically on their hall table. Looking on approvingly, he gave her a wink and left. Feeling buoyed up by the fact they soon had their twenty week scan she could not help thinking this baby was going to be a giant as she already looked seven months pregnant. Feeling invincible she walked to the kitchen, taking care not to knock herself or slip. She had a new McKenster to take care of now.

Sitting drinking a glass of water, she looked at the clock. On her way to work she had a pregnancy check-up and then an early meeting too. This was a follow up regarding Freddie Stoney's behaviour on the French trip. She sighed and tried to block the thought of all this stress from her mind and looked over at the forbidden mail.

'*No doubt just pizza delivery offers, gardening services but there's a red envelope with a handwritten address.*'

Going over she noticed that it had their flat number on it. Unsure which one of them it was for she opened it.

'*We have no secrets.*'

Inside was a valentine's card. She took a sharp intake of breath. There was a typed note.

"I can't accept this. I'm returning it to you."

Taking a gasp, she looked inside the card, nothing was written except three kisses at the end. Straight away she took a picture of the card and sent it to Marcus.

'**Recognise this?**'

'**No, what is it? Not Jesse sending you valentine's cards! xxx**' he pinged back.

She drew her breath and was taken aback. Whoever sent it must have got the address wrong. On her way out she decided to put it into the general hallway. '*It must be for one of the other flats.*' The card smelt of sweet perfume which she thought she had definitely sensed before.

Marcus

Already cold waiting at Newcastle train station Marcus grabbed a coffee and a croissant for his journey. Echoing announcements filled his ears and everyone was rushing to and fro. There was a particular chill only a busy railway station gave out. Marcus pulled his coat around himself to keep out the cold.

'*Gloves would've been a good idea.*' He thought as he cupped his hands around his coffee to warm them up. '*Alex should've been here ages ago, he's cutting it really fine, unlike him.*'

Finally, he went towards the platform for the 07:30 London departure. Checking his phone there were no messages. He moved to take up his seat on the train and assumed he would meet his consultant there. '*Nice a table, socket and all that! I can put the finishing touches to my presentation.*' Balancing his coffee and laptop bag, he popped his overnight case into the luggage area. With seasoned travellers moving swiftly past him, he got to his seat and was happy to see he had an aisle. Quickly he settled down in the packed carriage. He waited for Alex to join him in the seat next to him with its reservation ticket stuck lopsidedly into the headrest. Marcus heard a message ping through, it was from Noëmi, he was puzzled by it but answered it quickly. Next, he looked at his watch, it was now only three minutes to departure and he knew the trains always left on time. The whistle blew, the train set off and now Marcus assumed there was some other plan as he went to get his laptop out. The train picked up speed. The last passengers were walking through the train to get to their seats. Suddenly a figure was standing next to him, he looked up. It was Evan.

"Oh…where's Alex?" his mouth gaped open.

"Alex James can't make it so I've come instead."

"Right, of course," Marcus got up so she could sit down.
She squeezed slowly past him, her sweet, lily perfume filling the air and her bottom rubbed against him as she went to her seat.

'*That was no accident.*'

Marcus sat back down silently and focused on his laptop. He noticed that Evan had on a low-cut silky blouse in spite of the February frost. She took her coat off and preened herself. Marcus sighed as he noticed the man opposite look appreciatively at his new view. The train was absolutely packed so he could not move to a different seat.

"How's it going?" She arranged herself and looked over at Marcus who did not return her stare.

"Good thank you, how are you?"

"Very busy Marcus. Making decisions about the hospital, its future and of course staffing, pay grades, promotions."

"I'm surprised you've got time to come on a trip to London for a conference that's not part of your team's annual plan." He took a gulp of coffee.

"I need to support my staff, especially with this topic, what's the conference on?"

'*Your staff, really?*' he thought.

"The conference is the OoHGOD one."

"OoHGOD?"

"Organisation of Hospital Global Overseas Development. It's to support low-income communities. We're presenting our model of good practice. That is for a teaching hospital to support the global initiative to eliminate neglected diseases. But of course, you must know all about it right?"

Looking in his laptop bag, he ferreted around, '*Damn no earphones*'.

Evan settled into her seat and pulled her long hair out of its ponytail and tossed it around. The traveller opposite looked impressed; his already great view was improving by the second. Marcus opened his laptop and joined the Wi-Fi to check his emails. As he logged on to his emails, he noticed Evan watching him.

"What are you working on?"

"Just clearing my in box then I'll be touching up my presentation."

"Do share it with me when you finish," she said breathlessly.

He saw the email from Alex saying he would not be able to join as management had changed its mind about two medical doctors being away. Marcus replied:

"I'm sorry to hear this and surprised that ESJJ is suddenly involved in this project!"

Evan asked, "What plans did you have for the two days?"

"Just some things with my fiancée. Need to relax. We're both busy with work."

"Teaching's got those long holidays right?" Evan smoothed her blouse into her skirt.

Marcus turned back to his computer. His throat tightened.

'Why have I not told Noëmi about all this? Now it's me and Evan on a trip à deux to a hotel in London with a black tie dinner.'

He got his phone back out. *'N **I need to talk to you about something at work.**'*

His battery was running low so he had to ask Evan to plug in his laptop for him.

"Sure," she bent down to get to the socket and her body rubbed against his as she did. Sitting back up she did not adjust to put the space back between them. Marcus shifted to the side of his seat to remove the physical contact, he looked at the time, they were fifteen minutes into the three hour and ten minute journey.

Arriving at the hotel in London they checked in. Marcus was not surprised to see that their rooms were next to each other. Marcus had the agenda and the delegate list. He only recognised a couple of names.

'Jesse? Yep, of course he's here.'

203

The conference was based on dinners and meetings which would mean he would not escape Evan the whole time. He sat on his bed and looked at the London skyline. It reminded him of New Year and the surprise that Noëmi was pregnant. A warm feeling came over him.

"N, how's it going? I need to talk to you." He video called her.

"Oh Marcus, thank God, I'm so worried, I have to go for another check up tomorrow as my urine test was a bit iffy this morning. I hope nothing's wrong. Do you know what it could be?"

"If there's protein it can mean pre-eclampsia but that's rare, make sure you get an appointment asap and let me know."

"What's your problem?"

"Oh, nothing for you to worry about, let me know what happens, I love you, you know that."

"Of course, I hear it every minute of the day!" Through her smile, she seemed strained.

Looking at his watch, *'Reception in ten minutes'*. Raising his eyes to the ceiling, he thought about how to avoid the conference dinner. Determined, he set about looking up trains back home for the next evening. Suddenly there was a knock at his door and of course he knew it could only be Evan.

"Fancy a drink? I saved this for us! Someone special gave it to me! I did notice how expensive it was!" Evan walked straight in with the Secret Santa Pinot Grigio and two glasses. Putting them down on his bedside table she turned to him as he stood dumbfounded.

'The cheek of the woman. That wine! Oh God, I've really messed up. Noëmi must never know.'

"This dress was definitely the right choice, look at you!"

"No...no, it's not that!"

Cut down to the navel two strips of floaty white fabric seem to be glued on strategically to her bust. Being a halter neck, it was completely backless.

"I need a couple of minutes, do you mind waiting outside please."

Leaving the wine and glasses, she slipped out. Marcus joined her at last.

"We need to take photos for the staff magazine." She announced. "Not wearing your cufflinks then?" Evan sighed, "Never mind, you look good in your black tie, almost James Bond like!"

"Do you want to get a jacket, you'll be cold, it's quite drafty in the ballroom."

Tossing her head, she gave him a glance. Silently they went down to the reception.

Everyone turned to look at Evan, who stayed close to Marcus, touching his arm every now and then. He pulled away vehemently each time.

Having taken their seats, Marcus went to the bar. Suddenly he heard a voice, "Hey my man! What's up?"

"Jesse, good to see you!"

Top button undone, tie slightly loose and a drink in hand, Jesse was all ease.

"Got me an invite to this dinner. Nice one!" Jesse surveyed the room, finished his drink and ordered another.

'No! He's off the wagon.'

"You're still okay for the presentation tomorrow? It's just the two of us now. Alex was pulled off the trip at the last minute." Marcus explained. For once seeing Jesse relaxed him.

"Yep, all sorted. Ah I see you found another option! It's a shame things didn't work out between you two then." Jesse nodded over at Evan.

"I know I was shocked but I have to just get on with it now." Marcus sighed.

'I wish Alex had pushed back and told Evan how important this trip was.'

"It could all be a lot worse by the looks of things!" Jesse gave Marcus a slap on the back and took his phone out of his pocket.

The introductory dinner had a couple of interesting speakers on neglected tropical diseases and Marcus was keen to hear these. Evan looked at her phone throughout the speeches, drinking the bottle of wine that was meant for two. Marcus drank water as Evan grew livelier and gigglier next to him. After the final speaker had finished, he had an idea and he messaged his brother Jayden.

'J is there room on your sofa tonight? Can explain M'

'Sure did N chuck you out lol J'

'There about 10:30 say sorry to S for the bother thx bro x'

"Right, we need a photo!" Evan announced and she grabbed a waiter who agreed to take the picture of the table. "Okay everyone, smile!"

As the picture was taken Evan placed her hands on Marcus' hands.

"What are you doing?" He snapped at Evan. "Sorry, that's no good, can you take another please!" Marcus declared angrily, shaking her hands off his.

"Now, now this is not the time for a lovers' tiff," a merry looking delegate on their table quipped.

"No, we're colleagues, that's all!" Marcus bristled.

The waiter happily agreed and Marcus made sure his limbs were well away from Evan's.

"Can you delete the other one please Evan?"

"Sure, I'll do that later." She threw her head back and finished her drink.

"I'd prefer you to do that now! I didn't want you to grab my hands, it gives totally the wrong impression." He hissed.

"Don't be silly, we're colleagues at a conference in London, like you just said. Why would anyone think anything else? What are you insinuating? Are you hoping for more?"
The others on the table were wide eyed.
Looking over his shoulder he saw Jesse quickly avert his gaze.

"Definitely not!" Angry, he gathered his stuff and marched out of the ballroom, not caring that she was now on her own. *'She'll find her own entertainment I'm sure.'* Having got his overnight bag, he took a taxi to his brother's where he would be in no danger of being anywhere near Evan.
Jayden was pleased to see him and had invited Isaiah over. Relaxing together they all shared a few beers as Marcus explained his predicament which his brothers found hilarious. Whilst momentarily reassured by their amusement, Marcus remained unnerved. The night on the sofa was bliss compared with the stress of being in the same vicinity of the marauding Patient Care Manager.
Early the next morning, Noëmi texted Marcus.

'Seeing GP at 5pm today N xxx'

'Bit late but that's a relief, I'll call you just before my presentation at 6pm I love you M xxx'

CHAPTER 25 - WHO ARE YOU?

Marcus

He got back in time for the first presentation the next day and Evan looked confused. Meeting outside their rooms she was accusatory.

"I had a problem with my computer last night and needed you to fix it but I couldn't find you." She pouted.

"I went to see my brother in Battersea, he works in the City, is everything okay now?" He clicked his door shut.

"That's very unprofessional to abandon a colleague like that.

Tonight I'm arranging a table for us to have dinner together to debrief your talk."

"Sorry I'll have to debrief another time. I've got plans." Marcus turned away and walked off.

'There's no way I'm telling her I'm leaving on the 9pm train from Kings Cross.'

He was presenting at 6pm so he was sure he could make it. Confident and determined he passed by reception on the way to the day's sessions and cancelled his room for that night.

Arranging to vacate it at 7:30pm he was pleased to be able to get a refund for the hospital.

A packed agenda on global humanitarian medicine followed. Marcus was enthralled. Motivation turned to anger when he sat in the session about the patents and how certain communities were unable to access medicines because of the high prices. Finally he had his keynote to deliver on the outreach Newcastle RVI would be doing for the End Noma Campaign hospital. Racing to the ballroom to set up, Evan trotted close behind, Marcus had only a few minutes.

Jesse was ready to introduce him and leant against a catering table.

"Looking good doc! Hope you're not too exhausted from last night!"

"Yeah, I hardly got any sleep!"

Jesse's lip curled.

Quickly checking the slides were working he found that the annoyance caused by Evan had calmed his nerves. Marcus felt ready to deliver a strong presentation on RVI's support for the noma hospital. Already the delegates were coming in and all of a sudden he remembered he needed to phone Noëmi. It was ten to six and her appointment had been almost an hour earlier. He reached into his pocket for his phone.

"Damn!"

"What is it?" asked Evan, who was never far away.

"I need my phone. I've left it in the room."

"Time's a bit tight. I'll get it for you!"

'*For once Evan's useful!*'

"Thanks, it's by the bed." He gave her his key card and off she went.

"You two are quite the team when you're not arguing!" Jesse said as he moved forward to begin the presentations.

Evan

Arriving in Marcus' room, having picked up his phone, Evan had a good nosey round checking out his underwear and personal bits.

'I would have guessed Calvin Klein's, what's this aftershave? God even a photo of her by the bed he never slept in.'

She moved the bottle of wine and glasses in front of the picture to cover it up. Suddenly the phone started vibrating. It was Noëmi on video chat.

By the time she got back Marcus was already presenting to the packed conference. His slides were engaging and he really connected with the audience. Towards the end of his speech, he put up a slide of himself with his 'fiancée' from their trip to Nigeria.

"Our month there was life changing. Work needs to continue with the new RVI collaboration. At some point we'll go back to help."

Looking on, Evan smiled to herself. *'Mmm that picture of happiness will soon be shattered.'*

Marcus took a breath and moved out to the front of the stage,

"But this year we'll not be able to visit as my fiancée and I are going to be very busy with our first baby due this summer!"

A cheer went up from the audience and loud clapping started. Marcus could not stop grinning.

'Baby! What! No! Oh my God! That evil woman planned all this!'

Evan sat down, heart jumping, hands clammy, her body turning cold.

After an extended period of Q&A, Marcus shut down his laptop. He began looking at his watch.

"Here's your phone and key card."

"Thank you, that seemed to go really well! Are you alright?" Marcus noticed she looked pale.

"Yes, do you want a drink?" Evan shook her head.

"Just a soft drink, thanks, I'll get cleared up."

Marcus had an hour and a half to get to King's Cross. He went to phone Noëmi but she did not pick up so he texted her. '***How was the appointment? Let me know. Conf went well. Love you xxx***'

Jesse strolled over, took a swig from his beer and squared up to him. Jesse prodded his shoulder with his finger. "Man, before you leave, I'm gonna let you know exactly what I think of you!"

"Eh?"

"And I'm gonna tell her what you're up to! How could you cheat on Noëmi? And she's fucking pregnant, you're the shittiest lowlife I've ever met..." Jesse now gave his shoulder a shove with his fist. Marcus stopped packing his laptop bag and looked up at Jesse.

"Cheating? I'm not cheating!"

"Who are you? Slippery fucking toad. What's the deal with her then?" Jesse pointed over at Evan who was at the bar.

"Nothing, she's a work colleague!" Marcus' eyes were wide.

"Really? You've been sneaking around with her!" Jesse put his face right up to Marcus'.

"Never! Not me!"

211

"You said you and Noëmi were done!"
Marcus raised his eyebrows.

"No! Definitely not, we're getting married, having a baby together! Evan's an annoying colleague."

Jesse wiped his mouth and was pensive. He slammed his fist on the table. "I thought...yeah... great news about the baby, hopefully it'll look like her!"

"Sorry?"

"Man that's a joke, chill out! Right I'm off, see you around." Jesse grabbed his rucksack and headed off. Marcus saw him wait at the ball room door, as he was joined by a petite blonde woman. Jesse put his arm around her and they strolled off.

'What a mess!

Evan broke Marcus' thoughts as she replaced Jesse.

"Thanks for the coke. I'm leaving now to go back to Newcastle."
Marcus was all confidence.

"What about our dinner together?"

"Sorry, not possible. I checked, there's a group from St George's that you know. They've invited you for dinner so you'll be fine with them."

Once outside he flagged down a cab to the station. Running like mad, still in his suit, he jumped on the train buying a ticket online as he did.

"Thank God that's over!" He said to himself and settled into his seat. Again he tried Noëmi but no reply. *'N are you ok? I'm worried, call me xxx'*

Looking out of the window into the dark, his eyes reflecting back at him, his whole body uncoiled; he was on his way home.

CHAPTER 26 - HONEY I'M HOME

Marcus

Jumping off the train into the still darkness of the early morning, Marcus was desperate to see Noëmi. Finally home, he thanked the yawning taxi driver, took his bags and crept into the flat.

'Thank God I'm back!'

Just putting his phone light on, he slipped into their bedroom.

'Not in bed? Where is she?'

A cold feeling came over him and he checked the bathroom, then the front room.

'What happened at the GP?'

Finally going to the kitchen, he put the wine on the side. There he saw a note.

'More than coffee this time then? Hope London was worth it, gone to Dad's, N'

He took a deep breath. *'Jesse!'*

Despite the late hour, he rushed over to Donnie's. Already 1:30am, he rang the bell and finally a dressing gowned Donnie answered the door.

"Sorry Donnie, what's happened? Is the baby okay?" He whispered all at once.

"Well yes all that's fine…she's upset about something. You'd better come in. I thought you were in London."

"I was, I've come home early." He stepped into the hall.

"She said she never wanted to see you again." Donnie had a knack for repeating exactly what he was told.

"What? Do you mind if I go up and see her?"

"Of course, you need to sort out whatever this is."

Marcus went upstairs and found Noëmi lying awake on her old teenage bed. A thousand memories filled his head.

"N what did the GP say? Are you alright?" He sat on the end of the bed.

"You tell me."

"I came back early to see you, the conference went well."

"Or came back early because I found out?"

"Found out what?"

"Don't play all innocent with me, that Evan woman." She said bitterly.

"Oh God her, she wasn't supposed to be on the trip. Alex James was due to come. It was a last-minute change."

"Of course it was." She rolled onto her side.

"It was awkward but I managed the situation well. I spent my whole time telling her about you, us."

"She said it was exhausting."

"Said?" Marcus could feel his heart begin to race.

"You were in the bathroom."

"What?"

"Caught out? Do you need some time to get your story straight?" Marcus moved to the side of the bed so he could see her.

"I rang you. She was in your room."

Marcus was dumbfounded.

"When?"

"This evening."

"What time?"

"Around 6pm."

"Oh...oh God...N, I think I can explain." Marcus felt his colour rise as he realised what Evan had done.

"Don't bother, go away," she turned and began to cry.

"N, can I say one thing, at 6pm I was in a conference presenting to 500 delegates. I stayed at Jayden's last night and tonight I've come home."

"Sure whatever you say."

"She's been causing me problems. I wanted to tell you. Try and relax. We need to think about the baby." He reached out to touch her but she pulled away.

"You could have thought about that before you arranged that coffee with her and didn't tell me. Then you go off to London with her. I call you, she answers your phone in your room. Now I'm the one imagining stuff. So how do you explain this?"

Shoving her phone into his face, he read the message.

'Hey beautiful, looks like our window of opportunity is flinging itself open! I see it's all over between you and Dr Perfect! He's here at the conf 'working' with his new woman! When are we going to meet up?'

She turned over and away.

"What the? No, N, I told the whole room about us and the baby."

Silence stood and then she whispered, "How was the wine?"

"Oh Noëmi, no...no it's all a misunderstanding!"

Hiding under her hair he could hear her giving small sobs. He touched her arm but she pulled away. "Cruel, but you were before, or did you forget?"

"I know, please forgive me but please just remember how wrong I was." His chest tightened. Memories of their last misunderstanding erupted in his head. Pain tore through him.

Roles reversed, her words were now his, '*No chance to put things right, that hurts. Especially when it's us.*'

It was now 2am, he went downstairs and lay on Donnie's sofa until the dawn broke.

Noëmi

Wednesday at 7am, Noëmi left for a work meeting with Freddie Stoney's mother and Frank. She stomped to the station with Marcus walking next to her still in his black tie.

"N, please talk to me!"

She refused to say a word to him and left on the train. As the train pulled away, she saw him standing on the platform. He looked completely lost. She bit her lip.

Marcus

Wandering home, Marcus showered and went into RVI. Alex James greeted him. "You're back early! You look a bit rough, is everything good?"

"Oh yes, I didn't sleep well that's all," he thought about his two nights on different sofas. Images of Jesse and Noëmi filled his head. Nauseous, he could see Jesse's large hands holding his child.

216

"Yes, I got your message." Alex was logging onto the main computer to check the staff rota.

"I was just surprised at the change." Marcus did not want to talk about the conference.

"Great presentation by the way I dialled in just before six and saw the whole thing online!"

"Thanks, glad you could join for it." Marcus was distracted.

They got on with their day and half way through the afternoon Evan returned to the hospital. Marcus ignored her and tried to contact Noëmi but the latter would not pick up.

Alex

Towards the end of Wednesday Alex James began to hear some anecdotes about the conference. Marcus and Evan looked '*so good together*', '*spent all their time together*', '*taking selfies*', '*their rooms were next door*', '*a bottle of wine was ready*', '*he gave her his room key*', '*Dr McKenzie never slept in his own room*', '*cancelled his room for the second night*', '*One room not two*'. Concerned he called Marcus in to talk.

Walking into Alex's office Marcus sat down. He noticed Marcus staring at the desk picture of himself with his wife and three children smiling in a perfect portrait of domestic happiness.

Alex looked across from his desk and sighed. His colleague sat quietly, now examining his hands.

"Thanks for your time, I'll get to the point, I'm hearing rumours about you and Evan at the conference."

Marcus put his head in his hands. "That woman is out to destroy me."

Without drawing breath, Marcus delivered a whole landslide of evidence of her pursuit of him to his mentor. Alex James was not sure what to think. Having watched his young protégé closely he felt he believed him. '*All he ever talks about is Noëmi, which at this point is endearing rather than annoying, although it could become so.'*

"It's all a grey area. Her over attentiveness cannot be seen as an HR violation. It could be a coincidence that she's at the same gym and all the bars that you go to. However answering a personal phone call is definitely unacceptable behaviour. At that time I could see you were definitely in the conference so why do you think she wanted to do this?"

"To break up my relationship and it's working. Noëmi's gone to her dad's." Marcus leant back and exhaled deeply.

Alex James was stunned. "Okay, leave this with me."

"Here look at my phone, I've got nothing to hide." Marcus almost thrust the device into his boss' hands. Alex James looked at the time of the calls and also his messages with Marcus' full consent. In spite of the seriousness of the situation Alex James suppressed a smile as he saw all the loving text messages sent to Noëmi, especially as they were always sent outside his shift times. *'That's so Marcus.'*

Later on that day Alex James got an email from Jesse O'Donnell.

'Hey A

We're moving forward on the collab #exciting. Sokoto ENC hospital is all firing to go! They can't wait to host your docs and nurses. Got the green light from the Ministry of Health. Shame you weren't at the conf. Doc McK did well with the presentation, especially giving it that personal touch! But he's got a short fuse. Especially with that hyphenated blonde bombshell you sent from RVI.

218

Tempers like that don't fly in Nigeria so we'll need to look at some mindfulness training for him (actually anyone else going out). Yoga can help. Can you guys organise that your end?

Let's all jump on a call next week. Going out to fundraise now - wish me luck!

J'

'Marcus annoyed? I just can't imagine that!

Even more intrigued Alex James decided to play detective.

CHAPTER 27 - ANYTHING OF VALUE

Donnie

Wednesday evening, Marcus went to visit Noëmi. She refused to see him.

Marianna, Marcus' mother, messaged a now exasperated Donnie;

'*Are you unwell? I see Noëmi is staying with you? Is Marcus there? He's not replying to me.*'

Seeing a downcast Marcus walk away, once again, on the Thursday, Donnie decided to speak to his daughter. She was sitting at the kitchen table, staring into space. One of her mother's favourite songs was on repeat;

'*The Winner Takes It All*' by *Abba,* filled the room, over and over again.

He pulled a chair to face her. "Honestly N, you're being so selfish, you should at least talk to him. Are you going to ignore him at this ceremony tomorrow night? You both have to be there."

Noëmi averted her gaze. Donnie continued. "Then you've got the scan on Monday, you'll have to see him then. You're having a baby together, even if you two are not together. This baby is as much his as it is yours. You'll need to make arrangements to co-parent."

"C...co-parent?" She stuttered, her face suddenly white.

"Yes! Organise which days you'll have the baby and which days he will. Eventually, when either of you gets a new partner, you'll need to consider what responsibilities they'll be able to have. Will you allow them to have sole charge of your child? So much to discuss. To do all that you'll have to communicate, as adults." Donnie said no more and went out to his garden to check the frost coverings on his fruit trees.

Noëmi

"Co parent? New partner? Sole charge?" Noëmi repeated slowly. She paced the kitchen. Images of her baby with a red lipped Evan filled her head. Evan's manicured, red tipped fingers were clutching their precious child. She put her now nail bitten hands on her stomach. She closed her eyes. The doorbell rang. Noëmi stood frozen to the spot. Brusquely Donnie went to it. "Come on in, it's cold."

Looking round she saw Sarai with Lucia.

"Noëmi!" Sarai was all surprise.

"Hello, sorry I need to rest." She walked past her friend without catching her eye and went to her old bedroom.

Donnie gestured to Sarai to leave her be.

221

Rowing practice was intense as the next regatta was approaching. Tianna was tired but exhilarated. She had scored her fastest ever time with her rowing partner in the sculls and her coach was absolutely delighted. He knelt down by their boat, congratulating them heartily as the dusk drew in. Feeling a slight chill as she leant back, she breathed in deeply, smelling the wet mud. The lights of the local village glistened in the distance and there was a low hum of traffic. Kit had not been rowing and came out to see them, pint in hand.

He helped her out of her boat. She stumbled slightly and he steadied her, she saw him staring coldly at her. "Tianna, well done! There you go again winning races and showing the rest of us up! Just remember not to get too big for your boots, people don't like that!" His words froze her; she felt the hairs on her neck rising.

Kit downed his drink. The group pulled the boats in and went for a debrief in the bar. As they listened, a couple of people gave Tianna their social subs and she held onto these carefully. The meeting drew to a close and she noted the contributors on her spreadsheet. Knowing her father had arrived to collect her, she rushed to put the money in the safe. Tianna opened the cash box and gasped. An ice cold sweat covered her body, her heart was racing, and she felt sick.

'There should be over £300 and there's nothing.'

She thought back and could not fathom what on earth could have happened. Suddenly Kit was on her shoulder.

"Are you okay Tianna?"

"Yes...no...the money's gone Kit!'

"Tianna what?" He sipped his pint.

"I don't understand. I have no idea!" She shook her head.

"God no. Tianna, this is serious, that was your responsibility!"

Tianna began to tremble. Kit put his arm around her.

"Look don't worry, we'll get this sorted. I'll have a think. Can I meet you tomorrow?"

"Yes… should we tell… the Squadron Leader… what's happened?" She asked, beginning to hyperventilate.

"Tianna, that's not a good idea, we're the only ones with keys to that box. There's only one thing they're going to think."

She searched his face and he continued.

"I don't need money do I? You've seen where I live! Everyone knows you and your family are, well how should I say this, poor."

Tianna put her head down, shut the small box and nodded.

"I'll text you."

With a large lump in her throat, she walked across the car park to find her father. He greeted her brightly, asking her how she got on. Tianna answered monosyllabically as her mind raced with scenarios. *'I'll be thrown out of the club for theft. My parents' shame. The disgrace of everyone knowing. The club will tell the school. University won't take me.'* By the end of the ride home she was in jail.

Anthony

Tianna ran upstairs and shut her bedroom door.

"Something's not right…" he told his wife. "Marianna, something's worrying her. Normally she tells me everything but tonight it's like she's seen a ghost. She's terrified. Something's really not right." Anthony shook his head.

Friday 1 March 2019.

The whole Italian holiday group, from the summer before, was to meet up for a special honour. The five involved in the beach rescue were to receive an 'Award for Civil Valour' from the

Italian government in recognition of their actions. This was at the behest of the increasingly grateful mother of Matteo. She had campaigned tirelessly for them to be recognised somehow. The Italian ambassador to the UK was passing through Newcastle and would host a reception for them at the town hall.

Raeni

The McKenzies arrived, assembling on the steps. Donnie and Noëmi were last to appear. No one, apart from Raeni, clocked that Noëmi and Marcus had come along separately. Noëmi looked straight ahead and avoided Marcus' gaze. They all chatted quietly as the Mayor, Italian Ambassador and a photographer arrived.

Raeni sidled up to her grandson. "What's going on?"

"Nothing, why?"

"You and Noëmi have had a row, I can tell!"

"Grandma, it's just a misunderstanding." He looked around at the group.

"She's ignoring you! I've never seen this between you two before!"

"I did the same to her about two years ago, which was nice of me. Another miscommunication."

"What? You're both so even tempered!"

"I'm trying to sort it out, stop worrying."

Raeni studied the two of them and saw them both get tearful at different times. Marcus pressed his hands to his face to compose himself. Noëmi turned away from everyone, looked up and breathed deeply to avoid breaking down.

Before the ceremony Noëmi went to the toilet. Raeni followed her.

"Hey Raeni, the baby makes me go to the loo every five minutes!" Noëmi tried to be jolly.

"I can see you and Marcus have some problems." Raeni touched her arm gently.

Noëmi lowered her head. Raeni continued, "So, my dear, a clever lawyer, (Frank A Clark), once said, *If you can find a path with no obstacles it probably doesn't lead anywhere!*" Raeni washed her hands and looked tenderly at Noëmi. "But whatever has come between you two, you need to move together. Neither of you has the strength to do that alone." Raeni watched as Noëmi bit her lip as her eyes filled with tears.

Guy

Moving to the drafty auditorium for the awards, Guy was upbeat! *'I do love a municipal building or two, all this brown decor, it's a step back in time.'*

They went to take their places and naturally everyone moved so that Noëmi could sit next to Marcus. Guy and Yumi sat, hands held tightly, whereas Noëmi and Marcus were untouching.

A tight schedule had been arranged and whilst appreciative, everyone was a little embarrassed by the attention, none more so than Tianna. A video link had been set up to include the child's parents, who sat with little Matteo between them.

Noëmi's grandparents were with the young family too. The Italian Ambassador began with a long-winded summary of the rescue, including an account of the actions of each one. Behind Guy was Tianna, dressed in a sequin top that glittered in the soft lights. Guy bit his lip to avoid laughing when he heard her whisper.

"This doesn't feel like a celebration! It's beyond dull, I thought it would be more like the Oscars."

Marianna gave a big "Shhhh!!!" Guy looked round and smiled as Tianna raised her eyes and no doubt lowered her expectations.

225

Sitting in the musty, frayed, red velvet seats, they all looked at the two dignitaries lost on the vast oak stage. The ceremony was paused for a few moments. Marcus was looking rough. Guy, positioned on his other side, was concerned.

"Are you okay mate?"

"Not really, my boss called me in about the rumours he's been hearing about me and whatshername. N's gone to Donnie's; she won't talk to me. Everything's a mess."

Guy's astonishment took over his face. Noëmi was looking at her engagement ring, turning it round and round.

"That Evan woman from the careers' event?" Guy grimaced at the name.

"She got herself onto the conference. Just the two of us."

"God! What happened?" Guy stage whispered.

"Nothing! She set me up, answered my phone in my room, long story. N's obviously upset, the hospital all think I'm up to something."

"Ohhh and it's worse because you never said anything right? In spite of the good advice given!"

"I gave Noëmi's wine to Evan,"

"What the? I'm that confused. Are you of sound mind?" Guy took Marcus by the shoulders.

"Obviously not and now she's left…" Marcus wriggled uncomfortably.

"God, you absolute plonker. I'll talk to her. Marriage guidance is one of my specialities," he sighed, flopping back into his seat.

Presently the five congregated on the stage for handshakes, medals and photographs. Standing in a group, Guy spoke to a stern-faced Noëmi.

"I hear there are problems in the McKenster alliance."

"Your friend has distractions at work." Noëmi said with determination.

"She's after him but he's not after her."

"Three, two, one cheese!"
They fixed their grins.

"They shared a room at that conference."

"No, he stayed with Jayden the first night to get away from her. You do actually know that. Then came back early and slept on your dad's sofa." Guy reasoned.

"Big smile everyone."

"Why did she answer his phone?"

"He asked her to get it from the room so he could call you, he was presenting." Guy crossed his arms.

"You've seen her!"

"Yeah she's fit!"

Noëmi scowled at Guy who finished his sentence, "but you're the only one he finds fit. I've been out with him many an evening, his head never turns."

"She's fit, he's a bloke."

"Oh come on, you know how devoted he is to you!" Guy sounded exasperated.

"Arrampicarsi sugli specchi! It means you're clutching at straws! Just because he's *devoted*, doesn't mean he can't stray. It's always the ones you least expect." She glanced over at the clock.

"Actually, no, in the line of duty I'd say that a little previous always comes first,"

"That coffee? There's your previous, I rest my case. He got caught out then."

"I know but he never went."

Noëmi took deep breaths, occasionally wiping her eyes. Inhaling sharply, she stated to Guy. "She won't be allowed near the baby."

Guy laughed.

"I fail to see the funny side. Anyway you can tell him I'll give back anything of value he ever gave me. He's not to contact me."

Guy sighed under his breath. "Of course, I can just see you two living without each other."

"And can we have the two couples with Tianna in the middle now."

Standing rigidly, Noëmi did not look at Marcus.

"And with the certificates, now just the girls."

"And back as a group please for the final shots."

Guy was back next to Noëmi.

"I gave him your message. He says the only thing he's ever given you, of any value, is all his love and that you can keep every single bit, it's yours. Taking it back would be stealing."

"Big smiles everyone! And that includes you!" The photographer jabbed his pudgy finger in Noëmi's direction.

The rictus smiles on the faces of the group fell when huge sobs suddenly broke out and echoed through the rafters of the hall. Moving from her place in the line, Noëmi threw herself into Marcus' arms and cried hysterically. The others looked bemused apart from Guy, Donnie and Raeni who had large smiles on their faces.

"Just carry on, don't worry about her," Guy told everyone with a huge grin.

The photographer was pale with shock. "I'm sorry I didn't mean to... and she's pregnant!"

Guy explained, "No it's not you, she wanted to return something then changed her mind,"

Tianna muttered under her breath, "Can those two never just keep their hands off each other!"

The photographer shook his head, "I've never seen anyone get that upset about shopping before!"

Tianna

Buoyed up that she could join the couples for a post award drink in the city centre, Tianna had momentarily put her troubles to the back of her mind. Her sleep had been punctuated with nightmares; prison officers, strip searches and application forms asking about criminal convictions. She heard nothing in her lessons, she spoke to no one, she sat in the toilets at lunchtime crying. Suddenly she felt nauseous. *'They'll take my award away and use these newspaper photos for my conviction and sentencing.'*

They went into the bar which was busy with students and Guy came over to Noëmi and Tianna handing them a drink. "An exciting diet coke for you! And one for you!" Tianna rolled her eyes, "You could've got me a proper drink Guy, I'm nearly eighteen!"

'God will I go to jail or a youth offender prison?'

"Of course! Now Tianna just remind me what I do for a living!" Guy ruffled her hair affectionately and Tianna pulled a face at him as she sat down with her thoughts.

Guy turned to Noëmi.

"She's really a piece of work that manager. When did you call?"

"About two minutes to six." She sipped her drink through the iridescent paper straw.
Marcus joined them.

"I actually dialled into the conference too. We're looking to do a similar thing with law enforcement. At five to six, he was there on the stage, so I can vouch for the timings. What do you think of the evidence presented by my good self here?" Guy seemed proud of his skills.

"How do I know you're not just backing up his version of events?" she said playfully.

"Ah okay, I understand, he may be my best mate but you're the

best friend of my fiancée so that takes precedence. I'm on your side Noëmi,"
Guy put his arm around her in solidarity.
Marcus and Noëmi stared at Guy.

"What?" He asked, switching his quizzical gaze between them.

Marcus nudged her and continued, "Putting the girls before our brotherhood."

"Of course, you can make a formal complaint. Answering the phone is an invasion of privacy, harassment. You should probably think about a restraining order too. Anyway enough of all that, no one's got work tomorrow so which club are we going to first?"
Guy went off pleased with himself.

"I don't see a ring. They've just been to Paris not last weekend but the one before." Noëmi recalled.

"Her parents are coming this weekend from Japan, so I guess they're waiting before making an official announcement."

230

"They'd want to tell them first and in person."

"Guy's got the biggest mouth in the world! Never tell him a secret!" Marcus laughed.

Noëmi leaned next to Marcus and spoke. "What a week!" He stroked her cheek. Suddenly she looked at him, "Oh I need to reply to Jesse! What should I say?"

"Yeah let me help you with that text! God he never gives up does he?"

"I quite admire his determination!" She snuggled into his shoulder.

"N, it's not funny, make sure he gets the message?" Looking up at him she saw that Marcus' face was dark.

"Oh it's just Jesse, slipstreaming into an opportunity. And actually ditto. That Evan woman scares me, it's spooky that there's someone in the shadows thinking of you like that!"

CHAPTER 28 - FORTUNE HUNTER

Guy

Guy and Yumi did indeed announce their engagement that Sunday, once the families had met, blessings had been given and the ring finally placed on her finger. The actual proposal had taken place more than two weeks before. It was now a year since Yumi had decided to move to Durham and Guy had thought

Valentine's Day would be the perfect time to propose. As it was a Thursday, he would take her to dinner and surprise her. Then once she had finished work the next day, he would whisk her off to Paris on the Eurostar. This would be the perfect engagement celebration weekend.

Arranging dinner at a top Chinese restaurant in Newcastle, Guy had a cunning idea. Having finished his shift, he popped in to check the reservation arrangements. There he spoke to Ming, the manager, about his plan and the necessary steps to execute it to perfection. Ming, seeing the uniform was going to agree with whatever Guy wanted without question.

Not suspecting a thing, Yumi met Guy at the restaurant. As ever she was looking immaculate in a low-cut silk navy dress that skimmed her figure exquisitely, her hair was styled up and elegant earrings dropped from her ears. Equally smart Guy was excited and not at all nervous, this was all going to be so wonderfully unexpected. Chatting, laughing and thoroughly enjoying themselves they ate aromatic starters, fine noodle dishes and drank a good bottle of merlot together. At the end the manager came over and chatted with them and gave them a fortune cookie each. Guy gave him a wink. Ming smiled.

"I love a fortune cookie, let's see what ours say!" Yumi was all excitement.

"I'll go first," Guy said and opened his, **"You need to get down on one knee.** That's weird, do you think I should?" so duly he did. "Open yours, maybe you've got a yoga position too!"

Opening her cookie, she read it out **"Your first love has never forgotten you."** Yumi screwed her fortune up and threw it onto the table. Guy felt his colour rising and started hunting around on the floor.

"Is everything alright sir?" Ming rushed over as Guy was feeling the carpet with his fingers.

"Guy, are you okay?" asked Yumi confused, "You need to get up! Everyone's staring."

"Ah, just one minute." Guy went to one side with the manager. "That's the wrong one Ming! The message is incorrect and there's definitely no ring!"

Going pale with dread, the manager got all the fortune cookies out.

"I think we've given it to another diner...I'm sorry...I'll find it."

Back at the table Guy kept throwing looks to Ming who appeared to now be sweating. A smiling waiter brought some green tea to keep them busy. Yumi sipped hers, "Guy what's wrong with you? It's like you're sitting on a termites' nest."

Ming explained, as he brought over more tea. "I'm so sorry we're ringing, I mean calling round the guests who have left to check who has your property sir, please forgive me!" Finally he gestured to Guy to come over.

"Good news he says yes!"

"What Ming?"

"We've located the ring!"

"Great, which table?"

"Bad news, they're on a train to London with the ring. They can get it back to us next week at the earliest, they've sent a picture!"

Guy looked at his ring on top of its fortune cookie packaging. Next to it was Nigel, a smiling, grey haired businessman who had retrieved the unopened cookie from his pocket. Nigel had added a caption "Yes!"

"I suppose he thinks that's funny. Anyway when next week?" Guy sighed.

"Monday, I'm so sorry sir, he says he'll look after it and he's given me all his details. Nigel's a regular who works up here and lives in London. He's completely trustworthy. I've told him you're a policeman. You know, to scare him!" The manager handed Guy the contact information. Given that all the bookings for Paris were engagement themed, Guy had little choice but to continue, ringless, with his proposal.

"Thanks, can you just send that picture to my phone Ming?" he sighed.

Guy walked back to the table.

"Guy, what is your problem?"

Getting on one knee he looked at Yumi.

"Yumi, I've written you a poem, it's called *You and Me.* Do you get it?"

234

Yumi smiled, "No Guy! I've never heard your favourite pun before!"

"Concentrate this took a while! Okay here we go!"

The last of the diners in the restaurant smiled from a distance.

Yumi, such true love you and me share together...get it?

"It should be *You and I,* and why are you kneeling down?" Yumi interrupted.

"Yumi! It's poetry, I'm allowed to flex grammar rules so that the beauty of my words can shine through!"

"Oh sorry, Guy!"

"Right here we go, from the top!"

From memory Guy delivered his self-penned poem.

Yumi, such true love you and me share together
I know that I want to be with you forever
What you have done to my heart I cannot devine
I hope our fortunes and stars always align
So I look to those heavenly portents above
I give you this ring as a symbol of my love
And I promise I will adore you all my life
Tonight I pray you will agree to be my wife

Before she could reply he carried on to hide his nerves,

"I'm really sorry I can't give you the ring as it's on a train to London with a guy called Nigel but let me forward you a photo of it."

Yumi burst into tears.

"Ah now is that for how dreadful the poem is or that your ring is a few hundred miles away or because...oh God you're not going to say no are you?"

"Yes! I mean no! It's the most moving thing I've ever heard, you writing poetry and doing all this. Wait, let me reply in style!"

235

She wiped her eyes, flapped her hands, took a breath and began.

I love you so much and want you to be my guy ... get it?
To be with you so it is always you and I
Ever since I met you my life has been the best
So absolutely I am going to say YES!

"Just like that... you came up with a poem in rhyming couplets, correct grammar and with a name pun too! Do you have any idea how long my poem took me?"

"Oh Guy! I love you and I can't wait to marry you!"

He kissed her and explained about the ring.

"You need to get your passport as we leave tomorrow after school for a weekend away! Don't ask where, it's a surprise!

Nigel's bringing the ring back on Monday, we'll meet him here.

Yumi, you mean absolutely everything to me and I can't imagine life without you. You are the most beautiful person inside and out."

He forwarded her a picture of her sparkling, sapphire engagement ring with a grinning Nigel holding a fortune cookie saying '*Yumi will you marry me?*'. Yumi could not care less about the ring. She was ecstatic, although she did crop Nigel out of the picture.

Out of respect for her parents to be told first and in person they had to keep the news safe for a couple of weeks. Then the celebrations would begin.

CHAPTER 29 - SORTED!

Noëmi

Early the next morning Noëmi followed Marcus to the kitchen.

"You need to get ready; I'm taking you out for your birthday!" Hugging him, she noticed a fancy bottle on the side and gasped. "The wine!"

Marcus put his arms around her waist, he kissed her neck, "It's a bit travelled!"

"Secret stealer! You got it back!"

"It belongs to you! Oh, I've got an email from Alex James." Her brow furrowed as they read together.

Marcus,
Thank you for your time on Wednesday and for allowing me to look at your personal messages and phone call records. I can confirm that I have filed a formal complaint

regarding Evan St-John-Jones' behaviour towards you. Our Head of HR has also spoken to Evan St-John-Jones. She has admitted answering your phone. Using your personal device is not permitted. She will receive a warning but no further action, which is disappointing. HR state that it is 'her word against yours'. From my side it is clear that she deliberately changed the conference attendees, taking my place. She answered a personal call of yours at 17:58 on Tuesday 26 February 2019. Having dialled in at 17:55 I could clearly see you were in the conference ready to present and not 'in the bathroom' as she claimed to Noëmi. Other incidents of unwanted attention have been noticed by you, your friends and me but it is hard to quantify these. I would suggest that you keep a log of any future incidents.

However I must say that your professionalism won through and you delivered the most impressive keynote speech I have seen in a long time. I liked the slide at the end. Congratulations on the presentation and I hope that you can get on with your personal life, now that this is sorted.
Best regards
Alex James

Marcus gave a loud sigh. Noëmi was pragmatic, "That's the end of that then. Nothing more to worry about." Instantly she was on her mobile, giving Yumi an update, secretly hoping that her friend would offer up one in return.

Joel

That same day the local press had reports of the life saving 'famous five' splashed all over its front pages and social media. It would appear that the Italian Ambassador had made quite an impression and that their heroism was an uplifting story for the local community. Not having told anyone of the incident, the modesty of the group only magnified their life saving mastery.

Marcus had kept very quiet as he felt he had actually done the least. Joel and his family looked at the news with wonder and

Penelope had tears in her eyes as she read the account of the beach rescue. Everyone thought Tianna had done brilliantly in the part she played. Joel sent her a message.

'Tianna, well done, wow a life saving award!'

'I made a phone call and did a bit of swimming, that was it!'

'No you directed the emergency services and swam to save the baby. I need to be around people like you! You're awesome!'

Tianna

Gazing at the texts she felt warm and hopeful.

'Is that a hidden message?' Almost floating, she gave a start as another message buzzed through.

'Can we meet at 6pm? I'll send you a pin.'

Her imminent conviction crashed her back to reality. Now desperate to know what Kit had found out she raced to meet him, telling her mother she needed to pick up a textbook from a friend. He was at the park near their house, leaning against his mother's car. Finishing a cigarette with a friend, he gestured at her to wait. She watched as he moved in front of the lad, shook his hand and waved him off. He walked to her.

"I've covered the money. It's sorted!"

"What do you mean?"

"I had some savings, I've replaced the missing money. No one will ever know."

"Oh my God, thank you, but I just don't know what happened."

"Tianna we don't need to ask questions, everything's sorted and whatever you need the money for, it's okay." He stared at her.

"But I didn't take the money, it was in the box." She felt herself getting hot and clammy.

"Tianna it's sorted, don't worry, no one's asking any questions."
They sat down on the graffitied park bench. To the side was the bin for dog waste which was overflowing with plastic poop bags. Kit tried to kiss Tianna but she pushed him away. The grey drizzle seeped down. A whiff of dog pooh came upon her as she felt him move closer.

"I understand, we need to find somewhere more private." He murmured.

He was right next to her, she could feel him breathing, hot and sweaty. She wanted to go home. "I'll repay you, every penny." She vowed.

"Tianna, don't worry I don't keep scores!"

Later that evening, another message pinged through.

'I loved being with you today. I can't wait for us to be alone together.'

Tianna felt her stomach jump to her throat. She did not reply.

'Squadron Leader Kelly was asking for the money, I've got your back.'

'Thank u Kit.' Her hands were shaking.

'Hey don't worry about it. It's our little secret. You can pay me back like you said.'

'It's going to be a few months, sorry.'

'Maybe we'll find another way. Take our romance a bit further?'

'I don't know what you mean.'

He did not reply. Tianna knew exactly what he meant.

CHAPTER 30 - IMAGES

4 March 2019.

Marcus

Monday morning Marcus walked into work refreshed and optimistic. That Saturday had been his twenty-sixth birthday and today they had their twenty-week baby scan. Now that the horrors of the OohGOD conference were behind him, nothing could go wrong.

However, arriving at work, he noticed an eerie silence in the A&E department. Standing at the briefing desk he noticed that the receptionist suppressed a smile and one of the nursing assistants gave him a sideways look.

'*Very odd, I remembered to bring in cakes for my birthday so it's not that,*' he thought as he went to his pigeonhole. Amongst other bits of internal mail, he pulled out that week's hospital newsletter. This was the publication circulated to keep all staff and supporters of the hospital up to date on recent events. Marcus felt his heart stop. In a long, slow second he saw his smiling face on the front cover of the magazine. The picture captured himself and Evan at the conference, at the first evening function. Sitting at a table in their evening dress, a candle glowing between them, her hands

241

clasped over his. The photo had been cropped to remove the other six people who were originally in it to leave just the two of them. The headline read,

RVI Emergency Doctor and Patient Care Manager together in large font with a much smaller continuation 'at the Organisation of Hospital Global Overseas Development Conference.'
Marcus knew immediately whose work this was and banged the desk with his fist in frustration. The receptionist gave him a look over her glasses. He apologised.

A long, busy morning in A&E followed. Striding around, his face was war like. *'That newsletter will be all over the hospital.'*
Checking over the patient lists at the front desk, Alex saw his colleague's demeanour. "Clearly not happy about your star billing."
Marcus shook his head. "Just what I need. There were six other people in the photo and she put her hands on mine at the last minute. She was so fast!" He desperately explained.
"You're lucky she didn't get them anywhere else!" Alex quipped, eyes twinkling.
"It looks so…"
"Don't worry I can see what's going on, but she's terrifyingly good I'll give her that!"
Alex laughed and Marcus sighed.
"Thanks for your email and all that you've done on this. I do feel I should say my piece to her, let her know that she can't do these things."
"I understand but it's probably best to leave it, given that it's now an HR issue." Alex looked up from his notes.
"She's caused great upset to Noëmi and myself."

"I understand but I think in these kinds of cases the least contact the better. They get off on the attention, these scheming people." Alex was wise.

"No wonder it's called the OoH GOD conference!"

Alex laughed, "Don't worry I've let it drop to our very indiscreet admin staff that I've made an HR complaint because one of my doctors is being harassed by ESJJ."

Alex gave Marcus a knowing look and filed the morning's reports away.

At quarter to two Marcus finished the first part of his shift and was off for the twenty-week baby scan.

"Good luck, exciting times!" Alex called as he checked the treatment bays.

"Yes I can't wait!"

Almost on cue Evan appeared, the two men looked at each other.

"Hi Marcus, we need to find a time to debrief the conference." She had a red dress sprayed onto her figure.

"Sorry, got to go, I have an appointment." He walked off, to find the mother of his child; the woman who was making all his dreams come true.

As Marcus walked out of A&E, he saw Noëmi sitting in the corridor.

"Isn't that my shirt?"

Only three buttons were done up and the rest of the shirt was pushed out of the way by her growing bump.

"Nothing fits and why are all your shirts slim fit?" She pulled her mustard coloured handbag in front of her stomach to hide the undone clothes. "I don't want your work friends to see me like this!"

243

"Don't worry about that, but you need to get maternity clothes now!"

Evan strode past in her red dress and high heels.

Noëmi almost screeched, "What's she doing here? How is it I'm too scared to tell her that she's a fucking bitch to her face! Feel my heart, it's racing!" She pulled his hand onto her chest.

"Shhh, relax, Alex says it's more powerful to ignore her."

"She's impossible to ignore! I bet she's never been *ignored* in her life! Just look at her! I feel a real mess. I need to get some designer clothes, get my hair done, maybe nails, a facial, spray tan… is that safe when you're pregnant?"

"N, please stop, if you want to transform into her you'll need to work on developing a sociopathic personality with obsessive stalker traits. No more about her, come on we've got the scan it's just so exciting."

Noëmi

They hurried to the antenatal block, let the receptionist know they were there and waited in line. The team all smiled as they saw Dr McKenzie sitting there in his uniform.

"*Hey Marcus, good luck mate!*"

"*Ah nice one Marcus, get some good pictures!*"

"*Wow Marcus and Mrs Marcus a baby, lovely!*"

"It's like being with a celebrity," she giggled, as everyone who passed wished them well.

"You're the special one, it must be amazing to be carrying a new life."

Noëmi was proud to be at his side. Still terrified at the thought of '*co-parenting*', she held his hand tightly in hers.

"N, my fingers are going to sleep," he had to tell her.

All the other pregnant women were similarly dressed in leggings and large tops so she felt a bit more in place. Noëmi looked down at the low coffee table and caught sight of the hospital newsletter. She leant over and studied the front page.

"Yeah, that's the latest surprise, life just keeps giving!" Marcus commented, exasperated.

"So you had no idea that was going to be on the cover?"

"Nope. I told you about the hands thing." He looked to the ceiling, waiting for her reaction.

Noëmi gathered the pile of newsletters up and walked over to the reception desk, grabbing any other copies that she saw on her way. Marcus looked at her curiously.

"Do you have a recycling bin?" She asked.

"Yes over there." The receptionist pointed at a set of large receptacles labelled for different waste. Noëmi promptly dumped all the newsletters in the paper and card bin, pushing them down firmly.

"That's this week's copy, it's only just come out!" The receptionist sounded unamused.

"Yes but unfortunately no consent was given for the use of the photo on the front so they all have to be binned! Sorry!"

Marcus laughed as Noëmi turned and smiled at him.

"Miss McAllister," the sonographer called.

They went into the small dark room for the scan. Noëmi lay on the bed, Marcus sat by her side and held her hand tightly.

"Hello Marcus, I didn't know you were going to be a dad, this is exciting," smiled the sonographer.

"Noëmi this is Esme, she's the best so we're in good hands here."

"Lovely to meet you," Esme smiled and put gel on Noëmi's growing stomach. "That's a good old bump for twenty weeks!"

"I know, that's what I thought. I'm a teacher and all the kids at school have noticed I'm pregnant now!" replied Noëmi.

Esme spent some time going over Noëmi's stomach and did some measurements, clicking on the screen to record the data. "All good, growing well, on course for the 14th or 15th July, let me show you."
They looked towards the small screen next to the bed.

"Here's the first heartbeat....and there's the second, two placentas, so maybe identical or fraternal..." she smiled.
"What?" Noëmi and Marcus both said.

"Yes twins, did you not know? Sometimes the dating scan can miss this. Congratulations!"
They looked at each other astounded and she saw he had happy tears in his eyes as she did.

"Typical doctor, they always have to outdo everyone else in efficiency, two for the price of one!" Esme laughed. She went through the measurements and showed them the organs of their babies. They saw their faces but did not ask if they were boys or girls. Wiping the excess gel from her Noëmi's stomach, Esme smiled kindly at the pair. "Any questions?"

Suddenly Noëmi asked, "Yes, is it ok to keep having sex at this stage of pregnancy? Is there anything to avoid?"

Marcus
Marcus visibly cringed at the question; he was fed up with his private life, supposed or otherwise, being discussed at work.

Esme replied with a ghost of a smile on her lips, "Now probably is a good time, if your midwife or GP has no concerns, as later on in the pregnancy your partner may have trouble..."

Marcus interrupted firmly, "No, no, no, stop! You know there are some conversations I'm just not comfortable with."

Esme and Noëmi looked at each other and burst out laughing. They thanked Esme, got their pictures and left on a high. Whenever Marcus saw Esme around the hospital again, she would greet him with a huge grin. He suspected this was very much due to her continued enjoyment of his discomfort at their discussion of his conjugal life.

They walked back to his department.

"Come and see Alex!" He took her hands.

"I look huge! My clothes are awful!"

"Those are my clothes! You look wonderful, come on, he'd love to see you!" He took her into the department.

"How did everything go?" Alex James asked, beaming at them both.

"Brilliant. It's twins!"

"Oh wow congratulations, good job you're a Junior Doctor so you're used to hard work!"

"And no sleep!"

"You'll need to buy an industrial sized washing machine! My wife and I had our first about the same age as you. It goes very quickly, two of ours are at university now and one finishing school. Such a wonderful thing to have children together."

"I know, it was a happy accident too!" Marcus said.

"I'm not sure it's good for a doctor to admit that!"

"Obviously I don't take my work home with me then!"

Alex

Noëmi saw some more hospital newsletters and picked them all up. Alex was puzzled.

247

They chatted some more and the two men walked Noëmi to the A&E exit. As they got there she turned to this receptionist and asked her

"Excuse me, do you have a shredding machine please?"

"Oh yes!" The receptionist was behaving as the consultant was there.

"These all need to go through it." She plonked the pile of newsletters on the reception desk. "Unfortunately they did not get Dr McKenzie's consent to use his image and the picture was taken outside of the hospital so the usual HR consent doesn't cover it."

Alex smiled and the receptionist looked between them all wondering who was in charge.

"That's fine, shred the lot, burn them if it's quicker," Alex confirmed, "and any other copies you find."

Marcus

Marcus walked Noëmi out, "N, you need to take care, stay safe!" Suddenly a message pinged through to her mobile,

"This'll be Dad wanting to know the news already!"

She looked at it.

'Hello Miss McAllister' she read out.

"Who's that?"

"No idea, it's anonymous." She showed him. "Oh, it'll just be the kids messing about, I'll let safeguarding know and ignore it."

A moment later,

'Miss McAllister, how's your boyfriend?'

"'Honestly look at this. Those Year 8 students saw you kiss me!"

"That was ages ago, make sure you report it. I don't want anyone thinking I did anything inappropriate at the school event, not after all that happened there."

"Anonymous, I didn't think that was possible." Noëmi sounded confused. Suddenly her face blanched. Fumbling, she almost dropped her phone, "It's her! That Evan woman! She's trying to get at me!"

Marcus gave a start, "Let me see!" Examining the mobile, his brow creased, "But N, there's no way she could have your number. All your details, you've kept so well hidden. You're right below the line. You've hardly got any social media because you didn't want the students to find you. No, it can't be her. I'll ask Guy how people can send anonymous texts; we're playing squash later." His expression relaxed.

"I was scared for a moment then! It has to be those kids at school." She patted her stomach. "We'll be bringing these two up properly!"

His pager beeped, a quick kiss and he raced back to his department.

CHAPTER 31 – OMISSIONS

Evan

Tuesday morning, Evan sat in her manager's office and stared at the little cactus plant on the desk. Zena Walker, HR manager, was busy looking through one of her large folders for the correct flowchart required for '**Allegations of invasion of another colleague's privacy**'.

"Hello Evan, how are you? Can I get you some water?"
Evan did not reply but shook her head angrily. This was now the second time she had been called in to discuss her conduct. Zena huffed and puffed as she picked up another large ring binder. Still flicking through pages, she began.

"I'm afraid that we've had another formal complaint that you've been compromising the privacy of Dr Marcus McKenzie. The first allegation, as you know, was answering his personal mobile phone without permission. The second is the public use of a photo taken on your personal device without his consent. Now I'm sure there's a perfectly reasonable explanation for you answering Dr McKenzie's personal mobile phone..."

"He asked me to fetch his phone from his room, so I did. It rang, it was a friend of his and I said I would tell him they called."

"Right but starting with the actual basic passing on of the message, that didn't happen did it?"

"I forgot; we were busy at a work conference. His personal mobile should have been switched off and away."

"I understand it was in his room, so it was away." Zena threw her multicoloured, soft knit scarf around her shoulder and looked up at Evan.

"He told me to fetch it." Evan examined her nails. March sunshine caught the red acrylics.

"I'll note that, but the allegation is that you implied you were in a relationship with Dr McKenzie?"

"He's very flirty with me, but I believe the friend is pregnant. Maybe she's just a bit hormonal, imagining things? What proof do you have?"

"Indeed, that's it, none. It's your word against Dr McKenzie's. Tell me what happened."

"We were at the conference; the presentation was about to begin. He wanted his phone so he told me to get it and gave me his key card. I got his phone, took the message and went back to the conference."

"Yet Dr McKenzie was not 'in the bathroom'?"

"No, why would anyone think that? I said 'ballroom' that's where the meeting was."

"Right, I see, yes that makes sense, they sound similar. I'm just trying to understand the situation. Now with regard to the photograph..."

"I was desperate for a picture, he was supposed to supply something for the newsletter and failed. I improvised. I genuinely thought I was helping with that." Evan knotted her eyebrows to fake concern.

Zena made some notes.

"Right, we do have a flow diagram of how to ensure the correct permissions are obtained for image usage, it is folder 4576, chapter 39, section 8Q, paragraphs one and two."

"When we took the picture he said I could use it." Evan asserted.

"Okay but it would seem Dr McKenzie has forgotten this. Always necessary to get things in writing. It may be an idea to keep a set of permission forms on you at all times."

"Are we done?"

"For now. We have a situation here of allegations without proof so looking at the procedures I need to warn you informally. I advise that you avoid a situation where this kind of thing could arise again. As you know this is for your own protection. The steps would be to note the events that take place during an off-site meeting in a notebook with timings. It is also recommended that boundaries are not crossed. Answering personal phone calls, using pictures are examples of this. Be careful in future with your dealings with Dr McKenzie please." Zena sat forward and pulled the ring binder in towards her chest.

"Of course, I think he's feeling the vicarious stress of his friend's difficult pregnancy, maybe we should look at what support we can offer him?"

"Right, good idea Evan thank you for that, I'll do so."

She got up to leave and Zena pushed her glasses onto her nose and finished her notes.

Evan scowled down the corridor to her office. Shutting the door she flung herself in her chair and thumped the desk. Her phone pinged.

'Evs what's going on? I hear you've been stalking Marcus McKenzie. He's engaged to my friend. That's off limits? You need to end that affair now!'

'Bri, I can't help it if he comes onto me the whole time!'

'They split up because of you.'

'Oh yes! It's working!' Evan smiled to herself.

'They're back together now.'

'Damn that woman.' Evan slammed her hand on the desk.

'End everything and anything now. She's my friend and they're having twins together.'

"Then let battle commence!" Evan said with determination as she went onto her HR system for a bit of a deep dive.

* * *

Noëmi

Later that Tuesday, Noëmi was baking a torta di carote using her grandmother's recipe. The sound of the doorbell and Donnie arrived on her doorstep. "Dad come in, it's so great to see you, stay and eat with us!" she said, embracing him fondly.

"I saw you the other day N, it's not been that long," he replied with a wry smile. "You're obviously excited to be back home. You look like you're nesting already."

"Look at the pictures! Twins!" She showed him the computer screen with the scan images of the twins.

253

"My goodness that's wonderful!" he peered, having a good look, "Things have moved on from when we got a grainy black and white print of you at our scan. I take it everything's sorted out?"

"Of course, it was just a big misunderstanding Dad, don't worry.

Never use the phrase co-parent ever again please," she announced melodramatically as she placed some flour in a bowl. A white puff of flour dust followed.

"Is Marcus alright? He looked in actual pain."

"Yes everything's wonderful, someone at his work was after him!"

"That's tricky but I see in Marcus the same devotion that I had for your mother. N, you must talk things through with each other, not just react so impetuously. You'll face many of your so-called misunderstandings during your life together."

"I know, it was just… there are such scheming people in the world, Dad!"

"Well yes they hide in the shadows, but you must not let them get the better of you N."

Suddenly a message came through on her phone.

'Miss McAllister you're not good enough for him are you?'

"Oh no, no, no."

"What? Is everything okay?"

"Yes Dad, all fine." She turned her phone off.

They discussed some practical arrangements for the summer births. Her father told her he thought that they needed to move to a bigger place as soon as possible as 'a double buggy would not fit through the front door and certainly not up those three steps.'

She zoned out and wondered why the students would be sending her such weird anonymous messages.

CHAPTER 32 - RVI

Tianna

Heart pounding, Tianna arrived in Newcastle RVI reception. She brushed her skirt over her knees as she sat waiting. Marcus appeared, running, and scooped her up by the arm.

"Are you all signed in?"

The receptionist nodded at the doctor before Tianna could open her mouth and they bounded off to the research labs. Everyone seemed to move fast and as they hurried along the corridors. Alex came speeding towards them in the opposite direction.

"I'm sorry, I'll be right there in a sec," Marcus called out.

Alex stopped so Marcus did the same and introduced everyone.

"Alex James, this is Tianna, my sister. She's doing a few days' work experience in the labs, I'm just dropping her off." He was out of breath.

"Good morning, Tianna, come to do some more lifesaving? I saw that article in the local paper, well done!"

"Hello, pleased to meet you, sir, all I did was make a phone call!"

"Call me Alex!"

"Thank you. By the way I know your daughter, Louisa, from The Wear Rowing Club. She said you were the consultant in charge here!" Tianna was almost curtseying.

"Ah, not in charge of the whole hospital yet, give me time! Lovely to meet you too, did you tell Louisa your brother works here?"

"Oh yes!"

"Right! Enjoy your day! See you later Marcus!"

Tianna noticed Alex looked uneasy.

Alex

Later Alex sought out his youngest daughter. Louisa was lounging on their caramel leather corner sofa in their summer room. The late evening sun caught honey gold highlights in her hair.

"Dad!" She cried as she saw him and she put her arms out for a hug which he gave her. He undid his tie and began to talk.

"I met a friend of yours today, Tianna McKenzie. She's doing some work experience at the hospital."

"Yeah she's nice, we row together." Louisa was back to her book.

"Why did you not tell me her brother works in A&E?" His eyes were puzzled.

"Oh Dad, I'm sure you don't know *all* the porters there!" She gave her father a look.

Alex took a deep breath. "Louisa, her brother, is a junior doctor specialising in emergency practice. He graduated two years ago from Oxford with a first in medicine, one of the highest scores ever recorded. I'm his mentor and I can just about keep up with him on a good day."

Louisa looked suddenly drained of all blood, "Oh my God... I didn't realise...I'm so sorry."

256

"Plus he's a wonderful friend in spite of being half my age. If you want to go to Oxford, study medicine, or both, like he did, you need a big reality check. And anyway while we're at it, why would I not know all the porters?"

Alex said no more and left frustrated that his children lived in a privileged bubble and not the real world. He thought about Marcus, Joel and Tianna and wondered if private school had been the right decision for his daughters. He went into the kitchen, poured a glass of wine and thought for a minute.

Alex turned to his wife. "Tell the cleaning company we won't need anyone for the next month, we'll still pay. They can start again when the A Level exams begin but until then Louisa will clean the house."

"What about her grades for Oxford?"

"If she wants to go there or anywhere, she'll need to know about hard work. Noëmi did everything in the house as a teenager and she got into Cambridge."

"Great idea," Cathy agreed and she gave her husband a kiss.

Tianna

Whilst Marcus had suggested that Tianna apply for a week's work experience at the hospital, he had not done anything to facilitate this. Tianna did the application independently and was delighted to be accepted. She was to work in the labs of RVI Department of Blood Sciences for three days over the Easter holidays. Samples were brought up by the HCAs and on her first day Joel was running for the department. As she was being shown the automated analyser in the bright white laboratory, he came up with some specimens.

Joel gave a start when he saw her. Saying nothing he put his delivery down and turned to leave. Pausing he swung round.

"Shall I show you how the canteen works? About midday?"

Gleefully she accepted.

At lunchtime, Joel explained the set up as they queued with their trays. Sitting down next to one another Tianna felt a frisson of excitement. They chatted happily about hospital life. Then Joel sat silently for a minute, "How's the revision going? I don't know how you fit it all in; work experience, revision, rowing...seeing Kit." He examined his water bottle.

Tianna froze, "I'm not seeing him."

"Oh, sorry I got the wrong impression then." Joel took a swig of water.

Her embarrassment regarding the Christmas party returned.

"I wish I could turn the clock back; I would never have gone to that Christmas party. I don't actually remember anything apart from being vile to you, I'm sorry." Tianna dropped her head.

"Tianna stop, you've apologised a million times already. I was angry with him trying to get with you when you were drunk. I can't stand him, I'm glad you're not involved with him. Gives the rest of us a chance. Sorry I've got to get moving, need to take some shit to pathology, quite literally." He gave her a smile and he was gone.

Later that same day, working quietly checking some lab reports, Tianna was startled when she heard her name.

"Tianna McKenzie?"

"Yes?" she squeaked as a sweet, lily perfume overwhelmed her. The most perfect looking woman was blocking her view.

"Evan St-John-Jones, Patient Care Manager. I thought I'd come and check how you're getting on. I like to take a personal interest in all employees, including work experience students. You are

258

the future after all!" Tianna noticed her new colleagues looking on curiously.

"Thank you," she could not imagine how it must be to look like this. Tall, blonde, immaculately dressed. This woman had hair that swung.

"You know what I think, you should spend a couple of hours with me in management if they can spare you?"

"Oh, yes!" Tianna's voice was shrill.

"Great I'll get that organised and give you a proper tour of the hospital, we can have lunch too!" The blonde ponytail cascaded round and swung from side to side as it left.

Later that afternoon Joel re-appeared in her department as she was looking down a microscope at some specimens. He sidled up to her.

"Why did the germ cross the microscope?"

"Joel! I'm working!" Her voice was hushed.

"To get to the other slide!" He whispered to her.
Tianna looked up and gave him a withering look whilst trying not to laugh. Her whole body tingled with excitement upon seeing him.

"You find it funny, you do! I can tell!"

"I'm a scientist at a top teaching hospital, please let me get on with my work!" She looked back into her microscope. He put his elbows on the bench and she could feel his warmth as he bent down to the same height as her.

"I could give you a tour of this whole place if they'll release you from the cells! Get it?" He also tried to squint into the lens. Guard dropped, unable to hide her amusement, she replied, "Too late! That Patient Care Manager is showing me around tomorrow! I'm very important!"

259

"What ESJJ?"

"Yes! ESJJ plus two hyphens! Plus lunch!"

"God she's so moody, never talks to anyone unless they're a consultant, you're privileged!"

Tianna thought for a bit, '*Maybe it's because of Marcus being a doctor?*' Suddenly she was uneasy.

"Maybe we could grab a coffee after work some time?"

She froze, heart pounding. "Yes!" she squeaked. She cursed her voice.

'JR to reception, there's a delivery...repeat JR to reception immediately.'

"Have to go! See you! Load of crap waiting!" With a grin he was off.

CHAPTER 33 - TROUBLEMAKER

Tianna

The next day the tour with Evan was on Tianna's daily schedule. On cue the manager arrived to collect her. Too scared to speak, Tianna managed to look enthusiastic. Off they went. Tianna trotted behind the blonde ponytail. Suddenly Evan began to ask the youngster questions.

"So you're at Newcastle Green Academy? Did all your brothers go there too?"

"Yes and it's hard because the first two went to Oxbridge and

then the one just above me is at Imperial. They're hard acts to follow!"

"Do you get on with Marcus?" Evan asked as she opened the door to some more research labs, then shutting it before Tianna had even looked inside.

"Oh yes! He's such a caring brother. He and his girlfriend,

they're so good to me."

The next door was opened and shut, Evan marched on.

261

"Such a sweet couple, have they been together long?" Evan looked like she was smiling.

"Nearly two years!"

"Here are the mortuaries. That's where we hide the bodies!" Evan sounded amused. Tianna shuddered. The questions kept coming.

"And before that did he have lots of girlfriends?"

"I'm not really sure there was just one other at uni. She was unpleasant; a promiscuous, posh, blonde bi..." Tianna met Evan's eyes, "er yes a lovely person."

"Interesting! I love a man with a past!"

"Oh I don't think he's like that!" Tianna felt her neck tingling.

Quickly she added, "They're having twins!"

"Oh wow, fast moving stuff. How nice, well let's get you to A&E where you can see him at work!" Evan strolled forward. Tianna could not take her eyes off this golden hair that swished, the tiny waist and the tight suit.

Marcus

In A&E, Marcus was at the reception desk with Alex discussing the procedures for overdosed patients when they approached. He smiled broadly at Tianna as did Alex.

"Just showing this young lady the hospital, she's an impressive student, I think we have a future consultant on our hands here!" Tianna blushed and felt awkward. She wondered why Evan would say this when she had delivered nothing but information about Marcus. Evan proceeded to continue with Tianna on her tour. Alex looked knowingly at Marcus, "Lucky Tianna, Evan usually gets Lynn in reception to do the walkabouts."

Marcus sighed, "I'll check in with Tianna at lunchtime."

Striding into the canteen Evan walked to the front of the queue, forcing one of the porters to step backwards.

Tianna was aghast, "I'm so sorry to cut in. I must apologise."

The employee smiled knowingly at Tianna's embarrassment. Evan busied herself with ordering food and presented Tianna with a huge plate of spaghetti Bolognese, whilst taking just a bottle of water for herself. They sat down. By now Tianna's throat was tight as she faced this enormous plate of food.

"Do you not want anything Ms St-John-Jones?"

"Call me Evan. No, I don't eat at lunchtime, too busy." The super thin businesswoman replied as she watched Tianna tackle the edge of the pasta politely.

"So what's the best thing about Marcus, tell me about him!"

"As I said, soon he'll be a dad, that's exciting, they don't know if it's two boys, two girls or one of each. I'm a bit sad because I'll be going off to uni when they're about three months old which is when babies get interesting isn't it?"

"Absolutely I think that's so true! He's quite young to be settling down." Evan's eyelashes fluttered like large moths.

"Maybe, he's just twenty-six, but they're so perfect together! I can't wait to be an aunt."

The corners of Evan's mouth dropped. "I don't know, the other day he said he felt a bit trapped."

"What?" Tianna looked up from her pasta mountain.

"Oh sorry, I'm sure he didn't mean anything by it. He was talking to some of the nurses, some of them are very attractive. He's always telling them that! They all love it. He's such a flirt and very tactile, do you know what that means?"

"Y...yes of course...he says all those things to other girls?" Her mouth was gaping.

"Oh yes, all the time! He's got quite the reputation! Marcus always has a favourite nurse on the go. He's quite the stud! A real tease. Bit of a seducer if I'm honest. Disappearing off with them alone. Shift work is quite good for having affairs. There's always a spare room somewhere!" Evan's red lips twisted into a smirk.

Tianna's fork dropped into the pasta and remained upright. Her throat felt tight and her heart was beating fast. She felt sick.

"Ah look, here's your brother now. Right, I think we're done. Eat up!"

Evan wafted off, leaving a trail of scent and destruction.

Marcus

Marcus saw that Evan had got up to leave in accordance with the appropriate behaviours advice she had been given. Then he was able to join his sister for lunch.

"How's it going Tianna?"

"Oh yeah great." She glared at him.

Out of the corner of his eye he could see Evan watching and smiling from a distance.

"Looks like you've had the royal treatment!" Marcus was all amusement.

Tianna was silent.

"Did you like A&E?" Marcus made conversation.

"Yes, do you? Hope you don't feel trapped there?"

264

Marcus' face clouded with confusion. "Not at all, I love my job!"

"And what about Noëmi? Do you feel trapped with her?"

"No, why? Come on, cheer up."

"I've got to go back to the lab, sorry... bye," Tianna grabbed her tray and left.

The plate of pasta slopped into the food bin.

* * *

Marianna

Softly humming one of her favourite hymns,
"Emmanuel, Emmanuel..."

Marianna was feeling reflective as she put laundry away in her daughter's room. Suddenly she heard a message ping through.

Glancing sideways at her daughter's phone she was unable to avoid the message.

'Ready to take our romance all the way? Make sure you're prepared, we don't want any little accidents in nine months' time!'

A cry went up that would wake the hounds of hell.

Shaking with a combination of fear and rage, she dropped the pile of beautifully ironed t-shirts. Ripping the mobile from its charger, Marianna marched straight to see her daughter.

Tianna

Tianna was in the kitchen, sorting out the dirty clothes and processing Marcus' dirty laundry at the same time. All at once, a tirade of screaming stormed in. Marianna did not pause for breath. Presented with the evidence in front of her, Tianna's face resembled Munch's The Scream.

"Who sent you this? What have you been doing?"
Finally Tianna could stutter.

"I haven't done anything. That's just some guy being a creep, Mum."

"Who's being a creep?"

"Just some boy!" Tianna moved the laundry basket to one side.

"Why's he saying this stuff then?" Marianna's voice curdled.

"It's just what boys are like, I can handle it. They do stuff like that!" *'Your son, my own brother is a creep too.'*

"This is not funny! I don't believe you! There's no reason for him to say this unless you are going to sleep with him!"

Tianna was getting anxious. "No it's just some boys, being weird!"

A scream went up that would wake the dogs in the icy wastes of treachery.

Anthony came running and stood in the doorway.

"Who is this person?" Her mother's face contorted with disgust.

"I can't say!" Panic flew through Tianna's body.

"Tell me now!"

"No!" All eyes were upon her.

"Is he at the hospital?"

"I can't say!" *'She can't find out about the money I've lost.'*

"That means yes!"

"No!" Tianna felt sick.

"Have you been seeing him?"

"No!" *'Please just stop.'*

"Why does he send a message like this then?"

"I don't know!" Like an attacking dog, her mother would not give up.

"I know why, who?"

"No!" *'Kit will tell her I'm a thief.'*

"Tell me now!"

"A boy at the hospital!" *'Please someone make it stop!'*

"Who?"

"Joel." Unable to think of a name Tianna offered the only one on her mind.

"Joel who?"

"Joel Rivera!" Unable to lie, she gave Joel up.

Marianna paced the kitchen. Both wept. Anthony was unsure whom to comfort first.

"To your room now!"

Tianna was sent upstairs, sobbing, the phone was confiscated.

Marianna

Arriving at the Newcastle RVI hospital main reception Marianna was on a mission. She strode across the lobby area, heels clicking defiantly, on the newly polished floor. Each tap of her angry feet echoed throughout the entrance hall. Each click announced her imminent arrival. Stopping at the reception desk she waited until the woman on duty asked how she could help. Marianna informed the receptionist.

"I need to see a Mr Joel Rivera immediately, without delay and I intend to wait until he is free."

Looking through the staff list, the receptionist radioed through to the HCA office. "JR to reception please. Visitor in main reception for JR."

Around six minutes later Joel appeared, "I'm not stopping today!

What am I collecting and where's it going?" he asked nonchalantly, running his hand through his hair.

The receptionist pointed silently to Marianna who turned to face him.

"I take it you're Joel Rivera?"

Bewildered, Joel nodded in reply and went a bit red as he recognised her instantly.

"I'm Marianna McKenzie, Tianna's mother. Never in my life have I been so shocked and upset young man. I've seen your vile messages. I have discovered your dirty, evil tricks. She's told me herself that you've been attempting to force yourself on her. My daughter is a God-fearing Christian girl who will not be led astray by a depraved seducer like yourself. I'm in half a mind to inform your employer that you are coercing a young girl into sex and attempting to rape her. You're never to contact her again and if I find you have gone near her, I will inform the police. Is that clear?"

Ashen faced, Joel steadied himself on the reception desk. Marianna was clearly not inviting any conversation. She turned on her heel and left, marching defiantly to the main doors.

The receptionist looked sideways at Joel as did the other occupants of the lobby. A serious looking consultant peered over her glasses and one of the premises staff, who had been polishing the floor, gawped at him.

After a few minutes Joel was still standing silently. The receptionist asked kindly,

"Can I call someone for you Mr Rivera?" She pointed at a seat next to her.

"Yes, Mrs Penelope Rivera please. She works in A&E." Joel whispered.

CHAPTER 34 - SOLUTIONS

Jude

Kicking his heels Jude Stoney, Freddie's brother, sauntered down his front driveway.

"Good luck in the revision session!" Jude's mother, Honor, was all optimism.

Turning into the street, Jude threw his head back and laughed.

'Like I'm going there!'

Continuing onto the park he turned his music up.

He saw Kit, sitting on the back of a park bench, feet on the seats. Kit grinned at his friend.

"Nice are those Air Pods?"

"Yeah, the latest model."

"Glad you're enjoying the fruits of your labours!"

Jude joined him on the bench and Kit offered him a cigarette.

"There are a good few post exam parties, a lot of people asking for stuff. I'll need a bit more for mid-June."

"Sounding like a businessman there Jude, no worries, you'll have your gear. Oh, look out over there we've got company."

Strolling towards them was Guy with his new mentee and trainee police officer, Tariq.

"Tariq, you know you've made it in life when you spend your days in these parks on *recreational solutions and substances* patrol." Guy looked sideways at Tariq.

"Parks and recs eh? Not as glamorous as Luther then Guy!"

"Is that why you signed up? No, definitely not but a much lower body count thank God!"

"I want to be a role model. Make my parents proud. They love me being a copper!"

Guy put an affectionate arm around his mentee, "Better not tell them the day to day reality of dealing with the scrag ends of life who supply kids with drugs then! Tell them it's all top secret."

As Guy stopped speaking, they reached Kit and Jude.

"Mr Deehan, it's always a pleasure."

"Don't let me interrupt your hug! Parks are great places for hook ups!" Kit drew deeply on his cigarette, blowing the smoke towards the policemen. Guy saw Jude smirk.

Ignoring his comment, he asked. "How did rehab go?"
Kit shrugged his shoulders.

"According to my records you didn't turn up. Disappointing. Are cigarettes not expensive for someone with no job?" Turning towards Jude he asked, "Name please."
Jude remained silent.

"Gentlemen, you can cooperate or we have every right to take you to the station to answer these basic questions." Guy instinctively checked his stab vest was in place.

"I don't think so, stop and account, remember? We can walk away." Kit scuffed his trainer on the bench.

"Right here and now, given that this is a well-known meet up point for dealers, I can get you searched on suspicion of

270

supplying. You chose." Going forward Guy moved in front of Tariq, Guy switched his eyes quickly from one lad to the other. He watched for any movement.

"Jude Stoney."

"Jude they need facts to search us, you prick!" Kit said under his breath.

"Thank you. Plus you're both engaged in anti-social behaviour to sit on the bench like that. Feet on the seats. Blowing smoke in our faces. Date of birth?"

Kit butted in, "Are you saying that causes you *harassment, alarm or distress?*"

Jude laughed, "1 April!"

"Why are you not in school?" Guy checked his portable police computer, still blocking his colleague.

"Easter holidays. I've got nothing on today."

"Shall I check with Mum?"

Jude got up and started to walk off. Kit followed.

Watching them disappear into the distance, Tariq was puzzled.

"Can we not do anything?"

"No Tariq, our hands are tied, we have no proof of anything. As you saw, Deehan has a good grasp of the law. We know they're up to something but we have to catch them or get a witness. No one's going to risk giving a statement. The kids are all terrified of retribution."

"But we scared them off right?"

"Moved them on. Won't stop them dealing to kids. The weed problem in schools is out of control. We know county lines dealers are pushing more stuff onto younger groups. Like Kit they all stay one step ahead."

"I'll put a call into the mum of Jude Stoney though. Just to follow this up."

271

"Nice, good idea Tariq."

Walking off, Tariq turned to his mentor, "Guy, back there, I noticed you cover me, protect me."

Guy looked away and suddenly asked. "Which Luther series did you like best? For me it was the first."

"Yeah agree, definitely that one." Tariq nodded.

Tianna

Marianna would not stop ranting day and night about morals and lewd behaviour. Barely speaking to her daughter, she communicated her disgust through dark, defiant looks and unflinching stares. Tianna remained mostly silent and slammed doors in response to her mother's diatribe. Anthony attempted to get the two to speak civilly, no longer caring about the cause of this feud, but more upset by how they were behaving. Now on a curfew, Tianna was only allowed to go rowing. Marianna had not clocked that the scoundrel Joel Rivera was also a member of the club.

Arriving at rowing practice Tianna was glad to have escaped the house. Bouncing into the practice area, on the cool April evening, she spotted Joel. Her heart gave a few extra beats. He was in his training gear, ready to race and she could see his biceps as he warmed up. Now desperate to organise that coffee he had suggested, she greeted him warmly.

"Joel! Hi there! How are you?"

Without replying or looking, Joel simply walked away. Stunned by this clear snub, Tianna felt anxious and followed him. "Joel, hey what's wrong?" He turned and moved away from her, speeding up his step. She hurried to catch him but he moved too fast. Joel was gone.

Upset and tearful she wiped her eyes and went inside the clubhouse. She sat down on the dark oak bench in the changing room and stared at the grey breeze block walls. Beginning to feel hot tears and a large lump in her throat she wondered what she had done. Head on her knees she relived the last exchange she had with Joel.

'He invited me for coffee… what's happened? I need three hundred pounds…my brother's a cheat… there's no one I can trust'

Obliged to re-emerge as practice began, Tianna endured nothing but agony; Kit kept putting his arm around her, Joel refused to even look at her and Louisa kept 'snapping' at her. Tianna tried to follow Joel one last time to talk to him and he kept walking away from her or turning his back to avoid seeing her.

'He wants nothing to do with me.'

Anthony

Anthony collected his daughter later that evening to find her despondent and uncommunicative. He tried to cheer her up.

"Tianna, did you enjoy your time with your friends? You got that one past your mother!"

Tianna burst into tears. Anthony stopped the car and gave his daughter a hug.

"Shhh my dear, what is this? These tears are from the heart not the brain!"

Tianna nodded but said nothing. She cried desperately clinging onto her father for a good eight minutes as Anthony tried to console her. Her father held her until she had recovered. Then he drove home, wet shouldered. The silence in the car was permeated only by Tianna convulsing with hiccough like sobs every few seconds. Upon arrival home she fled to her room. Anthony saw her feet dash upstairs. Out of the corner of his eye he saw a picture of Tianna on the wall. Her first day of school. He sighed deeply as he recalled how proud she was of her uniform and how she wanted bobble ties for her hair. He had carefully arranged her little bunches himself as Marianna could not get the time off work.

273

'Time just steals her away from me.'

* * *

The next day, nineteen miles apart, Louisa and Tianna both carefully poured out cleaning solutions to wipe down kitchen surfaces. Both frustrated. Both busy. Both stressed.

Noëmi

Noëmi got back, carrying her laptop bag and a canvas bag of exercise books. Opening the door, she was exhausted after a busy day with five lessons. She went to the kitchen and found Tianna silently scrubbing her oven. Putting her stuff on the table she watched as Tianna gently moved the Brillo pad from side to side, without a word. Stretching out her back, Noëmi suddenly gasped,

"Tianna please stop! Stop right now! I can't bear it! I feel so bad about you cleaning, terrible in fact, you have your exams. Let me just give you money! Why are you so insistent on doing this? Why do you need money?"

Tianna, kneeling in front of the cooker as if she were praying, fell prostrate in front of the large steel altar. Her shoulders shook with huge sobs. Noëmi went to her.

"Ti, come on, is it the row with your mum?" She helped her onto a chair, which wobbled as Tianna convulsed. Inconsolable, she gave out long guttural cries of pain. Noëmi held her.

"That doesn't help...everyone hates me. I'm in trouble N, I've lost £300 of the rowing club's money. I have to pay it back."

Noëmi bit her lip; she had been worried when Tianna took on the role of U19 squad treasurer.

"You should've told me...hush now... stop... let's make some tea, tell me what's been happening."

274

Tianna worked her way through a box of tissues and explained about the missing money; Kit had helped her out but was now pressuring her to pay it back.

"I have to get rid of this debt, I'll do anything." She looked beyond Noëmi.

"Anything? No doubt Kit has ideas!"

Tianna nodded, face crumpled.

"If the rowing club finds out everyone will think I'm a thief and I won't be able to go to university," Tianna broke down again.

"Okay, listen, there's nothing here we cannot fix. You owe £300 but what do we do when we need to solve a problem?"

"Go back to the beginning." Noëmi had trained her well.

"The money was in the safe in a lockable box, you had a key, anyone else?"

"Kit."

Noëmi was stunned, "That was quick, there you go Tianna there's your answer!"

"But he's rich, why would he take the money? He said no one would think it was him!"

"Why indeed? Why indeed? Ignore him now please you don't owe a penny. No more cleaning, no more worrying and no more communicating in any way with that Kit person."

Tianna grabbed a final tissue, wiped her face and eventually stopped hyperventilating.

"N, is everything alright with you and my brother?"

"Yes of course we're just busy! Why do you ask?"

"No reason, but how do you know you can trust him?"

"Tianna we know each other so well!"

"It's just...I think...maybe you should ask him about work... just check everything!"

275

Noëmi's phone pinged.

'*Miss McAllister how rough was the sex that got you pregnant?*'

"Oh my God, do you know anything about how people send anonymous text messages Tianna? Some pupil has been sending me weird texts!"

She handed her mobile to Tianna.

"Can Guy find out?" Tianna asked as she looked at the message and pulled a face.

"Definitely looks like a student. I wouldn't care but I've spent ages with those sixth formers helping them!" Noëmi's voice cracked as she poured the boiling water into the cups.

"Not being funny N, but kids my age wouldn't send something like that! Not those words, no way!" Tianna folded her tissue and pointed at the phone confidently.

"It's so creepy to think someone is thinking about me in this way. I keep glaring at all the kids thinking '*is it you?*' Sixth form all think I'm really moody. I can hear them whispering about my hormones."

"That's not a student, N, sorry." Tianna took her tea.

"Senior Management are looking into it but they think it could be some kind of retribution against teachers for what John Dyer did, now that all the details have come out following the guilty plea."

"No, kids aren't dumb they wouldn't blame other teachers for that pervert's actions. Definitely not someone like you."

"Who is it then Ti?"

"I think you need to file a report with Guy. Sorry N, someone's trying to mess with your head."

Sitting close together; they discussed their troubles and both decided to take the other's advice.

CHAPTER 35 - COULD DO BETTER

Parents' evening; a highlight in everyone's calendar. A chance to review progress and set targets.

Frank

Frank straightened his tie in the staffroom mirror.

"The epitome of senior management suaveness." Noëmi called over to him from her itchy woollen seat. He looked round at her and smiled.

"You look all mumsy for parents' evening, very themed!"

"Enormous you mean, still another two months to go!"

Frank's face tried to comprehend this possibility. Unable to think how she even moved, he shook his head. "Anyway! Ready to face the enemy?"

"Stop! I have a double Stoney appointment. One for Freddie as his tutor and one for his brother Jude as I teach, or try to teach, him maths."

Frank's face blanched. "What time's their appointment?"

"Six forty."

"I'll hover by your table then, *I've got your back!* as the kids would say!"

Noëmi's face relaxed.

Sitting at her table she saw the Stoney family approach. Mrs Stoney strode towards 'Mzzz McAllister' and the boys scuffed behind. Finally sitting before her, Noëmi felt her hands get clammy.

"How lovely to see you all!"
Silence.

"Well let's start with Freddie! Hello Freddie! You've made better progress with your targets and your time keeping has really improved. Well done! Targets for this year are to really focus on English and maths as those subjects are compulsory for GCSE. Do you have any questions?"

Freddie remained silent. Honor Stoney began,

"Will you be his tutor next year?"

"As you know Mrs Stoney I'll be on maternity leave for a year…"

"Excellent!"

"… but I hope to pick up the class again for Year 10!"
"What!"

An awkward silence fell. Mrs Stoney's face darkened.

Noëmi had the impression some kind of hex was being put upon her.

"Shall we move onto Jude?" Noëmi fixed her grin.

"Exams are very soon so Jude you really need to attend the revision sessions we set up for you. They're one to one, which is very valuable and could make all the difference."

"One to one with?"

279

"That would be me as I teach Jude. He's not turned up to any of them so far." Mrs Stoney pursed her lips.

"Yeah, sure but I'll fail anyway so what's the point?" Jude spoke slowly.

"Jude you can do this! Honestly I saw last year with a student, these extra lessons can change everything!"
The Stoneys sat saying nothing.

"And homework, you need to do that too Jude! Remember there's homework club where we can help you!"
Silence.

"Mrs Stoney, could I have a word with you alone please?"
The boys slouched off.

"Mrs Stoney I really need your support, this is make or break for Jude, he needs maths, all the courses and jobs require something in maths!"

"It's your fault for being a bad teacher. That's why he's failing!"

"Mrs Stoney that's not true, he improved massively when I took over the class!"

"You're the teacher you need to do your job and sort it out, don't try and make me teach him!"

"I'm not but he's your son, you want the best for him! I understand the police were in touch about his absences. The revision sessions are formal lessons, even if they do take place in the holidays."
Mrs Stoney stood, stooped down and put her face right up to Noëmi's. Her low voice growled, "Fuck you!" Smelling the stale garlic on her breath, Noëmi felt nauseous. Throat tight, she watched Mrs Stoney walk off across the hall. She looked down at her papers and moved them around, willing the tears not to fall. Frank darted over, "What happened there?"

280

Noëmi's lip trembled as she explained.

"Leave this to me!" Frank, Assistant Head of St Wolbodo's School, put his shoulders back and marched off in the direction of Mrs Stoney.

Tianna

A message buzzed through on Tianna's phone.

'*Final meet up of the season. Committee meeting and novice squad BBQ at Kit's. Sunday 3pm*'

'*Hey guys bring your swimwear for the hot tub! Tianna, I'll pick you up*'

Louisa sent, '_("/)_/' *no swimwear*'. Joel did not reply.
Worried about what Kit had in mind, Tianna's skin was clammy. She quickly messaged him,

'*I can't do Sunday; I have to revise.*'

Straight back. '*Look don't worry I just want to forget about the money. All the others are coming too. I'll pick you up as arranged.*'

Tianna felt uneasy and started pacing her room. Her mum knocked on the door and brought her a smoothie. Sitting on her bed she asked Tianna;

"How are you my child? Still sulking?"

After a minute's silence Tianna finally opened her mouth,

"Mum I need…"

"Oh goodness Tianna don't start asking for things now! And just look at this room, clothes on the floor and empty cups everywhere!"

'*…to talk to you about that Kit person…plus I'm worried about Marcus and Noëmi*'.

"Sorry Mum, I'll tidy it all up." Tianna shut her mouth. Heart racing, palms sweating, she turned to her books but saw nothing; *'Exams, Oxford, Kit's messages, a cheating brother.'*

"Just so moody the whole time!" Marianna left sounding annoyed.

CHAPTER 36 - FACT CHECK

Anthony

Kit duly arrived the next day and shook everyone's hand as he collected a subdued Tianna. Marianna was content for her to go with Kit as his name was not Joel Rivera. Anthony looked him up and down. Inspecting the silver sports car, he asked to see Kit's driving licence and took a picture of it for no reason other than to intimidate the young man. He watched him drive off with his daughter.

"I'm going for a walk." Grabbing his jacket, Anthony took himself to see his eldest son, Marcus, who was on his sofa watching Match of the Day on catch up.

"Dad! Hey this is an honour, it's so good to see you! I'll get us a beer, don't tell me the result but I don't think Newcastle are going to beat Liverpool!"
He returned with two bottles of cold lager.

"Well that's not the only bad thing this weekend."

"Cheers! How so Dad?" Their eyes were fixed on the screen.

"Marcus, I don't like that boy who's hanging around Tianna."
Anthony sat forward on the sofa and played with his bottle.

"Who's that then?"

"She's gone off for a barbecue at that Kit person's house."
Marcus spun round.

"Oh no not him! He's been messing with her head, Dad. We
need to keep her away from him."

"Bit late now! It's a rowing club meeting and he comes and picks
her up, all the way from Durham."
Marcus thought about what Noëmi had discovered. Grabbing
his mobile, he texted Tianna.

'Why r u at Kit's ?'

Tianna

Tianna arrived with Kit. About twenty of the U19 rowers were
present. A few were cooking burgers and sausages. Louisa was
organising buns and ketchup. The atmosphere was calm.

"Where are your parents?"

"Away visiting my brother in London, I've made the most of a

free house, had some mates over last night." Kit's lips curled

into a smug, self-satisfied smirk. "Drink?"

"Just some water please." Tianna's throat was tight.

"Chill, have a proper drink, did you bring your costume?" They
walked through to the garden.

"No, of course not." *'All men are perverts, like my own brother.'*

Kit's face dropped. He went out to get a drink. Tianna gazed out
at the smart, lawn striped garden. Joel was lounging on a garden
hammock talking to a couple of the single scullers. Tianna's

heart jumped to her throat. He did not acknowledge her. *'Nothing goes my way.'*

Joel

Listening to his friends' training plans, Joel noticed Tianna arrive.

'Those two are well suited. Both liars, both drunkards, both idiots.' He saw her smile at Kit.

'Well done Tianna drinking water, finally getting your act together.' Giving the hammock a swing, he could feel his teeth grinding. The conversation around him changed to protein powders. He kept glancing round at Tianna.

'Still on the water, that'll annoy Kit.'

Joel noticed her suddenly push Kit away, *'Ha she's strong, she's actually putting him down, literally!'* He found himself smiling as Kit picked himself off the floor and Tianna walked off into the house.

'Oh lovers tiff! Serves them right.' His eyes followed her. She stumbled slightly.

'What a surprise she wasted. Just like at Christmas. Kit can clean her up this time.'

Looking at his phone Joel sighed. *'I'm done, I don't need to be around this lot.'*

"See you guys I'm off!" He gave them a hug and grabbed his hoodie.

"Louisa, you have to come too if you want a lift!" He yelled. Louisa rolled her eyes and followed him to his car.

"Rubbish atmosphere anyway, plus I have to revise." Louisa was nonchalant.

Striding to the front door, he tugged it open, cursing under his breath. In an instant he almost tripped over Tianna, who was now sitting on the doorstep, alone, trying to use her phone. Her eyelids were heavy.

"Was she drinking before she came? Look at her, she's not been here long. What a loser."
Joel commented loudly to Louisa, as they went past Tianna.

"You're a bit mean! She's been on water the whole time. Just hold on will you!" Louisa snapped.

Joel walked across the lush front lawn to his car. "She's not my problem."

"Yeah, but you can be nice." Louisa yelled.
Slowly he opened the car. Looking back, he saw Tianna staring into space and Louisa trying to talk to her. Joel stood at his car.

'*...been on the water the whole time. What's going on? Something's not right.*

God, why do I have a conscience?' He went over to the pair.

"What have you taken?" He asked without looking at her.

"Dunno... few sips."

"For God's sake you're so useless. Come on, I'll take you home."
He put his arm out, refusing to give her eye contact.

"Stop being a jerk Joel." Louisa folded her arms and glared at him.

Yawning, Tianna grabbed onto Joel.

"You have to come too. I'll drop you back after." Joel barked at Louisa.

"What! All the way to Newcastle? I have exams and parents who'll go ballistic if I don't get into bloody Oxford!"

"Yeah!"

"Why?"

"Just because."

286

Louisa rolled her eyes as Joel helped a sleepy Tianna into the car. They left.

Marcus

'*Someone gave Tianna something. She's fine but we're taking her to A&E in Durham to get her checked over. My mum will meet you there.*'

"Oh God no! Joel's just messaged me, Dad. We need to collect Ti from Durham. Can you come with me?" Marcus jumped up off the sofa.

"Joel? But…is she okay?" His father was wide eyed as he stood up.

"He says so, he has medical experience, so let's trust him."

The men collected Marianna and drove as fast as possible to the emergency department of University Hospital of North Durham. Despite Marcus' reassurances, Marianna was getting hysterical. Swinging into the car park, Marcus screeched to a halt and dumped the car. They all ran. Breathless, the trio finally reached the resus unit where Tianna was being observed.

Sitting outside the curtained off area was Joel. His face flinched as he saw them approaching and then head down, he rushed off. They hurried into the treatment bay and found Penelope who was with a silent, downcast Tianna.

"Joel brought her here," Penelope did not look at the McKenzie's.

Marianna's mouth opened. "What's he done…"

Marcus interrupted. "Is Tianna okay and Louisa? Is she alright?"

"Yes fine, Joel's just dropped her back too."

Marianna began to hyperventilate. "What's he done to her?"

Anthony put his arm around his wife and took in the scene. Penelope got up, head held high and left the family alone.

A nurse was taking blood for testing. Tianna, hooked up to a drip, rolled her eyes,

"I'm alive, we don't need all the drama." She fiddled with the cannula going into her hand.

The nurse finished up and smiled at them as she took the samples off.

A junior doctor appeared, reading her notes.

"Hello you're Tianna's family, her friend said you were on your way. Where's he gone? He was here a second ago! Right anyway, I'm Dr Page, very nice to meet you. She's totally fine, but obviously traumatised, it looks like traces of GHB, date rape drug. Tianna's not reported any assault. When we get the definitive test results back, we can let the police know."

"Thank you, are you F1 or F2?" Marcus asked, smiling.

"F2 emergency specialism!"

"Me too! I'm at RVI! Lovely to meet you."

"And you, we often help each other out, don't we? You've got more emergency surgery places than us I think!" She popped the notes back at the end of the bed and left them with the nurse team. Anthony held tightly onto his daughter, Marianna stroked her drip free hand.

Seeing she was in good shape, Marcus left his parents and went to move the car. Strolling around the hospital grounds in the late spring sunshine, his thoughts overwhelmed him. Finally sitting on a bench outside the hospital he stared at a raised bed of blue and pink flowers and contemplated Tianna's recent troubles.

Soon she would be eighteen and going to university. How would she cope?

Penelope was preparing to leave. Suddenly catching sight of Marcus, she went to join him.

"I hear she's okay and no assault? Joel said she wasn't there long." She sat next to him. Marcus took her hand and she rested her other arm around his shoulders,

"Penelope thank you. What would've happened to her without Joel's help? I can't bear to think of it."

"He set her up, from what Joel's told me he's been pressuring her."

"It definitely looks that way. I'll guess we'll find out when she talks to the police."

Penelope looked straight into Marcus' eyes. "My friend, I know this is a worrying time for you and probably wrong for me to ask, but I need you to sort something out for me please, I'm actually quite desperate."

Marcus turned, still holding her hand, he assured her. "Of course, Pen, just name it, absolutely anything you need."

A couple of hours later, Tianna was discharged and Marcus drove everyone home. There was only silence. Blanket wrapped around her Tianna would not meet anyone's eyes. His parents got out slowly of the car, Marcus spoke.

"Do you mind if I just chat to Tianna for a minute?"

Marianna and Anthony nodded, they both weary and looking years older all of a sudden.

"How are you feeling?" Marcus asked his sister.

"Pretty stupid, a bit weak..."

"Do you have any idea what could have happened..."

289

"Oh don't start! All I did was take a few sips of water! You're not so perfect you know," her eyes were glaring.

"Yes I'm very aware of that!" He did not return her stare.

"You're such a fake, you make out you're some kind of saint saving the world, but really you're a liar and a cheat!" Tianna hissed.

"What?"

"I know all about your flirting, your affairs!" She snapped, putting her shoeless feet on the glove box.

"I'm sorry?" He turned, eyes now owl-like.

"Telling the pretty nurses how much you like them, I hear that you have a different favourite each week, you're very tactile, disappearing off with them for affairs and that you feel trapped with N?" Tianna spat out her words.

"Whoa what is this?" Marcus put his hands out to make her finish.

"Evan told me! You go around at work, saying you're too young to have babies and get married! That you feel suffocated by your relationship…" She snarled like an angry vixen.

"Stop right there! I've never cheated in my life!" He clenched the steering wheel.

"Of course you're going to deny it! So full of your perfect self!" Tianna looked away defiantly.

"No, just stop and listen. Tianna we've both been played. All that is a load of lies, Noëmi is the best thing that's ever happened to me. That Evan woman has been causing me hell from the day she arrived. She's been wanting to get with me. To do that she's trying to destroy my life. Anything she can do to split N and I up."

Tianna wriggled under her blanket and seemed pensive. "I just don't know how you could do that to Noëmi...the woman who saved you from being the most useless man on earth. And she's pregnant!"

"Well done Evan." Marcus' face was dark. "When did she say this?"

"She took me on that tour." Tianna's feet tapped the glove box. "What a surprise! I've had to complain to work about her harassing me. There's a whole thing going on with HR. I've not told anyone, not even Noëmi, because you can imagine how upsetting it is."

"Is that why you had that row?"

"Yes, all thanks to that woman spreading lies." Marcus clenched his jaw. "In the same way Kit's been destroying your life to get with you. When scheming people want you for their own purposes, we are just pawns in their game of chess."

"I'm so stupid, why did I not just ask you about it? Sorry Marcus. All she did was ask weird questions about you. Nothing about me, just fishing for info about you! I should've seen it was a lie but it's because she's so high up..." Tianna's voice began to break.

"And because someone is important, we automatically believe them?"

"We're trained to do that in life!" She sounded exasperated.

"'I get that but we have to fact check. Sometimes the more important the person, the better the lie!"

"The pawn and the king end up in the same box at the end of the game."

"Very wise." Marcus felt his muscles relax.

"Joel taught me that, he remembers Noëmi saying it at school when she was teaching him."

"Indeed, but Tianna, I need you to do one thing tonight. Could you tell Mum that Joel is not involved in coercing you in any way. Please can we just put that one thing straight? For his sake?"

Awkwardly, she pulled her blanket tighter around her.

"Why would anyone think that?" She looked away from her brother.

"You told Mum it was him,"

Tianna froze visibly.

"How do you know?"

Marcus looked at his sister.

"God Tianna, Mum went to RVI and confronted Joel. Told him exactly what she thought of him. Right in the middle of RVI reception. Yelling at him, calling him a rapist. You can only imagine what that would have been like for him." Marcus put his hand across his mouth and lowered his head as he pictured the scene.

Tianna began to shake. "No! Not Joel!" She cried out, "Oh my God, that's why..."

She began to wail loudly, "No, no, he must really hate me...no...what have I done...no!"

Marcus hugged her and in time she was still. Between breathless sobs, her voice was small,

"I need to apologise to everyone and in person."

Tianna

With Marcus' support Tianna confessed what had happened to her mother. However before Tianna could draw breath, Guy and Tariq were on the doorstep.

292

"Nice colour front door!" Tariq commented. Guy gave him an old fashioned look.

Having been called in by the emergency department Guy and Tariq walked into the McKenzie living room.

"Oh God!" Tianna cried out. '*Can this day get any worse? Of all the policemen in Tyne and Wear, it has to be my brother's best mate.*'

She saw Guy look around and nod at the family.

"Hello, we all know each other, not sure if that helps. Tianna, this is Tariq, he's in charge. As you're a minor, one of the adults needs to be present. Tariq has to go over the legal implications of the test results with you...if this is a good time?"

No one moved. Tianna sat on the sofa, still under her NHS blanket and she nodded. Tariq got started.

"Okay, in your system was found, via blood and urine tests, GHB, or gamma-hydroxybutyric acid. Sometimes it's called Liquid Ecstasy. This is a class C drug. It's illegal to possess, you can get up to 2 years in prison, an unlimited fine or both. Tianna, you told the doctor you did not have it in your possession when you went to Mr Deehan's house."

She squirmed, eel-like, in her chair. "No of course not, he gave me some water which tasted funny, but I only took a couple of mouthfuls."

"The Sexual Offences Act 2003 states that it's an offence to administer a substance, like GHB, to a person with intent to overpower that person to enable sexual activity with them. This is punishable by up to 10 years imprisonment." Tariq recited the exact wording.

"I wasn't going to have sex!" Tianna hid her face in her knees. Her parents were silent.

Guy leant forward sympathetically. "Tianna no one suggests that you intended to, that's the very point, someone wanted to render you defenceless. From what our first responders have said, there would've been nothing you could've done about it."

Tianna put her head under the blanket.

"Luckily Joel Rivera was suspicious." Marcus added.

Tianna and Marianna both bristled.

"This Kit, who invited her, lives in Oxford?" Anthony asked.

"We have another address, where Tianna was taken. We're sending a car with a warrant to search the place and to take him in for questioning now. What do you know about him?"

Anthony showed Guy the picture of the driver's licence.

"Mmm, I think I know what that is all about. We need evidence. I have to warn you, given the complexities of the law, it's unlikely we can make an arrest just like that." Guy sighed as he made some notes.

"What! How's this allowed? He could've killed my little girl." Marianna stood up and shouted.

"It'll take time. There were a number of young people at the house it transpires. We need to gather statements and evidence. He'll have a restraining order not to come near Tianna but there's simply not the capacity to keep all those suspected of or even accused of drug offences locked up. He'll not be able to leave the area whilst we need him for our investigation."

"Well how comforting." Marianna sat back down on her sofa and gave a loud tut.

"Tianna we'll need a more detailed statement from you as soon as you can give it to us. Background to your relationship with Kit..."

"It's not a relationship." She now wanted to teleport anywhere away from her front room.

"I mean how you know him, how you came to be at his house as I understand you went willingly?" Guy's eyes were kind.

"Yes but no...I'm such a fool." Her head returned under the blanket.

"I think you'll find it's coercive control. We can come back with a chaperone, Karen, if your parents give permission for us to talk to you alone? I'm not trying to cause a family argument but it may be easier at first. We need to make sure we get all the details." He looked understandingly at the family who all nodded in agreement.

Marcus went with his friend as they left the house. Guy turned to Tariq,

"Riqqi, can you do this one with Karen? I'm too close to the family."

"Sure Guy, I'll prepare everything. I love that scarlet, I really do! My girlfriend wants a new colour for the door to our flat, that could be it!" He said as he shut the McKenzie front gate.

PART THREE - RESULTS

Pour aimer, pour haïr, il faut se donner - Les
Mouches, Jean-Paul Sartre

.

CHAPTER 37 - YOU'RE NOT WELCOME HERE

Guy

Guy picked Noëmi up and they drove over to The Wear Rowing Club for a meeting with Squadron Leader Alan Kelly. They wandered into the club house and looked around. The bar server was polishing the optics and a couple of track suited rowers were having a discussion at a table on the far side of the room. A youth, with his back to them, was at the bar, drinking a pint and browsing on his phone. An older man was next to him, watching the evening news on the small television positioned precariously above the shelf for wine glasses.

Alan

Alan scurried, mouse like, out of the office. He was an athletic man of around 48 years whose background as a marine, made him an excellent leader. He loved the discipline, both physical and mental, that rowing demanded. Having little time for emotions and feelings, his manner was direct and decisive. Upon seeing Guy's uniform, he morphed into full commando mode. Standing to attention, he was ready to uphold the law. He ushered them efficiently into the bar area.

"Is this private enough?"

"Behind closed doors would be better if that's possible, thank you." They transferred into a back office and Alan moved a number of folders so he could write some notes. He began by taking their names, job titles, contact details and connection to the club. The room was dingy with a bulky desktop computer and a number of metal filing cabinets with misfitting drawers. Previous rowing club chairmen stared down from the walls in their lopsided, dusty frames.

Guy got started. "This concerns one of your Under 19 squad, Christopher Deehan."

"Good kid, talented rower, how can I help?" Alan's eyes were bright.

"I'm afraid I have to tell you that Kit, as you may know him, has been arrested and released on bail. That is for possession of a class C substance and he is also suspected, more seriously, for administering this to a third party. We're currently investigating."

"Class C? Not that bad is it?" He replied, brow furrowing.

"All drug charges are bad."

"Yes, yes, very serious, we take a dim view of drugs here. We have a full safeguarding policy which I'm happy to show you." He was vehement.

"Thank you, I don't doubt that but as Mr Deehan is on bail, he is technically free to carry on with life as normal. The conditions are that he does not leave the country and that he reports to the police station once a week."

"Okay I get it innocent until proven guilty and all that." Alan was now a legal aficionado.

"Indeed, I believe that's the idea. However I really need to advise you to ban him from the club as the victim of the second allegation is also a member..."

"Oh yes of course, absolutely! No need to name names!"

"You see, I cannot force you to do this. I can only strongly advise that you take this action. If you don't, you'll be encouraging him to break the law. Kit is prohibited from being within two hundred metres of the possible victim. This is incompatible with him continuing to be a member here."

"I get it, we'll issue the ban on the grounds of...?"

"Unacceptable behaviour perhaps?"
Alan scribbled furiously.
Noëmi now added her concerns.

"There's something else. The U19 social fund subs were mislaid. They were kept in a locked box and then put in the club safe. Only Tianna McKenzie and Kit Deehan had keys to the box. Kit, sorry Christopher, took the money and has been threatening to lay the blame on Tianna. She did nothing wrong. I understand the money has been fully returned by Kit Deehan."

"So that's good?" Alan hesitated.

"Yes but it gives the ban for antisocial behaviour some more strength does it not? He has been trying to blackmail her."

"Absolutely! Please don't worry, I'll issue the paperwork and talk to him." Alan nodded emphatically. He finished his notes and shook their hands. Alan showed them out and went straight back to the office to get on with the job in hand. That day he issued Mr Kit Deehan a formal ban via a letter, to be signed for on delivery. Receipt of this notice would enforce its legality.

Tianna

The next day Marcus dropped Tianna off and waited in the car. Knowing this could take some time he put the seat back. Headphones on, he listened to acoustic pop and shut his eyes. Getting out of the car, Tianna trembled. She walked to the marigold yellow front door of the small terraced house and knocked with determination.

Joel's father came to the door and smiled.

"Hello, is Joel there please?"

"Er yes, who can I say is asking for him?" Luis was friendly, wiping his hands on a red chequered tea towel, he gestured to invite her in.

"I'll wait here if that's okay sir."

Joel appeared. Seeing Tianna he did not hold back, "Really? You're not welcome here!"

He then turned away from her saying loudly, "Will you tell her I'm not in please, Dad."

Embarrassed, Luis looked at Tianna imploringly.

"Please can you tell him I've come to apologise." Tianna said sincerely.

Joel overheard and shouted back. "Again? Tell her this is getting a bit boring. You really love doing this don't you? A real, live sorry gif, do you ever get a day off?"

"I've made many mistakes and I need to talk to you." She remained at the doorstep accepting her punishment.

"Okay fine, if you've got something to say you can do it in front of all the people you've hurt. Take responsibility for your stupid games." Joel stepped aside so she could come in. Luis looked ever more embarrassed but remained silent.

Walking into their family home, Tianna took a deep breath ready for retribution. Her throat constricted as she saw Joel's smiling face in the family portraits. Warmth and affection glowed in their innocent faces.

Joel's mother Penelope told her youngest son, Gabriel to go upstairs. He put his exercise book down and groaned, visibly disappointed to be missing more of the drama. The three other Rivera family members stood in the narrow kitchen, silent and stern faced. Luis had been chopping a chilli. Penelope had been unpacking bags of supermarket shopping, and washing their hospital uniforms, after long shifts at RVI.

"I have to beg forgiveness because I told terrible lies. I've explained all this to my mother. She'll send you a letter of apology for her actions but obviously those were my fault. I'm sorry Joel. I was caught with compromising messages from Kit Deehan, bad stuff. When confronted by my mother I said they were from you. There's no excuse. The whole thing is made worse because, Mrs Rivera, you and Joel were the ones who rescued me, twice, once at the Christmas party and then from Kit's attempts to drug me. You saved my life. I cannot thank you enough. Joel has only ever been the kindest friend. I'm selfish and immature. I'm truly very ashamed." Tianna bit her lip to stop the tears. "From what I know of you Joel I realise how much these accusations will have hurt. You're such a decent, honourable and honest person."

Joel turned his back on her. Penelope glanced at her son. Suddenly she indicated for Tianna to move into the hall and she shut the kitchen door.

"Thank you Tianna it means a lot that you've put things right. Joel took it badly but now we can all start afresh." Tianna heard Joel's father comforting his son. Wretched and remorseful Tianna saw herself out and got back into Marcus' car. She burst into tears. Unplugging himself from his music he handed her a tissue, "I know it hurts but we all have to look into the mirror of our mistakes and see our grotesque reflections."

They sat a while. Eyes puffy, throat swollen she quietly put on her seatbelt and gave her brother a nod.

302

The following day, Tariq and Guy were busy in a review meeting.

"Well done Tariq, you're making excellent progress. You're a fine policeman and a valued colleague." Guy commented as he sent his mentoring report to his trainee who was sitting at his side.

"Guy that almost sounded touching!" Tariq said deadpan.

"Yeah, don't push it! I'm a mess if I get emotional!" Nodding his approval at his colleague. "And here you go!" Guy got up from his office chair and plonked some folders in front of Tariq. "Paperwork for the Kit Deehan case!"

Already late for his squash match with Marcus at the end of a long week, Guy gave his emails a final check. A copy of the letter that Squadron Leader Alan Kelly had sent to Kit Deehan had arrived in his mailbox. He looked at his watch and quickly clicked on it.

Following a visit by DS Guy Castle and Miss Noëmi McAllister, who informed me of your recent charge of administering a class C drug to a vulnerable person with the intention of rendering them unable to decline sexual activity, I hereby inform you that you are banned from The Wear Rowing Club with immediate effect. You are not to come within 200 metres of the club or contact any of its members herewith.
Squadron Leader Alan Kelly
The Wear Rowing Club Chairman

Guy leant back and gave a long sigh, "What a bloody stupid thing to do. What an idiot. He's not been charged with that yet! Kit knows me, we have history, but to put her name on the letter is unsafe."

Agitated, he grabbed his kit bag and turned out his office lights as he left to get some well needed cardio exercise.

Inevitably beating Marcus, the two showered, changed and went for a drink. Marcus passed him a beer and they sat at the bar. A guitarist was setting up for a live session and they arranged to come back later with some friends. Guy asked after Tianna.

"She's fine, bit quiet but she's got support. I know you can't talk about the case but this guy seemed so charming."

"You're answering your own questions there mate. Luckily her friend was vigilant. I hate to say this but he could've carried his plan through. Victims often have little memory of what's happened."

Marcus took a deep breath, "Doesn't bear thinking about. Thank God for Joel."

"He's on bail and has to report once a week to us. He's not allowed near Tianna, your parents' house and the rowing club. It'd be difficult for him to cause any more problems...but not impossible, sorry."
Feedback screamed in their ears.

"Thanks Guy, we all appreciate it."

"Hold on, there's one other thing. He's got Noëmi's name thanks to that idiot in charge of the rowing club."

"Yeah but I doubt they're going to come into contact again now." Marcus sipped his drink.

"Hopefully not."

"Do you want to come back to ours to get food? It's N's turn to cook tonight, then we'll see everyone back here later?"

"Sounds good, Yumi's already at yours I think!"

Drinks finished and they walked out into the night.

Tianna faced the rowing club one last time for the final regatta before the summer break. The weekend coincided with Marianna's birthday so all the McKenzies were there to watch.

Tianna channelled a year's nervous energy into her two thousand metre single scull event. Her style and strength ensured she was a worthy winner and the congratulations flowed. In the midst of noisy celebrations, Tianna's smiles were forced. Nauseous and light headed, all that was in her head was the sound of Joel upset.

Marcus

Meeting back at the clubhouse the McKenzies were all chatter and laughter. They were getting ready to leave when Marcus did a double take. He noticed Kit drinking a pint at the club bar, talking to the barman who was changing a beer keg. Marcus felt his blood rise and he went to his brothers. Within seconds the three had parked themselves behind and either side of Kit.

Kit clearly noticed them. The three moved closer in. The barman wiped his counter and sounded worried, "I don't want any trouble."

"Three black men in a bar and you suddenly think that means *trouble*?" Isaiah said angrily.

"Sai leave it, let's focus on the real problem here!" Jayden advised.

"Don't worry there won't be any *trouble*, not from us, but I thought our friend here was banned?" Marcus pointed at Kit.

"You'll have to ask the club chairman about that."

Kit finished his pint and turned to leave. Immediately he saw Isaiah was right behind him.

305

"You're not supposed to be anywhere near this club, remember?" the youngest McKenzie brother said.

"Or what?"

"Or you'll be sorry." Jayden replied, standing tall.

"Is that a threat?"

"We're just making sure you know the terms of your bail."

Isaiah widened his stance. "Stay 200 metres away." He stared Kit out.

Kit squared up to him. "She's a thief, she stole £300, I had to cover up for her."

Marcus saw Isaiah flinch slightly so he moved between the two. "We know what you did, setting her up. You stole that cash and you've gas lighted her all this time."

Kit put his face close up to Marcus' and smirked, "How did you come up with that? She's all about the money, she'll do anything for money you know what I mean...anything."

Marcus' whole body fired up. Jaw locked, muscles tensed, he raised his arm only to feel Jayden pull him away. He let out a scream of frustration, doubled over and put his arms on his head.

'Everyone has a point at which they'll go. I'd never thought I'd get that close.'

Taking a deep breath, heart still racing, slowly he righted himself and said his piece.

"Wrong, we know she never stole a thing. She took the serial numbers of all the notes of all the subs she collected. So scared she was of losing any of it. Meticulous. When the club leader checked the money, it's the same notes. It was never stolen by

Tianna, whoever *covered* it as you say, had the money the whole time."

Kit paled and had no reply.

"Keep away from this club, keep away from her and keep out of our sight. Got the message?" Marcus finished, unblinking, fixing his eyes on Kit.

Kit remained silent but stumbled as he left the bar. He swore under his breath and marched out of the main door into the car park. The brothers watched him leave and returned to the rest of the family only to see Guy's police car pull up outside. Entering the club bar, he saw the McKenzies chatting and walked over to Marcus smiling.

"Got a call, something about three men intimidating a member of The Wear Rowing Club. Did you see anything?"

"Really? No idea what that was, mate, must've been someone's imagination." Marcus looked over his shoulder.

"He was one of them!" The bar man called over to Guy.

"Can I ask what happened sir?" Guy moved to speak to the barman.

"One of our members at the bar, minding his own business and those three black men came, stood next to him, spoke to him and then he left."

"Big crime!" Marcus said under his breath, not looking at the barman.

"I see. Any altercation? Or threatening behaviour or physical violence?" Guy asked professionally.

"No, they just stood next to him!"

"Right, can you give me the name of the club member upset by these three men standing next to him?" Guy took his notebook out.

"Mr Christopher Deehan."

"Thank you for reporting this crime, Deehan is not allowed within 200 metres of one of your club members who is about two metres away from me now. You should also know he's been officially banned from the club. I can forward you a copy of the chairman's letter to that effect. Although it may be quicker just to ask Squadron Leader for a copy. I'll need to record this incident as Deehan is breaching the terms of his bail."

"Aren't you going to arrest them?" The barman narrowed his eyes.

"Sir it's not a crime to stand at a bar, if it were, our jails would be full and you'd be bankrupt." Guy replied.

"But there were three of them and…"

"Well I'll be on my way then. If you need any advice or education on anti-racism I'd be happy to come and talk to you."

"You're alright."

"But clearly you're not," Marcus said under his breath.
Guy turned to the McKenzies.

Tianna

"How's everyone? Hello Tianna, how did you get on in your race or whatever what you posh folk call it in rowing?"

"Yes, a race and I won, my fastest time ever!" Her words contrasted with her feelings of lethargy and her eyes were dull.

"Congratulations! How are you feeling? You look tired."

"I'm much better thanks, I didn't see he was there. Luckily my brothers scared him off."

"Useful for something then those annoying older brothers eh?" Guy gave her a nudge and a knowing look.

Tianna almost smiled. Suddenly she saw Joel whom she had not come into contact with since her latest apology. She felt hopeful that all was forgotten, maybe even forgiven? Their eyes met, he gave her a nod and quickly looked away. She watched as he then continued his conversation with Louisa who was preparing for her race. Tianna gazed as he obviously explained some improvement on a stroke to a smiling Louisa. Crestfallen she reminded herself she was very lucky that he had even accepted her regrets. Now his clear indifference to her somehow seemed harder to bear than his anger.

CHAPTER 38 CONFESSIONS

Wednesday, 26 June 2019.

Noëmi

"Everything's perfect! That's your final scan! Good luck!" Esme, the sonographer wiped her probe and grinned. The future parents thanked her and kissed goodbye. Beyond excited, Marcus sprinted back to his department.

Wandering heavily towards the entrance of the hospital, Noëmi thought of all that she needed to do before the births. The sky-blue linoleum floor was freshly polished; she landed her slow steps with care. Suddenly uneasy, a shadow seemed to be on her shoulder. Stretching her head round, a blonde ponytail swished past. Sweet lilies filled the air.

"Evan!"

The smartly dressed manager stopped.

"And you are?" Evan rolled her eyes.

"You know exactly who I am." Noëmi gasped. The two women faced each other.

"Are you alright? You're shaking! Can I get someone to help you back to the psychiatric ward?" Evan turned her back on Noëmi.

"Do you want to apologise to me for what you did at that conference?" Noëmi stood feet apart, resting her hand on the corridor wall. Chipped paint dug into her palm.

"I have no idea what you're talking about."

"Answering his phone, lying to me, trying to cause a problem between me and Marcus?"

"Do I need to call security?" Evan tapped her foot.

Taking a deep breath, Noëmi spoke. "I can't stop you pursuing him, that's your choice. But surely, as an intelligent woman, you must've worked out that you're wasting your time? Nothing will break us up."

Evan crossed her arms and spun round, "My relationship with Marcus is none of your business." Sunshine, peeking through the skylight, caught the outline of her glistening red lipstick. Noëmi bent forward slightly as she took a breath, her silky hair fell gently over her shoulders as she pulled herself up. A couple of chattering HCAs strolled past them.

"You're lucky. He's decent and professional. If everyone knew the truth, you'd be sacked but he'd never do that to anyone; not even you. So once again, I ask you, do you want to apologise to me?"

"There's nothing to apologise for, we can't help our feelings!" Evan pulled her jacket smartly around her slender waist and did up the button. Her eyes flickered onto Noëmi's expansive stomach. "Do you want a chair? You must be getting huge stretch marks! Those ankles must be elephant like by now?"

"I'm fine, thank you. One last time, will you apologise?"

Evan smirked and put her hands on her hips. "He's only with you because you're pregnant. He feels sorry for you."

311

"Just remember I gave you a chance to apologise. That's all I've asked of you."

"You two can't have too much longer to go? Soon it'll all be over." Evan said with a scoff.

"Evan, you need to think very carefully about what you do next."

"You're absolutely right! Now leave this hospital before I have you removed by security for harassing me!" Her voice was mocking.

Sweat on her brow and feeling a chill come over her, Noëmi continued laboriously towards the hospital entrance.

Evan

Evan proceeded smartly to Zena Walker's office. Outside she waited, messaging on her phone.

'*Bri when can we meet?*'

'*Evan leave them alone, I'm warning you.*'

'*Bri fancy big birthday drinks?*'

'*Bri why are you ignoring me?*'

Invitations to drinks and meet ups had been ignored by hers and Noëmi's mutual friend. '*Bri's a bitch. How dare she take sides. That woman's taking my man and my friend.*'

Zena Walker, HR manager, was a rush of colour and confusion as she appeared at the end of the corridor. Mumbling profuse apologies, she padded, flat footed to her door and unlocked it. Evan was offered a chair and readied herself for her meeting with her line manager Zena.

The small office was filled with plants of all types; a little cactus was again directly in front of Evan with its spikes poking out. It looked dry and thirsty. Zena, a flamboyant woman of an indeterminate age between forty and sixty, settled at her desk.

312

Busily she rummaged amongst the files and folders on her desk, collecting all she needed for the meeting. Repositioning herself on her seat and rearranging her glasses on her nose, she began.

"Thank you Evan for coming to this review meeting. How are you? By the way, many happy returns."

"Thank you."

"Remember at any time you feel you want to pause the meeting you just let me know. Now at this stage I have to discuss some allegations about your conduct. I believe you were issued with a warning to ensure your behaviour did not upset others, is that correct?"

"It is, although I wish to comment further on this as I felt extremely pressurised in that meeting to tow the party line."
Zena took furious notes in a brightly coloured jotter.

"Now those allegations concern your conduct towards one of our junior doctors, Dr Marcus McKenzie. If you allow, I will read the statement…"

'*Between the dates of 3 September 2018 to present it is reported that Evan St-John-Jones has been breaching the expected professional boundaries in her conduct towards Dr McKenzie. The reported incidents are:*

1. *Answering his personal mobile phone.*
2. *Creating an article in the staff newsletter that gave an unprofessional image of the complainant and using an image of him without his consent.*
3. *Contacting him outside of work hours.*

"Now, I'm afraid there have now been some additional complaints."

Evan rolled her eyes. Zena pursed her lips, "I'll read this statement we've just received," She cleared her throat. "Telling a work experience student that Dr McKenzie is *a seducer, likes affairs with pretty nurses and that he always has a favourite nurse on the go.*"

"Did I say that?"

313

"Indeed, I wish to hear your side of this. Do you mind if I record your statement? Makes it so much easier to get everything accurate!" Zena pressed her voice recorder and indicated to Evan to start.

Evan nodded and dabbed a tissue to her eyes.

"It's just been relentless. I'm so glad to be able to talk about it finally. I've tried so hard to ignore it and all I wanted to do was to protect that poor pregnant fiancée."

"That is so thoughtful of you Evan, please go on." Zena leant forward.

"From that first meeting, he had his eye on me. I felt uncomfortable but to be honest I've got used to men admiring me. However, this was different. Very soon on the way to work he started stopping and giving me a lift. Such a coincidence! Had he been stalking me? I wanted to say no but the way he looked at me was intimidating. Then he made me feel so awkward, there were conversations about women putting things up their vaginas. So inappropriate. Finally, I got my car back on the road and that stopped but then things got more intense. I found out he lives not far from me and every time I went out, he would be there! In a bar staring at me! Offering me drinks, kissing me on the cheek without invitation! Even at my gym, he would turn up. So scary. We helped at a school event and he insisted I travel with him. I couldn't say anything at work as I was uncertain if I was imagining it all! Eventually it became too much. He started messaging me on my emergency work phone, look here are some messages. Absolutely terrifying. One evening, he engineered a meeting out of work hours. I was so scared, but I managed to talk to him, and calm him down. He messaged me to meet him the next day, which I refused as I was terrified. Next thing he's trying to give me expensive presents. I told him I cannot accept these as my partner would be upset, plus I didn't

314

want to encourage him. However, the secret Santa he manipulated meant I had to accept one. The nightmare continued when he got on that conference and there was the whole phone and room key thing. By then I was worried. There was a heavily pregnant fiancée to consider so I didn't make a fuss. I wanted to protect that poor woman, as who knows what he could do to either of us? As for the photo that was his idea, he got someone to take it at the conference and made it look like a romantic date, I guess to feed his fantasy. He refused to delete the photo when I asked him to. Clearly, he was hoping for more and got angry when I told him 'no'. He just won't stop!

He corners me at work, tells me which weekends he's off and what he's doing. He tells trainees I feel 'trapped' in my relationship. He questions me incessantly about my private life and keeps asking to go out with me under the pretext of getting to know the area. I'm going to have to move house, it's just too much. I don't want to leave my job, why should I? But I just can't take it anymore!"

Evan sobbed and fell forward dramatically onto the desk, pricking her forehead on the cactus. Annoyed, she sat up, shoved the plant away. Before it toppled off the desk, Zena caught it protectively with one hand. Evan rubbed her temple and imagined herself stamping on the ridiculous little plant. A small drop of blood fell from her brow onto the desk.

Zena, open mouthed, went to her handbook to check the next step.

"Right, let's look at this flowchart, shall we? *Allegations of a threatening nature against a colleague*."

Evan smirked to herself. Finally free from the meeting, she stormed out of Zena's office.

Slamming her door, Evan arrived at her desk. Stretching her hands out she steepled her fingers. "Bri, let's give you something to get upset about, shall we?" Evan took a deep breath and made two phone calls. Caller ID hidden, the first was to the A&E main reception. The second was to Bri.

"Bri, don't hang up, it's me. Look, let's meet for a drink, I've seen how wrong I was, I want to confess everything."

Marcus

Head full of final scan, Marcus was buzzing. '*We're going to be parents! We could see their little limbs!*' He sped around the department and saw to his patients. '*Everything's in such fine shape, the locum should have no problems filling in for me when I'm on paternity leave.*' As he walked past the main desk, the receptionist interrupted his thoughts. "Marcus, someone called Val has left a message for you to meet at 7pm in La Ilusión, that tapas bar." The receptionist curled her lip. "Are you going to tell us who Val is?"

"Val's my mate and he's a bloke! Valentino! Thanks for letting me know!" Marcus laughed, '*I wonder what he wants; maybe a final drink for the condemned man! He could've sent me a text!*'

Shift over, Marcus sped down the street to the little tapas bar, eager to tell Val about the scan. '*I saw their tiny fingers…*' Running down the steps he entered into the dimly lit bar and searched for his friend. Unsuccessful, he ordered their usual drinks and waited at the table where they had sat on the previous visit. He was tapping his foot.

"Marcus!"

Seeing Evan stop at his side, he jumped.

"I need to apologise, there's been a huge misunderstanding!" Her dress clung onto her body. "Of course there has." He said under his breath. She sat down next to him. "Excuse me, that seat's taken, I'm waiting for someone." He snapped.

"Me too, they should be here in a moment but I wanted to tell you how sorry I am for what happened at the conference." She put her hand on his arm. Slowly he pulled away. He could feel her getting closer. Her sweet lily perfume filled his nostrils.

"I need to go." Marcus stood up. Grabbing his phone from his pocket he strode out, jaw riveted, eyes burning. Headlong he rushed, bumping into a waiter as he dialled Val's number. He apologised. Finally, Val answered "Pronto!"

"I can't meet you in that bar, let's meet in the Kings Head."

"What? Marcus? Are we meeting up? I'm home with Frank working on a fine Malbec!"

Giving a growl, he knew he'd been played. *'Will she just never leave me alone?'*

Bri

Arriving at La Ilusión, Bri gave a start. *'What's Marcus McKenzie still doing with Evan? How could he be so cruel? She has to see this. This has gone on too long.'* Bri stared at the two of them close together sharing drinks. Evan's hand was on his arm as they drank each other in. His eyes were dark and fixed on her, she was in a low-cut dress.

'You know what I'm done with the pair of them!'

Bri did not give the lovers a second glance. Turning on her heel, she texted as she stomped up the stairs

'Evan, you liar, if you don't stop this affair with Marcus McKenzie right now, I'll make sure his fiancée knows everything!'

Evan

'Now why would I have any problem with that Bri? You go for it!' Evan stirred the cocktail intended for Val. Like a potioneer, hopeful of alchemy, she knocked it back. Wiping her mouth, she gave a throaty, drainlike laugh.

Noëmi

Shutting the front door Marcus exhaled sharply. Noëmi was lying on the sofa, stroking her tummy, she stretched her hand out to him.

"T minus 108 hours! Our last weekend of just us before we're a family!" Her face lit up.

"What did you do after the scan?" He asked, cuddling up to her on the couch.

She put his hand on her stomach. "Nesting! I've prepared hot pepper shrimp. Your grandma's recipe!" She bit her lip, *'I'm not going to say her name. She'll cast no shadow over us when everything is this perfect.'*

Marcus

She repositioned herself and put her head on his chest. "You? Good rest of day?"

He closed his eyes. *'I just can't face an Evan conversation when this is such a perfect time for us.'* He felt her breath and pulled her closer in, "Yeah, all good."

They lay for a while; their love would keep them safe.

CHAPTER 39 - NEW LIVES

Thursday, 27 June 2019.

Joel

Joel was excited. Having spent nine months working as a Healthcare Assistant at RVI he had now been promoted to an Emergency Care Assistant in A&E. Stationed at the Emergency Ambulance Entrance, he was ready to help bring in the most serious cases. These were major trauma victims. Time was of the essence. Each morning they practised and timed their drill; from ambulance to treatment bay. Next they would double check all the supplies on the trauma treatment trolley according to a strict list. Joel's senses were heightened in this critical environment. Seconds separated life from death. Joel enjoyed the fact that he was on the frontline.

Tianna

The exams were over and Tianna was straight back to the hospital, having taken a job as an HCA. This was her first day and she was to shadow an experienced HCA so that she could learn the ropes.

'If I could just regain Joel's lost approval this will all be worth it.'

Getting up extra early, she had all her clothes clean and pressed. Hair and make-up done, a touch of cologne but not too much, she remembered how Louisa was always fresh. Mints in her bag for after coffee and clean hands. In anticipation she had carefully prepared some conversation starters that would immediately make Joel know she was a fine, decent, clever person; "Isn't it terrifying that Mount Ulawun has erupted? Climate change is the real emergency now isn't it? So much plastic! When will this world learn?" She practised in front of the mirror.

Tianna arrived at the HCA office and was shaking with nerves as she caught sight of Joel at the door.

"Oh! You're working here now?" He was surprised.

"It's terrible...er... Mount Ulawun!" Tianna spluttered without even saying 'hello'.

"Are you okay? Is that in Newcastle?"

"Papua New Guin..."

"Right.... have a good day everyone!" And off he went to his new department.

Tianna wanted to curl up into a ball and cry.

Marcus

Everything was ready at their small flat for the two new arrivals. The caesarean was booked for Monday 1 July at 9:30am. Then a new challenge of two weeks of paternity leave with two newborns and a fiancée recovering from a major operation. Having set up the two baby car seats, Marcus had some time before work. Noëmi was resting as the heat was exhausting her. Sitting, taking up most of the sofa, she was fanning herself when her phone buzzed.

'*I hope your baby dies*'

Sobbing, she handed her mobile to Marcus.

Marcus cried out in anger. Holding her, he rang Guy to ask for help. Finishing the conversation, he spoke to Noëmi.

"He says it's a malicious threat so it's higher up the priority list.

He needs access to your phone account; he'll bring the form round later to save you having to get yourself to the station." He stroked her huge bump adoringly.

"That's so kind of him. Who does stuff like this?"

Eventually Guy arrived, took off his stab vest and sat down. Noëmi stared into space.

"What's been happening?"

"Since September, Noëmi's been getting brochures about divorce services, plastic…"

"No!" she gasped.

"… and other stuff." Marcus noticed her lower her head. "All addressed to Noëmi personally, with notes saying '*here's the information you requested*'. Of course, she's never contacted anyone about anything like that."

"Have you kept any of it?"

"No, we chucked it. Plus, there was some valentine's card returned to us that neither of us sent."

Guy started to make some notes.

"If anything else comes, keep it. Something's not right. Now these texts. When you put everything together it looks like someone's got a grudge. What's been sent to your phone?"

"Messages like 'Miss McAllister how rough was the sex that got you pregnant?' we've reported everything to the school, but they're taking ages to sort it out,"

"Have they got a number? It can't be that hard surely?"

"The texts are anonymous," Noëmi spoke for the first time. She showed him her phone.

Guy looked through the messages.

"What are you two like!" he looked up cheekily and smiled as he scrolled through them. Stopping at the anonymous ones his brow furrowed.

"No, this is more serious than I realised, that's not kids."

"What? Oh God! It's that woman! Evan! Or maybe Sophie?

Neither would apologise. They're lining up all those people who hate me..."

Marcus shook his head, he thought about Evan in the tapas bar. Guy glanced between them.

"Bunch of ... sorry. Noëmi, if you can sign these permission forms, I'll get it booked into technology forensics for a full search. Can I pick it up tomorrow? No point taking it now, especially if you're going to be on your own tonight, when Marcus is at work."

Guy took the paperwork and the mobile account details. "Right, I'm on duty tonight too, an all-nighter."

"You'll be looking forward to the delights and devastation caused by the thirsty Thursday crew!" Marcus quipped. Both men stood up and began gathering their things.

"Ha! Maybe I'll see you in A&E when I bring them in!" Guy joked and he gave Noëmi a big hug. "And I can just about get my arms around you! Have you measured that bump?"

Smiling, Marcus slapped his friend on the back to say goodbye.

Turning to Noëmi, Marcus tried to cheer her up.

"Okay baby seats are ready! Should we choose some names?" He picked up the name book Sarai had returned.

"We should make a list. We don't know if we need two boys, two girls, boy, girl. Does it matter to you?" She brightened up.

"Not at all, as long as they play football. You make a list and I'll see what I like on it!" He looked at her and smiled. "I guess you'll choose in the end though!"

"Oh they're fighting!" She grabbed his hand to feel the babies moving and kicking as they changed position.

"Are you sure there's only two in there! Monday we're all systems go!" He laughed. "You won't be able to get up if I don't help you. I could just leave you there."

"Stop it, these are your offspring I'm carrying, clearly going to be McKenzie size! I'm going to bed to stock up some sleep before these two make their break for freedom." He helped her up.

"Good idea, I love you, stay safe!" he replied as he left for work.

Lying in bed, unable to get comfortable, Noëmi tossed and turned. Inside her the babies were agitated. She sat up, grabbed her phone and texted her list to Marcus.

Boys
1. *Bruno*
2. *Enrique*

Girls
1. *Emmanuelle (called Mani a bit for my mum)*
2. *Geneviève (pronounced the French way)*

A message pinged in from Bri.

'Noëmi, can I have Marcus' mbl no? I've got a medical question x'

'Sure but I can pass on a msg x'

'Never mind, look I need to talk to you about Marcus. He's hiding things from you, sorry x'

323

Noëmi tried to call both Marcus and her friend, but neither picked up. Mind racing and unable to sleep, she grabbed her laptop and started doing some admin.

Marcus

Marcus arrived at work, went to his pigeon hole and found his paternity leave permission forms. *'Yes! Alex has signed them now!*

He saw Noëmi's list ping through, amused, he turned his phone off and put it in his locker. He looked at his watch.

'If I'm quick I can get these documents up to HR now.'

Running to drop off the necessary papers, he was daydreaming of the very upcoming moment they would meet their children.

'Enrique honestly! God, I don't know if I'm shaking with excitement or terror! What will they look like? Boys? Girls? I actually don't care! I thought I'd always want a son but a daughter would be cute. Can't wait to take them to football. They'll need to support Newcastle. Get them those little babygrows we saw that time in the stadium shop. That was years ago, my eighteenth! We joked about it, now it's real. I knew then. It was always meant to be us!' Marcus was inside his head.

Evan

Striding down the HR corridor Evan's whole body suddenly froze. She could see Marcus coming towards her with some papers in his hands.

'Looking so hot in those scrubs.'

Pushing out her chest, she slowed to a stroll. Removing her glare and fixing her smile she looked hopefully in Marcus' direction. Marcus walked on by. Not a flinch. Not a flicker. Nothing. It was not a snub; she had not caught his eye. His face was serene and his eyes lost in thought, no doubt imagining his new life as a father.

324

Fists clenched, Evan marched into her own office, slamming the door behind her. She let out a howl. Flinging herself into the oversized office chair, she threw her papers down. One jumped out at her immediately.

A and E staff rota week commencing 1 July 2019.

Picking it up, she studied the 'personalised' spreadsheet she had demanded the team keep. **Dr Marcus McKenzie - paternity leave from Monday 1 July to 15 July 2019.**

Evan stood up and paced about her office. Grabbing her psychology manual, she flung it across the room, and cried out.

"Why is he with some plain, unwashed nobody! I'm prettier, sexier and richer than this insignificant boring woman."

Storming back to her desk, she grabbed her briefcase and walked out of the building. Driving home in a blind fury she parked her car. A cyclist had to swerve as she threw her car door open. She screamed at him, "Oi! Watch it you fucking wanker!"

Once inside she kicked her front door shut behind her and poured a large glass of Pinot Grigio. Evan sat at her kitchen island and opened her briefcase in a frantic fury, chipping her nail varnish. Sitting at her laptop Evan was determined.

'He needs to be with me.'

She opened a number of tabs and logged onto Marcus' email account. *'Of course, I know your password!'* Her lips twitched. She looked at his recent activity and saw a few emails forwarded to Noëmi McAllister, regarding his paternity leave.

"Why leave it there, let's give you both more to read!" Evan laughed out loud. The gulped wine had made her lipstick bleed into the skin around her lips. Feeling invincible, Evan typed two emails one to Marcus and one from Marcus. She waited and as she had predicted a reply came through. *'Perfect!'* Next, she carefully deleted all these emails from Marcus' inbox and sent

325

items folder. In this way, she could leave no trace of her activity at all.

"Easy to keep in contact with them now!"

Looking at the clock it was 5:30pm, she finished her drink, gave a loud belch and poured herself another, ready to get back to her scheming.

CHAPTER 40 - CODE RED

Thursday 27 June 2019.

'*Your driver will meet you at the corner of Osborne Road and Osborne Avenue at 17:45*'

Looking at the pin on her phone, she reached the pedestrian crossing. She could see the taxi waiting to meet her. Traffic lights red, green man flashing, she could cross.

She stepped out, focused on her cab. She gave the driver a quick wave and a smile.

'*Noise. Revving. Faster. Not stopping. No! Move now!*'

Guy

'**RTA immediate response required, junction Osborne Road and Osborne Avenue, one pedestrian down, one walking wounded, ambulance service aware, car did not stop**'

"On my way." As soon as Guy got the call, he set off.

"Come on Tariq, our first job, it's a minute away. Request more details." Guy blue lighted away, sirens screaming.

The paramedics were arriving and a couple of passers-by were helping. The ambulance team rushed to the unconscious victim. Blood covered the tarmac, Guy shuddered; "This job gets no easier."

Guy parked up to block the road. Hurtling out of his patrol car, leaving the lights flashing to warn other road users, he sprinted over to the first responder.

"What've we got?" He shouted, continuing to assess the security of the scene.

"Car didn't stop, witnesses say the casualties were on the crossing and it was green for them to go. A car sped through a red light. Hit the one lady at full force on her leg. Looks like she fell and hit her head. Unconscious and bleeding heavily from a leg wound, we're stemming the bleeding. It's a severed artery; not looking good for her."

Guy went to the scene where belongings were strewn on the road. He began to retrieve whatever he could to identify the victim. He saw an older lady sitting in the back of an ambulance with one of the paramedics who was treating her for shock. The unconscious victim was being put carefully, but swiftly, onto a stretcher; a heavily pregnant woman.

'*My God!*' he said to himself. "Tariq can you see to the lady over there, calm her down but get an initial statement quickly. Any details of the car that didn't stop is what we're after. They could be a danger to others."

A taxi driver walked over to speak to Guy. He obviously felt reassured by the policeman's presence as he left his cab running.

"I think it may be the woman who ordered a taxi, she waved at me, plus the mobile phone on the ground over there was ringing out when I called to see where my fare was. The cab was ordered to get to RVI urgently. I'll get you the name if that helps."

'*She's off to RVI alright.*' Guy grimaced at the irony.

Guy checked through the belongings. The sirens of an arriving support unit faded away as he found a purse. He put an arm on his car door to steady himself. His blood went cold. Almost immediately the taxi driver confirmed his fears. Guy quickly took the taxi driver's card so he could keep in touch then rushed to his car radio.

"There's no time, I need to get in touch with the A&E department right now."

Guy phoned through and then prepared to leave for the hospital with the belongings.

"Guy, you're suddenly so pale and look! All sweaty!" Tariq's eyes were wide.

"I need to get to A&E right now. Stay with the other patrol car!"

"Sure Guy, we're getting the CCTV from the crossing camera, to identify the car, it should be through soon..." Tariq's wave stalled.

Brakes screeching. A flash of blue. Guy was gone.

Presently statements were collated. The scene was checked for evidence, photographs taken of where the casualty had fallen and estimations made about the speed of the vehicle involved. The road was then given back to users and the bystanders dispersed. Within the hour, Osborne Road was back to the usual Thursday evening run of things.

Marcus

At the forefront of the emergency department were Alex, Marcus and Madhav, the resident A&E specialists. On the rota this week, Marcus was down as the second doctor in charge after Alex, the lead consultant. Beginning their shift Marcus and his team had a number of tricky cases; the queue was building up.

Marcus was focused on his first patient '*eight year old, fallen from*

329

his bike… stable but pain in upper thorax, check possible clavicle fracture…' He wrote up the X-ray request and sent the youngster for imaging.

Suddenly the emergency phone rang. Penelope ran to it. Without taking breath, she relayed the message. "Code red, RTA, female, six minutes. Full situation, background, assessment and recommendation."
As she put the phone down it went again.

"Urgent, we've now got two code reds. Another separate RTA coming in, limited SBAR. Four minutes, casualty female and pregnant! I don't believe this! Get ready everyone!"
Marcus then just ran. Everyone knew that this was one of the worst scenarios as it was a case of meeting the ambulances with whatever they had. The short time meant information was scarce in spite of urgent details being radioed ahead to help the receiving doctors.
Frantic, Alex ran to the main desk to alert other units; " Two Code Reds. We need a full obstetric team ready in theatre for a caesarean and help down here now! Neonatal intensive care on standby too. Hoping for a live birth." Off the phone he charged over to his teams.

Alex

"Code Red, trauma protocol times two, if you can believe our luck. Double up the trollies and call now for more bloods." Alex announced to the quickly assembled colleagues.
"Right now, we're at rapid response with these two. Marcus, you take the first, stabilise and get straight to theatre for that caesarean. Madhav the second. Be steady, control your teams, they need you to lead. When it's this panicked be extra careful if shocking. Marcus, remember the drill for pregnant women and resuscitation, plus the four minute window. I'll move between the two and assist as required. Okay go!"

330

Frantic preparations continued. Scrubbed up they could hear the sirens approaching the emergency ambulance entrance. Marcus knew the first thing would be possible resus, major haemorrhage protocol, bloods and a main line. A pregnant woman made his skin go cold.

'Thank God Noëmi's tucked up safely in bed'. This was the reality of his work, he needed to save lives.

Pacing at the emergency ambulance entrance, Alex received an urgent bleep from the main desk. His face darkened and he charged to the A&E receptionist who had taken Guy's call. The briefest of exchanges and together they sped to Marcus' team.

Bursting through the crowd of assembled nurses and assistants, Alex was breathless.

"Dr McKenzie, you're relieved, report to the main desk now," Alex said sharply. They could hear the ambulance teams working quickly to bring the patients in.

"But I'm in charge here according to you, I've got this." Marcus was making his final checks.

"Dr McKenzie, return to the main desk, right now, that's an order!" Alex's voice was firm.

"What's going on?" Marcus was confused, as the outer doors of the emergency ambulance entrance swung open with their patient ready for treatment.

"Marcus, please just go."

Something in Alex James' eyes made Marcus relent. Hands falling to his sides, he turned and allowed himself to be ushered to the main desk by the clerk.

'*What's the problem? Does Alex not think I'm up to the job? Is it because the victim's pregnant like Noëmi? I've got no problem separating work from my personal emotions,*' he thought to himself, feeling suddenly hot.

'*To be so publicly dismissed like that! What will everyone think? Will it affect my authority when dealing with the teams in the future? Why was Madhav allowed to lead and not me? Madhav has tended to be the one who needs support…*' All sorts of thoughts ran around his head.

Joel

Joel was ready as the first ambulance screamed into the bay. The team raced to get their patient down, shouting that she was unconscious and losing too much blood. Getting into position he was listening carefully to every instruction. When he glanced down at the bloodied face of the casualty, his heart jumped. Once they had delivered her to the treatment bay he sat down in shock, unable to comprehend what had just happened. Explaining to his supervisor that he felt unwell, he asked to be excused.

Marcus

Marcus waited, unsure what he was supposed to be doing at the main desk. He looked at the case lists to see where he could help. Should he start seeing to the minor cases?

'*Why's the receptionist hovering by my side?*' Suddenly she spoke,

"Marcus, why don't you wait for Alex in his office?"

At that moment, Marcus saw Guy enter the main A&E reception area. The receptionist rushed over to talk to the officer. Realising his friend was undoubtedly coming in with one of the RTAs, Marcus was momentarily distracted.

"Mate! Finally we meet in the line of duty! First time ever! You predicted it earlier!" He shrugged his shoulders and smiled.

Guy had not seen his friend at first and looked up as he heard his voice. They stood at the main desk a few metres apart. Marcus waited leaning on the counter. Guy spoke in a hushed voice to the receptionist.

332

Pausing Marcus realised. '*He'll be giving her the details of the casualty for the registration system*'. A second officer arrived to do the same for the second RTA trauma patient. In the background Marcus could hear the teams working, one quieter than the other. Alex James was suddenly shouting furiously.

"Securing the airway. Get that IV line in! Hurry! Come on! Prepare for anaesthesia, we need to get her to theatre now!"

'*I could lead like that.*'

He saw Esme hurtle past on her way to do an emergency scan, no doubt as for the pregnant victim.

"She's losing more than we can get in…"

Intermittently Marcus heard the team shouting out. An eerie sound of controlled frenzy.

'*They need to get the bloods in urgently. The patient must still be haemorrhaging badly. An initial tourniquet until surgery will help. Will I be part of the debrief? Will I get an explanation? Sounds like they're shocking now. I could've handled this. I'm sure.*'

Marcus' thoughts were interrupted by Alex buzzing through more details on the department radio. "Code red. Two fetuses, anecdotally informed 37 or 38 weeks or thereabouts, require two NICU cots in theatre, repeat two, going straight up now, we need to move, where is everyone? She needs to go now!"

Guy had finished registering the casualties and had the few possessions, retrieved from the scene of the accident, put into clear plastic bags. Marcus looked across again and moved towards Guy.

"Guy, you're with one of the RTAs?"

Guy nodded, he was silent and looked down. Finally he whispered, "Mar…"

Pointing at one of the plastic bags, Marcus interrupted.

"That's just like the bag I gave Noëmi! We got it in Italy for her birthday a couple of years ago. That mustard is quite an unusual colour but she uses it all the time, look it's even got the same beaded charm thing like the Nigerian one she added..."

Guy just looked at Marcus; his face said everything.

A thousand thoughts raced through Marcus' mind and he turned and hurtled back to the treatment areas for patients brought in by ambulance.

Areas now clear, a nurse was completing the accident reports on the system.

"Where is she?" His eyes were wild.

"Sorry?" The nurse looked up and jumped back slightly.

"The RTA casualty that just came in?" Breathless, bent double, he was convulsing.

Seeing a junior doctor, she pulled herself up straight and replied.

"There were two. Both taken to emergency surgery, one still in. I've just been notified that one died on the operating table so a DOT. The other one's not looking good either so we need to get the chaplain up there for possible last rites. No relatives informed yet I'm just working on that. I just need the formal identification of the deceased and then I'll be getting the death registered on the patient record system..." Clearly she assumed he wanted the cases followed up quickly and that her procedures were being checked.

Guy

Guy had quickly followed and caught Marcus as his legs crumbled. Urging the nurse to call for help and he held onto Marcus who was now sobbing uncontrollably. Bewildered, the nurse stared at the scene in front of her.

"What's even going on?" She stammered. Then she put a call out for assistance.

"We don't know what's happened yet," Guy held onto his collapsed friend. Hearing him now start to scream, Guy's whole body began to shudder. *'God there's no good option…last rites, emergency surgery. Pregnant with twins, what are their chances?'*

Esme

Esme was packing up her portable scanner. Feeling numb she began to hyperventilate.

'It's her, his partner. Just the other day they were in for the pre-caesarean scan. Are they all dead?'

A few of the team who had worked on Noëmi were slumped around the department, recovering. In a corner by an IV pole, Penelope used a soggy tissue to wipe her tears away but more kept coming. All at once, Marcus' panicked screams filled the trauma bay. Heads in hands, they looked at one another unsure what to do.

'How's that sound even human?' Never had Esme heard such pain.

She put her hands over her ears. *'This is unbearable.'* Finally taking a deep breath, she rushed to help. Penelope did the same.

Guy

Together with Guy they got hold of Marcus, who was now shaking, gasping and muttering incoherently. Gently they moved him towards one of the relatives' lounges. A dull room, with no natural light and tired pale green walls. A dehumidifier hummed in the background. The room had nothing else but a low brown Seventies sofa and a coffee table. A fresh box of tissues sat on this small table with a jug of water next to it, but no cups. Sitting him down, Guy held Marcus in a tight embrace, he could feel his friend's tears soaking his neck. Esme alerted the front desk. Numerous checks were made and after what felt like forever, an administrator appeared.

335

Marcus was now slumped forward, shoulders shaking.

"So you are the next of kin of?"

Guy took over and gave Noëmi's details.

"How are you related?"

"They're engaged."

The lady took notes, over her glasses she mumbled, "That's not a formal next of kin."

Guy gave her a look of exasperation. "As the police officer in charge I'll take responsibility for that."

She acquiesced and continued. "Anyway we just need to confirm the identities of the two casualties, do you have a picture?"

Marcus did not look up. Guy searched his pockets and found his wallet. Opening it Guy grimaced as he saw a picture of Noëmi smiling on one side and a print of the baby scan on the other. He passed the whole thing over to the administrator.

"Okay thank you, can you confirm if this is her jewellery?" She handed over a small plastic bag which contained Noëmi's eternity and engagement rings plus her silver heart necklace. Marcus started shaking violently and Guy nodded simply.

"Just one minute," the lady went out.

Guy appreciated that they needed to ensure they did not mix up the casualties but was astounded at how excruciating this was. His own heart was racing. Guy knew exactly what his friend was thinking.

"Maybe a CT scan, removing artefacts and all that. Or because they're operating, you know, hygiene rules." Guy struggled to find an explanation. His own emotions on hold, Guy could only cling onto his weeping friend.

CHAPTER 41 - KITH AND KIN

Alex

Alex James had received the message from Guy that Marcus' pregnant fiancée was a Code Red, RTA victim arriving at RVI within 4 minutes. Full speed Alex had dashed to replace Marcus on the team. As Alex sent his junior doctor away, he steeled himself for the harrowing realities of what made emergencies just that; too much to get right in virtually no time, otherwise his patient would die. He felt the hairs on his neck.

Thirty odd years of training were leading up to this; one of his most difficult trauma cases. Pregnant with twins. RTA injuries: fractured leg and catastrophic haemorrhage from severed popliteal and femoral arteries. Whilst all patients were treated equally the fact that she was engaged to his colleague and friend, made it all the more real. Although he had met her himself a few times, he knew he was the only one who could take responsibility for this. Shoulders like lead, skin clammy, he took a breath. Quickly he reminded himself of resuscitation for women in advanced stages of pregnancy, tilted up, leaning to the left. Theatre was ready, their patient was coming through the emergency ambulance doors. Now time to lead. Calling the team to order, he began work. Airway, ventilation, IV line in, bloods, stabilise, vitals check. Then she was gone. Time to shock. In four minutes if she still had no heartbeat, caesarean section there and then; the reality was that brutal.

The team worked as one, hopefully unaware of the connection. Alex grimaced as Esme's face blanched as she monitored the babies. '*She scanned her the other week.*'

"They're okay but heartbeats are racing, could be distressed, we don't have long." Her voice trembled.

Mother stable he shouted for the team to get her to theatre. He followed until she was handed over to the surgeons. Exhausted, he collapsed in a chair in the corridor. An HCA sauntered past whistling and a visitor was complaining loudly on their phone about a car insurance claim. Life rolled innocently on.

With a jolt, Alex pulled himself up and hurried to the relatives' room. Outside, the receptionist briefed him. Clenching his muscles, he entered. Marcus was shaking uncontrollably as Guy held him. Alex went and sat next to his young colleague.

"Okay, your fiancée is Noëmi McAllister. Date of birth 26/8/93, age 25 years, resident at your address,"

Marcus nodded. Whilst Alex knew all this perfectly well it made her like every other patient, setting a boundary so that he could cope.

"She's alive. Noëmi's in surgery, they're doing everything to save the three of them. I'm sorry but I have to be honest, things are very difficult."

Alex's breathing was shallow, his face red. Desperately he wanted to protect Marcus from the grim reality of the situation.

'*If they don't make it'll be me who has to deliver the news.*'

"We've stabilised her, central line, bloods, we did need to resus as she went into cardiac arrest because of the haemorrhaging."

Marcus grabbed Alex's hand and fell into his body.

"But we got her straight back and both fetuses were alive when we transferred to theatre. Strong heartbeats, some distress but we moved quickly."

Silently Marcus gave a nod that he understood, still clenching Alex's hand.

"The emergency caesarean is underway; you know you can't be there. Then we need to assess Noëmi. Unfortunately, at this stage there's no guarantee of the outcome for any of them...I'm sorry for earlier, there was no time." Alex was clear; Marcus needed the truth.

"You know how this works; you need to wait here. I'll get any news to you as soon as I have it." Marcus clung onto him and Alex enveloped him in a hug.

"We're all in this with you and praying for your family." He whispered simply, meaning every word. Head down, Alex left the small relatives' room.

Guy

"What happened?" Marcus did not look up. "Why was Noëmi out? Why did the car hit her? I don't understand, she went to bed, I *saw* her in bed."

Guy told him what he knew, "According to witnesses Noëmi and another pedestrian were using the crossing when the car didn't stop, she did nothing wrong, the light was green to cross."

Marcus gasped "Guy I'm so scared."

Yumi entered the room.

"I know mate, me too." Guy swapped places with an ashen faced Yumi. She took Marcus' hand and put her arm around him. Guy knew he had to get Donnie.

Donnie

Donnie had received a message from Noëmi and had rushed straight from his badminton club to the hospital. Not knowing where to go and not being able to contact his daughter he headed for the main reception.

"Good evening. I need to find my daughter. Her fiancé is a doctor here and he's been taken ill."

"Names please."

"Noëmi McAllister and Dr Marcus McKenzie."

The receptionist looked through her systems, tapping through a number of screens.

"Do you have some ID as a next of kin?"

Donnie handed over his driving licence. The receptionist looked through her records.

"Mr McAllister, go to A&E immediately. They will be able to help you. Here's a hospital map and the directions you need to follow." She handed him a print out with the route highlighted.

Racing to A&E Donnie arrived and saw Guy walking away.

"Guy, hello! Is Marcus okay?"

"Donnie! Thank God! ...no, not at all."

"Oh my goodness, what's happened, what can I do?" Donnie put his kit bag over his shoulder and gestured openly with his arms.

"Donnie..."

"Where's Noëmi? Is she with him?"

"No, no, Donnie, come with me."

Guy led Donnie towards the relatives' room.

"I got Noëmi's message telling me something was wrong with him, but I've not heard anything else." He explained reaching for his mobile from his pocket.

"Donnie I'm sorry there's been some misunderstanding, it's Noëmi who's injured."

"No, no you've got it the wrong way round, she messaged me, she's worried about him. Marcus is ill or something..."

"No, he's in the relatives' room, I need to take you there." He put his hand on Donnie's arm. Donnie looked at him open mouthed. "Donnie, Noëmi's been hit by a car, it's serious she's badly hurt. They're operating now, hopefully a caesarean. We just don't know if any of the three will make it..."

Guy watched as Donnie's face fell. He lurched suddenly forward and held onto the wall. Disturbingly silent, he began to cry. Gently Guy took him by the shoulders and got him into the family room then fetched some more chairs. Yumi took Donnie's hand, her other arm still around Marcus.

Guy

Guy sat with them all and tried to figure out why Noëmi would send a message saying that Marcus was ill. Nothing made sense. Marcus sat forward not speaking, Yumi was rubbing his back gently.

"Donnie, can I see the message?" Guy asked quietly. Donnie nodded and handed his phone over, wiping his eyes.

'**Dad something's wrong with Marcus, I'm going to the hospital, plse call, I'm upset**', Guy noted the details of the text, '*Noëmi*

341

sent it earlier that evening, maybe twenty minutes before the accident. She was rushing to the hospital. Why had she thought that Marcus was ill?

Marcus put his head on Yumi's shoulder and she gently stroked his hair and mopped up his tears.

Joel

Joel went quickly through the main wing of the hospital to the HCA admin office to find out where Tianna was. His manager slapped him on the back with a big hand.

"Well done your first proper stretcher!"

Joel could not speak a word.

"It's carnage down there! What was it that got you? Once a guy came in with his arm missing. Ripped off by a grain sifting machine, nasty sight, you could even see the tendons hanging next to it. How that bone got sliced through is quite unbelievable..."

Hearing the commotion Tianna and her supervisor diverted into the office; she smiled shyly.

"A&E, takes its toll." The manager sneered his lip as he gestured to a ghost like Joel. "You have to man up if you're going to be an ECA. You can't get the cases to order. No one ever said life was pretty...or death for that matter and of course we're all going to end up in a body bag one day." The manager turned back to his computer and took a bite of a chocolate digestive.

Finally, Joel gasped, "T..T..Tianna, it's Marcus' girlfriend, my old teacher, she's been in an accident, she's down there in A&E, it's really bad."

Tianna screamed and fell back against the door.

Not having listened properly their manager turned and glared at them.

342

"Can you two imbeciles not shut up? Pull yourselves together! I'm trying to get this rota done. A hospital is full of ill and injured people. It's not some joyride you know."

Tianna burst into tears and Joel held her by the shoulders as the manager tutted and went back to his screen.

Tianna

Joel and Tianna arrived at the A&E reception. Tianna was shivering as she sobbed.

A crowd of people were now around the reception desk and two phones were ringing out constantly. A receptionist and a nurse were attempting to deal with the confusion.

"I'm sorry to disturb you but we got a call that our daughter's been involved in an accident..." A middle-aged man, dressed in a dark suit spoke for the group. An anxious lady of a similar age hovered behind, tissue in hand which she used to dab her eyes.

A woman pushed through, leaving a pale looking child with an iPad, sprawled on the blue padded plastic seat behind her.

"Excuse me! I've been waiting three hours with a very sick child and this lot have barged in front of us!"

With no option but to wait, terrifying images went through her mind. More family members of the casualties were arriving and the receptionists were struggling to find rooms for everyone. Joel finally managed to explain why they were there.

"The sister of a fiancé is not a next of kin." The exasperated receptionist stated firmly.

"But he needs her support." Joel insisted.

"Okay but we'll need to check with the official next of kin who is now there, hold on."

After more toing and froing, they reluctantly allowed just Tianna into the family room to join Marcus. Devastated by the desolate sight of her brother and Donnie, she hugged them both tightly. Shaking, she rang her parents to join them at the hospital and

343

messaged her other two brothers. From then on, her phone did not stop and trembling she swapped places with Yumi and handed her the mobile. Tianna reached out to Donnie, who was crying quietly and held his hand. Within the hour Marcus' parents and grandmother had joined them.

The receptionist had now given up on whatever limits and rules were in place. She brought in some extra chairs and a fresh jug of water with some plastic cups.

A phone pinged.

"Jayden and Isaiah are travelling up from London together immediately," Yumi related in a whisper. An eerie silence filled the room punctuated only by Tianna's and Donnie's small sobs. Marcus had barely moved and remained head down elbows on his knees, unable to talk.

Marcus

Suddenly the door swung open. Alex James returned. The whole family looked at him half with dread, half with hope.

"Good news, the babies are well, no complications. Marcus, you and Noëmi have a son and a daughter, congratulations. We're getting there! We'll get you all up to the Neonatal Intensive Care Unit very soon to meet them. We'll have an update on Noëmi before long, she's still in theatre for vascular surgery on her leg."

Raeni let out a gasp of relief, "Thanks be to God!"

"That's wonderful news, thank you!" Yumi spoke for the family. Marcus rubbed his hands on his face and looked up for the first time.

His consultant went to him and hugged him as Marcus whispered, "Alex thank you."

Eventually a nurse came and led them up to the Neonatal Intensive Care Unit. Marianna held onto her son, supporting him, Anthony took Donnie. They made their way through the hospital corridors in silence. Arriving at the NICU, the unusual site of two cots with no mother made everyone uneasy. The expectation was always to see a proud new mum sitting up babe in arms. However, they could see the infants were well, each with their own nurse attending. Marcus was unable to hold his children as they were still on drips and oxygen. Instead, he had to stroke them through the arm holes of the incubators. There they lay, little knitted hats on their heads to keep them warm. He was enthralled to see their tiny faces and bodies. He gasped as he felt the most almighty, overwhelming rush of unconditional love. He checked their tags; male infant N McAllister, 27/6/19, 18.02 and female infant N McAllister 27/6/19, 18.03. His heart pounded with pride and panic.

"Bruno and Emmanuelle."

He prayed. '*N you did it, they're safe now just get back to me, I can't live without you. God please help her.*'

He said simply to Yumi "I'm staying here," and sat down in the plastic cream coloured armchair between the cots. The nurses, busy around the incubators, gently explained how the infants were improving.

Taking some video and pictures, Yumi seemed determined to be positive,

"Taking this for when she's better, she'll be gutted that she's missing this. You know how she is!" Yumi hugged Marcus firmly and set about recording every inch of the babies. Marcus occupied himself quietly, watching the babies, touching their tiny limbs and praying. Donnie did the same.

Alex James sprinted to the NICU group. Breathless he could hardly get his words out.

"She's out of surgery...comminuted fractures in right tibia and fibula. Both plated successfully but she's still unconscious. Until we do a CT scan, we have no idea of what is going on there, you know that. Stable but critical. Infants are doing well here, let's go,"

Marcus and Donnie got to the intensive care unit. Amidst an array of monitors and displays Noëmi was lying in a web of tubes and cables. A nurse smiled at them as she finished her observations, popped the notes at the bottom of the bed and moved to the side. Marcus' heart sank, he knew none of this was good, Donnie felt more optimistic and cried out, "Just looks like she's having one of her deep sleeps!"

Marcus went over and stroked her hair and face. He kissed her forehead, told her he loved her and sat down by the bed. Donnie did the same. The ventilator mask was fixed across her nose, a drip went into her arm as well as various cannulas for giving sedatives and antibiotics.

Alex explained quietly. "Her leg was shattered as it took the full force of the impact. It's now been pinned back together. It's suspended to avoid movement. Her abdomen's healing from the emergency caesarean. Plus she has a head injury. In order to allow her body to heal from so much trauma, she's in a medically induced coma and that'll be for a week at least."

Marcus held her hand.

Alex stepped back.

"Is she going to be okay?" Donnie whispered, voice breaking.

Amid the familiar sounds of ICU, Marcus closed his eyes. '*Will I walk his path? Am I beginning to understand his pain?*' Reaching

346

across to take his hand, Marcus replied, "Donnie all I know is that we need more than medicine, we need so much love and prayers."

CHAPTER 42 - STATEMENTS

Frank

Friday, 28th June 2019, was a bright, breezy, blue skyed day. St Wolbodo's was all finished with exams. Staff were endeavouring to engage their energetic students, whose thoughts were on nothing but the summer holidays. Streaming into school, the youngsters were all noise and nonsense. Freddie Stoney was bouncing along the main corridor on his way to his locker. At the top of his lungs he was singing, "Ding dong the witch is dead! Ding dong the witch is dead!"

Frank walked past, '*Of course this cacophony is caused by Stoney junior*' and turned to him, "That's enough of that thank you."

"Will you cry sir?" The thirteen-year old's eyes were glinting.

"What are you talking about Freddie?"

"Miss McAllister's dead sir."

"Don't be ridiculous, that's a truly awful thing to say, get to registration."

Frank shuddered at the grotesqueness of Freddie's comment.

As Frank reached his classroom, one of his inspirational quote posters reminded him, "There's no accounting for taste - *De gustibus non est disputandum.*" Freddie seemed to be more of a moral vacuum by the day. He decided not to share this comment with Noëmi as it sent a chill through him and he knew this was her last day before maternity leave. Settled at his desk, he opened his emails. Next, he checked through the schedule of the following two weeks where students would be off timetable, absorbed in '**complimentary studies**'. Frank sighed heavily as he composed a reply to get the spelling corrected.

'*Whilst I appreciate that these activities are indeed free, the only cost being the one taken on our teachers' mental health, their main purpose is to go along with our curriculum. The name should hence be corrected to complementary studies.*'

Moving from his computer, he noticed a small student come to his door and knock. He put down the rack of test tubes he was sorting out for his lesson and opened the door.

"Yes Daisy, how can I help?" Daisy promptly burst into tears.

"Whatever is the matter Daisy? If it's about the homework, why don't you and I come to an arrangement?" Frank ushered the student into his laboratory and sat her down.

"Miss McAllister's dead." Daisy's face crumpled.

Frank lurched forward onto his desk and took a second to absorb this comment.

"W...what? Who told you this?" He could hardly speak.

"That's what everyone in Year 8 is saying. Everyone in her tutor group is crying, apart from Freddie Stoney."

Finally, he composed himself enough to tell her, "Let me find out what's happened my dear," gesturing to one of her friends, waiting at the open door, to look after little Daisy.

Heart beating, skin sweating he rushed to the staffroom with terrifying thoughts that she had died in childbirth filling his head. Suddenly he bumped into Guy who was coming out of the Head Teacher's office. Frank gave a scream upon seeing Guy, assuming this confirmed Daisy's account. Guy looked ashen.

Frank became petrified. '*No, this has to be wrong.*'

"Guy, is everything okay?" Frank stammered, white with terror, dreading the reply.

"Frank, no, not at all, have you got a sec, can we go somewhere?"

"Oh my God, please don't say it's true!"

Guy explained what had happened and Frank struggled to comprehend. "But she's alive?"

"Yes, but critical on life support and the babies have been born, they're in intensive care but fine."

"And Marcus?"

"As you imagine, terrible. I've just spoken to the Head Teacher; he'll deal with it and explain to staff. However, students will be told that she's had the children but is unfortunately still unwell. I can tell you more when you come in to see her, we're all based over at RVI now."

"A child has just told me she's died!"

"What? But only the immediate family knows, even her grandparents have not been told anything yet. Hospital staff are not allowed to talk about their patients, they all know that."

Guy's brows were knitted in shock.

"Very odd, if I hear any more, I'll tell you."

"The worst thing is that we're pretty sure this was not an accident." Guy looked beyond Frank.

The investigation continued to find the car that had not stopped.

Noëmi's phone had been retrieved from the scene of the RTA. Having already obtained signed permission from Noëmi to investigate the anonymous messages, the police team was able to analyse it.

Guy got back to the station and saw Tariq going through papers on his desk.

"How's that CCTV footage looking?"

Tariq fidgeted. "Bad news, the camera on the crossing wasn't working, being fixed next week. No other CCTV in the area."

Guy banged the desk, "Will nothing go our bloody way! Tariq, what do the witness statements say?"

"Not much just that it was a small car, silver coloured."
Guy looked to the Heavens.

"Can we get them to look at some examples?"

"We did that but they all identified different models of car, nothing we can really go on."

As a grown man Guy had little reason to cry but now he was on the verge with sheer frustration. He walked to his desk, sat down and clenched his jaw.

"I need that car…"

He thought about the enormous job of going over CCTV from any cameras in the wider area leading to the crash site. All he had was the unlikely possibility that any footage would have picked up the car that none of the witnesses could recognise.

Time limped on; medical reports and numerous witness statements indicated that the actions of the driver were deliberate and yet no evidence, to identify the car, was giving itself up.

351

As Guy pursued the car, HR was pursuing Marcus. In an untimely display of efficiency, Marcus was summoned to a meeting to discuss Evan's allegations against him. Guy went directly to RVI to support Marcus in this meeting with Zena Walker. They were joined by Alex who had been called in as Marcus' line manager. Marcus was sitting in the same chair that Evan had occupied. He looked gaunt as he stared blankly at the cactus, cupping his face in his hands. Summer sang happily outside the blind covered window, via the chirping of a sparrow. Zena Walker opened the venetian blind with a scraping that scared off the small bird. All they could now hear was the low hum of traffic.

Zena

Before anyone spoke Alex asked.

"Is this really the right time to be doing this?"

Zena Walker gave a sympathetic shrug of the shoulders and explained.

"This is a serious case, when you read the victim's statement, we need to get this resolved. The accused could be a safeguarding threat to others in the hospital. I appreciate the timing is awkward, but the directive states that…"

"Let's be quick shall we?" Alex turned his head.

Zena got started.

"Dr McKenzie, thank you so much for coming to see me. DS Castle, Mr James thank you too for joining us. I appreciate this is a difficult time for you personally so I'll keep this brief. Evan St-John-Jones has given us the following statement. It's basically a transcript of her interview where she describes the allegations she's making against you. According to our HR procedures, I have to get a response within seven days, so the dead.., sorry, time limit is today, it's hospital policy."

Zena Walker, HR Manager, handed the men a typed copy of Evan's words, which they read in heavy silence. Guy commented sarcastically under his breath, "Poor Evan".

After a few more minutes of quiet Marcus spoke next.

"Yes that all looks about right, absolutely correct, there's just a couple of things." His voice was thin but firm.

Alex looked up confused. Guy was even more bemused.

"Alright what are they?" asked Zena smiling, delighted that this was making everything extremely easy for her. Indeed, '**agrees with statement**' was one of the options on her flowchart.

"If you change the 'he' to 'she' and alter the 'him' and the 'his' to 'her', then it's accurate and I can sign it as my own statement."

Guy smiled and added "Do you want to change the bit about men finding you attractive?"

"Not at all." Marcus shook his head.

Alex sent Marcus back to his vigil. He and Guy then gave Zena their own extensive statements in support of the true victim. The HR manager checked the '**Witness statements in support of a harassment case**' flowchart to see what to do next.

CHAPTER 43 - MY PLEASURE

Marcus

The medically induced coma had been brought to an end. Noëmi was moved to HDU (High Dependency Unit) as she had not yet regained consciousness. Another CT scan was planned for that week. Feeling tense at the thought of what it may reveal, Marcus tried to settle in a hospital chair next to her. Their lives were suspended but the outside world went on.

Alex visited and gently told Marcus he needed to respond to HR's query about his absence from work. In order to help, HR had moved Marcus onto compassionate leave so that he could take his paternity allowance later when Noëmi was recovered. However informal conversations were never enough and HR required formal execution of all procedures.

The flow diagram only allowed a week for '**serious illness in a family member**' so he had to extend the time. Of course Alex had endeavoured to do this but the HR directive required '**a communication from the affected party**'. Whilst this procedure had been established to prevent misuse of the policy, it was distressing in certain cases.

Marcus fully understood and moved to the neonatal ward. There he went onto his laptop to his emails to quickly sort it all out. Not having checked in well over a week, his inbox was overflowing. Ignoring the mass of communications, he quickly replied to HR and pressed send. He was about to shut his laptop when he noticed messages in his deleted items folder. Anyone who knew Marcus was aware how meticulous he was. He always cleared emails from his recycle bin and deleted items folder immediately. Suddenly as he clicked into this folder, he saw three messages from the evening of Thursday 27th June.

'I was working...nowhere near a computer...I never went on my email...what's this?

An email I never received and another one I never sent to Noëmi? And her reply...just before the accident...Oh God! No!' He cried to himself as he clicked them open.

The blood drained from his face. He looked at the time of the emails.

'Was this the last thing she saw? Had she believed all this. This is why she had got out of bed. This is why she was coming to the hospital. This is why she was hit by the car.'

Marianna was with him and was feeding Bruno and Emmanuelle. Marcus gave out an agonised scream and his laptop fell to the floor.

"My son! What's wrong?"

One of the babies began to whimper.

Marcus heard nothing.

He stood up, kicked the door open and marched along the foyer. Flinging open double doors and banging them shut he crashed along the corridors. Growing in stature with every step, he gave out a tortured cry. This figure of fury, striding forthright on his warpath, frightened all who saw him. As Marcus swung into the administration corridor, one of the nurses screamed and sprang against the wall to get out of his way. Seeing the blind anger on his face, she ran to the first telephone point she could find and called security. Throwing the door of the office open Marcus stormed in and stopped dead in front of her desk. He stared at her.

Evan

Evan was sitting at her desk behind two screens. One had her business emails and the other had her social media. The gentle buzz of building work was taking place in the background and the day was peeping through the soft grey venetian blinds. Evan was sipping a cappuccino and writing a list of what Marcus would like about her.

'*Firm breasts.*

Small waist.

White teeth.'

Marcus

Marcus, whole body shaking, eyes staring, screamed at her.
"Those emails! Those lies! Why did you do that? What kind of a demented evil low life does that?"

Hearing the disturbance, two of Evan's colleagues sprinted to the room and stood open mouthed as they saw Marcus looming before her.
Evan jumped back in her seat.
Marcus put his hands on the desk and leaned towards her. Face burning, cheeks shaking, voice gasping, he let her have it.
"Why can you not leave us alone? Do you know how much you've ruined my life? Do you see what you've done? Have you

sneaked up there to look? Are you planning to turn off the machines that are keeping her alive? Is that your next move? Does all this make you happy? Are you diagnosing yourself with that psychology book? Let me help you with that!"

He picked up the huge, unread book and flung it back down on the desk with a loud crack. He yelled at the top of his voice, "...dangerous, psychotic, social deviant with a fucking full on personality disorder, nothing borderline about it, it's the full fucking works, fully fucking loaded, there you go that should help you. You complete fucking bitch, you absolute fucking troll, you foul fucking witch. You need to be locked up, removed from society, not allow..."

"Mate, come on, leave it. Let's get back to the ward." Leo, an HCA friend who knew Marcus well, had seen him striding, incandescent, down the corridor. Amidst the gasps of the HR team, Marcus' fellow healthcare worker pulled him firmly out of the room. Evan sat, eyes wide, stunned at the display of searing emotion.

'*Good hair.*'

Marcus collapsed in the HCA's arms sobbing.

"Shhh mate, it's okay, we'll get this sorted, shhh, come on let's go." Leo reassured him. His colleague took his arm and led him back to the ward. Marcus walked lamblike beside him.

Guy

'*DS Castle we have another allegation against Dr McKenzie. He is now rampaging around the hospital and terrorising other staff members. Please can you come and deal with this as I believe it is a criminal offence. Zena Walker*'

Within the hour Guy appeared. Eventually finding Marcus feeding one of the babies, he and Tariq went to him. As Marcus gave Bruno the bottle, Guy saw he was stroking the baby's cheek with his little finger. The sight of this 'terrifying brute', as Zena had described him in her subsequent call to Guy, with his tiny child made Guy almost smile.

"You again! All of this is confusing my trainee. Okay not funny..."

Marcus was focused only on baby Bruno. Tariq looked on, doe eyed.

"An allegation of affray with possible intent to..." Tariq began but Guy gestured for him to stop. The policemen settled in the spare chairs and Guy took Marcus' laptop.

Guy logged on to look at the emails. Next, he took the account details and Marcus' laptop to start an investigation into who sent them and from which device. Tariq busied himself with the technology forensics permission forms.

Having packed everything away, Guy sat close to Marcus and stroked the baby's head, "Nice head of hair, but then you both..." Guy sighed, "...anyway you need to keep away from *whatshername* with all the hyphens. Your outburst is being put down to stress for now but it's supporting her version of events." He put his hand on his friend's shoulder, "I'll get this sorted, just focus on Noëmi. Right, Yumi's organised some knitted hats for the neonates, I just need to drop them off on the way out."

Marcus did not reply. He gently put little Bruno down, rearranging his cot to ensure he was comfortable. Next, he carefully picked up a restless Emmanuelle to feed her. As Guy left, he saw a tiny hand grasp Marcus' finger.

Unsurprisingly, later that day, Marcus was back in Zena Walker's office. Shutting the door behind them Zena sank into her big executive chair and popped a multi-coloured rug over her knees. Once behind her desk she rearranged her poncho and moved a number of thick information folders so that she could be seen. Sighing loudly, she looked over her glasses at Marcus, who was staring ahead not blinking. Also present was Alex who looked pointedly at his watch.

"Terribly difficult all of this, I understand this is a trying time..." Zena picked up her pen.

"Trying? No way! Really?"

"Marcus, not now." Alex put his hand on his arm to calm him.

"As I was saying, under the circumstances we can appreciate that you are under a great deal of stress. However, this does not mean that you can intimidate, threaten and verbally abuse a member of the RVI team. Is that clear?" Zena did not hide her exasperation. "The language reported was highly offensive and I'm not talking about the profanities. As a medical doctor you must be aware that mental health and psychological disorders are not fodder for your infantile tantrums. The hospital has been fully accommodating of your needs."

Seeing Marcus open his mouth, Alex jumped in, perfectly able to predict his mentee's upcoming reaction.

"Alright, I know Marcus is very grateful for the help. I think the stress has been a factor here and the police are investigating the actions of all parties involved. The lead investigator has just taken some devices for technology forensics."

Marcus did not look at anyone, but suddenly said. "I'll write a letter of apology."

"I don't think Ms St-John-Jones desires any ..."

"...to Alex James, here, it was wrong of me to let him down given all the support he's provided..."

"You know Dr McKenzie this case is still your word against Ms St-John-Jones. In spite of your friends' accounts of all your innocence, it's getting harder to distinguish between the perpetrator and victim. For now, I have to issue you with a warning to remain at least 20 metres from Ms St-John-Jones at all times."

"It'd be my pleasure." Marcus stood up and walked out the door.

Zena sighed again. "He really needs to watch it Alex, his professionalism is clearly being called into question here. If he continues to behave like a crazy madman, a deranged lunatic, we'll need to take serious action."

Alex stood up and grabbed his notes.

"Yes indeed, what was that you were saying about correct use of language?"

"If you read poor Evan's account, it's most distressing."

"It's all so out of character, but unfortunately no one prepares employees for dealing with the attempted murder of their entire family and the ensuing inconvenience of their partner lying in a coma. Maybe we should look at popping that training into our new starters' induction programme?"

Alex strode angrily out of the office and slammed the door behind him.

The HR manager flinched then sighed as she checked the **'Strained dialogue between colleagues'** flow chart to see what to do next.

* * *

As Marcus and Alex sat grim-faced before Zena Walker, Val joined Donnie's vigil at Noëmi's bedside. Looking at the numerous machines and monitors he evaluated the scene before him and took a deep breath. Donnie would chat quietly to Noëmi then he would stroke the parts of her face and head not covered with tubes. Val pulled a chair next to Donnie's.

"Ciao, come stai?"

Donnie put his hand on Val's shoulder and smiled weakly. Val put his arm around his friend.

Suddenly Donnie's mobile rang. "Hello!"

A burst of Italian followed. He handed the phone to Val.

"Pronto!" Val listened intently as the voice on the other end spoke without drawing breath.

Nodding and answering from time to time, Val began to take some notes. Suddenly the voice on the other end sounded shocked. Finally, he finished.

"Who was that?"

Val sat forward as he put the mobile back on the bedside table.

"You know when we were in Italy and the five of them helped save that little boy, Matteo?"

"Of course, yes."

"An Italian TV company's doing a documentary on people who, kind of come back from nearly dying…yeah." His voice faded as the two men's gaze turned to Noëmi lying before them.

"Anyway, they love the story of how Matteo was saved and wanted to get some interviews. I had to explain that given the situation it was not possible."

Donnie nodded and returned to his thoughts.

Suddenly his phone rang again. Val answered and a burst of Italian followed. Val went into discussions and left the room.

361

Eventually returning, he replaced the mobile and turned to Donnie.

"That was the film production company again. They have an agency in London. They want to help. They're suggesting a TV appeal to find the car."

Val looked at Donnie with his body hunched, eyes red, hair matted; this man had not slept in days. Val quickly added.

"Sorry, I wasn't thinking, it won't help her recovery. Forget it."

Donnie's dead eyes flickered.

"No Val, it's a great idea, we need to catch whoever's done this.

Help Guy's investigation."

Slowly nodding, Val thought some more. "They need your agreement Donnie, as the official next of kin."

"Marcus is really the one, who..."

"Neither of you will have to do anything, they're suggesting Guy. Whilst this is a wonderful offer, we do have to remember that the company could be making a whole documentary about the rescue and this. They're genuine but it's TV so they're all about the drama. The series is called Ricambia L'Amore..."

"I know it! N and I sobbed through an episode the other summer." Donnie gave something resembling a smile for the first time in weeks, "In English it's **Return the Love**."

"They'll not do anything yet, they just want to help with the appeal." Val rubbed his hands anxiously.

Donnie looked back at Noëmi.

"She was the one who saw little Matteo first. Whatever Matteo can do to help her is fine by me. Val, I can't lose her. I promised Manon I'd look after her. I swore that I'd protect her and keep her safe. It was Manon's only wish. If only I could take her place..." Donnie's shoulders shook as his body crumbled.

Val felt his eyes well up, his throat tighten and his heart get heavy. He put his hand on Donnie's. Presently, once Donnie was dozing quietly in his chair, he went to discuss the TV appeal project with Guy.

CHAPTER 44 - RICAMBIA L'AMORE

Alex

Personal suffering did not halt life marching forward. Sitting in his office with Zena Walker, Alex had to do the final arrangements for the Nigeria skills exchange.

"Jesse O'Donnell's already out in Nigeria. We're joining him on a video call as we need to go over the paperwork our staff need to take. Just give me a minute, I've got to open Marcus' spreadsheet." Alex, brow furrowed, clicked through his files. Zena prepared her notebook.

Jesse popped onto the screen.

"Hey Alex! How's it going? We're all ready for your doc and nurse practitioner! Exciting!"

"Hello Jesse, good to hear from you, what's the weather doing out in Sokoto?"

"One of our coldest months so only 33 degrees! Ha! Yeah but you need to tell them it's raining the whole time too!"

Alex saw the soles of Jesse's feet appear on the screen as he popped his feet on his desk and stretched back into his chair.

"Thank you Jesse, we've done the documents but I just wanted to check the paperwork they need to bring."

"Doc McK can tell you all that stuff!" Jesse gave a stretch.

Alex looked at Zena, "Unfortunately he's not on duty for a while…"

"Oh the baby! Of course, I wondered why I hadn't got this month's blog from Noëmi! Boy? Girl?"

"Twins, a boy and a girl."

"Nice one! How's she doing? Bet she's right on it knowing her!"

"Mmm did you not hear?" Alex's face was grim.

"Hear what?" Jesse put his hands behind his head.

"She's been involved in an RTA, hit and run, she's been in a coma ever since."

Jesse's soles disappeared from the screen. "What the fuck?"
Zena shot a look at the laptop.

"I know it's difficult. Prognosis is unknown. We're doing all we can. There's a TV appeal going out to catch the driver." Alex rubbed his chin with his hands, Zena lowered her glasses as Jesse now peered at them from the screen.
"What can I do?"

"The medically induced coma is done now, so it's a waiting game. It's hard to believe the babies came through. Makes you wonder if her whole being was willing that to be. Especially as she crashed in the trauma bay."

"God that's…" Jesse's head was in his hands.

"Jesse, do you want a minute?" Alex's voice was calming.

"Sorry, I'll get the team here to pray. They do that, I kinda believe it works, everyone knows her from last summer."

"Thank you." Memories of having to shock her filled Alex's mind. His hand trembled. In those heavy seconds as he had waited for her heartbeat to return, he had been praying too.

"We're friends, as you know, but I almost had a chance with her, we went on a couple of dates but it was a car crash, I was off the wagon and she was in love with Doc McK...sorry, Marcus, she always has been... car crash...yeah that's not good, I didn't mean to say that." Jesse was nothing but openness.

Zena gave the screen a disparaging look as she fidgeted with her hot pink mohair scarf.

"I thought they'd split up at that conf earlier this year. Turns out it was just that Evan woman hounding the dude the whole time. We all joked about it! She wouldn't leave him alone, desperately trying to get those shiny red nails into him. He had to escape to his brother's."

Pushing her glasses back, Zena moved her loose knit blanket back over her knees.

"Are you able to provide more details on his behaviour?" Zena asked in a nasally tone.

"Man, he was just doing his job, did a great keynote right? It was a bit of panic as he was all stressed about not having his phone. Evan volunteered to go get it for him. She was gone for a while. He was with me, he never did anything unprofessional. Apart from getting annoyed with Evan when she was putting her hands all over him at dinner. I'd have told her exactly where she could shove her hands, he's way too polite."

Zena asked, "Most helpful, could I get a statement from you?" Jesse agreed, paperwork was confirmed and the meeting was closed.

Gathering her blanket, notebook and Overseas' Visits folder, Zena's eyes met Alex's.

"We'll look at the whole range of evidence together and then go from there. It's disappointing to hear that he's been getting angry with her for a while now! Clearly she's been suffering in a climate of toxic masculinity."

"Zena, I need to borrow one of your trusty folders, it's the one entitled, *how to help your colleague get their head out of the sand*. Would that be a problem?"

Bristling, Zena removed herself from Alex's office.

Guy

Time dragged on; it was now ten days since Noëmi and her unborn twins had been mown down. For Guy, this was an eternity. The CCTV from the routes leading to Osborne Road gave nothing of interest; so many cars at that time and no vehicle make to go on. All the witnesses could say was that it was a silver car that went through the red light and hit Noëmi. The fellow pedestrian on the crossing stated that she had definitely heard a car speed up. Unfortunately, she had no idea what the car looked like, she said she had only heard it 'rev its powerful engines.'

Sunday, 7 July 2019.

Having found out about the attack on Noëmi, the Italian production company had contacted their UK team to see if they could help. Everyone knew that news passed quickly; today's traumas were soon tomorrow's trivia. Budgets and the sheer number of cases meant it was impossible to launch media appeals for all investigations.

Guy agreed a televised plea for help could help enormously.

The TV production crew arrived within the hour. Suddenly a large meeting room seemed tiny. Boxes of equipment, multiple crew members and constant chatter filled the space. Guy was to give a TV appeal to find the car.

"Right Guy, you've got your script?" The Production Assistant was doing the final checks.

"Don't need it, I've learnt it all,"

"Amazing, I love it! If only everyone else we filmed took it as seriously as you do!"

"I want to look behind the eyes as it were. Catch the bastard,"

"That's what it's all about, results! Sundays are great days to reach a big audience. Ah no swearing on prime time though Guy. Lots of little old ladies!"

An assistant put some powder on Guy's face.

"Do I need that?"

"TV can be cruel, Guy!"

"Right, we're ready to roll," the camera operator called out and the filming began.
Guy looked into the lens.

"On the night of Thursday 27th June, at around 5:45pm, a heavily pregnant woman was deliberately knocked down by a silver car. She was legitimately using a pedestrian crossing and we know from witnesses that the car sped up and intentionally hit her. It was a clear attempt to murder the young woman and her unborn twins. The silver car would no doubt have some kind of damage, given the speed at which it hit the victims. We are appealing for anyone with any information to come forward."

* * *

Donnie and Marcus were at Noëmi's side talking as Tianna sat with the babies.

"Today is Manon's birthday. Noëmi's like her mother, they both hate missing out on things. I remember when N was six, Manon and I went to celebrate the new millennium with friends in Edinburgh. Noëmi was desperate to come with us. She kept stamping her foot to be allowed to join. 31st December 1999 was the end of a century, actually a millennium right?"

A cough and a voice distorted by a tube, "Wrong... day..."

They looked round and although her eyes were still shut, she had spoken.

"Noëmi?" Marcus said softly.

Donnie rushed to alert the nurse. Alex James arrived. Gently they removed the tube from her mouth.

"...two thou...sand ... not new mil......" Her eyes still shut.

Marcus touched her face gently. "Can you open your eyes?"

"... slee...ping."

"Okay, just rest, you're in hospital."

Suddenly she was more lucid, eyes open.

"Alex...keeps saying...stay with me Noëmi...come on, stay with me, please come on Noëmi, please..."

Gently her eyes closed.

Alex gave a cough, "Sounds good, typical post coma confusion but with enough cognitive ability and knowledge for us to be extremely hopeful. For her it's like a weird dream, the main thing is she's talking about real things and seems to know who you are."

"Alex, I don't know how to thank you, there are not the words to give it justice, especially as I know what it must have taken..."

They both fixed their gaze on Noëmi.

Alex brushed his cheek. He gave Marcus a pat on the shoulder. "We're all good, and she's right about the millennium thing, but obviously only a few of us maths geeks really cared about that!"

Monday, 8 July 2019.

The sunny day outside did not reflect Guy's mood as he sat in his office playing the 1010 game on his mobile. Mindless clicking was supposed to help him forget, but as the puzzle blocks mounted up, they only reminded him of the actual brick wall he was facing with this investigation. He took a sip of his coffee and grimaced as it had gone cold. Jolted out of his trance he wondered how long he had been playing on his phone. Would the appeal work? Nothing had come in overnight. Was the news and the case already cold? Deciding to stretch his legs, he went into the main office area. Sighing, he moved to get ready to meet his team and think about what they could do next. Going into the open plan office he recognised the unfamiliar sound of people laughing, something he had not heard in the last couple of weeks.

The team were huddled around a computer screen enjoying a video of a driver 'freaking out', as one colleague put it. Guy looked over and smiled. Tariq stood to attention.

"Very silly," he said, but Guy gestured to him not to worry. Looking over their shoulders he could see the road user apoplectic with rage. Walking away a thought came to him,

"Tariq, that video, how's it recorded?"

"It's from a dashcam, Guy, DashCam Dramas on the web, people upload their funny dashcam footage…bit immature really, sorry, we were…"

"Tariq that's it, hunting in his pocket he pulled out a card and called the number."

Within minutes he was on his way to see the taxi driver who had been due to pick up Noëmi that evening. His car was a typical taxi with the yellow fir tree air freshener, but it also had cameras anywhere and everywhere. Having been shocked by what he had witnessed, he had kept a copy of his dashcam footage. Assuming the police would have all sorts of CCTV at their fingertips; he had never thought to let Guy know about his recording. With much gratitude Guy took the video from the driver and went back to the investigation centre to review the footage.

Tariq got on with downloading the file and then called out, "Look at this!"

The team crowded round to watch the video, which clearly showed the silver-coloured car speed up towards the pair of pedestrians. Noëmi had avoided taking the impact full on, but was clearly dealt a severe blow; slamming to the ground by the force of the speeding car. Having now seen the incident Guy sat down for a minute. Tariq noticed and asked quietly.

"Are you okay?"

"Yeah, it's just not easy to see whoever the victim is, but worse when… yeah, we now know it was definitely a deliberate act, thank God they survived."

"How's the mother doing?"

"'Still in a coma, no longer medically induced...but Tariq... I know that car!"

"We're checking owners of all this type of vehicle in the area and we should have a reading of the last part of the number plate any minute now."

"Good work, but I know that car. Tariq." Guy thought hard. Suddenly it came to him. He scribbled some details on a piece of paper and handed them to Tariq. "We need to pick up this person urgently. Let's go!"

Grabbing his keys and phone, Guy was readying to leave.

371

A call came through to Tariq's desk. Guy was impatient.

Tariq listened and related the call to his mentor.

"Guy, hold on, a call's come through with some information following the appeal!"

Tariq took notes. Guy hovered.

Finally putting the phone down, Tariq studied the information before him.

"Guy, it's the same address!"

Tariq took another call, "Guy, some kid's been on the phone and gave us a name. Do you think it's a prankster? They rang off straight away!"

Guy looked at the name before him.

"Tariq, same name! Let's move, now!"

CHAPTER 45 - HERE TO HELP

Alex

Over the next ten days Noëmi continued to make progress. Similarly the babies grew stronger and no longer needed to be in hospital. The support system worked well with either Donnie or Marcus at Noëmi's side day and night. By now her four grandparents had travelled to Newcastle to help.

The A&E department had returned to near normality with a locum standing in for Marcus. One morning Alex was enjoying a relatively stress-free moment. Standing at the front desk of his department he was sipping a coffee, chatting to the receptionist.

"Tuesday nine am a bit early for all the A&E madness," he commented with a wry smile. He looked through the cases from the evening before and was deciding which ones he needed to follow up. In an instant, an apparition came before his eyes.

"Good grief!"

Marcus, dishevelled, dressed in hospital scrubs appeared at the main desk.

"Alex, I can work today, I've had too much time off." Marcus was fidgeting around picking up papers and clipboards.

The receptionist, mouth open, gazed between them.

"Time off? You mean like you've been on a holiday!" Alex said with kind sarcasm.

"I need to help here. Do my job." Disoriented, he looked round.

"Where on earth did you get those scrubs?" Alex stifled a guffaw.

"The machine. Where's the patient list?"

Penelope hurried past with some cannula packs, stopped suddenly, dropped half of her load; her face aghast at the sight before her eyes.

"Sorry you're going to be of no use to us here, you should be

back up in that high dependency unit with Noëmi. She's the one who needs you now." Alex exhaled deeply. He put his hands on Marcus' shoulders and turned him round.

"But I've had so much time off, I need to pull my weight." Marcus attempted to rotate back and was trying to stretch his arm out to get the patient list clipboard.

"You know what Marcus, when she's better, you just tell me all

those extra shifts you want and you'll be more than welcome,

for now I'm taking you back up to Noëmi. Let's go!" Alex now

had his arm around his colleague's shoulders and was walking him back to the ward. Blankly Marcus stared ahead. On his return, Alex stopped off at the well-being hub and discreetly organised some more support for his colleague.

* * *

Donnie

One morning Donnie was woken by Noëmi's guttural screams. Rushing to her bed, she was thrashing her head violently from side to side and her body was shaking. For a minute she tried to speak.

"N, it's okay, you're in hospital, shhh," he tried to calm her. Her hand clawed onto his. Finger nails tore his skin.

"The babies are dead aren't they? That's why I'm here? Tell me..." Her voice rasped. Her eyes were wild.

"No, no they're fine, they're alive, N, they're three weeks old." He gently held her hand and felt her relax, she began to sob.

"You're lying!" she howled and started trying to get out of bed. Dislodging two of her monitors a nurse rushed in to help Donnie.

"Shhh no, N, they're fine, doing so well, they're with Marianna."

"What? Why Marianna?" Her voice curdled. Her head flung itself from side to side. Muttering incoherently for a few moments she suddenly screamed, "Marcus is dead?" She tried to sit up but fell back onto her pillow as her visceral pain echoed throughout the ward. Together the nurse and Donnie held her as she convulsed.

"No, no he's here, looking after you. I'll get him."

Donnie left his daughter being comforted by the nurse. Stumbling over a treatment trolley, he ran to fetch Marcus. It was time for her to meet her children.

Marcus

Still moaning and giving small sobs, Noëmi was clutching the nurse's hand. The door opened and Marcus arrived backwards with the pram. Straining her neck to see, he saw her eyes regain their life as she saw them all.

"Marcus!" she stretched her hand to reach him.

"You need to meet these two. Here they are, a boy and a girl. Bruno and Emmanuelle, I just took the names from the top of your list. They were my favourites too, they're three weeks now, they've grown so much, we've videoed everything for you. That was Yumi's idea!"

"Our babies!" She leant her hand out trying to touch them. "I...I don't remember giving birth, what happened?"

"I'll explain everything, just have a cuddle with these two first, I'll take some pictures?"

She nodded, breathless with joy as she looked at her children.

"I can't believe it, we're parents! They're so perfect!"

"They are but they cry all the time and at different times! Those lungs are overdeveloped! I've had enough! They need their mum!" He handed her the first baby.

"Here you go! Over to you!"

The nurse had the biggest grin on her face as she left the room. Numerous arrangements were made to get the new McKenzie family home to their flat in Newcastle. Noëmi's leg was in a brace and it needed to be laid flat. She went home with a barrage of crutches, sticks and a wheelchair. Marcus soon realised they would not be able to go outside all together as he could not push a double pram and a wheelchair at the same time. None of these wheeled devices would get up the three steps leading to their flat so he had to make numerous journeys transferring babies into car seats and Noëmi onto a sofa, then bringing all the equipment up behind. All he could say to himself was, *'there's no way life could get any more logistically challenging, but I don't care one bit. They're all here with me.'*

* * *

Guy

Back at the police station, the digital and technology forensics team met Guy with their analysis of the emails sent from and to

376

Marcus' accounts that Thursday evening. Given that Marcus had been in work, with a number of witnesses, it was soon found that another user had logged onto his email. The location of the computer used to do this was found to be in the Newcastle area. As his colleagues were leaving, they added.

"Also, those anonymous text messages you asked us to look at came from a mobile registered at a Durham address. We have that report here too."

"Thank you, that clears it all up. We'll get a car to pick up the residents," Guy now understood exactly what had happened. Looking over the reports he could picture the series of events.

* * *

Thursday, 27 June 2019.

Kit

Thursday afternoon, Kit was pumped up. Grabbing his mother's car keys, he jumped in the car. '***On my way Jude!***' he texted as he took a bend at speed.

Pulling up outside St Woldbodo's he waited, engine revving.

Jude appeared and jumped into the passenger's side.

"Exams finished then?"

"Yeah, I've failed the lot, wrote nothing in that maths exam." Jude threw his head back.

"That'll show those stupid teachers, right let's go and get fucked up!" Kit's voice was excited.

Off they drove, music blaring, towards Newcastle looking for amusement.

Rolling along the pair exchanged gaming tips and jokes. Next, they pulled up in a local field where they smoked a couple of joints. Windows open, the orange glow of the late afternoon bathed them in warmth and light. The soft sound of birdsong was all around.

"This is stronger than the usual stuff, a special celebration!"

"It's calm!"

The boys chatted as they watched the low red sunset shimmering over the golden wheat field as they got wasted. They strolled back to the car and set off with nowhere to go.

Noëmi

Thursday late afternoon, Marcus had just left for work. Brow furrowing, Noëmi was sitting in bed with her laptop in front of her huge pregnancy bump. Having chosen names she had logged on to check what she needed to do for her maternity leave. Her arms were aching from stretching past her stomach. Emails from Marcus sent that evening jumped out at her. He had forwarded them to her personal email from his work account. All the communications he had sent were about his paternity leave.

She started to click through them in case there was some reason she needed them.

'Dates submitted to HR, that's the same as he told me, what's this one?

Ah information in case of illness or complication, God don't want to think about that. What's this?'

Her back was feeling the strain. There was one more email from Marcus:

'N I'm running out of time, it's easier if you just log onto my work emails and pick out the ones you need, you know the email address and the password is M&N26810.'

"Makes sense, although he didn't need to write out the password, he knows I know the usual one!" she said to herself as she logged on.

Now she could see all his emails. The most recent one jumped out at her.

'*Dr McKenzie - Sexual misconduct tribunal*', she cried out "What's going on!"

Looking at the email it had been sent to Marcus from **HR Gen user RVI.**

Dr McKenzie,

You are aware of the ongoing cases against you. On the one hand these relate to sexual misconduct on your part towards a number of female staff members. We have now examined the testimony of each complainant. The hospital board has confirmed that owing to the extremely serious nature of these allegations that further action must be taken. Therefore the police will take over. Criminal charges are more than likely to follow.

The other cause for concern, for which the hospital board wishes to discipline you, is your continued misuse of contracted working time and hospital accommodation to pursue sexual affairs, albeit consensual, with a number of colleagues.

We appreciate that you are about to go on paternity leave but you are to report to an extraordinary meeting tonight at 6pm in the **HR Director's** office. During this we will go through the official warning process. This will be on your employment record, along with the warning you received in February, following your conduct at the London conference.

HR Manager Z Walker."

Babies kicking, heart pounding she began to burn up. Tears streaming down her face, she tried to call him. No reply.

'Marcus would never do that! Tianna told me to check if he had work problems! Bri said something was going on too! Is this what she meant? Dad said, talk, don't assume. I need to see Marcus, sort this out. There's some mistake. He would never do anything like this. I have to get to this meeting; I must speak out for him. I have to defend him!'

Quickly she tried to ring Marcus again. No reply.

'I'm on my way to the meeting.' She replied to Marcus' email quickly.

'If I hurry, I can get to the hospital in time.'
Hauling herself round, she caught her breath. Holding onto the headboard she strained to pull herself out of bed. As quickly as she could she put on the maternity dress she had laid out for her last day of work. Now the evening was cooler she grabbed a light coat and her handbag and headed out. Feeling scared she sent her father a message.

'Dad something's wrong with Marcus, I'm going to the hospital, plse call, I'm upset.'

She knew it was badminton practice and he probably would not see the message for a bit.
Ambling slowly along she could feel the weight of her pregnancy pushing down on her pelvis. Arms protectively over her bump she made laboured progress. There was no time to find a lift.

'Guy's working, Anthony's on lates, I'll get a cab.' Reaching Osborne Road, she saw her taxi waiting for her on the other side of the road. She waved to the driver and stood at the crossing waiting for the green light.

Kit

"Woo hoo! Newcastle needs us," the boys raced along Osborne Road aiming for the city centre. Kit was doing a steady thirty on the residential road in spite of being stoned.
Approaching the crossing he saw a woman waiting.

"Fuck it's that snitch McAllister, she got me banned from rowing."

"She got my mum banned from the school premises. Isn't she about to spawn?"

"That or she's just fat!"

"Buzz the hell out of her! Put your foot down for the bantz!"

Kit revved his car to speed up. Suddenly time stopped. '*Her fiancé saved my life. It's not right. I can't!*'

Kit began to swerve to avoid her.

"Get her!" Jude's cold hand grabbed the wheel.

Kit wrestled it back.

"Jude no!" Kit swung the car away from her.

Hearing the car Noëmi froze. She threw herself forward, twisting onto her back. Her right leg took the full blow of the weaving car as it sped past. Landing on her back she held her stomach. Her head carried through and hit the tarmac with a thud.

"No!" Kit screamed.

"Her fault for not getting out of the way!"

"Jude, we need to stop, get an ambulance!" Kit's voice shook, he clenched the wheel.

"Are you mad? We'll get arrested. Drive!"

Kit began to tremble. Suddenly feeling very sober he looked in his back mirror to see another driver go to her. '*God what kind of a monster am I?*' Memories flashed through his mind of Marcus treating him at RVI. '*Christopher stay with us! Come on. Christopher, we need you.*' Christopher's skin was clammy. '*He saved me. Everyone wants the best for me.*' Other voices began to fill his head, his teacher. '*If I didn't care about you, I'd let you do what you liked!*' The policeman, '*We value you and I'm not giving up on you.*' He saw his mother's love for him in her eyes as he screamed in her face. His father's quiet pain as they drove back from Oxford. Now his tears were unstoppable.

'*I didn't want to hurt her. The baby! What the fuck have I done?*'
The silver car sped off down Osborne Road.

Donnie

Thursday evening and Donnie was feeling splendid. Now he had won the last of the qualifying matches and was into the knockout stages of the Heaton Leisure centre badminton tournament.

"Well done Donnie! You get stronger by the minute! Not sure what you're taking but it's working!" His opponent joked, shaking his hand and patting him on the back.

"Ah, just good living! And plenty of practice! You know I've been a member here for nearly nine years! Thanks for the game!" Unable to stop smiling, he showered and relived a few shots he was particularly proud of, recalling how his opponent could not get anywhere near them. Drying his hair with a towel he checked his phone.

"N! What's this? In labour maybe?" He gasped. His skin tingled with excitement.

Reading the message, he took a deep breath! '*Oh my, what's happened to Marcus? He's so fit and healthy? Maybe he's been attacked in A&E! That documentary the other day showed how dangerous it can be on the frontline! I need to get there.*'
Feeling his heart race, he prepared himself speedily to go straight to the hospital.

Ultimately the TV appeal had done its job. By Monday 8 July two arrests had been made.

Having been told by Jude what had happened that night Freddie Stoney had thought it was all a big joke. Like one of his video games, '*extra points for a teacher!*'

Freddie had watched the Sunday night appeal with wide eyes. Feeling sick he realised that it was real people.

'*I want that secret out of my head. It's freaking me out.*'

Freddie resolved to merely '*forget about it*' when a memory flooded his brain of the last time he had been this frightened.

'*Miss McAllister, she put her arm out and saved me from walking into the path of that car, when we were in France on that school trip.*'

Freddie looked at the number at the bottom of the screen and memorised it. He used the technique his tutor, Miss McAllister, had taught him to remember long numbers. The next day he delivered the name of the car owner in a brief, nerve wracked call, made in the school toilets, during morning break.

Rufus

Rufus Deehan was ordering Italian marble tiles for his new ensuite bathroom when he saw two police cars draw up to his front drive. Pressing the button to open the gates, he sighed to himself, wondering whether they had done the right thing. He remembered clearly having to book the car in to have a dent repaired on Friday 28 June. Christopher had given no explanation and simply said, '*We think we knocked over a deer.*'

Bothered by this Rufus had wondered how many deer he had ever seen in Newcastle city centre.

The TV appeal had been compelling. Christopher had watched it with him and had begun to sob hysterically. "I tried to avoid her! I swerved! Then Jude…"

Held by his father he confessed. Together they sat as Rufus made the call.

'Have we done the right thing? Of course we have. If I love my son, it would

be the only thing I could ever do.'

Letting the officers in, they unsurprisingly asked to speak to Christopher and also to look over their silver-coloured sports car. Two officers took statements from the parents about their movements on the night of 27 June 2019. Silently Christopher was arrested.

Guy

Tariq was looking at statements. Swivelling left and right on his chair, hands on his head he knotted his brow. "Guy it just makes no sense, why would Christopher Deehan want to harm Noëmi McAllister. Why did he go for her? What made him want to drive his car into her?"

"Christopher Deehan?"

"Looking at the witness statements Jude Stoney states she *'got Kit*

banned' but from where?"

"The rowing club, remember I went with her to report Deehan for the drugging of Tianna McKenzie."

"Ah that's why, Kit and Christopher, the same person…of course

they are, Jesus is there no one in that family he's not harmed?"

Tariq banged his hands on his desk.

Guy sat stupefied and looked at the two charge sheets in front of him.

Prosecution charges for suspect A:

- Attempted voluntary manslaughter of persons known to them.
- Actual bodily harm.

- Driving whilst intoxicated.
- Administering GHB with the intent to commit sexual assault.

Mitigation
- High on drugs so not in complete control of senses.
- Urged on by a third party.
- Third party took control of car.
- Evasive actions.
- Genuine remorse.
- Prepared to plead guilty to a lesser charge.

Prosecution charges for suspect B:
- Inciting another to commit attempted voluntary manslaughter of persons known to them.
- Actions contributing to the attempted voluntary manslaughter.

Mitigation
- Age 17 years.
- High on drugs so not in complete control of senses.

There was one more charge sheet being completed. All would make it to prosecution.

Guy handed the sheets to Tariq, who poured over them intently. Moving to the window of the office Guy stared out at the road. Life trundled on; cars queued, the odd pedestrian sauntered past and a couple of cyclists weaved in and out of the traffic.

"I should've pushed to get Deehan held in custody." Guy was pale. "If I had then…"

"No Guy, don't do this to yourself. There was no evidence that he was a threat. And definitely not enough proof that it was even him who put the drug into Tianna's drink, there were twenty odd youngsters at the barbecue. Remember, I was there when the Superintendent refused the order. *You* keep telling me about the burden of proof."

Nodding reluctantly, Guy continued to observe life's monotonous progress, "Why are people like that Riqqi?"

"Dunno Guy, everything's always someone else's fault!"

Tariq began to gather the papers together.

"They're too young to throw their lives away, but first they must accept they've done wrong." Feeling more optimistic, Guy smiled at Tariq. "Are you coming for a drink later?"

Tariq gave a thumbs up and they closed their files.

Guy headed off to pick up Yumi. He told her about the arrests as they got to their flat.

"Deehan? Has he got a brother? It was a Deehan who made fun of my name and made those vicious comments to me in my first class at Mountford."

"First name?"

"Christopher'

"Kit is a shortened version of Christopher, they're one and the same, no surprise there."

"He was sent down from Oxford within two weeks of starting, that's why he was back in Durham. Possession and unproven administering of GHB to two fellow students. No case could be brought because of a lack of evidence." Yumi explained. "It was felt kicking him out of Oxford was bad enough. A fall from grace."

"Indeed, we have a number of new lines of inquiry. Plus he's confessed to drugging Tianna. There *is* a seed of hope. His remorse seems genuine. He's taken full responsibility for his actions." He was wringing his hands, she took them in hers.

She kissed him, "Be still. You've got justice."

PART FOUR – RECKONINGS

Je ne te quitterai pas - Le Petit Prince - Antoine de Saint-Exupéry

CHAPTER 46 - IT'S US!

Noëmi

Guy and Tariq went to visit Noëmi and Marcus at their flat once they were settled back in. The front room was arranged with two navy carry cots, two yellow changing mats and multi-coloured baby changing bags, neatly lined up next to one another. Babies fed and settled, the new parents were ready for their visitors.

"These babies are so cute. Can I hold one?"

"Tariq, they're not pet rabbits!" Guy said.

"Sorry Guy, kind of forgot we have a job to do, but look how tiny they are!"

Guy grinned, "No they're lovely, here pass one over! Which one's this he teased?"

"Emmanuelle."

"My girlfriend's keen to start a family," Tariq explained. "I think I need to get qualified first but seeing these two makes me want to be a dad."

"Yumi and I will be doing things the right way round, you know, wedding first," Guy gave Noëmi a wink.

She threw a soft toy fluffy chick at him which jingled as it bounced on his shoulder.

"Tariq arrest her for assaulting an officer, will you!" His eyes twinkled.

The two uniformed men cuddled the tiny infants and a good ten minutes was spent passing them between each other. Finally, Guy and Tariq put the babies back in their cots and began their work. Tariq kept stealing glances at the children.

"We're here in a formal capacity to let you know where we are with the investigation." Guy began very professionally. "Thank you for allowing us into your home."

"Guy?... it's us…you and Yumi spend most of your time here!" Marcus looked incredulously at his best friend who just turned up whenever he wanted, knew exactly what was in the fridge and actually had a key.

"Only doing my job," Guy replied defensively.

"Shall I do this then Guy?"

"Sure, go for it Tariq."

"Right Marcus, Noëmi, let us take you through the events of Thursday 27th June. Noëmi you received an email from Marcus that prompted you to get out of bed to go to RVI."

"But it wasn't from him, was it?"

"Correct. It was Evan St-John-Jones who logged onto Marcus' email account from her home at about 5:15pm. Marcus was dealing with a basketball player who'd got a finger in the eye, sounds nasty that, was he alright?"

Guy gave Tariq an old fashioned look.

Noëmi shut her eyes and grabbed Marcus' hand.

"Anyway, the IP address confirms it was her. Marcus, she noted your password when she sat next to you on the train going to the conference in London. She sent those fake emails to and

389

from your account. Noëmi replied and next Evan deleted all the emails. As we know emails never go away! Noëmi you then got up to go to RVI. By chance Christopher Deehan and Jude Stoney were high, having smoked a few joints and were cruising to Newcastle when they spotted you, Noëmi they decided quite deliberately to frighten you, but knocked you down. They hit you at fifty miles per hour."

Marcus looked away.

"Why?"

Tariq replied, "Deehan blamed you, not his dreadful actions, for getting him banned from The Wear Rowing Club. He was high so we have to go for attempted involuntary manslaughter.

However, that's for two lives as he admits he knew that you were pregnant."

Marcus' face said what he did not.

Guy took over, "I picked him up last year, suspected drug driving but results were clear. Then his mother told us he nearly died last year when he overdosed on GHB, he was treated at RVI..."

Marcus realised, "Oh my God, now I remember. It was me, I got him back, he was half dead...self-administering GHB, we put him on a rehabilitation programme..."

Noëmi added, "That's such a weird chain of events..."

Tariq went on, "I'm afraid there's more. In the car with Deehan was a Jude Stoney. You taught him maths and his brother Freddie is in your tutor group Noëmi."

"Him?"

Guy replied, "I know, this is also difficult to hear. I understand from witness statements that Freddie is a disruptive student and that you have had to speak to his mother on a number of occasions."

"Yes, but I have dealt with everything according to school policy, nothing's personal."

390

Tariq explained. "Yes, but at home the mother has been constantly bad mouthing you. The oldest Stoney boy also recognised you. It seems Deehan changed his mind and swerved to avoid you. It was Jude who took the wheel and aimed the car at you."

Noëmi cried for the first time. "All I was doing was my job."

Guy held her hand as he explained. "Noëmi, you've done nothing wrong. Mrs Stoney has a record for actual bodily harm against a primary school teacher. She held that teacher up against the wall by his neck, calling him all sorts of unpleasant things because he put Freddie into a behaviour support group. Another teacher, at St Wolbodo's, received a cake baked with some unpleasant ingredients."

"Never eat anything homemade!" Tariq added wisely.

"Stoney is facing incitement to cause actual bodily harm." Guy finished.

Marcus asked "Which one, the boy or the mum?"

Tariq agreed, "Ah yes indeed, the boy this time!"

Noëmi said, "The weirdest set of coincidences ever!"

Guy added, "Like finds like. However, there are more things."

Marcus was incredulous.

Guy finished, "There's an offence under the Malicious Communications' Act. Those anonymous texts, they were courtesy of Mrs Stoney. Freddie and Jude's mother."

Noëmi's head fell forward. "So much hate...how did she get my mobile number?"

"It seems you gave it to her by accident. When you wrote your work telephone number for her on a slip of paper from your handbag..."

"...my change of address slips...did she send all those brochures too?" Her voice was breaking.

391

Sighing Guy finished. "No, the mysterious leaflets were courtesy of Evan St-John-Jones. She's up for harassment, invasion of privacy, infliction of emotional distress, cyber bullying, computer misuse and anything else we can get to fit. She'll have a record, lose her job, but won't go to jail. Since she's confessed, that's all a given."

Marcus fell back in his chair, "I'm exhausted just listening to this. Plus we mustn't forget what Tianna went through."

Tariq agreed, "Absolutely not. That'll be a separate trial for Deehan. We're hoping he just pleads guilty."

Guy then leant forward. "Noëmi do you remember anything about the accident."

"Not really, I remember seeing the green light to cross, then nothing."

"As you saw the car coming you moved quickly. You twisted onto your back to protect your pregnant stomach."

Marcus gave her a squeeze.

Tariq finished up, "The appeal worked. Deehan confessed. Also, a kid rang with the name but we couldn't trace that number, it was too quick."

"I'm pretty sure it had to be Freddie Stoney. He knew about the accident before it was public knowledge. That's my hunch."

Noëmi looked reflective.

Tariq smiled. "You didn't do anything wrong; it was extremely bad luck. Dominoes falling over."

They thanked Tariq who then left, having had one more cuddle of each baby.

"Where are they all now?"

Guy told them, "Deehan's being held. Stoney, Mrs Stoney and St-John-Jones are on bail but all have restraining orders against going anywhere near you both. In spite of their actions, they're remorseful, obsessive behaviour got out of control. St-John whatsit is showing a great deal of contrition. Although her tears seem a bit for herself. However, as with all offenders we need to offer the chance for rehabilitation and support their eventual reintegration into society."

Marcus nodded reluctantly.

"Three, two, one... 6pm and now I'm off duty." Guy looked at his watch and undid his top button "What a bunch of whackos, I'd lock them all up in a room together for eternity and throw away the key if I could. Damn waste of tax payers' money spent on defending all these fucking low lives who aim cars at pregnant women. That conniving bitch at your hospital's not much better, she knew you were pregnant too."

"I love how spectacularly you turn into the voice of angry Britain once that shift is over!" Marcus laughed.

"Sorry I didn't mean to swear in front of the babies, that was bad! Don't want them exposed to all that!" Guy covered the ears of the nearest baby with his fingers.

"You need to take your Godparent duties carefully in future!" Noëmi added.

"Oh really?"

"We thought you and Yumi, plus Alex and Cathy, would be great Godparents to our son because obviously we want him to turn out like you. Sarai, Lucia, Frank and Val to our daughter..."

"Because you want her to turn out like Frank!" Guy grinned.

"Could be a lot worse!"

Marcus handed Guy a beer and for a minute he was lost in thought, "Actually, Guy, what are you doing the bank holiday weekend, Saturday the 24th?"

393

"I'm off that weekend because it was your wedding, but I'm not babysitting, I'll be out out!"

Marcus laughed "No, I'm not stupid, but can you be my best man?"

He turned to Noëmi, "If your dad was holding you how far could you walk then?"

"I don't know maybe a few steps, but I'd need help."

"Actually, you need to weight bear on that leg now, so I think we should keep that date and get married. I don't want to wait until next year."

"Yes! We'll give everyone a great party to say thank you for all they've done for us."

That agreed, they busied themselves with the necessary arrangements.

* * *

Tianna

15 August 2019, A Level results' day had arrived. Having a break from work, babies and hasty wedding arrangements, Marcus picked up Tianna from his parents' home. She shot out of the front door, tugged open the car door and jumped inside. Staring ahead, her face was frozen in terror.

"Just go!" She put her feet on the glove box.

"Why can't Mum and Dad come? McKenzies always go en masse." Marcus looked inquiringly.

"I'm too nervous, I think at this moment I would rather die than get my results. I can only feel my feet when I stand up, my legs have gone." Her hands were shaking.

"I remember feeling like that too, but you'll be the first McKenzie to get results without the whole clan present. I hope that's not a bad omen."

"Stop scaring me! Okay they can come." She threw her arms in the air. Marcus beckoned at the rest of the family, all standing in the hallway, to join them. Marianna, Anthony, Raeni and Isaiah grabbed their jackets and ran to their car. The convoy departed. They heard their mother shout, "Anthony get Jayden on video chat!"

"This McKenzies assemble is the worst ever!" Tianna's voice was almost screaming.
Arriving at Newcastle Green, Marcus gave her some water and told her to breathe. They walked through the grey school gates. The hall was a mass of bubbling excitement. Messages started pinging through to Tianna's mobile.

'Yay! Going to Oxford to study MEDICINE!!!' Louisa sent.

'I'm off to Oxford Brookes :) but I kinda already knew that!' Joel replied.

Marcus took her phone from her. Tianna's whole body was trembling. Her head filled with images of Joel and Louisa, all dressed in white, sitting in a punt on the river, falling in love with each other. Within seconds they were drinking champagne, feeding each other strawberries and exchanging rings.

The system had not changed in the eight years since Marcus had picked up his results. Tianna lined up in the M queue with Marcus at her side; the rest of her family waiting further back with the other relatives. Isaiah got Jayden on a video call. Some teachers came and chatted with Marcus, pleased to see him. His and Noëmi's Oxbridge success and then Jayden's two years later, had really changed the school's image. Tianna got to the blue melanin table as one of the admin team looked through the envelopes for hers. Hand shaking, she took it and passed it straight to her brother.

"I can't look."

Marcus

Marcus did not want to either but he opened the envelope.

He smiled. "You're going to Oxford to study biology! Congratulations!"
Tianna fainted. Amidst the gasps and shrieks of horror, Marcus calmly put her into the recovery position and checked her pulse. Very quickly she came round. One of the office staff rushed to get some water. Marcus thanked them and gave Tianna a drink. Marianna and Anthony rushed over as Tianna sat with her head between her knees.

"It's okay, she got two As and an A* in Biology. She's going to

Oxford, she's just in shock." Marcus explained.
Her phone pinged, it was Joel wondering why he had not heard anything from Tianna. Marcus rang him back, having explained he heard the relief in Joel's voice. Joel also had a message for Noëmi from a former pupil.

Noëmi

A celebration lunch was instantly arranged by Marianna so Marcus left to collect his own family. Laboriously he got all the McKensters into the car. Noëmi flopped into the passenger seat and sighed as both the babies began to grizzle.

"That was an Olympic event! How are we ever going to leave the house again!"

"One day at a time, eh? Oh, the windscreen's misted up given the increased number of lungs in the car, some more active than others! N, can you pass me the shammy, it's in the glove box."

Noëmi opened the glove box and felt inside. Her heart stopped.

'*Lace?*

Slowly she drew out her hand and held up a red satin thong. They looked at each other. "Euh!" She dropped it on the floor and used a nappy sack to prepare it for the bin. "Where's the hand sanitizer?"

Together they burst out laughing. "Right, the challenge is to work out how she did that! Extra marks for when! We have two Oxbridge degrees between us! We've got this!"

Noëmi turned, took his body to hers and kissed Marcus, with everything she had.

CHAPTER 47 - X BOX

Saturday, 24 August 2019.

Marcus

Despite Marianna's mutterings about childhood churches, the wedding was to take place at St Oswald's in Durham. The great advantage was that everyone, apart from the bride, could walk to the reception at the Indigo Hotel next door. The Italian cohort were firmly established in the hotel and thoroughly looking forward to a joyful celebration. The weather was fine for the 4pm service, which would then carry on late into the evening. Attila Varga, the Priest, was ready as Marcus arrived with his family and Guy, his best man. The church was packed as the young couple had spared no expense and had invited all their friends, family and work colleagues.

The church was bedecked in glorious, late summer flowers with lilies reclaimed. A red rose was the choice for the buttonholes. Heart pounding, Marcus sat down and adjusted his jacket.

'Nearly twelve years. I remember noticing her in class. I wanted to talk to her. Then we met properly that afternoon in the November drizzle, the absolute best day of my entire life. I can remember every

word of our conversation. She's still as feisty. I can see her pretty eyes

looking curiously at me.'

As everyone settled, Guy, excited grin on face, turned to his best friend and gave him a huge bear hug.

Noëmi

Feeling hot she sat in the church side room giving her babies a final feed.

"Dad, most brides effusive effortless elegance and me? Breast milk!"

Despite the colour and warmth of the church, the room was everything dull and tepid. Grey brown chairs, carpet and walls. Untouched books filled the vast shelves.

Her mind raced, *'6 November 2007, the day that changed my life. His smile, his voice, how he knew me even then. It's scary that we could have passed each other by.'*

A tiny hand flinched into the air. She let Mani grab her finger.

"Dad I love these babies so much, I didn't know it was possible.

I thought the love I have for Marcus was infinite, but there's even something more!"

Her father put his arm around her, "I know, Mum and I often had that conversation! The love for our children does have an extra dimension." She felt her throat get lumpy.

Presently, he helped her get the infants changed and settled. She touched up her make-up. Next, he took her dress from its carrier and held her as she stepped into it. Silently he did her buttons up and helped her with her veil. Both looked at each other. They knew the other's thoughts.

"Noëmi, you're beautiful. I'm so proud of you."

She nodded, "Mum and I used to plan this day together! It's turned out very differently...but the love is here. That was always at the top of our list."

Eyes already welling up, he opened the door and took the double pram into the church to position the babies with Marianna and Anthony. Returning with Frank they pulled Noëmi up onto their arms.

"Noëmi! Exquisite! Stunning! Quite a transformation from the hospital gown look!" Frank's eyes glistened.

"Let's go! Time for me to gain a very lucky son in law!" Donnie's face flushed with joy.

Marcus

Excited chatter moved through the congregation, then the church fell silent apart from the odd whimper from one of the eight week old babies.

The click of a walking stick made him aware that Noëmi had arrived and he smiled to himself. Of all the things she had wanted to float graciously down the aisle. Now she was using the stick whilst being held by Donnie and Frank; one on each side. Guy gave his friend a firm squeeze around the shoulders and they stood looking over towards Noëmi. With her dress shimmering and hair flowing she arrived smiling irresistibly.

"Offloading to you Marcus!" Frank whispered

"Frank, I'm a bride not a cargo pallet!"

"Well my arm's going to sleep!"

Marcus' heart was bursting. "Noëmi you look so beautiful, you could never imagine how much I love you."

"I can because I love you the same, Marcus. You really are holding me up, as you've done all this time,"

"I'm never letting you go!" Marcus whispered, then suddenly he changed the subject, "Noëmi...I've just realised there's one thing you don't know about me...oh we're starting."

Noëmi

Noëmi was confused, *'After all these years, how can there possibly be anything I don't know about this man?'*

Attila smiled and began the ceremony, Tianna, Sarai, Yumi, Val and Lucia were also bridespeople along with Frank. The whole altar area was packed with the ten of them. The whole way through Donnie kept wiping his eyes with his free hand.

"Do you Noëmi Donna take Marcus Romeo..."

Noëmi looked at Marcus in amusement. At the same moment she saw Guy smirk, look up to the ceiling and enjoy the moment they all found out Marcus' middle name.

Wedding complete, baptisms finished, everything was good in the eyes of God and Marianna.

"Romeo...you've kept that quiet mate!" Guy said as he slapped Marcus on the back, coming out of the church.

"For good reason with friends like you."

"You know, some people ditch their given name and are known by their middle name. It's quite the thing, could work well for you."

"Why do I think you may be enjoying this?"

"No worries Romeo, I've got your back, oh and congratulations by the way!"

No one had been able to come up with a sophisticated way of getting Noëmi to the reception. So much to her horror, she was pushed in the old wheelchair, hastily re-borrowed from RVI. It was decorated with some silver horseshoes from Poundland, a hot pink bow and a just married sign.

"Not quite the horse and carriage I used to dream of when I was ten." She sighed.

She resolved to save her strength for the first dance as she was determined to do that at least. The photographs, drinks and mingling started amidst happy chatter. Then the group entered the main room for dinner and dancing.

In time, Donnie stood to talk as the tradition demanded. The mood was buoyant and a few cheers went up.

"Those of you who know me appreciate there's no way I'll get through a speech, I'm far too emotional. Today I could not be happier or prouder. I know Noëmi's mother, Manon, would be feeling the same way. In place of a speech, I've teamed up with Marianna and Anthony. We've prepared this little visual representation to say how much we love you both, well all of you now that you've become four."

To go along with the slideshow, Tianna stood to perform an acoustic version of 'You're still the one.' Years of singing in church had prepared her well. Isaiah accompanied beautifully on his guitar and all the guests were enraptured by their soulful performance.

Starting with pictures of the pair as babies, Noëmi felt choked. *'Mum, if only I could hug you and tell you how much I love you.'* From age 14, all the photos included the two together at various family get-togethers with dates and funny captions. In their school uniform, at the beach, the beanies selfies and of course Oxbridge success. There was a slight hiatus over the first few years of university with only a couple of stilted photos. Then the Japan shirts, the fun run, the charity ball, numerous graduations, engagement photos, the Nigeria visit, moving in together, Noëmi pregnant, Noëmi in hospital, Marcus with the newborn twins, and finally the young family together safe and happy. Marianna had also managed maximum guest inclusion in their photo display.

Marcus

Once Noëmi and Marcus had given a speech together, it was time for the best man to take the floor. Guy fidgeted as he waited for quiet. Noëmi whispered to Marcus.

"He already looks particularly pleased with himself before he's even begun!"

"Don't worry, he's banned from singing the stag anthem..."

"What? *Living next door to Alice!*"

"Yeah but Guy had his own version!"

Before she could answer, Guy was off. "Okay we've had enough of all this romantic stuff. Now my job is to dish the dirt, all the stuff he's been trying to hide. This is a challenge! These McKensters are quite perfect; Oxbridge degrees, key workers and charity supporters; genuinely great people. I sigh, there's going to be nothing! Undeterred, I ask Marcus Romeo a few basic questions.

"*How did you meet?*"

"*November 2007, on the way home from school when we were fourteen.*"

"*When did you get together?*"

"*July 2017*"

Sorry what? Ten years? If you ask their families, as teenagers they were inseparable and it took how long? I ask Marcus, '*Did you ever go there?*'

He avoids answering. Big mistake. I'm a detective. In the family pictures I see something in a photo taken nine years ago in Zen, just round the corner from here!"

Guy popped a photo up of the two of them as teenagers, looking lovingly at each other. Noëmi, startled like a baby deer, whispered, "What does he know?"

"He said he's quoting French and Chinese philosophy, it'll be fine!" Marcus, beads of sweat appearing on his forehead, leant in close and put his arm around her.

"First he's writing poetry, now highbrow quotes, nothing to worry about hey?" She replied, snuggling into her new husband. Marcus felt his throat tighten.

Guy went on, "I take our boy to the pub and show him the evidence. Now this works really well with criminals; they squirm and try to deny everything. Marcus Romeo attempts to do the same. Tell me about this photo? He gives the tiniest of flinches...it's there...I persist ...and finally he cracks..."

Marcus avoided Noëmi's questioning eyes.

"So our little love birds are seventeen in this photo. I'm after motive and opportunity. Motive, by now they're best friends, study buddies, helping each other revise. Yeah, there's nothing like a bit of advanced level calculus to stir up all those feelings. That summer, Noëmi decides she's had enough of all this friendship stuff and she creates opportunity. Now I'm going to be a little bit scholarly here and quote the great Albert Camus. Noëmi likes a bit of philosophy. This famous French thinker once said, 'There always comes a time when one must choose between contemplation and action. This is called becoming a man'. And basically having spent more than a year contemplating his feelings for Noëmi that's what Marcus did. He chose action and became a man. You know a proper one!" Guy was enjoying himself immensely. Marcus, arm around his new wife's shoulder, studied a ceiling rose intently, '*How did Guy quoting a French existentialist not ring alarm bells?*'

Noëmi could not have sunk any lower in her chair.

Anthony said under his breath, "All that *revising* together!"

"I had no idea, by the way, you got away with it!" her father whispered.

"That was kind of the intention Dad, I'm sorry."

Her father gave her a smile and a comforting hand which she grabbed.

"It was only ever Marcus, no one else, just so you know."

Through the fingers of her other hand covering her face, she saw Deanna's look of absolute incredulity. She and her posse had been rendered totally speechless when they had heard about Noëmi and Marcus getting together in the first place. Then engaged. Then babies. Then a wedding. Now this! But this was far bigger than anything. The missing piece of the '*Marcus McKenzie always being single*' puzzle, had finally fallen into place. No wonder, he had begun his romance with Noëmi when they were in sixth form. Neither of them had ever said a word.

Tianna was equally horrified, her sensible older brother. She recalled their conversation,

'*Have you ever done anything like out there?*'

'*Nothing that I'm going to tell you about.*'

Peeking through her hand Noëmi saw everyone she knew thoroughly enjoying Guy's speech. Buoyed by the laughter, off Guy went again.

"They kept this new hobby to themselves, worried that their parents would put a stop to him spending every waking moment at her house if they realised. So, they snuck around during that last year of sixth form...playing Xbox together...I'm not sure what you all thought I was talking about but clearly you've got the wrong idea."

"Honestly I'm so gullible!" Donnie said shaking his head

"No, no, Dad I really did love the fact you were playing badminton!"

"Of course you did Mrs McKenzie!" he smiled at her.

Guy went on. "Obviously revealing this to you all I had to check in with their parents. I didn't want to cause some kind of family brawl. Happens a lot up north! Not like the civilised south where I'm from! Anyway they just said *go for it!*"

Immediately, every one of the McKenzie siblings had the same open-mouthed look of incredulity at this unjustness.

'Only Guy could get away with that!' Marcus thought to himself as he imagined the moment his mother learnt of Guy's speech plans.

"A year later, Marcus, still besotted, tried to convince her to tell everyone that they were gaming together, but she did that whole *'time to move on'* speech. It was game over. There were a number of wilderness years where they wandered through life, lonely, as single players. Neither of them was into casual gaming and they began a quest to reunite. During this time, they encountered a number of obstacles and quite a few people with *'criminal tendencies living outside the norms of accepted behaviour'*. I have to say that because I'm not allowed to say the word I want to use. I had to arrest a number of them. Actually, to date about four or five, I think. Finally, just over two years ago they decided to play Xbox again as they were still very much in attract mode. Now to make up for time lost, and their lack of practice during these wilderness years, they kicked off with a twenty-hour revision session. I hear Marcus did suggest going for a drink or a meal but Noëmi was having none of it and was just desperate to get her hands on that joystick again."

Guy was on a roll. Marcus focused on some very interesting coving towards the side of the room. Noëmi now wanted to crawl under the table and never be seen again. Through her hand she caught sight of all the grandparents looking bemused, apart from Bruce McAllister who was chuckling merrily. Val, pursed lipped, was translating for Noëmi's Italian grandparents; "As seventeen year olds they would enjoy studying, discussing philosophy and playing computer games together."

Guy was back on it, "So enthusiastically returning to their action game, they were back to being inseparable. In spite of being older, Noëmi still struggled with some basic game rules and their team expanded unexpectedly with the arrival of the adorable Bruno and Emmanuelle. Not that our emergency doctor here was much better as he completely failed to notice that she was pregnant. I'm not really sure these Oxbridge degrees are worth it given the track record of these two. There you have it! As a fortune cookie once stated, '*In the end all things will be known*' and those of us who know how unpredictable a fortune cookie can be, fully respect this!"

'*And there's the 'Chinese philosophy'...a fortune cookie...*' thought Marcus.

"The stars aligned for my two best friends and true love won through. The dark times this summer did make me realise how much I love my friends here, and now after this speech you can imagine how much they love me!"

The best man did the toasts, thanked the bridespeople.

"Time for a night of dancing and celebration!" With laughter and cheers, everyone watched as Marcus carried Noëmi to the middle of the room for their first dance. He held her up the whole way through.

Later Guy met Marcus and Noëmi in the bar and put his arms around them.

"That went well!"

"Only you Guy, from existentialist to fortune cookie," Marcus scoffed.

"Had to keep it intellectual, all those Oxbridge guests, I'm just a bit worried your Grandparents don't know what an Xbox is."

At that moment Noëmi's Italian grandfather asked Val,

"Cos'è una Xbox?"

CHAPTER 48 - YOUNG LOVE

Noëmi

It was not quite true that no one had ever been told about the teenage trysts between Marcus and Noëmi. A week before her planned caesarean, Noëmi had arranged to go shopping with Marcus' mother, Marianna. They were to get the last things for the babies. As they entered John Lewis, Marianna got Noëmi a trolley to lean on.

"You're very quiet, are you worried about the operation?" Marianna felt the quality of a set of bibs decorated with pandas.

"Marianna, I have to sit down, the babies are kicking, I'm sorry."

"Okay let's get to the cafe, it's just over there, they've thought it all through it would seem."

Hauling herself into a seat Noëmi was relieved, the babies were agitated. She took Marianna's hand and put it on her stomach to feel them move and the future grandmother gave a frisson of excitement. Marianna went to fetch them a tray of tea. Returning she breathed with joy. "This is so wonderful. You know Noëmi, in the past twelve years or so I really have seen you as my own."

"That wouldn't work now would it Marianna!" She laughed.

"You know what I mean, child. You had a rough time when you were younger. You were so awkward but by seventeen you really blossomed into a happier teenager."

'*And I know exactly why…*' Noëmi said to herself.

Marianna

Marianna was fully aware that Marcus' friendship had been a catalyst, but she also appreciated that Noëmi's kind nature anchored her son. On top of this, she was delighted at how focused they both were on achieving academic excellence.

Noëmi looked at her tea for a minute and suddenly said; "I have to sincerely apologise to you Marianna."

"What do you mean?"

"I'm sorry. I have to say that, after your reaction to Tianna, to be fair to you and to her. I have to confess, maybe I shouldn't bring it up because it's in the past. You have to know that whilst it was consensual, it was all my fault, not his."

Marianna sat back in her plastic cafe chair and chose her words.

"Is what you're referring to something from way back, maybe nearly nine years?" Marianna gave Noëmi a knowing glance, as she added more hot water to her cup.

Noëmi hung her head, "Yes it wasn't meant to turn out like that. It was disrespectful to your values."

Marianna sighed. "I love that you wait until you're very pregnant with my first grandchildren! Thank you for saying sorry but what do you expect me to say now?"

"Are you not angry? It was only supposed to be a kiss." Noëmi fiddled with a sugar sachet.

410

"Well child of course! I would've been as angry as I was with

Tianna! You're lucky to have time on your side! I had suspicions but no proof. I could see how you were attracted to each other. Your idea of a little kiss would have been like lighting a touch paper beneath a bonfire of emotions, carefully layered up over three years."

At the beach that day Marianna had seen the pair getting ever more affectionate; leaning all over each other, play fighting and whispering shared secrets.

Noëmi

"That day... it was just a tsunami of feelings, we were so close." Her mind wandered to them lying together, their bodies entwined, not wanting to let the other go. How entirely they had loved each other that day.

"First love, eh?"

"First and only love, first kiss, first everything for us both." Noëmi was enthralled.

Marianna looked at Noëmi in her reverie and rolled her eyes, muttering. "Your father, the enabler of all enablers! Leaving you two alone the whole time! All that taking him to church... ruined."

"I'm sorry, Marianna. We kept our relationship secret. We were

worried you'd stop us working together, seeing each other, if you knew we were more than friends."

"Absolutely correct. He would've been locked in his room!" Marianna was almost certainly not joking.

"Then I ruined everything. I hurt him." She took a sip of tea but grimaced as it was already tepid.

"What do you mean?"

"I finished our relationship. I said a long-distance romance

wouldn't work. I thought he was too good for me. We were in a

411

mess." Noëmi picked up another sugar sachet, held it in her hand.

"When is a man ever too good for a woman! I wish I'd known. Girl you need to hold your head up high, be proud and be seen. I say this to Tianna all the time! Why did you think you knew what he wanted?" Marianna looked strained.

"I didn't want to hold him back."

"Noëmi I know Marcus, I could see that even then you two were in love but you did not know what all those feelings were now did you?" Marianna gave Noëmi an old-fashioned look.

"There were some little slip ups down the line, like the jacket fiasco."

"Oh Marianna...jacketgate..." Bursting out laughing, Noëmi returned the sugar to its bowl.

"Ah you make all sorts of excuses for yourself don't you! But you know what Noëmi," Marianna thumped her hand down on the table, "I'm glad you got there first!"

"Marianna!" Her heart and babies jumped.

"That one I never met! I heard all about the shenanigans, from my boys and even Donnie. Plus she made Tianna cry. Anthony had to stop me from going down there. We have a word for women like that, a sketel. She was a true one. That all upset me so, so much, him being treated like that, her saying these racist insults."

"He had no idea, Tianna only told him last year, I wish I'd known. Unfortunately, I created a vacuum for Sophie to fill." Noëmi nodded and leaned into Marianna.

"Thankfully you found your way home to each other. I'm sure my boys are loved by good women, but I worry for Tianna, I don't want to think about all that happened to her."

Noëmi took her hand. Marianna rubbed the back of Noëmi's appreciatively.

"It's been an awful year for her. Scheming people are everywhere it seems." Noëmi sighed in agreement.

After a few minutes, Marianna lightened the mood. "And you were one back then! But thank goodness you worked it out. You need to get that wedding done...in the eyes of God."

The women had a long hug.

Tianna

Throughout the Wedding Day Tianna had been stealing glances at Joel.

'*Broad shoulders, fresh haircut, smooth skin. He's looking chilled in that smart suit. Stylish too, the short stand-up collar shirt, slightly open at the neck.*'

Joel was relaxed. Leaning back in his chair, sipping a beer from the bottle, chatting happily with everyone; he was evidently enjoying himself.

'*Always with Louisa, but I'm not seeing any sign of them being close. If she liked him, she wouldn't be lolling back in her chair on her phone, ignoring him like that.*'

Tianna felt hopeful, '*I'll go and chat with them. No! What if I get put forever in the friend zone too.*' Her throat tightened.

Sitting as the first dance began, she looked wistfully at her brother and new sister-in-law, '*They're so in love.*'

Past them she kept eyeing Joel. Her heart kept beating a little faster each time she spotted him. Suddenly he was gone. Carefully searching she could no longer see Luis or Penelope, his parents. They had left. Tianna sighed and looked down. She smoothed her perfect, rose gold, silk dress over her knees and

413

examined her new nails; '*Of course I don't deserve him. I've been a liar. I betrayed him horribly. It was unforgivable. I hate myself.*'

Couples started joining Marcus and Noëmi as they continued their first dance. ***Escape*** by Enrique Iglesias played out.

"Got any more updates on far off volcanoes?" Joel sat down next to her with his beer.

"Joel my God, I thought you'd gone!"

"No we're all having the best time, you sang beautifully Tianna. You're truly gifted. I had no idea!"

She blushed. "I hope to do some open mic nights at Oxford."

"Nice! Make sure you invite me!"

"Deal!" she squeaked. Her heart was thumping.

"I've just been chatting to my old form tutor, Frank Sprague, he's so pleased with how I'm getting on. I think he's quite drunk! Funny seeing my old teachers actually enjoying themselves, like proper human beings!"

"Frank's a legend!" She began to relax.

He leaned in and whispered to her. "Your brother's a dark horse, always seems so sensible."

"I don't need to hear any more about all that! Makes sense, he never dated in sixth form and he was at Noëmi's house the *whole* time. Everyone liked him. People used to ask me for his number, I was ten! God knows why they wanted to get with him!"

Joel laughed. "She's no better, she used to give us all these talks in PSHE, 'Just say no!' was her favourite strapline!"

"Such hypocrites! Look at them!" Tianna laughed, waving at an excited looking Noëmi who was attempting to dance with Marcus on the other side of the room. Joel burst out laughing.

"This is such a funny wedding song!"

"It's N, she's into all this old music! Ah I think it's what her mum liked. He'll do anything for her! I want someone to love me that much one day!" Tianna sighed.

"And I'd love someone to love me as much as she loves him!"

"I know right! Sums up all my brothers actually! Look at them all. I may be sick...oh God, I don't mean…"

"Been there, done that!" He finished his beer.

"Stop, what I mean is I'm the odd one out!"

"Ah well you don't have to be." Joel turned towards her. "You look beautiful Tianna as always. I've been wanting to talk to you for ages, but at the rowing club you were surrounded by all those brothers and the police dude, the funny one." He glanced down, fidgeting with the empty bottle in his hands.

"Joel, you didn't have to help me at Kit's. Why?"

He looked bashful. "True I was still angry with you but I had a feeling something wasn't right. I couldn't leave you like that."

"You never even spoke to me."

"I wasn't talking to you, remember! Your mum was coming for me!"

A laugh caught in her throat. Memories of her rudeness filled her head. He gently put his finger under her chin to lift her head and fixed his eyes on her.

Feeling her body tense she asked, before he could, "Actually Joel, do you want to dance?"

"Only with you, come on!"

415

She led him to the dance floor and they held each other tightly.
"Joel I'm so..."

"We've had this conversation Tianna. No apologies,"

"...so happy to be going to Oxford, you'll be there."

"I can't wait to be there with you. You've done so well after all that happened to you." Joel twisted a strand of her hair with his finger gently.

"I'm so naïve, I don't know who I can trust anymore."

He hugged her tightly. "Me, trust me!"

Pulling him away from the dance floor and away from all the eyes of their families, she led him out onto the patio. The evening was beginning to draw in and the far-off sound of others faded away. She kissed him gently as he put his arms around her. Electricity flowed through her body, this was it, this was how happiness felt. She melted into him.

"It's been tough for both of us. Seeing you go through all that, I felt so helpless!"

"Joel, I really like you!"

"And that makes two of us then doesn't it! I really like me too!" he smiled at her as she laughed.

Marcus

Everyone was dancing and thoroughly enjoying the party. Anthony returned from settling the babies with their minder. Arriving in the bar Marcus went to him.

"Dad! Time for father and son to share a beer!"

Behind him, Marcus noticed Joel, looking apprehensive. He saw his young friend go over to Anthony, hesitate then move away. Seeming suddenly more determined he returned in front of Anthony, hopping from foot to foot.

Finally remarking Joel, Anthony moved next to him. Watching, Marcus could see Joel talk seriously to his father who looked intently at the young man. A wide grin broke on his father's face. Anthony hugged Joel who looked a little overwhelmed.

Moving to join them Marcus handed a beer to Joel, who thanked him and sped off.

"What was all that about Dad? Looked serious!" Marcus laughed. He passed a beer to his father, "Cheers!"

"He wants to take Tianna out. How old fashioned of him to come and ask me properly! I love that!"

Marcus threw his head back, "Brilliant, that's the best news! You can trust Joel completely."

"She's liked him for a while!" Anthony sipped from his glass.

"Oh, did she talk to you about him?"

"No, I could just tell!" His father looked knowingly at him.

"All this time I thought it was only Mum with the sixth sense!" His father gave him a mystic smile.

Marcus glanced across at Joel chatting with his sister and thought how lucky they were to be going to university together. Suddenly his throat felt tight as he remembered the lonely years apart from Noëmi.

CHAPTER 49 - ALL THINGS WILL BE KNOWN

27 August 2010.

Donnie

The day after Noëmi's birthday beach trip, Donnie's parents had driven over from Leeds for the bank holiday weekend to celebrate with her. They invited Marcus, his parents and grandmother, Raeni, to join them for dinner at Zen, a fine Thai and pan Asian, restaurant in Durham. Bruce and Morag McAllister were keen to do this, given the endless McKenzie hospitality they had all enjoyed over the past three years. Marcus and Noëmi sat next to each other at the restaurant. Part way through, Marcus asked to be excused to use the bathroom. Noëmi almost immediately followed suit.

"Such lovely manners!" remarked Bruce McAllister, Donnie's father.

Marianna saw the two disappear and sighed. "They're both off their food." She nodded to their barely touched plates.

"Same yesterday, they ate no pizza and usually I have to fight to get some!" Donnie agreed, "Do you think they're sick?"

418

Marianna rolled her eyes and muttered something Donnie didn't quite catch.

"He's such a good-looking boy!" commented Morag, Donnie's mother. "I take it Noëmi has finally settled in Newcastle?"

Donnie replied, "Now yes. She was always doing well academically but obviously struggling emotionally. When she met Marcus, things began to improve and this last year she's been a different person. They're very good friends, they have this routine where they do their studying and then he comes round and they do extra work. I think she's quite chuffed because at sixth form he's quite the heart throb and with her being so quiet, she feels flattered."

Anthony interrupted, "Noëmi is a very fine girl in every way. They care for each other. He's lucky to have a friend like that."

Donnie nodded his head vehemently, "Yes! Yes! I agree. Even during the holidays, when all the exams are done, it's so good that they can relax together too!"

"Isn't it just!" Marianna gave a sigh.

"Let me see where they are." Raeni got up from the table and Marianna smiled approvingly.

"Dad, look, I got her a mobile phone! I picked it up yesterday late-night shopping, a bit late but she still got it on her birthday! Here it is, a Blackberry Bold, she's wanted one for ages." Donnie took the handset and showed his parents, feeling proud he had treated his daughter. A message stream was on the screen.

N - *Miss you <3*

M - *Miss you 2 <3*

Embarrassed her grandparents were seeing this he scrolled back and got to the start of the messages.

26 August 2010.
N - My new phone!!!
M - :) <3<3<3
N - ;) Miss u <3
M - Miss u 2 <3
M - MOS brb
N - DOS 2
N - They must never know :E
M - Never :#
N - So much <3 4 u :x
M - All my <3 4 u 2 :x :x <3

"We can't read the screen Donnie without our glasses, give us a sec." Donnie's mother reached for her handbag.

"Don't worry Mum, it's just to show you the phone is quite the thing! They all want one!"
Donnie quickly put the phone back before Marianna could see and felt a bit guilty reading his daughter's messages.

'Noëmi and MMcK. That's Marcus. <3 is that the symbol for a heart? Love? Or both? :x and : both mean a kiss, I saw that before. Sometimes I do wonder how much I really know about N. She has a place she goes to I can't seem to reach. No, these texts must be something to do with how much they love school work! That's it! They're gearing up for their final exam year, always so ingenious those two!*

"She gets more like Manon every day," commented Morag.
"She definitely has her mother's spirit." Donnie wondered what :# meant.

"I'm glad things are working out Donnie, it's been a tough time for you both. Prawn toast anyone?"

Raeni could not find her grandson and Noëmi near the bathrooms so she went out of the restaurant and immediately saw them kissing, locked in a tight, loving embrace. They did not see her. Leaving them to it she returned to the table.

"Did you find them?" Marianna asked.

"They're just chatting outside, something about university choices, they'll be back in a moment."

Marianna nodded and presently Marcus and Noëmi returned to join the group. Bruce chatted with them about their plans for university.

Marcus kept looking over his shoulder.

Suddenly a rush of movement and a darkening of the lights heralded a birthday cake. Bursting into song the group grinned as Noëmi was overwhelmed by the pretty cake with its seventeen candles.

"Smile!" Bruce all but yelled at his granddaughter as he clicked away with his camera.

"Ah, thank you! That's so kind." She looked at them all, eyes bright in the candlelight.

"Happy Birthday!" Marcus said quietly to her and she took in his face. Holding the other's gaze their eyes spoke. '*You mean absolutely everything to me.*' Her heart was racing.

Under the table she took his hand. He squeezed it back.

"Gorgeous picture! I'll send you a copy Donnie," Bruce blustered with delight and put his camera away.

"Lovely cake, well done Marianna!" Donnie nodded in appreciation.

421

"I'm not the one to thank!" She looked at Raeni who shook her head. Anthony looked puzzled.

"Mum, Dad! Nice one!" Donnie tried but got blank looks from both.

"Whoever got this organised, loves you very much Noëmi!" Bruce exclaimed, winking at his son!

Donnie fidgeted with his chopsticks and whispered to his father, "Dad I feel terrible I ran out of time. I was at the phone shop yesterday evening. Then at work today but I did make her favourite carrot cake yesterday on her actual birthday!"

"Donnie! We all know what a devoted father you are!" Bruce patted his son on the back.

Marianna

Noëmi went bright red. Marcus sat back in his chair, doubling over his napkin. Marianna noticed the pair flinch. An awkward silence fell upon them all.

"Come on, let's have some cake then!" Anthony filled the quiet. A waiter sorted the cake and the group finished up.

Having paid the bill, Bruce gave everyone a fortune cookie.

"So exciting, maybe this will tell us your A level results! Let's see what they say! Mine is, **'Embrace this love relationship you have'** well there we go, one for the lovers!"

'*Is every McAllister out to corrupt us!*' Marianna said to herself.

Donnie opened his, **'Your home is the centre of great love.'**

"Isn't it just!" Marianna said under her breath.

"Wonderful, I like that, Noëmi, what do you have?"

Noëmi read hers out **'You can keep a secret.'**

"And just how many?" Marianna sighed.

"Interesting, Marcus, what do you have?" Bruce asked.

'Stop searching forever, happiness is just next to you.'
Sitting on the end of the row he glanced to his other side to see Noëmi beside him.

"Marianna?"

'In the end all things will be known'. Okay I think we've heard enough fortunes for now!"

"Fortunes, success, love, Noëmi, I hope you have time to find yourself a nice young man when the moment comes!" Bruce was merry and bold with wine.

"Oh I doubt it, at Newcastle Green they're a bunch of cruel bullies. Marcus is the only decent, in every sense of the word, guy there." Noëmi was straight forward.

All of a sudden Marcus turned to Noëmi. "You're the best girl there, or anywhere actually."

"Oh listen to this, you never know, maybe then you two, the music, the moonlight, the moment..."

"No Granddad you've got it wrong, we're friends. We get along because we study together, that's all."

"Yeah, we've been good friends for a while." Marcus could no longer fold his napkin.

They did not look at each other. Marianna sighed again. '*Stable door, horse, bolted,*' she said to herself and realised there was very little she could do as her teenage son grew older.

"The pink cherry blossoms are so perfect; they hang so exquisitely!" suggested Raeni. The conversation and everyone's eyes moved on.

Noëmi

Marcus and Noëmi kept their secrets, with the very self-disciplined plan to make their romance public once their exams were done. However, Noëmi was too self-sacrificing and

423

Marcus, although heartbroken, conceded defeat too readily. Both regretted it.

CHAPTER 50 - TO SEE LOVE

Noëmi

September was giving in to October. One Saturday, Donnie, large plant in arms, arrived to see his daughter.

"Marcus at work then?"

"Yes, he's doing as much as he can. It makes him feel better, like he's showing everyone how grateful we are!"

Donnie's face was far away.

"Dad don't go there, we had bad luck and then good luck! It happens in life."

He shook his shoulders and kissed her on the cheek.

"Any news on buying a place N? When these two start moving, you'll know about it!"

Donnie looked around at the flat packed with babies and supplies. He moved a packet of nappies and sat down.

"Yes we're searching around here, problem is so many places are student flats. Marcus is looking at one tonight on the way home, we've got the deposit now that's the main thing."

Smiling at the carry cots, he jiggled the jungle animal mobiles which loomed over each tiny child. He did not return her gaze. Presently, he sat down close to his daughter as she began the twin feeding ritual. They listened to the little sighs and whimpers the first hungry baby made. The second baby was restless, stretching and kicking.

"You were like that!" Donnie pointed at the impatient infant. "Never still!"

Donnie helped her change the children and they settled in their cots. She limped to the kettle and made tea. Looking at the white and yellow colour schemes, he commented, "I like that you're not doing that pink and blue thing, N."

"Actually, it was only because we didn't know the sex. I like all colours. Rainbows are best!"

"Indeed, and I've got you a Japanese cherry tree just because I wanted to! This one has white blossoms. It'll be glorious in spring! It can stay in a pot now and then go to a garden when you get one."

"Dad, thank you so much!"

He pointed at the planter, which was covered with some brown paper. "I'll leave it here!" Suddenly restless he moved it onto their small terrace, outside the kitchen. The other potted plants were bare but the Japanese maple tree Donnie had given them for their engagement was a fiery bronze red. Noëmi walked over to see her gift and began to unwrap the plant.

"No! You can do that when I've gone, N!" Donnie's voice was high pitched.

As she pulled the paper off an envelope fell out to the ground. Her name was on the front.

"A letter?"

Donnie looked at his hands.

"It's just...N... I feel sometimes I can't say things, so I've written some stuff down. Some of it I wrote when you were in the coma, so it may be a bit over the top!" He tried to laugh it off.

"Dad! Can I read it?"

"I'll be off!" He stood up from their garden bench.

"No! You're going nowhere Mr McAllister!"

She pushed him down and plonked herself on his lap. She opened the letter.

'My dear Noëmi,

Forgive this self-indulgent outpouring of something resembling emotion! It is of course badly written; your mother would have sorted it out she was the clever one!

Since Manon was taken from us, I know I have been consumed with my grief. From that young age you looked after me, you walked beside me, you gave me comfort. Being just the two of us I got scared. My terror that something would happen to you has been a dark shadow alongside me all this time. In my darkest moments I asked myself, would it have been easier to never have loved anyone as then I would not feel such fear? The greater the love the greater the joy but also the greater the fear. I reasoned, if I'd never loved anyone, I would be safe and protected from pain.

This summer those dark shadows loomed over us. A self-fulfilling prophecy some would say. I looked into the face of my greatest dread and saw only myself. I had to find a way. How I prayed. How I wracked my soul. Slowly the image changed. I began to see love. Our love for each other. That was what mattered. I realised that we cannot protect ourselves from love and indeed nor should we.

427

My relief that you all came through cannot be put into words. During my vigils at your bedside, I began to wonder how you had coped without Manon. How quietly you have borne that sorrow. How much you hid your hurting. In some ways I was the lucky one being able to work through my grief, whereas you have sheltered me from yours. How did you do that? How could you be so giving, all this time, whilst in such pain?

I believe that I now know, Noëmi, that you have seen love for a long time. Your love for others is greater than your love for yourself. Your ability to give love and your capacity to show love has held you up. It has astonished me. You have proved to me that I could never have been more loved by you or Manon. I know I have not said it enough but I could never love you more. My love for you and for Manon could fill eternity. As we pass into shadows our love never does. It continues to shine brightly.

Thank you Noëmi. For being you and for being everything.
All my love
Dad

PS: Honestly, as for all those sixth form antics, do you have any idea what Marianna could have done to me if she'd found out?

Bursting out laughing, Noëmi's tears fell as she hugged her father. She kissed the top of his head and ruffled his hair. Slipping onto the seat next to him, he put his arm around her. Together they watched the blazing autumn leaves skit along the ground in the gentle breeze.

THE END

(To be continued...)